THE

DARKEST

GREEN

THE DARKEST GREEN

RAMONA BAILLIE

Based on the screenplay by Ramona Baillie and Olivia Gottlieb

IGUANA

Copyright © 2025 Ramona Baillie

Published by Iguana Books
720 Bathurst Street
Toronto, ON M5S 2R4

Publisher: Cheryl Hawley
Editor: Amanda Feeney
Front cover art: Suzanne Courtney

ISBN 978-1-77180-727-2 (paperback)
ISBN 978-1-77180-739-5 (hardcover)
ISBN 978-1-77180-726-5 (epub)

This is an original print edition of *The Darkest Green*.

CONTENTS

CHAPTER ONE

HOUSTON, TEXAS

Gabriel sat in his parked car, eyes closed, drumming his fingers on the steering wheel to Led Zeppelin's *Whole Lotta Love*. The next song to come on was one of the latest hot songs. He opened his eyes and turned down the volume. "Boring crap."

He hated the new music. The tripe being churned out had no soul. Even his favorite band, the Stones, hadn't come out with anything worth listening to since *Goats Head Soup*. He hated anything new because, like everything else, it disappointed.

He ran his hand across the dashboard and smiled. Something he rarely did. His Chevy was the only thing that had never let him down. He'd bought it when they were making cars to last, and it had a lot of good years left. It was obvious that he loved the car from the pristine shape he kept it in, even though he was not a tidy man by any stretch of the imagination. "We'll go to the scrapyard and graveyard together in the end," he whispered.

At fifty-one he felt old. Old and tired. He'd been a recluse for the past twenty years, not by choice, but by necessity. He was no longer just another face in the crowd. He looked at his reflection in the rearview mirror and quickly looked away. It was the face of a man who inspired shock, disgust, even pity. Pity. That was the worst. His was a face that could frighten small children. The face that used to be his greatest asset.

He remembered when people were drawn to him because of his face. When he was handsome, even men tended to want to be near him. All he had to do to get laid was smile at any woman in the room. Now he couldn't smile. Now he wore a two-faced mask. The left side a reminder of the power beauty elicited, and the right side a cruel reminder of his sins. Deep scars forced the eye to droop and pulled his lips down to a half-grimace, creating the illusion of a Freddy Krueger mask. No, not a mask; the real thing.

Gabriel turned off the radio, leaned back, and pulled a folded letter out of his pocket. He read it for the tenth time, still not understanding why he'd been invited. He shoved it back into his pocket and scanned his surroundings. He was in the underground garage of a downtown office building. There were plenty of cars parked near him. Gabriel looked at his watch. It was almost 10 a.m. Hopefully, everyone would be settled in their offices, and he could get to the elevator and into the lawyer's office without bumping into too many people.

He grabbed a baseball cap out of the glove compartment and ran his fingers through his hair to smooth it down before putting the cap on. A habit from before the accident, unnecessary now that he wore his hair in a crew cut. He'd purchased a hair clipper on Amazon to avoid having to visit a barber.

He pulled the key out of the ignition and slowly got out of the car. He pulled the knot in his tie closer to his throat, tucked his shirt in, and buttoned the jacket of the charcoal-gray double-breasted wool gabardine suit he'd bought to wear to his father's funeral more than two decades ago. Gabriel was thin-framed, and no matter how much he ate, his weight stayed the same, so the suit still fit perfectly. He figured he looked presentable enough, not realizing the suit was now considered "vintage" and quite stylish. Actually, his whole wardrobe was vintage.

He walked, head down, to the nearest elevator and pushed the button repeatedly, willing it to arrive quickly. The doors opened. The elevator was empty, thankfully. He got in and pushed one of the buttons, sighing as the bland elevator music engulfed him.

***

The dark wood paneling, plush leather chairs, and mahogany furniture in the lobby of Benson, Swartz & Sumner gave the impression that clients would be well taken care of, for a price.

The young girl at the reception desk was unable to take her eyes off Luke as he paced impatiently in front of her desk.

"Can I get you anything, Mr. Verde? Coffee? Water?" It didn't matter that she'd asked the same question only minutes earlier, when he and his mother had arrived. The girl couldn't help herself. Luke oozed a bad-boy confidence that was irresistible to most women. She needed to get him to look at her, to make a connection, and could think of no other way.

If any man could be described as beautiful, it would be Luke. He was tall and had full lips, ice-blue eyes under dark lashes, and thick black hair that framed his face. He usually favored a polo shirt and casual slacks, but today he wore an Armani suit that he felt fit the occasion. And, as a bonus, it accentuated his perfect twenty-six-year-old physique to the best advantage.

When it was time for college, Luke chose one just far enough away from his father to make his own mark on the world. He'd found getting top grades at UT Austin easy and making an impressive income selling molly and cocaine to his rich college friends and their fat-cat parents even easier. When the Wall Street boys started coming around with the big orders, it made sense for Luke to stay in Austin and expand the trade after he graduated. That was until the news of his father's death. Luke would be more than happy to swim in a bigger pond, especially when the pond was filled with bigger fish.

He stopped in front of the desk, leaned in, and purred, "Maybe later." The receptionist turned a bright red and, unable to think of an appropriate response, nodded enthusiastically. Luke had no intention of seeing her "later."

"Luca? Sit with me?" He heard his mother ask, barely above a whisper. Luke sat next to her and watched her toy distractedly with the double strand of pearls at her neck. Meredith Verde wore a black Chanel suit and pillbox hat. She owned the same outfit in various colors, as it was her church attire, and she went to church a lot. She had the posture and grace often associated with years of ballet lessons or strict private schooling. Meredith took great care in her appearance, but it was doubtful she took the same care when it came to her health, as she was uncommonly frail for her fifty years.

When Luke was asked if she was unwell, he'd jokingly say it was obvious that all the praying she did was sucking the life out of her. In truth, it was most likely the physical manifestation of having been married to Joseph Verde. In one way or another, they'd both been victims of his father's dominance.

But now Joe Verde was dead, and Luke would return to Houston to take control of the family businesses.

"How're you holdin' up, Mother?"

"I'm fine. It's you I worry about. This was all so sudden and unexpected."

"Hmm."

"It's good to have you home. I hope you plan to stay on at the ranch. At least for a little while." She smiled and touched his cheek.

"We'll see." He didn't want to make promises to her that he wouldn't keep.

He squeezed her hand, glanced at the platinum Rolex on his wrist, and frowned. He let go of his mother's hand and stood. "Why are we being made to wait?" he asked the receptionist.

"I'm sure he's very busy. Perhaps he's forgotten we're here," Meredith mused.

"He wouldn't dare," Luke growled.

Before the receptionist could respond, the door to the inner office burst open.

Benson, a portly man in his sixties, entered the room and approached them, smiling. "Meredith, how good to see you. Sorry it's under such terrible circumstances. And, Luke, pleasure to finally meet you. I'm Thomas Benson, sorry to have kept you waiting." He held his hand out, which Luke ignored. Instead, he helped his mother to her feet. The lawyer, uncomfortable now, changed his tone from congenial to all-business. "Yes, well, follow me." He pointed to the open door and the three of them continued to his office.

The room reflected the decor of the lobby with the added benefit of a panoramic view of city skyscrapers behind Benson's desk. Three matching chairs faced the antique ebony desk. Gabriel was seated in one of them, apparently appreciating the view. He didn't acknowledge their arrival.

Benson quickly made introductions. "Luke, Meredith, this is Gabriel Douglas. Mr. Douglas, Luke and Meredith Verde."

Surprised to see Gabriel, Luke snapped at the lawyer. "What is my father's bookkeeper doing here?"

Without looking at him, Gabriel retorted snidely, "I asked the same question." He'd met Luke once when he was fifteen and took an instant dislike to the spoiled brat. He figured his father hadn't thought too highly of him either. The lawyer confirmed as much when he'd read portions of the will to Gabriel earlier. He was looking forward to Luke's reaction.

"Mr. Douglas has been invited to the reading of the will because it concerns him as well."

"Yeah? How?" Luke asked, glaring at Gabriel.

"It will all become clear momentarily." Benson sat at his desk and motioned to Luke and Meredith to take a seat. Luke helped his mother to one of the chairs and remained standing.

"Please have a seat, Mr. Verde."

Luke sat but watched Gabriel surreptitiously as Benson opened the leather-bound folder on his desk and began to read the contents of the will.

"*I, Joseph Verde, of Houston, Texas, being of sound mind and not being under duress or undue influence, do hereby make, publish, and declare this to be my Last Will and Testament, and revoke all Wills and Codicils heretofore made by me.*"

Luke tapped his foot and mumbled under his breath, "Blah, blah, blah."

"*I nominate, appoint, and direct my executor, Thomas Benson, to pay from my estate all debts and expenses of my funeral and the expenses of the administration of my estate. I direct that all taxes shall be paid—*"

Luke interrupted him. "Get to the good parts, please."

"Yes, certainly." Benson adjusted his glasses and looked down the document. "*I give, devise, and bequeath to my son, Luca Verde, my stallion, Thunder, and one hundred thousand dollars.*"

Luke leaned forward. "What about Club Vox?"

"Ah, yes. Your father included a conditional bequest with regards to that property." Benson waited for Luke to respond and, after a moment, cleared his throat. He was nervous, not knowing what kind of backlash would be directed at him by the hotheaded son. "*I hereby bequeath a forty-nine percent share in Club Vox to my beloved son, Luca Verde, and, in return for his years of unwavering loyalty, a fifty-one percent share to Gabriel Douglas.*"

Luke jumped up. "What the fuck!" He scowled at Gabriel. "How the hell did you get him to give you controlling interest in my club? What did you have over him?"

Gabriel continued looking out the window, but he could not help smiling. Why bother answering. There was no need. This was definitely the most fun he'd had in years.

Luke clenched his fists. "I swear, I'll—"

"Luca. Please." Meredith reached up and touched his hand. He looked down at her and she nodded toward his chair. He sat, glaring at Gabriel.

Benson continued. "*In the event of either Luca Verde's or Gabriel Douglas's death, my executor shall have full power, without requirement of any order of court, to liquidate and sell the property and assets of Club Vox in order to donate said estate to Saint Patrick's Church, currently located at 32 Mountain Street, Houston, for its general purposes. The receipt of an appropriate officer of the church shall be a sufficient discharge of my executor.*"

Luke looked at Benson. "What the hell does that mean?"

"In other words, if either you or Mr. Douglas die, for any reason, all shares are bequeathed to the church."

Luke snorted. "That doesn't sound legit. He has no power once we own the shares." He added dryly, "He's dead."

"Luca, really," uttered Meredith. Luke ignored her, barely able to keep his anger at bay.

Benson continued. "Both of you will have to agree to this stipulation in order to receive ownership of the shares. If you do not, we are instructed to liquidate and sell the property and assets of Club Vox and donate the proceeds to Saint Patrick's immediately." Benson took two sets of documents out of a drawer and placed them on his desk along with two pens. "I'll need your signatures."

Gabriel stood and straightened his jacket. Benson pointed to the signature lines on the documents, and Gabriel signed them. *Oh, so much fun*, he thought. He couldn't help smiling.

"I'll send you copies, Mr. Douglas."

"Fine." Gabriel left the room without looking at either Luke or his mother.

"Terrible man," Meredith whispered.

Luke went to the desk, signed the documents, then returned to his seat.

Benson read on. "*I give, devise, and bequeath all of the rest, residue, and remainder of my estate to my beloved wife, Meredith Louise Verde. In witness whereof I have hereunto set my hand to this, my Last Will and Testament, this thirteenth day of April, two thousand and twenty-two.*"

Luke rose, took his wallet out of his pocket, and removed a business card. He dropped it on the lawyer's desk. "Have the documents sent to my lawyer today along with Thunder's registration papers. He'll let you know where to deposit the hundred grand."

Benson stood. "We can complete your paperwork at the ranch if you'd like, Meredith."

She smiled. "Of course, Thomas, that's very thoughtful."

Luke helped his mother to her feet. "We'll be in touch."

***

Gabriel always entered the club through the back door. From there he was able to get to his office unseen, so it was easy to avoid running into one of the cleaners or one of Joe's goons.

He'd been Joe's accountant for the past twenty years and only went to the Vox when necessary, slipping in and out when the club was closed. Mika, the club's manager, would meet him in the afternoon when he had questions that would take more than a quick text or phone call to answer. She had no problem with the way he looked and had even touched his face once.

He looked around with a new perspective, that of someone who had a hand in the game. He now owned the hottest nightclub in the city.

Club Vox had an irresistible attraction. Half sleaze and half class. It was located in a seedy-looking building in an even seedier part of town and promised more of the same inside. At night, people lined up for hours, desperate to gain entry. Who wouldn't? It was important for anyone who was anyone to be seen there.

He walked to the center of the spacious Art Deco interior. He placed his hand on the circular bar and pictured the place at night when it rocked. The bar would be staffed with the best-looking bartenders in town. Equally beautiful, barely clad go-go dancers would undulate on silver-caged pedestals as the DJ of the moment spun the latest and hippest sounds. VIP booths would fill with patrons ordering only the best champagne.

Gabriel walked over to the staircase. There was a private VIP room at the top of the stairs furnished with a lush, white, U-shaped leather couch surrounding a black lacquered table. Customers rich enough to be served there were offered companions-on-demand and all the discretion one could ask for.

He climbed the stairs, passed the VIP room and continued down the hall to Joe's private suite. He wasn't surprised to find the door locked. It was Verde territory. He'd never been invited there. When Joe wanted to communicate, they would meet in Gabriel's small office under the stairs.

He returned to the staircase and stood for a moment taking everything in. "Fifty-one percent ownership. Fifty-one percent!" He laughed. He hadn't laughed like that in twenty years. It felt good!

He knew Luke would try to make his life a living hell. So what! Now he could finally start making some real money! He returned to his office and called Mika. "Mika, it's Gabriel. Can we meet before your shift?"

***

Sam drove his classic black sports coupe onto the property. He whistled in amazement as he approached the main residence, a three-story Colonial Victorian home surrounded by lush landscaping and majestic oaks. A huge barn and paddocks were off to the right with what seemed like acres of pastures and forest in the background.

Sam and Luke had roomed together at university and had fallen into an easy friendship right away.

When Sam was ten, his parents were killed in a car accident. Being an only child with no other relatives, he was thrown into the system overnight. There he quickly learned that he would not only have to fight to survive, but it would also be in his best interest to take advantage of every opportunity that came along, regardless of the nature of the opportunity. This attitude, coupled with a keen intellect, kept him fairly unscathed and out of juvie.

He was a natural athlete and played defensive end on the high school football team. He excelled and received offers of a full-ride scholarship from some of the top Ivy League colleges. But Sam chose UT Austin to get as far away as possible from New York's South Bronx.

He quickly became a Longhorn favorite, complete with NFL buzz. His future was bright but, again, his life would change drastically. Sam's dreams were cut short when he sustained a devastating neck injury his senior year. After months in the hospital, it was made clear to him that he could never play football again.

Sam had helped Luke out a few times for a little extra cash, when he needed muscle, so it seemed natural to offer that muscle full time when he was faced with having to find something else to do with the rest of his life. And, if the occasion called for more than a beating, Luke was more than happy to take care of it himself. Their relationship naturally evolved into a partnership that suited them both. Luke relied on Sam to watch his back, and Sam relied on Luke to share some of the profits. This afforded Sam a comfortable lifestyle and helped to cover any gambling losses he might incur.

When Luke left for the funeral, Sam had remained in Austin to make sure the business would continue to run smoothly while Luke made plans for the transition to Houston.

Sam got out of the car and stretched. He was twenty-six and ruggedly handsome, with deep ebony eyes under long lashes. A white T-shirt accentuated his broad shoulders and muscular build. He always wore the latest trainers and used to wear a do-rag over his shoulder-length tight dreads, but Luke told him it wouldn't fly here. "Casual conservative" was the look Luke wanted them both to adopt in Houston. Sam didn't care either way.

He walked over to the new BMW 7 silver-gray sedan parked a few feet away and admired the lines. The front door of the house opened and Luke stood smiling.

"Sammy."

Sam pointed to the house. "Impressive."

"Belongs to my mother's family. How was the drive?"

"Unremarkable. How was the funeral?"

"Unremarkable." Luke held up a key fob. "Seems I've inherited Joe's car."

"Nice." Sam grinned from ear to ear.

"Thought you'd like it." Luke walked over to the passenger door and then, a little less enthusiastically, said, "It comes with the condition that my mother gets driven to church." Sam shrugged. Luke clicked on the unlock button, threw the fob to Sam, and got in. Sam always drove. Luke liked it that way. He felt having a driver gave him status. Again, Sam didn't really care one way or the other.

They drove to the club and parked in front. Luke unlocked Vox's front door with the extra set of keys the lawyer had for him. Inside, Sam looked around and whistled. "Quite the place!"

Luke noticed the door to the small office was open. He figured Gabriel might be there. He led Sam to the bar. "Make yourself a drink. I have something I need to do."

Luke went over to the office and leaned against the door frame, his hands in his pockets.

Gabriel was working on his laptop. He looked up. "Luke? Can I help you?"

Luke scoffed, "Not likely. Just thought we should get a few things straight."

"Oh?" Gabriel had never had to interact with Luke before his father's death, but he knew everything about him. Joe used to come to his office every now and then to chat. He'd bring a bottle and they'd sit for hours. They'd argue politics and religion, and Joe would fill Gabriel in on his son's antics. It was unclear whether Joe was proud of his son for being so like him or if he simply assumed it would be a waste of time to try and persuade him to act differently. Gabriel knew he wasn't expected to judge either father or son. So, he just listened no matter how graphic it got.

Luke drew an imaginary line with his foot. "I wanna make sure you realize your influence in this club stays within these four walls. Anything that happens outside this office doesn't concern you."

"Unfortunately for you, your father's will says otherwise. Wanna take another look?" Gabriel reached to open a drawer. "Joe knew you would destroy the business. That's why he gave the controlling half to me. Obviously. And I plan to make sure you don't fuck it up for either of us."

Luke glared at him. He walked to the desk, leaned in toward Gabriel, and said in a low, menacing voice. "I'm gonna find a way to make your fucking miserable little life even more miserable!"

"Good luck with that," Gabriel snapped back.

"As it happens, I'm a pretty lucky guy," Luke declared as he left, slamming the door behind him.

Gabriel knew Luke wouldn't rest until he found some way to get rid of him. "Just try," he said aloud. "Just try." He went back to working on his laptop. He had to admit, he was rattled.

Luke returned to the bar, cursing under his breath.

"Everything okay?" Sam poured Luke a drink.

"Just having a chat with my new partner." Luke chugged it back. "C'mon, lemme show you upstairs."

They went up to the suite and Luke unlocked the door. The office was furnished in the same opulence as the club, with floor-to-ceiling windows that accessed a fire escape. He walked behind the desk and rested his hand on his father's worn leather chair as he approached the window. "I wonder how often my father stood here." He looked down at the alley and laughed. "Get this. Nothing but garbage."

Sam joined him at the window. He chuckled. "Appropriate." He sat in one of the two chairs in front of the desk and pointed to Joe's chair. "Try it on."

Luke regarded him a minute before sitting. "You know, I never once sat in his chair." He shimmied in the chair; then tilted back. "Feels good."

"Check the drawers." Sam leaned back and put his feet up on the desk.

Luke opened a few drawers, taking note of the contents. Aspirin, brass knuckles, rubbers, a bottle of twenty-five-year-old scotch, glasses, a gun. He checked the barrel. It was loaded. "Nothing of real interest." They laughed. He put two glasses on the desk and filled them with scotch. "Here's to Joe. Look out hell, here he comes." They chugged them back.

"Amen," coughed Sam.

Luke ran his hands along the top of the desk. "Fits. Fits fine."

"So, whaddya gonna do about the bookkeeper?"

"Well. Obviously, I can't kill him. I just have to find another way to get rid of him. And I will. Believe me, Sammy, I will."

"Hmmm." Sam poured himself another glass and downed it.

Luke pointed to the bedroom. "There's more." He went to the door, found the appropriate key, unlocked it, and pushed it open. They stood in the doorway, taking in the scene.

"Joe showed me this room once. I was eleven." Luke said, almost in a whisper.

That explains a lot, thought Sam.

It was obvious the furnishings were very expensive, but the room could not have been tawdrier. A king-size bed was situated in the center of the space atop an antique Persian carpet. The only illumination came from two Atollo glass lamps on the bedside tables. The walls were dark and the shades had been pulled down on the floor-to-ceiling windows. Tangled red silk sheets hung off the mattress and a spanking paddle lay on the floor near the bed next to a black lace bra. The paddle had an elevated "V" on the surface, which would have been sure to leave a lasting reminder of Joe's affection.

"Did the tour come with a lecture on right and wrong?"

"Less of right and wrong. More of how-to." Luke laughed, picked up the paddle, and swung it back and forth. "Whaddya think he got up to in here?"

Sam smirked. "Doesn't take much imagination."

"Nope." Luke slapped his hand with the paddle. "Ouch." He winced. "Joe told me the only way for a woman to know her place was to put her there. A little roughing up was not outta the question. How else do you earn their respect."

"Great influence," Sam remarked.

"Right," Luke harrumphed. "He stopped having to show my mother her place after I was born. I only know this because he told me."

"Jesus."

"He said he was content that she'd borne him a son, for then he could, in good conscience, simply ignore her." Luke slapped his hand with the paddle again, harder this time. His eyes squinted in pain. "He spent family time with his whores." He turned to Sam. "You know, my mother never complained or even mentioned him. Ever!"

"Victim syndrome?" Sam shrugged.

"I guess. I'm surprised she's even acknowledged his death."

They looked around the room. There was an antique armoire in the corner. Sam opened it. On the top shelf was a digital camera set up to film through a small hole in one of the doors. Sam checked the camera. "The memory card's gone."

"Too bad," Luke mused ironically. "We will never experience the joy of Joe's artistic endeavours."

"Yeah, that is really too bad."

In the space below, at eye level, were two monitors displaying views of the rear parking lot, the street outside Vox, the main floor, and the VIP room.

"Looks like your father was serious about security."

"Comforting," Luke murmured. "I don't think we need the camera in here though."

"No. And we can get the security cameras to feed directly to our phones. Get rid of the monitors."

"Make it so, Sammy."

Sam stood at attention, saluted, and said, in a very poor Scottish accent, "Aye, Captain, sir."

They laughed.

***

The outer door of the suite opened. "Hello? Anybody here?" Charley called out as he entered. He was a veritable Dapper Dan in great shape for someone sixty-plus who ate and drank as much as he did. He wore flashy jewelry and well-tailored, neatly pressed suits. He was an enforcer, and no matter how messy his jobs got, and they could get pretty messy, he never seemed to get a drop of blood or anything else on himself.

Luke and Sam exited the bedroom still laughing. Luke looked Charley up and down then embraced him. "Charley, how are ya?"

Charley stood back and patted his stomach. "Never better. Keepin' fit. As you can see." He chuckled.

"I can." Luke grinned.

Charley had worked for Luke's father, as his second, for decades and knew where all the bodies were buried. Luke wanted him on his good side. He wanted to know where those bodies were and if he'd need to add a few now that his father was no longer running things.

"More importantly, Luke, how you doin'? Sorry 'bout your dad. A real shocker. Real unexpected, you know. Thought the bastard would live forever."

"Yeah."

"How's your mother?"

"Hangin' in."

"Good. Good to hear."

Luke walked over and sat behind the desk. "This is my associate, Sam Hayes." Sam plopped down in one of the chairs.

Charley gave Sam a bleached-teeth grin. "Howdy, Sam. Good to meetcha."

Luke pointed to the chair next to Sam. "Take a load off, Charley." He took another glass out of the drawer.

"Sure." Charley sat, pulled out a cigar, and lit it. He took a long drag and leaned back.

Luke filled the glasses. Sam handed one to Charley and they sat quietly, savoring the liquor.

"Joe certainly had good taste in scotch," Sam said, almost to himself.

"Among other things," mused Charley.

"Many other things," Luke quipped.

They all chuckled.

"Did you find the call button?" Charley pointed to the center of the desk.

"Call button?" Luke felt along the underside and found a button.

"It's an alarm. Rings directly to the bar. Within a minute, the troops arrive."

"Cool." Luke pushed the button.

"Joe had it installed a few months ago. No doubt you've seen the monitors in the bedroom. Got security cameras in the club and around the perimeter of the building."

"We found them. Joe expecting an assault? Or simply smart club management tools?"

"You never know," chuckled Charley.

The door opened and two burly bouncers rushed in. "Just testing." Charley waved them away.

The bouncers nodded and left.

Luke knew that one of Charley's special skills was that he could ooze charm when it was called for. He could get anyone to believe anything he said. Perhaps it was because he looked like a beloved granddad or kind uncle. The adage "he could sell ice to an Eskimo" could have been coined by someone who'd been swindled by him. The truth was that most of the ice was in his veins. Luke had known Charley all his life, so he knew he couldn't fully trust him, but he definitely wanted him on his team.

"So, Charley, what are your plans now Joe's gone."

Charley knew Luke was running a lucrative drug operation in Austin and had a few ideas on how he could help him out in Houston. But that could wait. There was a more immediate concern. "I guess that depends on you."

"Really?" Luke wondered what he meant by that and how much he knew about Joe's will. "Did you know he left fifty-one percent of the club to the bookkeeper?"

"No shit. To Gabriel Douglas?" Charley figured something like that might happen. He didn't care. He had no interest in the club apart from the fact that it attracted beautiful women and, as a VIP, he drank there for free. Hopefully that wouldn't change.

"Gabriel Douglas," Luke repeated.

"Hmm. I did not know that. But, to be honest, I'm not surprised. Joe always figured he owed the guy. The scars, ya know. The warehouse? He was kinda responsible."

"How's that my problem?"

"It isn't, I suppose," mused Charley.

"So, Charley, gonna help me out here?"

"You want me to get rid of Gabriel?"

"No, that would not be a great idea at this point. I'll find a way to take care of him."

"Right."

"I wanna meet Joe's contacts, where his shipments come in, etcetera. Obviously, I plan on merging our operations."

"Hmm. About that." Charley sat up straight.

Luke raised an eyebrow at Sam as he repeated Charley's words. "About that?" He couldn't believe Charley would give him the run-around or try to take over Joe's operation himself. And he didn't have the patience to play games with him, especially after being screwed out of the club. He had assumed Charley would want to take on the same role he had with his father. He'd hate for things to get violent, but they would if Charley tried to fuck him over.

"Drop-off location, no problem. Merging operations. That'll take a little time."

"How so? Grass, cocaine. What's the difference?"

"Joe closed his drug operations months ago."

"Now why would he do that?" *Here we go,* thought Luke. *I can't believe he's gonna try and fuck me over.* He gave Sam a sideways glance.

"There's no future in it. Cocaine, sure. Grass, not so much. Besides, the cartels were making things difficult."

"Cartels don't scare me," Luke scoffed.

"They should. Anyway, Joe found something even more lucrative."

"Like what?" Luke was losing patience. What was Charley playing at?

Charley knew things that Luke didn't, and he planned on making good use of that knowledge. He could have simply taken over the other business himself, but he knew if Luke found out, and he would find out, he'd be a dead man. He'd heard Luke had killed men for less. He decided it was best to bring him up to speed right away, thus ensuring another win-win relationship.

"He ever mention the cottage?"

"Cottage?"

"Yeah."

"No, Charley. He never mentioned the cottage." Was this more fucking bad news? He leaned forward. "Care to enlighten me?" he said, finding it hard to keep the sarcasm out of his voice.

"How about I show you?" *So far, so good,* Charley thought to himself. He chugged his scotch and heaved himself up off the chair. "I'll drive."

"No. We'll take my car and follow you." Luke didn't like surprises, and this was the second one today. Besides that, he wasn't sure how much he could trust Charley.

"Suit yourself. Black SUV parked across the street. I'll wait for ya," Charley said as he left the office, closing the door behind him.

"Cottage?" Sam asked Luke, who knew it was rhetorical.

"Right. What fucking cottage?" Luke took the gun out of the drawer and slipped it into the waist of his pants.

They left the club and followed Charley's SUV.

***

Charley led them ten miles outside the city limits and turned onto a dirt road that weaved through a wooded area ending at an old fifties-style waterfront bungalow. It looked innocuous, just another family vacation home along the Brazos River.

They parked next to Charley and followed him around the back. "No neighbors for at least a mile on either side," he boasted.

Luke stopped and nudged Sam. "Check that out."

"Knew you'd like it." Charley led them down the gravel path to the floating dock.

How beautifully convenient, thought Luke. He'd wondered where Joe unloaded his shipments. "The river leads directly to—"

Charley interrupted him. "Yep. Directly to the Gulf of Meh-he-co. Oh, yeah. Almost too easy."

"Easy?" Luke echoed.

"Deliveries arrive in the middle of the night. Nice and quiet. Power boat, retrofitted with an electric engine, pulls up to the dock, makes the drop, and they're gone in a matter of minutes."

Sam knew nothing was easy. Especially when it came to receiving product. That's when people made the most mistakes. Selling it was actually a lot easier. "Isn't cottage country patrolled?"

"Not as much as people think." Charley snickered. "Besides, we got a guy who has access to the schedules."

"It's all in who you know, isn't it, Charley," Luke said dryly.

"Yep," Charley concurred. He'd share all Joe's contacts with Luke. Just not yet. Knowledge equaled power, and he wasn't sure how generous Luke would be.

"What about distribution? Still viable?" Luke asked.

"Leave everything to me." Charley patted him on the shoulder.

Luke gave him a hard look. "So. This is what you wanted me to see."

"This and… follow me." They followed Charley up the path to the cottage. He took keys out of his pocket and unlocked the back door.

The decor inside the spacious room was reminiscent of an old-fashioned men's club. Two plush couches faced each other in front of an oversized fireplace. Six wooden, straight-back chairs were stacked next to it. A leather-covered bar, with matching stools, was at the back of the room across from a regulation-sized pool table. A bedroom and kitchen were visible through two open doors at the back of the room. A third door was closed and padlocked.

"How about a drink?" Charley went to the bar and began looking through the bottles. Luke watched him as he took his time deciding what he wanted. He chose a bottle of Herradura Silver Tequila and poured three long shots.

Luke went to examine the pool table. He was impressed. "Sam, this is a Brunswick nine-foot, slate table." Joe did have good taste when it came to the important things.

"Anyone want a game?" Charley asked.

Sam went to the locked door and shook the padlock. "What's this?" They both looked at Charley.

"The mother lode," Charley crooned and grinned.

"Mother lode," Sam repeated.

"Yep." Charley picked up their shots. "Have a drink. Then I'll show ya."

Luke was getting impatient. Enough already. "What mother lode?"

Charley laughed and handed them their glasses. "Here. Drink up, then I'll give ya the ten-cent tour."

Both Sam and Luke threw back their drinks, slapped their glasses on the bar, and walked over to the door.

"I can see patience isn't a virtue you both share." Charley reached into his pocket, pulling out another ring of keys as he approached the door. He unlocked it and led them down the stairs.

The walls and floor of the unfinished basement were concrete. Cameras had been installed close to the ceiling in two adjacent corners. The room was bare except for four folding metal chairs and a seventy-two-inch quaker-style table. A large pack of cable zip ties, some duct tape, burlap bags, rope, and empty fast-food cartons covered the table. Three unopened cases of bottled water were stacked against the wall next to another locked door.

"What's in there? Sam asked.

"That's where we store the merchandise," Charley said matter-of-factly. He unlocked the door and Sam and Luke looked in.

The space measured about twelve by twelve and had no windows. Mattresses were spread out on the floor with a few metal buckets lined up against the wall. The room smelled rancid; it was obvious the buckets, even though they'd been rinsed out, were used as makeshift toilets.

Sam whistled and whispered, "What the fuck?"

Luke nodded. "You can say that again."

Sam repeated, "What the fuck?" He scratched his head and asked aloud, "Is this what I think it is?"

"It's what you might call a way station, Sam. We source the merchandise, ensure quality and, once delivered, our hands are clean. They're never here for more than a few days. Not enough time to get caught with our pants down, so to speak. In fact, we just delivered a shipment, and I have another two-week deliverable we're looking to fill."

"Where do you find them?" Luke asked.

"Fair question. Used to be you had your pick of runaways at the bus and train stations. But that meant you had to spend time hanging out there. Now, it's like picking low-hanging fruit off a tree. They're online just waiting for you to find them. I've got an internet sleuth on the payroll. He tracks the girls on sleazy sites like OnlyFans. Even TikTok, believe it or not. Unfortunately for some of them, apart from having no talent, they aren't very smart either. They're willing to meet you anywhere, do anything, if they think you'll make them famous."

"Sounds too easy," Luke murmured.

"It is. And they're getting younger and younger. Fuck, I'd hate to be a father nowadays," Charley added.

"Right," Sam replied sarcastically. He picked up a roll of duct tape. "Who's buying this merchandise?"

"The Saudis. But they're picky."

Sam went over to the buckets, looked into them, and gagged. He rushed out of the room, bending to catch as much fresh air as possible. "Christ. How long have you been at this?"

"A while."

Why am I not surprised? Luke thought. Joe chose the worst line of work he could find. Human trafficking. Pretty much beats 'em all. He turned to Charley. "What else has he been up to? Kidnapping babies, killing old ladies?"

Charley laughed. "Your dad negotiated the sale of all his other businesses when he realized the profits that could be made. This is it, apart from Vox."

"Who owns the place?"

"You do. In a sense."

"Does my mother know about this property?"

"Did you?"

"Good point. What do you mean 'I own it in a sense'?"

"Joe insisted my name be put on the deed. That way, if anything happened to him, no one would come to see the property. I always assumed he expected you to inherit it. Just not in the legit, on-paper sense."

"Joe's gone. You didn't have to tell me anything about this, Charley. You could have simply taken the reins and run the operation yourself."

"Wouldn't do that, Luke. I'm loyal. To your dad and now to you." *And I prefer to stay alive*, thought Charley. Now was the time to begin negotiations. "I figure we keep things 'status quo,' so to speak," he said casually as he led them up the stairs.

"What *is* the status quo?" *This should be interesting*, thought Luke. *I wonder if he's honest as well as loyal.*

"Partners. Sixty-forty. I run the operation, and you get sixty percent of the profits." Charley figured Luke wouldn't want to get his hands dirty at this point.

"Sixty. How am I earning my cut?"

"Firstly, your reputation, Luke. Secondly, you're Joe Verde's son and heir. It's like having a celebrity lend their name to a brand."

Luke, eyebrows raised, looked back at Sam.

Charley shut the door behind them and locked it.

"Why keep it locked?" Sam asked. "Doesn't look like anyone could escape."

2 to party sometimes. Wouldn't want anyone accidently goin' down there." Charley smirked.

"Wouldn't be able to let them back up," Sam remarked, half-joking.

"Exactly." Charley shrugged. Sam realized he was serious.

Luke laughed. Somehow this seemed funny to him. The big black hole in which no one escapes… except to go to another big black hole somewhere in the Middle East. "Who else knows about this? Who else is involved?"

"Couple of trusted men."

Sam didn't know how he felt about all this and hoped that Luke would be just as conflicted. But the thought didn't last long.

"What's the money like, Charley?" Luke asked.

"Can be up to a hundred grand each, sometimes more, depending on their age and looks. The prettier the face, the nicer the ass, the better the price."

"Does this bother you at all?" asked Sam.

"Not really. Dope or dopes. What's the difference?" Charley went to the bar and poured them another shot.

Sam took a flask out of his pocket and filled it with the expensive tequila.

"A hundred grand each," Luke mused.

"Sometimes more," Charley quipped.

"Sometimes more," Luke repeated, looking at Sam.

Ah shit, thought Sam.

After downing another shot in silence, they left the cottage, each engrossed in his own thoughts.

"I can make introductions to get distribution back on track tomorrow, Luke. And fill in more of the details of this operation." Charley got into his SUV and waved. He figured it went well. He couldn't have been more helpful, now could he. Smiling, he took out his phone and began texting.

Sam, on the other hand, wasn't crazy about this new business. He and Luke had to have a serious discussion. "Calling this place a cottage is like calling Auschwitz a spa resort," he said as soon as they were in the car.

Luke grinned. "Charley is rather laissez-faire about what he's doing, isn't he?"

"Yeah. You could say that. I mean... depending on their age and looks? Their age? Where does he draw the line? Ten, eleven?"

"I'm pretty sure he doesn't pick them off the street on their way to school, Sammy. If they're on the internet, they're sure to be at least twelve." He snickered and smiled wickedly at Sam.

"I don't think it's funny, Luke. I mean. Where *does* he draw the line? It's a nasty business."

"The women he's talking about already sell themselves online. The difference is someone else is getting paid," Luke said, serious now. "Sixty percent and we, to quote Charley, don't get our hands dirty. Where's the downside?"

Sam just shook his head.

Luke hadn't decided if this was something he wanted a part of, but he needed to know if Sam would be on board if he did. "I haven't decided I wanna be part of this, Sammy, but if I do, are you with me?"

"Jesus, Luke." Sam sighed.

"Are you?"

Sam nodded. "Uh huh." He took the flask out of his pocket and took a deep drink.

CHAPTER TWO

BIRMINGHAM, ALABAMA

Tessa sat motionless in a corner of the small living room, her eyes red and puffy, oblivious to everyone in the room. Mourners milled about eating finger sandwiches and petits fours brought by well-wishing neighbors. Every now and then someone would come near and mumble a platitude, but most left her alone in her grief.

Frida, who'd been hovering nearby, approached and knelt in front of her. She and her husband owned the ranch Tessa and her mother worked and lived on. Frida knew how close Sarah and Tessa had been and was concerned that Tessa would not get over this devastating loss.

"How are you holding up?" She took her hand. Tessa focused on her but couldn't seem to respond. "Not to worry, dear. You know we think of you as our own. That means whatever you need, whatever, you just let me know." Tessa tried to give her an appreciative smile, but her mouth seemed to turn down into a grimace instead. "There,

there. I know," Frida cooed. "You go upstairs. I'll take care of things down here." She touched Tessa's cheek gently, then rose and stationed herself by the doorway to say goodbye to departing guests.

Tessa slowly got to her feet and, as in a trance, went upstairs to her room. Exhausted, she dropped face down onto her bed. She had no tears left but couldn't stop herself from letting out a small wail. She closed her eyes. Hopefully she'd wake up tomorrow and this would all have been a bad dream.

She'd wake to her mom calling in a singsong voice from the kitchen, over the sound of one of her favorite records. "Get up, get dressed, and get on down here, baby." Tessa would throw her clothes on and rush down to watch her dance as she cooked breakfast. *Yes,* she thought, *tomorrow this will all have been a dream.* She fell into a deep sleep.

Except when Tessa woke the next morning, the house was quiet. No music emanating from downstairs. No call to breakfast.

She pulled the covers close and looked around the room. Ordinarily, it was a reflection of her happy life; but now it would be a reminder of better times.

It was a typical teenager's room, decorated in pale pinks and greens. Campy pictures of friends she'd made at the ranch and church choir were wedged into the frame of her vanity mirror. Trophies and competition ribbons were lined up on shelves above the bureau. A *Twilight* film poster depicting the human, Bella, wrapped in the arms of the vampire, Edward, took up a sizable portion of one of the walls. Her mom introduced her to the film franchise, and Tessa had watched each one at least a dozen times. Her mom used to tease her, saying it was proof that she was a hopeless romantic.

They'd arrived at the horse ranch just outside Birmingham, Alabama, when Tessa was a baby. The owners offered a decent wage plus room and board and had a stellar reputation that assured their stalls were always full.

As soon as Tessa could walk, it was obvious she shared her mother's affinity with horses. She loved to groom and exercise them, and when she was old enough, she was put on the payroll. She was eventually able to buy a mare of her own, whom she named Pepper for no reason other than it sounded like peppy, which wasn't a great name for a horse but described the mare's personality perfectly. She began competitive riding soon after, at which both she and the mare excelled.

There were two framed photos on Tessa's night table: one of her atop Pepper, dressed in full riding gear, proudly holding a trophy, and the other of her and her mother laughing as they posed in silly, matching Halloween costumes. If not for the age difference, they could have been twins. Both had large brown eyes, a peaches-and-cream complexion, and pouty lips, all highlighted by their blonde tresses.

Tessa took her cell phone out of her pocket and looked through photos of her mother. She thought it might make her feel better, but it didn't. It just hurt. She held the phone to her chest and cried. She'd been crying for four days. She knew her mom would have wanted her to pull herself together, but she didn't think it was possible. She didn't know how.

Her mother had always joked that, apart from having Tessa as a daughter, she'd never been particularly lucky. This was proven true when she was stricken with a rare and terminal illness that afflicted only 0.1 percent of the country's population.

They'd been saving money to eventually buy a small ranch of their own, but all the savings had to go to hospital bills. The only time she'd ever seen her mother cry was when she found out Tessa had sold her beloved mare to buy the needed drugs. But Tessa knew the loss of Pepper, though painful, could never compare to her mother's suffering.

She left her room, still wearing her black funeral dress, and went down the hall to her mother's bedroom. She stood outside the room and put her ear to the door, listening, not knowing what she expected to hear. She slowly turned the knob and opened it.

Her mother's room was simply decorated. The only pieces of furniture were a bed, a night table, a bureau, and a waist-high bookcase. A framed photo of Tessa and a small lamp with a horse-shaped base were on the night table. A record player and a dozen or so LPs stacked between two bronze horse bookends were on the bureau. Her mother said the only way to listen to music was on vinyl, where the sound was raw and pure. She was right.

Frida had removed all the medical paraphernalia, put fresh linens on the bed, and tidied up. It was as if the last six months hadn't happened. She knew the woman meant well, but she resented her for assuming life would continue as though nothing had happened.

Tessa stood in the center of the room. "Mom?" The silence was deafening.

She opened the closet door. She gathered some of the hanging clothes, held them to her face, and breathed in deeply, then dropped to the floor. The clothes she wouldn't let go of came off their hangers, falling with her.

After a while, she pulled herself up, wiped her eyes and nose on her sleeve, and gathered up the clothes. *What am I doing?* she thought as she put the clothes back on their hangers. "As though nothing happened," she said aloud. She looked up at the closet shelf and spied a shoe box. She picked it up, sat back on the floor, and emptied the contents of the box out in front of her. It was full of every birthday and Christmas card Tessa had ever given her. Tessa looked through the cards, fighting to hold back more tears.

As she was about to put the cards back, she noticed an envelope stuck to the inside of the box. It was unopened and addressed to Sarah Begley from a Gabriel Douglas. Both recipient and sender had Houston addresses. Who was Gabriel Douglas? Why hadn't her mom read the letter? She ripped open the envelope, pulled out the letter and read it.

My Sarah,
I know you're mad. You have every right to be. I want to marry you, if you'll have me. I want to marry you right away. You're so beautiful. Please return my phone calls. Let me talk to you. Or, if you don't want to talk, write back and tell me what you're thinking.
Gabriel

Tessa picked up the envelope. The postmark was dated eight months before she was born. Could this man be her father? Her mom told her they'd separated shortly after she'd become pregnant. They'd both been orphaned young, so neither had any family. But she wouldn't tell her anything about him, just that they were both better off on their own. Maybe her mom just didn't want to explain things.

Who was Gabriel? It sounded like he really, really loved her, and the timing fit. Tessa took out her phone and searched "Gabriel Douglas." No social media presence at all. Not surprising. If he was alive, he'd be kinda old. She knew where he had lived from the envelope and searched the address on Google Earth. The house was in Houston, Texas. She wondered if he still lived there. It was nineteen years ago, after all. Then she searched his name and found a cell phone number. She dialed and it rang a few times before a man answered gruffly. "Hello?"

Tessa was trembling but forced herself to speak. "Mis-mister Douglas?"

"Yeah."

She listened for a few seconds not knowing what to say.

"Hello?" His voice louder now.

She hung up. It was him. It was Gabriel Douglas. She put the letter in her pocket and placed the box back on the shelf.

She knew she couldn't stay at the ranch. She had to make a life for herself away from all the memories that were too painful, and the search to find this man would be a place to start. "I have to know if he is my father, Mom. And, even if he isn't, he needs to know his Sarah is gone."

Tessa pulled an old suitcase out from under the bed and opened it. She gathered the record albums and bookends and put them in the suitcase. Then she opened the top drawer of the bureau and removed a small velvet jewelry box. She opened it and checked the contents. It held a gold cross necklace that matched the one she wore, a silver dove-inlayed purity ring, pearl earrings, the ticket stub from a Fleetwood Mac concert, and a baby's tooth. She put on the ring and necklace then closed the lid and placed the jewelry box in the suitcase.

She opened the second drawer and removed a pink cashmere sweater. She held it to her chest a moment before placing it in the suitcase. She took one last look around, shut the case, and left the room, gently closing the door behind her.

She went to her room and changed into a sweatshirt and jeans. She filled the suitcase with the two framed photos, a few keepsakes from friends, and only enough clothes that she'd need in the foreseeable future. She put her phone, iPad, the photos plucked from the frame of her vanity mirror, and what little money she had into her backpack and threw it over her shoulder. She stopped in front of the *Twilight* poster, put two fingers to her lips, and pressed them against Edward's cheek. She whispered, "Wish me luck," and closed the door behind her.

She stopped at the top of the stairs. It felt like she'd left something important behind. She returned to her room and looked at the poster. "You're coming with me." She took the poster off the wall, careful not to rip it, rolled it up tightly, secured it with an elastic hairband, and placed it in the flap on her backpack then left her room, dragging the suitcase, wheels bouncing down the stairs, to the main floor.

There were noises coming from the kitchen. Frida was tidying up. A warmed-over casserole sat in the middle of the table with a place set for Tessa.

Frida turned and gave her a bright smile. "I thought you'd be hungry. Please sit and eat. There are enough casseroles in the fridge to feed an army, I'm afraid. Don't know how you'll get through them all." Frida paused, noticing the suitcase and backpack. "Going somewhere?"

Tessa sat and dug into the casserole. "I'm going to Houston to meet my father."

Frida sat across from her. "Your father? But I thought—"

Tessa cut her off. "He lives in Houston. He has a wife. I've been in touch with him before, so I called to tell him what happened. He asked if I would come visit them. He's expecting me." She knew if she told her the truth, Frida would try to talk her out of it or even stop her from going. It was just a little white lie. But a necessary white lie.

"Well, you're eighteen. Old enough. I can't stop you from leaving. But wouldn't it be better to stay a while. Give yourself time to think things through?" Frida knew the girl was headstrong. She'd been that way from the time she could walk. She knew she wouldn't change her mind, but she had to do her best to dissuade her from making such a rash decision. "Even if just for a month or two?"

"I can't stay here, Frida. It hurts too much. I've always wanted to meet my dad. And he's so anxious to meet me." Part two of the white lie. *I'll go to confession as soon as I get settled*, she thought.

"What about your friends? Surely, you'll miss them."

"I'll keep in touch with them."

Frida sighed. This was a battle she couldn't win. She reached into her purse and took a wad of bills out of her wallet. "Here, take this. It's just a little to make sure you get there safe." She put the money next to Tessa's plate. Tessa opened her mouth to speak, but Frida put her hands up. "Won't take no for an answer. And you make sure you call me as soon as you get there, or I'll call missing persons. I swear I will. Your picture will end up on a milk carton. Understood?" Tessa got up and rushed over to hug her. Frida held her tightly and only let go of her reluctantly.

"Now finish eating. You're not going anywhere on an empty stomach. What shall I do with all your mom's things?" Frida looked toward the stairs.

"Please give everything to charity. My things too. I'd really appreciate it."

"But you might want them someday. When…"

"I won't. Honestly, Frida."

"Call me when you arrive?"

"I will." Tessa finished eating, and after another bear hug from Frida, they walked to the screen door. Tessa opened the door then remembered she had something for her. She took her mom's necklace off and put it in Frida's hand.

"What's this?"

"Mom would have wanted you to have it. To thank you for all the kindnesses. It matches mine. This way we'll always be connected."

"Oh, sweetheart. I'll cherish it… And keep in touch. You hear?"

"I will."

"Promise!"

"I promise."

Frida checked her watch. "Bus'll be here in fifteen minutes." Tessa nodded and turned to go when Frida grabbed her hand. "Wait." She rushed to the kitchen and filled a paper bag with leftover finger sandwiches, cookies, cheese, and an apple and rushed back to Tessa. "Here. You'll get peckish on the way." Frida hugged her again.

Tessa walked along the gravel road away from the only home she'd ever known. She was about to get on a Greyhound bus to a city she'd never been to before to find a man she didn't know. To top things off, she was on her own for the first time.

She stopped to look back at their small cottage next to the sprawling ranch house and stables where she had known so much happiness. She pulled out her phone and took a picture then waved at Frida, who stood on the porch watching her, and continued to the main road.

She reached the bus stop as the Greyhound was pulling up, brakes screeching. Tessa felt as though she was in a film, the lone female standing at the bus stop, unable to move. But the hiss of the door opening brought her out of her reverie and seemed to urge her onto the bus. She stepped up to the driver, reached into her pocket, pulled out her money, and handed it to him.

"I'm going to the terminal," she said.

He nodded. "Yep, I figured that, miss."

Tessa blushed. "Oh, of course." She continued down the aisle. There were only a few passengers, so she was able to claim the seats at the back and stretch out. She lay with her head comfortably positioned on her backpack and put her earbuds in. She pictured the kind of man Gabriel Douglas might be and, in a best-case scenario, how her life might be with him. That's all she had now. The dream of what was to come.

***

HOUSTON, TEXAS

After two buses, a train, and an expensive taxi ride, Tessa finally arrived at the address on the letter. She exited the cab and stood facing the house. She took it all in, somehow surprised at how normal everything seemed. It was a typical two-story suburban home with attached garage and well-manicured lawn. There were neighbors on either side whose houses were almost identical.

Yep. Perfectly normal, she thought. *What was I expecting? A castle with a dungeon and moat.* She giggled. *It's the suburbs for heaven's sake.*

She pulled out her phone and took a picture. Then she remembered she had to call Frida and dialed her. "Hi, Frida, it's me ... Yes, I'm here ... He's a great guy with a really nice family. Turns out I have a little brother *and* a little sister ... Uh huh. A whole new family ... Look, I gotta go. We're having a birthday barbecue for Noah and they're lighting the candles ... Yes, I'll keep in touch ... I promise. Bye." Tessa put her phone away. She hated lying, but she didn't want Frida to worry about her. The lies were adding up. She'd make sure to go to confession as soon as she could.

She removed her earbuds, straightened her clothes, and knocked on the door.

A million questions flashed through her mind. *What will he look like? What will he say? Will he be nice? Kind? Will he remember my mom? Will he believe he could be my dad? Will he even care? What if he doesn't like me? Or he actually does have a family? I never really thought of that. What do I do then? He wouldn't want someone showing up claiming to be his long-lost daughter. Maybe this was a mistake. But where would I go? Back to the ranch? That would make Frida happy. But I don't wanna go back; I have to move forward.*

She smiled up at the half-hidden camera mounted near the door.

Gabriel was at the kitchen table reading the paper when he heard the knocking. He was wearing his usual at-home garb — a faded, oversized, brown T-shirt, scruffy fleece sweatpants, and tattered sneakers — all worn in and extremely comfortable.

He picked his phone up and checked the security app. He saw Tessa smiling up at the camera and the suitcase behind her. She had the cherub-like features of a young girl and exuded an innocence that couldn't be camouflaged no matter how worldly she tried to act. *Probably selling Girl Guide cookies,* he thought. The knocking continued. Gabriel sighed. Might as well buy a couple of boxes. He slowly made his way to the door, stopping to take his wallet out of his pant pocket. He removed a few dollars, hoping she would have left by the time he opened the door.

Twenty years ago, Gabriel had made the decision to live a hermit-like existence. He didn't invite anyone to his home, and therefore, he never expected anyone to show up. Bad enough he sometimes had to interact with people at the club now. At least they had the decency not to stare and were smart enough not to ask questions.

Tessa continued knocking. *Maybe he's just not home,* she thought. *I'll have to come back later.* She turned to leave, wondering where she'd go to wait for him. She looked around and saw nothing but houses. She would have to find somewhere to wait and might even have to spend the night in a hotel. She hadn't planned for that. Why did she think he'd simply be there waiting to welcome her with open arms. She removed her backpack, placed it on the ground and rummaged around for her wallet.

The door opened and Gabriel stood there. His face was turned to hide his scars, and he held out a few bills. On closer inspection, he realized she wasn't young enough to be selling cookies, so she had to be selling religion. The backpack was probably full of brochures and the suitcase full of bibles. Irritated, he slammed the door while bellowing his usual response to anyone who knocked, "I'm not buying what you're selling. Go away."

Tessa hadn't heard the door open and looked up as it closed. She stood and knocked again. She was relieved. At least he's home. "Hello!"

Gabriel returned to the kitchen and picked up the paper, mumbling, "I gotta get a dog. A Doberman. Knock on *my* door... bite your goddamned hand off."

Tessa banged on the door. "Mr. Douglas! I'm not selling anything!"

He tried to ignore her. "Get a 'beware of Doberman' sign so they won't even step onto the property."

Tessa remained unphased. *It's okay. This is a challenge. I love a challenge. He probably thinks I have the wrong address.* She banged on the door again with even more force.

She's not gonna leave, Gabriel thought to himself. He returned to the door, walking slower this time, hoping she'd be gone by the time he got there but knowing she wouldn't be.

The door opened wide, and Gabriel didn't bother to hide his face this time. He barked, "You got one minute." Then he looked at his watch.

Tessa stared at him, unable to speak. Gabriel was used to getting this reaction when people saw him for the first time, so he allowed her a moment to collect herself. Tessa recovered quickly and gave him her biggest smile. "Are you Gabriel Douglas?"

He didn't reply, still looking at his watch. She continued, speaking faster now, "My name is Tessa Begley. You knew my mom, Sarah."

Gabriel's gaze snapped up from his watch. "What?"

"Sarah Begley. You knew her. I think you were friends."

Gabriel didn't respond. Tessa continued. She didn't want to give him a reason to shut the door. "I realize that it was a long time ago, but I know you wouldn't forget her."

Gabriel studied her face. She could easily be Sarah's child. Almost an exact replica, except that she was taller. But how did she hear about him? Where did she come from? Why was she here on her own?

"Where's Sarah?" he asked, looking up and down the street, hoping that she might be waiting for the girl in her car.

"She's not here." Tessa wasn't ready to tell him. She just didn't want to say the words out loud. Not until she had to. "I have the letter you wrote her. So, I know you were friends." She pulled the letter out of her pocket and held it out to him. He looked down at it but didn't reach for it. She held it out further. "I don't know if you wrote more than this. It's the only one I found. She never opened it."

Gabriel saw the handwriting on the envelope and knew he'd written it. "Where did you get that?"

"It was with my mom's keepsakes. It has your address on the envelope. That's how I found you." Tessa realized he wasn't going to take it so put it back in her pocket. "I just wanna talk to you."

"Does she know you were coming here?"

"I think she does."

"You think."

"Uh huh."

Gabriel remembered writing the letter and how he'd felt when Sarah hadn't written back. Then she just disappeared. He had no idea where she'd gone. He looked up and down the street again before stepping out. He picked up Tessa's suitcase and took her backpack from her. "Come in."

Elated, Tessa followed him into the house. The main floor consisted of a living room and a kitchen separated by stairs leading to the second-floor bedrooms. Patio doors in the kitchen opened to a small, untended garden.

To say the house was furnished sparingly would be an understatement. The only things in abundance were books and newspapers. In the living room, the couch sat across from a large flatscreen, an old record player with LPs lined up against the wall next to it and piles of books, obviously used as end tables, on either side of the couch. The furniture in the kitchen consisted of a table and four mismatched chairs. Gabriel was old-school about where he got his news and didn't trust anything he heard online or on television, so he had three mainstream newspapers delivered daily. He only threw the papers away when they were piled so high on the kitchen floor that they fell over.

Gabriel left things exactly where he had used them last. Pots and dishes were left in the dishrack, as he expected to use the same ones for the next meal. It was painfully obvious he was a man of simple means and didn't believe in hiring a cleaning service.

They entered the kitchen, and Gabriel pulled a chair out for her. "Sorry 'bout the mess."

So far, so good, Tessa thought to herself. *Doesn't look like a wife and kids live here. Maybe he's divorced. Anyway, now that I'm in his home how could he not let me stay.* She looked around the room. "Your home is nice. It's really cozy." Somehow, Tessa felt completely comfortable here. From the look of the place, she was sure she could make his life more comfortable. She saw herself cooking, cleaning, and generally taking care of him. His face didn't matter. She believed everyone had a story to tell and his was probably a doozy.

Gabriel put her suitcase and backpack in the corner and sat across from her. Not really knowing what to do or say, he simply leaned back with his head turned a little to show the unscarred side of his face.

"Should I make us a cup of tea?" Tessa went to the stove. She wanted his first impression of her to be positive. To show him how nice it would be to have her around the house. She picked the kettle up off the stove, shook it, and found it empty. She filled it and put it back on the stove. She opened a few cupboards and found them bare except for some boxes of cereal and a few tins of beans and soup. "Where do I find the cups?"

Gabriel pointed at another cupboard. She opened it to find one cup, sitting alone on a shelf and two mismatched plates below it on the next shelf. "Looks like you probably don't have many dinner parties," she said lightly and looked back at him.

Gabriel didn't respond and, keeping a straight face, nodded his head. *That was kinda funny,* he thought. *But I don't want her getting too comfortable. What does she want? Does she expect to stay here? Well, she can't. We need to get this straightened out right away.*

He watched her put the cup on the counter and take one from the sink and wipe it. "Tea bags?"

Gabriel pointed to another cupboard where she found a small box of tea bags. The whole time, she was thinking to herself, *You can do it. You're smart. Strike up a conversation. Let him know you can be interesting to have around. But whatever you do, don't ask too many questions too soon.* "Ever been married?" *Oh my god, I can't believe I just asked him that.*

"What? No." Gabriel was surprised at how forward she was.

That's good, she thought. "Got any kids?"

He harrumphed, "No. Not that it's any of your business."

Change the subject quick. He looks mad. "You have a very nice home," she said again.

Gabriel couldn't help but laugh. "You think?"

She smiled, relieved. "Oh, yes. It really feels lived in. I love it." Tessa dropped a tea bag into each of the cups and filled them with water from the boiling kettle. She turned to him. "Milk or sugar?"

Gabriel shook his head. "Black."

"Me too," she said. She opened a drawer where she found a few pieces of mismatched cutlery. Tessa took two spoons of different sizes and brought the teas to the table.

Gabriel noticed the ring on Tessa's finger as she placed his cup down in front of him. Sarah had worn one just like it. He remembered the day she got it. She was so excited. The symbolism meant everything to her. But as far as he was concerned, its only purpose was to brainwash teens into abstaining from the joys of endless casual sex. He pointed to it. "Sarah wore a ring like that."

"This was hers." Tessa blushed and turned the face of the ring around. "You know, I could make a much better cup of tea if you had a tea pot."

"Probably." Gabriel ignored his spoon, took the teabag out with his fingers, squeezed it, and put it on the table.

Tessa used her spoon to stir her tea and remove her tea bag. She picked up both tea bags, put them in the sink, and returned to the table. "My mom and I had a ritual. We'd have afternoon tea at precisely four o'clock everyday. We'd pretend we were royalty. She'd be a cousin of the Queen, who she detested, by the way, because she was the rightful heir to the throne and it had been stolen from her."

Gabriel smiled. "And you?"

She giggled. "I was her spoiled daughter who wanted both of them out of the way so I could rule."

Gabriel couldn't help but warm to her. *She is charming, in a childish way,* he thought to himself. Then he asked, "Wouldn't you be at school at four o'clock?"

Here was Tessa's chance to tell him all about herself and she jumped at it. "I was home-schooled."

"Home-schooled? That's odd. Figured the Amish, Quakers, and hippies in communes were the only ones who home-schooled their kids. Did you escape from any of those?" he asked.

Tessa giggled. "No. Of course not. We lived and worked on a ranch that boarded and trained horses. There was always lots of work to do tending to them. We fit my education in whenever we had time in the day. I'm pretty smart, you know, and a quick learner. I aced all the required courses. I have a four point oh GPA. I graduated with honors." She jumped up. "Wanna see my transcripts?" She grabbed her backpack, unzipped it, and reached in.

"I believe you." Enough chitchat Gabriel decided; time to get to the point. "Why are you here?"

She sat back down, serious now. "Sarah. Mom. Passed away last month."

Sarah dead? It hardly seemed possible. She was always so full of life. So… Gabriel still dreamed of her every now and then. He'd picture them happy. Married with a bunch of kids. She wanted kids. A whole litter she'd say. But gone? He couldn't picture that. It hurt even more than he would have expected. "Sorry." It was all he could think to say.

They sat in silence drinking their tea for a while before he could bring himself to ask how she died.

"What happened?"

"Paroxysmal Nocturnal Hemoglobinuria the doctors called it, or PNH to everyone else. It's sort of like anemia but so very much worse. A bone marrow transplant is the only potential cure that might save someone's life." She did her best to hold back her tears but couldn't. "I wasn't a match, and I'm the only family she had."

"Where's your father?"

"Never in the picture." Which was the truth, though she believed he was sitting across from her now.

"Oh."

"And no brothers or sisters either. Just me."

He studied Tessa's face, trying to guess how old she was. She looked fifteen but could be older. He had no idea. He couldn't believe anyone would let a woman like Sarah get away. Especially if she was having his kid.

They sat in silence for a few minutes.

Tessa struggled to get control of her emotions, but she couldn't hold back her tears. She dried her eyes and blew her nose. "Sorry."

"It's okay."

She put the tissue away, gave him her best smile, and sat up straighter.

"It's not genetic, you know." Tessa didn't want him to think she could get sick one day. "It isn't a condition that's passed down to children. I'm fine. Healthy as a horse. And that's something I know about."

There was another uncomfortable silence as Gabriel struggled to think of something to say. "You know horses?"

Tessa cheered up. Here's a topic she could go on about for hours. "I adore them! They're wonderful! Did you know they can sense how you're feeling?" She didn't wait for him to answer. "Because they have feelings themselves. And they're very affectionate, believe it or not. They don't judge anyone. Unless that person mistreated them, of course. Then look out!" Wanting to keep Gabriel's interest. "Did you know they can sleep standing up?"

Gabriel smiled. "No, I didn't."

Tessa leaned forward and, in a lowered voice, said, "Well, they can."

She saw Gabriel check his watch. She wanted desperately to keep his attention. "I had a horse, Pepper, a beautiful black mare."

"Had?"

"I sold her after mom got ill."

"That's too bad."

"No, it's okay. I knew I probably wasn't gonna stay on at the ranch without Mom anyway. Too many memories. You know?"

He nodded. Gabriel knew what she meant about wanting to distance yourself from certain memories. Still, he had to dissuade her from wanting to do that here. She was so young. Weren't friends really important at that age? "What about your friends?" he asked. "Won't you miss them?"

Tessa took her phone out of her pocket and waved it at him. "We keep in touch."

"Do they know you left? Where you were going?"

"Uh huh. My friends understand that this is important."

"They do. Do they? Hmm."

What else could she say to make him like her. *Oh,* she thought, *tell him you can sing.* "I'm a pretty good singer. I was the soloist in our church choir. I sang every Sunday. Want me to sing something for you? I'm sure I know lots of songs you might know. My mom played piano and—"

Gabriel interrupted her. "I remember Sarah could play."

Excited now, Tessa went on. "Yes. She was a real fan of old rock bands and Dolly Parton."

Gabriel couldn't help but laugh. "Dolly Parton?"

"Uh huh. We sang every night after dinner."

Gabriel looked at his watch again and knew he couldn't make her leave now. It was dark out. Besides, where would she go? He stood up.

Tessa watched him, afraid he was about to ask her to leave. But instead, to her relief, he said, "It's late. I think you should stay here tonight. You can have my room. I just have to change the sheets."

Tessa grabbed her backpack. "Where will *you* sleep?"

"There's a sofa in the other bedroom."

"A sofa?"

"Yeah."

She picked their cups up and took them to the sink.

Gabriel thought to himself, *Careful, she's already getting comfortable.* "What are you doing?" he asked.

"I just want to clean up a little."

"Please don't." He took her backpack from her and carried it and her suitcase up the stairs. Tessa followed.

There were two bedrooms and a bathroom on the second floor. All the windows in the house had cheap plastic blinds. *This guy doesn't believe in curtains,* Tessa mused. *He needs my help.* They passed a room with a worn-looking sofa and an exercise bike with jackets strewn over it and continued to his bedroom.

Gabriel dropped the backpack and suitcase on the floor and began stripping the sheets off the bed.

"Let me help." Tessa pulled the pillows out of their cases. Gabriel went to the linen closet in the hall to get clean sheets. They were the only extra linens and were in their store packaging. He couldn't remember when or why he'd bought a second set of sheets but was glad he had. He returned and they made the bed together.

"The bathroom is down the hall. I'll be in the next room if you need anything."

I'm here for the night and that's a great beginning, thought Tessa. "I'll be fine. Thanks for letting me stay."

"Yeah." Gabriel left, shutting the door behind him.

***

The next morning, Tessa rose with the sun. She rushed to get dressed and go down to the kitchen, hoping to make breakfast for Gabriel before he woke up. She was disappointed to find him at the table reading the newspaper.

"I was hoping I could surprise you with breakfast." She went to the stove and put the kettle on.

Gabriel looked up from his paper. "I don't usually eat breakfast." He pointed to the cup in front of him. "Just coffee."

"Oh." She sat across from him. "Want some more?"

"No." Gabriel folded the newspaper and put it on the table. He was awake most of the night, and not just because that couch was bloody uncomfortable, which it was, but because he needed to figure out how to get her out of the house and on her way back to the ranch. And the sooner the better.

"Why are you here, Tessa?"

Here goes, she thought. "Because I think I have proof that you're my dad."

"What? Why?" He had to admit to himself that it could be true, even if they'd only made love that one time. But if it were true, what then? What would he do with a kid. Never mind a teenage girl.

"I'll show you." Tessa ran upstairs and returned with the letter. She put the envelope in Gabriel's hand. "Look at the postmark on the envelope. I'm eighteen. Read the letter. It seems like you and mom were…"

"Okay." He believed he remembered every word he'd written. Holding it brought back the guilt of their last meeting. Of her leaving. Of not knowing where she'd gone or how she had been all these years. He read the letter, folded it, and handed it back to Tessa.

"You think that means I'm your father? Don't you think she would have told me if I'd gotten her pregnant? Besides, we were young. I doubt I'm the only man Sarah ever slept with." He regretted saying it as soon as it came out of his mouth.

Tessa tried to hold back the tears. How could he say that. "You think she slept with someone else? That it could have been just any guy who got her pregnant?" Her voice rose uncontrollably. "My mom wasn't like that. I know that for sure. And so should you. I only ever saw her with one man, Shawn. And they dated for the longest time. But… but he died in a car accident, or she would have married him. She would never think of dating more than one person at a time." The kettle was whistling, and she was happy for the excuse to get away from the table. She wiped her eyes and made the cup of tea, keeping her back to him.

Gabriel felt bad that he'd upset her, but he had to get her to leave. "You're right. I'm sorry. Sarah would never do that. What do you think you can expect from me?" He asked, even though he thought he knew the answer.

"Nothing. I just wanna get to know you. To get to know my dad. Just let me stay here for a little while."

"Look at me."

She turned to him. He spread his arms then pointed to his face. "You don't want me for a father. And I wouldn't know how to be one anyway."

She went to the table and sat across from him. "But I do. I do want you for a dad. I know mom ghosted you; but I would never do that."

"Ghosted?"

"She never answered your letter."

"Oh. Yeah." Gabriel shook his head. "Doesn't matter."

"It does. And you'll see, I'm really easy to get along with. You don't have to take care of me. Just let me stay, for now. I can take care of you."

"I don't need taking care of."

"But I could anyway."

"It's just not a good idea. Sarah would not have been happy about this. I'm not a good guy, Tessa. I'm definitely not father material."

"I don't believe it."

"Well, believe it. I have enemies. If they found out I had a daughter, you would be a welcome target for them. They would use you to get at me. To hurt me."

"Enemies? What kind of enemies?"

"The kind no one wants to have."

"I don't understand."

"This isn't something you should have to understand."

"But I—"

"Look, Tessa, the people I associate with are not nice people. They're dangerous. Leave it at that."

Tessa stared at him, wanting desperately to come up with a solution. He was trying to scare her off. Even if he did have enemies, she was sure she could never actually be in real danger. Still, she had to play along.

"Then no one has to know I'm here."

"And how would we pull that off? What about college? What about your singing? Choir? Do you think you can just hide in this house? For how long? That's no life for a young woman." *That'll scare her,* he thought, pleased that he'd come up with enough reasons why she wouldn't want to stay.

Tessa's mind was racing. *How can this work. Think. You're a good storyteller. You aced that MSU online writing course.* She thought for a moment, then replied, "Easy peasy."

"Easy peasy?" Gabriel chuckled. *She's definitely not your typical urban teen,* he thought.

"Easy peasy lemon squeezy. We don't tell anyone I'm your daughter. I would be the maid."

"Why would *I* have a live-in maid?"

Tessa looked around. "Right. Not a maid. You could be sponsoring me. From, ah, I don't know yet, but from somewhere far away. I'm a very distant relative from Canada. You're letting me stay with you until I get my work permit."

"You'd still be related. Therein lies the problem."

"Right. Let me see… How about, instead of that, I'm the daughter of an old friend. He's in the army and is stationed far away. His wife, *my mother,* passed away and I have no other relatives. So, he begged you to take me in until he finishes his tour of duty and can come home. That would be my story."

"That's some imagination you got."

"You don't have to tell anyone anything. Your enemies wouldn't know I'm here at all. You don't ever have visitors. You said that yourself. So, that's not a problem."

Gabriel looked at her for a long while. Living on one's own wasn't all it was cracked up to be. He had to admit he was lonely most of the time. She was already growing on him. It might be nice to have some life in the house. And, after all, she most likely *was* his daughter. Maybe they could make this work. "Okay, we'll give it a try," he conceded.

Tessa jumped up. "Yeeess."

"Whoa. Hold on. First, you have to follow my rules. And you may not like them. Second, you have to swear that the minute I think you're in danger, this arrangement is over. Understood? This is temporary. If I say you have to go, then you have to go."

"I swear." She crossed her heart, rushed around the table, hugged him tightly, and kissed him on his scarred cheek. He leaned back, surprised at the unexpected intimacy. She returned to her chair. "Now. What do you want for dinner, Dad?"

"Dad?" That was a word he had never expected to be called.

Tessa nodded. "Dad."

***

Luke and Sam stood on the dock, smoking in silence as they waited for their delivery. They were appreciating what a beautiful, balmy night it was. The only sounds that broke the quiet were the serenade of katydids and the chirping of crickets in the distance. Luke had a flashlight and Sam a metal briefcase.

Almost silently, Luis and Diego pulled their boat up to the dock. They were professional drug runners and were adept at making deliveries at night. They used a Navionics app to navigate without lights and wore black clothing with knitted caps pulled down to their eyebrows, rendering them almost invisible.

Luis jumped off the boat and Diego passed them four cardboard boxes filled with plastic-wrapped, one-kilogram bricks of cocaine.

Luke took out his stiletto and made a small cut in a random brick from each box to taste, then nodded at Sam. Sam handed the briefcase to Diego, who opened it and, using his flashlight, did a quick count.

Luis looked around before pulling out a cigarette and lighting up. "Can't smoke on the boat," he complained.

"Long night?" Luke asked casually.

Luis took a deep drag. "Just one more delivery," he said through a veil of smoke.

Luke looked at him sideways. "I'm thinkin' of upping my order by 20 percent. Think you can do that for me?"

"No."

"No?"

"No. This territory belongs to Carlos. I can deliver only this much. More and it would be noticed."

"What difference is a few more kilos gonna make?"

"I'm risking my life delivering anything to you in Houston, Luke. I would be a dead man if Carlos found out. This much can go unnoticed. More would not."

"I'm not worried about the cartels."

"I am."

"I'm willing to negotiate a price."

"Sorry, my friend." Luis, eyebrows raised, shrugged his shoulders.

Diego turned on the ignition. "We gotta go, Luis."

Luis dropped his cigarette and stomped it out. He hopped back onto the boat.

"Pleasure doing business, Luis." Luke saluted him as they sped away, then growled, "Shit."

"It was worth a try," Sam quipped.

Luke scoffed. "Fucking cartels. Well, it's not our only option, is it?"

Sam sighed. "Nope."

They carried the boxes to the cottage, where two of their crew met them to help carry the load to the basement.

The room had been set up to process the cocaine to sell on the street. The table now had bags of flour, a digital scale, and hundreds of transparent ziplock dime bags lined up on the table. Snake took a few bricks out of one of the boxes and put them at one end of the table.

Luke looked at his watch. "Gentlemen, we will leave you to it."

CHAPTER THREE

The electric strains of a guitar riff almost covered the screams of the woman in the bedroom as she tried to elude the man chasing her.

The man was Luke. It would be reasonable to assume he didn't know her name. He'd slept with most of the women who worked at or frequented the club and usually didn't exchange more than a few words before, during, or after taking them to bed. Luke didn't date women. He didn't hit on them either. He didn't have to; they came on to him. Many women mistook his interest in them for real affection, but they were inevitably proven wrong.

He did, however, know this woman's name. It was Mika, and he enjoyed playing with her more than the others. She had skills — skills worth returning for.

Mika was twenty-five with doll-like features, alabaster skin, and long, silky hair that fell to her waist. Her slender frame made her seem delicate, almost fragile, but anyone who thought this would be very wrong. Mika was not a woman to be trifled with.

She'd been managing two very successful "rub 'n' tug" massage parlors when she ran into Joe Verde a few years back. She had the reputation of being a smart businesswoman, and when he met her, he decided right away that she'd be the perfect person to manage the Vox. So he offered her a salary and bonus that no one in their right mind could turn down.

He'd chosen well. Mika ended up attracting a more high-end clientele, and these customers would often invent trivial complaints requiring management's presence. She was always happy to play along. They insisted on tipping the exotic beauty, even though it wasn't called for, so she never left the club with less than a grand in her pocket.

Mika was second-generation Japanese and was related to a senior member of the Yakuza, one of the largest organized crime syndicates in the world. It was something she didn't tell anyone, as it wasn't exactly the greatest calling card when she met a man she wanted. It would be the quickest way to scare them off.

But not Luke. She had other reasons for not telling him. She figured Luke could hold his own against anyone, but she was smart enough to realize he'd see the connection as an opportunity to get into a much bigger game than the one he was in, whatever that was. She also knew it wouldn't even dawn on him to consider the repercussions she'd face for having introduced him if he screwed up. So, hopefully, he'd never find out.

They were both naked except for Mika's gold cuff bracelets and anklets. She circled the bed, laughing and screaming simultaneously, with Luke in hot pursuit. She picked up one of the lamps, yanked the cord out of the wall, and made as if she was going to throw it at him. Luke grabbed for her and she threw it. He was able to deflect it with an arm and it hit the wall falling, in pieces, to the floor.

"Oops," she pouted. "Thought you'd catch it. Honest."

He grabbed her arm, but she slipped out of his grasp. He caught her again and pushed her up against the wall. She raised her arms above her head and posed enticingly. "Do you think I'm beautiful?"

"Yeah." Luke grabbed her wrists with one hand and pulled her ass toward him with the other.

Mika whispered back, "I wanna be your girl. Your *special* girl."

Luke backed away and turned. "Why," he said, almost to himself.

"Because. Because I can make you happy like no one else. I know you. I know what you want." She pressed herself against him from behind and grabbed his cock. "I know what you need."

He removed her hand and turned to face her. "You do?"

Mika ran her hands down her body seductively and danced erotically. She reached out to him. "Make me yours."

Luke smiled. "Be careful what you wish for."

Mika cooed, "I know exactly what I wish for."

Luke shrugged. "I see we're about to get serious." He picked up his jeans, reached into one of the pockets, and pulled out a stiletto. He flicked it open. The slender blade curved to a needle-like point. He ran the length of the blade across his tongue then puckered his lips and kissed it.

Mika went to the bed, sat, and spread her legs wide apart. She beckoned him over with one of her red lacquered fingernails. Luke slowly walked over and knelt in front of her. "You wanna be mine?" He smiled wickedly and put the tip of the knife to her belly.

"Yes." She threw her head back and arched her torso, thrusting her taut abs toward him. "All yours!"

"Then stay still; this will only take a minute." He fondled one of her breasts as he carved a "V" below her belly button with the stiletto. Drops of blood trickled out of the wound. He wiped the knife on the sheet. "Does it hurt?"

"Yes," she whispered.

"Shall I kiss it better?"

"Yes."

Luke pushed her gently back on the bed as he bent and kissed the wound. He continued kissing her, leaving a path of blood as he made his way to the spot between her thighs. She moaned in delight and grabbed his hair, pressing him to her.

***

Riki sat on the sidewalk curb across the street from the Vox. His restless right leg belied the fact that he had been waiting patiently for the last hour.

He could always be found wearing the same uniform: Doc Martens, skinny jeans that only served to accentuate his skinny legs, and a white T-shirt with a black skull and bones embossed on the front. His sleek ponytail hung the full-length of his vintage aviator jacket.

Riki made an effort, unsuccessfully, to look tougher and older than his twenty years. His slender facial features and smooth skin didn't help. He made an attempt to grow a beard, thinking that would make the difference, but failed because what little facial hair he had grew in tufts that made him look like a wannabe hipster. Nothing could be worse than that, so he quickly gave up on the idea.

He pulled out his phone and checked the time. It was four o'clock. Riki had heard that Luke usually had a quick shag after lunch with one of the many willing waitresses or dancers, then spent the rest of the afternoon alone in his office. Hopefully, he'd be able to sneak up the stairs and find Luke there.

Riki knew he was one of Luke's most connected distributers, and yet it was impossible to get a face-to-face with him. He'd only ever been allowed to talk to his crew, and it was made abundantly clear that he wasn't welcome at the club. Not up to Vox's standard of clientele. Which was a joke because their most favored customers were well-known criminals and lowlifes.

Even when Riki was able to get past the doormen, Luke was unreachable, as his men kept an eye on the stairs to Luke's suite.

But, this time, Riki had to get to him. If the rumors were true that Luke was investing in a new venture, Riki wanted in on whatever the action was. He had skills. Even more importantly, he had drug connections he figured Luke couldn't access without him.

He took a vial of coke out of his pocket and snorted a few lines off the back of his hand. He sniffed, coughed, and wiped his nose on his sleeve as though it were the most natural thing to do. He pulled an inhaler out of his pocket and used it. Twice. Riki was dumb enough to be a cokehead who suffered from bad asthma.

He stood, wiped the sidewalk dust off his jeans, and crossed the street.

***

Gabriel was working in his office. Now that he had ownership of Vox, he liked to come in and audit the prior night's receipts from time to time. Just good business practice. The club's reputation as a hot spot continued to increase exponentially, and the books were in even better shape because of his vigilance. Now, if he could only get rid of the obvious criminal element.

A thud and shriek from the suite above penetrated the quiet. He looked up at the ceiling and shook his head but continued working on his laptop. Gabriel entered the last figures, stretched, and rubbed his arm, extending his scarred fingers. He grabbed a bank deposit bag and left his office to make his way to the cash register behind the bar. Not surprisingly, many customers paid in cash. And they were the ones who spent the most.

He stopped outside his office to survey the men assembled around the bar. They were Luke's so-called trusted associates. Snake and Joey were two misfits who reported to Charley. They were as deadly as vipers and as easily riled up.

Snake's demeanor was that of a rattler about to strike. One of his eyebrows had been replaced by a deep scar when, at the tender age of eight, his mother took a swing at him with an iron frying pan. He had no idea which of his many misdemeanors it had been for. He had a scruffy goatee and parted his greasy hair too low on the side. This, together with the one eyebrow, gave his face an unusual tilt. He always wore a bolo tie, black shirt, black chinos, and snakeskin boots. He never spoke, but no one had much to say to him anyway, unless he was hurting them, which was more often than not.

Joey was the more volatile of the two. He was short and stocky but could move like a panther when necessary. He always wore T-shirts, baggy jeans, and Nike Cortez trainers. He still lived with his parents. When he'd decided he wanted more privacy, it was suggested he could have the basement all to himself. Instead, he insisted his parents move down there. They acquiesced. Joey had a way of asking people to do things that would never produce a negative response. He had the reputation of not caring whether he lived or died. Everyone knew that a man who didn't value life was not to be trifled with, even if he looked harmless enough.

Snake was fast asleep at a table near the bar. His mouth was wide open, arms and legs crossed, with his feet resting atop the table. A scruffy, brown-and-white mutt was asleep under his chair. The dog looked like it had seen better days.

Joey was leaning back, balancing on a chair across from Snake, cleaning his nails with a penknife.

Charley sat at the bar and nursed a beer while idly watching the bartender, TJ, play solitaire.

TJ had been fifteen and homeless when he showed up at the club looking for work. Joe saw potential in him, so gave him a job sweeping up. He even let him sleep in the cellar until he could save up enough money to get a place. He eventually had TJ trained to tend bar, for which TJ was eternally grateful. It hadn't necessarily been out of the kindness of his heart, as Joe knew you couldn't buy that kind of loyalty. And now that loyalty extended to Luke.

TJ was the Vox's most popular bartender. He looked and acted like a clean-cut preppy working his way through college. It got him the most tips. He'd even bought a varsity jacket online, which he hung on a hook next to the bottle display behind him to complete the facade. Both female and male patrons loved him, and he had his pick of women to take home every night. This irritated Joey to no end.

TJ could usually be found behind the bar long before his shift was due to start because he knew they'd be there. He was out of his league when it came to these men, so he treaded carefully. He tried to keep his mouth shut and be respectful, whether he thought they warranted it or not. But he did listen furtively when they talked shop, hoping to learn the game.

He was always up for a money-making opportunity when offered. Bartenders saw and heard even more than people realized. The men expected him to have an ear to the ground for information that might benefit them. They also had him keep an eye out for anyone they were looking to make an example of. That sometimes meant that person would disappear. *Not my problem,* he'd say to himself. *I just pass on the information; what happens after that is not my business.*

Gabriel walked behind the bar and opened the cash register. TJ grinned. "Hey, Gabriel."

Gabriel mumbled, "Hey, TJ."

The other men ignored Gabriel as he emptied the tray and began counting the money. Without looking up Joey said, "TJ, get me a beer."

TJ continued his game. "Feel free to get it yourself." He figured he could say that to Joey as long as Charley was there to protect him.

Joey, pissed now, yelled, "You're the fuckin' bartender. Get me a fuckin' beer."

"Shift doesn't start for 'nother hour, Joey." TJ's eyes stayed on his game.

Joey glared at him.

TJ looked up and quickly looked away, thinking he might have gone too far. "Okay, chill."

Charley, who did have a soft spot for TJ, said matter-of-factly, "Joey, take it easy on the kid."

TJ brought Joey the beer. Joey chugged it and griped, "It's his fuckin' job."

Sam entered the club. He walked to the table and kicked Snake's chair. Snake snorted, opened his eyes, focused on Sam, and sat up quickly. Sam glanced up at the suite. "He upstairs?"

Snake nodded. The men looked at each other and laughed. Sam went to the bar, took his phone out, and started watching the screen intently.

Charley leaned over, trying to see the screen. "Who's playin'?"

"Orioles and Rays. Fourth inning."

"Skin in the game?" Charley leaned closer.

"Yep."

Charley moved his stool over and both men concentrated on the screen.

TJ poured Sam a shot of tequila and placed it in front of him. Sam drank the shot. TJ grabbed a stein. "Beer, Sam?"

"Sure." TJ poured a beer from the tap and put it in front of Sam before refilling the shot glass. Sam chugged it back, and TJ refilled it.

Joey gave TJ a dirty look. "Kiss ass."

TJ ignored him and returned to his card game. However, after a minute, he poured another beer and put it on the counter. *Better not push my luck,* he thought. *Don't wanna find a knife in my back.* "Use another one, Joey?"

Joey snarled at him, then yelled, "Hey, Charley, how much those twins cost ya last night?"

Without looking up, Charley responded good-naturedly, "I don't pay for it. I'm so pretty, chicks naturally flock to me. Ask your mama. She'll tell ya. Right, Gabriel?"

Gabriel ignored them. None of them ever passed up the chance to annoy him. But they were always careful not to go too far. Joe had made it clear he was not to be trifled with, and now Luke even said he was off-limits. Both directives were given without explanation, so they assumed he had been a major badass in his day. No one knew why he would merit that reputation or how he got his scars, but there seemed to be something not right about him regardless.

Joey grabbed his crotch. "How would Gabriel know? He ain't had pussy in decades. Probably shriveled up and fell off. Huh, Gabriel?"

Gabriel looked at Joey with a cold, dead-eyed stare. Joey immediately regretted what he'd said and shrugged innocently. "Just kiddin', Gabriel. You know I'm just kiddin'."

The dog woke up and crawled over to sniff Joey's crotch. Startled, he threw his hands in the air and yelled, "Get this fuckin' dog away from me."

He'd been bitten as a kid and was afraid of dogs, regardless of their size. He knew if the men found out, they'd tease him mercilessly. He might even lose some street cred, so he pushed the dog back, stood up, and kicked it hard, pissed that he'd been put in that position. The dog yelped and limped over to Charley.

Riki entered quietly. He saw them and quickly ducked behind a table. He berated himself. *Shit. They must have come in through the back door, you fucking idiot. Shit. I didn't even figure that in. Shit.*

Gotta go slow on the blow, man. Can't plan things if I'm too high. I know that. Shit. He crouched lower.

TJ came out from behind the bar and picked up the dog. He said quietly, "You're such a fuckin' tough guy. She's just a dog."

Joey growled, "What'd you say?"

TJ replied louder, "Nothin'."

"Keep it away from me, or I'll slit both your throats."

TJ answered, in a voice just loud enough for Joey to hear him, "You're a fucking ass." Joey lunged at him, grabbing him by the throat. "What'd you say? You little punk." TJ dropped the dog and tried to pull Joey's arms away.

The dog yelped. Sam and Snake grabbed hold of Joey and pulled him off.

Riki couldn't believe his luck. Taking advantage of the ruckus, Riki rushed by them unnoticed.

Gabriel saw him sneak past the men and climb the stairs. He smiled to himself, put the bills into the bank deposit bag, closed the cash register, and returned to the office.

TJ whined, "Didn't say nothin', Joey." He quickly retreated behind the bar.

Joey returned to his seat and stared daggers at TJ. He pulled his pistol out of the back of his pants and aimed it at TJ. He pretended to pull the trigger. "Ah, pow. Ah, wow."

Charley sighed. "He's just playin' with ya, man. And, if it makes you feel better, we all know he's wrong. You actually look more like an asshole than an ass."

Joey winked at TJ and put the gun back into his waistband.

Sam added, "Leave the kid alone, Joey."

Joey shrugged, closed his eyes, and leaned back in his chair.

***

Riki reached the suite unseen. He listened at the door, wiped his nose across his sleeve, and straightened his clothes. He paced back and forth, gathering the courage to enter, and murmured to himself as though reciting a mantra, "Come on. You can do this. He owes you. You can do this. He owes you. You *can* do this. He *owes* you."

Riki put his ear to the door again. He turned the handle and pushed the door open. "Hey, Luke, my good friend." He entered and looked around. Empty desk, empty office. *Shit. He's not here. Just my fuckin' luck.*

He went to the window and opened it to access the fire escape, not wanting to take the chance of sneaking past the men again. He was about to climb out the window when he heard noises coming from the other room. Riki went over and leaned against the door, pressing his ear to it. He held on to the handle and it turned accidently. The door swung open and Riki fell into the bedroom.

Luke was on his back. Mika was riding him. Luke smiled. "Deep enough for ya?"

"Never, never!" she screamed.

Riki scrambled up off the floor. He recognized his sister's voice. "Mika?"

Luke heard him and pushed Mika off onto the floor as he sat up. "What the fu—"

Mika stood up. The blood from Luke's carving had smeared all over her belly.

All Riki could see was the blood and all he could think of was protecting Mika. He lunged at Luke, pulling out his knife. "You cut my sister!"

Before he could reach Luke, Mika punched Riki in the face. It was hard enough to knock him out, and he dropped.

"Sorry about that, Luke. No idea why he's here." She stood over Riki, shaking her head.

Luke took Riki's arm and dragged him into the office.

Mika wrapped a sheet around her waist and followed him.

Luke lifted him onto one of the chairs and sat at his desk, not bothering to get dressed. He peered at Riki and saw the resemblance. He wondered why he'd never noticed it. "I didn't know you had a brother."

And that's the way I wanted it, thought Mika. She shrugged. "Can't pick your family."

She had been cursed with a brother who wasn't very bright, who did way too much blow, and who would never amount to anything except to have his face plastered on the front page of some newspaper because he was one of the victims of the latest mob hit. The family had written him off long ago, so she did feel responsible for him, often letting him sleep on her sofa and even tossing him a little money and intel now and then. But the last thing she wanted was for anyone to know he was related to her, and she'd made it abundantly clear to him that she'd write him off if anyone found out.

Riki slowly regained consciousness. He saw Luke smiling at him from across the desk. *Shit. I'm gonna die. Luke is gonna have me snuffed. I tried to kill him. Fuckin' coke. I tried to kill Luke fuckin' Verde. Fuckin' coke.*

Leg shaking uncontrollably, he reached into his pocket, which didn't seem to worry Luke at all. He pulled out his inhaler and took a deep breath. Riki turned to see Mika leaning against the bedroom doorframe looking as though she would kill him herself. It was now obvious she'd been in no danger, and he had jumped to a very wrong conclusion.

"How the fuck did you get up here?" Luke asked. He had Riki's knife in his hand. "I don't remember inviting you, and I don't think Mika wanted you to join us."

Riki couldn't answer and avoided looking Luke in the eye. *I'm a dead man. Oh fuck. I'm a dead man.* The words kept repeating on a loop in his mind.

Luke put the knife in a drawer. "If there's one thing I expect from people, it's loyalty. Well, two things really: loyalty and respect. Invading my private space? Attacking me? Is that your idea of loyalty and respect? And now I have to make an example of you. That really pisses me off! You were such a good earner. You knew your place."

The tense he used wasn't lost on Riki. *Were such a good earner? Knew your place? Oh, I'm a dead man.*

Riki looked at Mika pleadingly, as if she might have the power to help him. Mika gave him a look that said, *watch what you say!*

Luke lit a cigarette with a gold lighter that had the letter "V" engraved on it. He took a deep drag and exhaled.

Riki coughed and wiped his nose on his sleeve, careful not to look at Luke or antagonize him in any way.

"I believe I asked you how you found yourself in my bedroom. How you could ever have the balls to come into my private suite without being invited. My private suite? My bedroom? And it had better be a very, very good reason." Luke's voice dropped to a whisper. "Look at me."

Riki gathered all the strength he had, thinking all he could do was beg and play even more stoned than he was. He must be really stoned. How else could he have done such a stupid thing? And maybe tell a few good lies. That might keep him alive. He could do that. He leaned forward, looking directly at Luke, and whined, "So, so sorry. Luke, I didn't know you were there. Just gonna wait 'til you came to your office to talk to you. But I heard a noise. Thought maybe it was a burglar." He pointed to the bedroom wildly.

"A burglar?" Luke laughed. Riki really was an idiot and an even worse liar. "So, you were trying to protect my property." *This is fun,* he thought and decided to toy with him. "You came into my suite uninvited to protect my property."

"No."

"No? You wouldn't protect my property?"

"Ah. Yeah. Sure. I would."

"I still don't know what you're doing here."

Riki tried to laugh nonchalantly. "Too much blow." He wiped his nose. "Got the idea I could talk to you mano a mano."

Luke scoffed. "Mano a mano? Do you even know what that means?"

"Wanted to talk."

"You could have passed your message on to the men downstairs. I'm sure they would have been more than happy to relay it to me." Both of them knew this wasn't true. Riki used to be a good earner, but he was so stoned most of the time now that it was hard to imagine he could be capable of coming up with a plan or an idea worth listening to. Luke couldn't believe that Mika and Riki had come out of the same womb.

"Enough." *This is boring.* Luke pressed the hidden buzzer. He went to the front of the desk and leaned on it, causing Riki to shift even more uncomfortably. Luke took another cigarette out and put it into Riki's mouth. He lit it. Riki didn't smoke, he couldn't smoke because of his asthma, and Luke knew it. Luke took a deep drag on his cigarette and looked at Riki, who knew he had to do the same. He did and coughed. "Again." Luke took another drag and Riki followed suit, coughing uncontrollably. Luke butted out his cigarette. He took the cigarette from Riki and did the same with it.

Riki wheezed, struggling to breathe.

"Trouble catching your breath?"

Riki reached into his pocket to get his inhaler. Luke took it away from him. "What did you wanna talk about?"

Riki struggled to answer. "I heard…" Riki wheezed.

Luke smiled. "What did you hear?"

"New… opportunity… Oxy… maybe?"

"And who told you that, little monkey?"

Riki wheezed, "No one… I hear things… I could help… I'm a good earner. You owe me."

"I owe you? I. Owe. You?" Luke growled.

The office door opened. Joey, Snake, Charley, and Sam rushed in with guns in hand. Luke returned to sit behind his desk.

He threw the inhaler at Riki, who used it repeatedly.

Luke put his feet up and lit another cigarette. Looking at the cigarette, he said in a gentle voice, "Why do you think I would ever wanna involve you in my business? You're a parasite. You only survive because I let you, because I choose to be your host. And now, the feast is over."

Mika knew that Luke was about to have his men dispose of her brother and thought she might be able to save him. She cleared her throat. The men, who hadn't noticed her, looked at her now appreciatively. "Hey, Mika, looking good." Charley grinned sheepishly.

"Thanks, Charley." Mika winked at him and smiled at Luke. She pouted and, in a little girl's voice, said, "Luke, I'm getting lonely. Come back to me."

"Coming, sweetheart." Luke rose and went to Mika. She whispered in his ear, "Please, don't kill him."

He looked at her for a moment, then smiled. He hadn't had his fill of her yet and killing her brother might lower her enthusiasm a little. Without taking his eyes off her, he said, "Snake, show him why it was a mistake to enter my suite. And make it hurt."

As he pushed Mika playfully into the bedroom, he added, "You're lucky someone gives a shit about you, Riki."

Mika yelled, "Go home, Riki."

Snake lifted Riki out of the chair, and he and Joey dragged him from the room. Sam and Charley followed. All four understood Luke didn't want him killed. They figured it was because, even though the kid was a cokehead, he had moved a lot of product without skimming off enough to count. That was worth more than rubbing him out because he pissed off the boss once.

The problem was that Riki didn't know this. He didn't believe his sister actually had the power to save his ass. He was sure he was a dead man.

They dragged the squirming, yelling Riki down the stairs. "Come on, guys! Let me go! This was just a little misunderstanding. Never happen again. Stop!"

Hearing Riki's shouts, Gabriel opened his office door and shook his head. *What are those halfwits up to now?*

He watched as Snake and Joey threw the squirming Riki over a table onto his back. They held him down and Sam and Charley sat on stools at the bar to watch.

"TJ, Riki needs a drink," Joey shouted. "Cognac. The best for Riki. Right, Riki?"

Riki squirmed harder and stretched his neck to look at TJ. "Just a beer to go, thanks, TJ."

Joey fake laughed. "Thinks he's funny. Like a real comedian."

TJ took a bottle of cognac from the shelf behind him, removed the top, and put it on the bar. "Should probably use the cheaper stuff."

"You're right, TJ." Charley took a swig from the bottle. "Is there such a thing as bad cognac, though?" He took the bottle to the table and gave it to Joey. Snake pulled the cord off Riki's ponytail, put it in Riki's pocket, and patted it.

Joey snickered. "Won't be needing that no more." He poured the contents of the cognac bottle over Riki's head and chest. Riki frantically shook his head, sputtering and gasping for breath. He struggled harder, imagining what they planned to do next.

Gabriel, unnoticed, walked to the bar and grabbed a pitcher of water.

Snake pulled a lighter out of his pocket. He flicked it open and stared at the flame as though in a trance.

Riki screamed, "No! Please. Don't."

Joey punched Riki in the stomach. "Don't spoil the ritual. This is serious business."

Riki gasped for breath as Snake lowered his hand closer to Riki's head. He screamed again, "NO!"

Joey sneered. "What's a matter? Scared?" Don't your people come from the tropics? Think you'd be used to scorchin' heat."

Riki screamed, "I'm from Brooklyn, man!"

TJ piped up. "Japan isn't considered tropical, Joey. They have four seasons, just like us. Summer, fall, winter, spring." And under his breath, he said, "Idiot."

Joey shot daggers at TJ. "Shut the fuck up or it's you next."

Snake moved the flame closer. Riki fought even more frantically to free himself. "Stop," he whined, "please!"

The flame licked at Riki's ponytail; it caught fire, and the flames rushed toward his scalp. The pungent odor of sulfur invaded Gabriel's nostrils. Cringing, he reached the table and emptied the pitcher over Riki's head and hair. Surprised, Snake and Joey let go of Riki.

Gabriel pulled him up off the table. Without looking at the others, he muttered, "Point made, boys." He pushed Riki. "Get outta here."

Riki ran through the club without looking back. *Fuck, I almost died. I almost died. Motherfuckers! Burn me alive?*

Gabriel put the pitcher on the table and walked back to his office, shaking his head. The smell of burning hair lingered.

Joey yelled, "Just havin' fun, Riki." The other men laughed.

Riki stumbled out of the club and continued to the other side of the street. He pulled his inhaler out and took a deep breath. *Okay, so that wasn't a great idea. I gotta get smarter.* He gathered his hair together; a large portion had been burned away. Pricks. Think they can mess with me. "Pricks," he yelled. He took the cord out of his pocket and tied what hair he had left, then he took the vial of coke out of his other pocket, poured a line on his hand, and snorted.

Gotta find out what they're up to. But how? He paced back and forth before stopping, smacking his brow, and shouting, "Surveillance!" *Twenty-four seven. Yeah. Surveillance. That's it. That's what I'm gonna do.* He snorted another line. *Gonna surveil the motherfuckers. Think they can treat Riki this way. I'll show them. I'm gonna surveil the motherfuckers.*

***

A week after Tessa arrived, she had asked Gabriel to go to church with her. She wanted to attend mass and, hopefully, see if she could join the choir. He knew she'd be safe there, as there was no way Luke would be caught dead in a church and neither would any of his minions.

He told her he was happy for her to go, but he didn't go out in public unless he had to. She asked what he did when he had a toothache or felt ill, and he explained that his doctor and dentist had agreed to after-hour appointments a long time ago. He even ordered his groceries and clothes online or over the phone. He only left the house for work, as sometimes it was important that he be there. But, even then, he only had to interact with a few people he already knew.

"The reasons are as obvious as the nose on my face," he'd added.

Gabriel did, however, insist on driving her the five blocks to the closest church and waiting for her in the car. After the mass, Tessa had introduced herself to the priest and asked if she could join their choir. She did a quick audition, and he happily invited her to the next rehearsal. When she returned to the car, Gabriel had her recount, in detail, everything that had happened. It was obvious he was proud of her. It took another two weeks before he would let her walk the five blocks on her own.

Tessa had lived with Gabriel for almost a month now. She was sure he'd gotten used to having her around, even liked it. They'd merged Sarah's LPs with his and spent hours lazing around listening to the old rock and roll albums. He definitely smiled more.

Now it was time to turn the house into their home. A comfortable home. Gabriel had been sleeping on that old sofa, and she knew it bothered his back even though he never complained. She wanted a room of her own with place to put her things and wanted the same for him. And some new blinds and window dressings could definitely brighten up the place.

No matter what threat might occur, she never planned on leaving him. She'd already grown to love him.

Gabriel was in the living room, engrossed in a Houston Astros playoff game against the St. Louis Cardinals. Every now and then a bit of mustard would escape the hoagie he was eating and fall onto his clean T-shirt. He'd grab the T-shirt and try to lick it off, but all he did was spread the mustard further. He felt guilty about the stains because he made an effort to look his best for Tessa most of the time. Before her arrival, he could go a whole weekend without showering or changing his shorts.

Today, however, there was nothing more important to worry about than the outcome of the game.

Tessa stood at the doorway with an iPad under her arm and a cold beer in hand, smiling as she watched him yell at the television. She plopped herself down next to him, handed him the beer, and positioned the iPad on her lap. There was a furniture website displayed on the screen.

She watched the game with him, but as soon as there was a commercial break, she grabbed the remote and muted the volume.

"Dad, I've been window-shopping online. The house needs an upgrade." She raised her hand before he had a chance to react. "I know, I know. We don't wanna waste our money—"

"We?" Gabriel put the sandwich down on the plate beside him, wiped his hands on his shirt, and picked up the remote. "The place is fine as it is."

Tessa put the iPad down on the couch, stood up, and put her hands on her hips. "Seriously? I mean, seriously?"

Gabriel laughed, keeping his eyes on the television so he'd know when the commercials ended. "What do *you* think we need?"

"A bed." She slapped the couch arm. "A new couch. Curtains." She picked up the iPad and put it up to his face. "Here's a beauty. Only four hundred dollars. You'd be so comfort—"

"There's nothing wrong with this one." Gabriel quipped as he pushed the iPad away and turned the volume back on. She'd lost him to the game again.

"Puleeze." Tessa stood in front of him, blocking his view of the game. He stretched to see around her.

"Pretty please."

"Okay, okay, get what you think we need." Gabriel took his wallet out and handed her a credit card.

"Thank you, thank you, thank you." She took the card, kissed his cheek, and ran out of the room to the kitchen.

The truth was he would give her anything she wanted. She made him happy, and he had not been happy for decades. He wondered what it would have been like to have had her in his life all of her eighteen years. With Sarah. He pictured the three of them together sometimes. A family, a real family. A fantasy. He had Tessa *now*, and that was enough.

He smiled and yelled, "Only what we need."

"What we need," she yelled back.

Be frugal, she thought. *You can do that. No problemo. I should probably make a list first, so I don't get carried away.* She grabbed a pen and pad out of a kitchen drawer and sat at the table to make the list. *Let's see... Bookshelves, queen-size bed, new bedding, new towels, set of drawers, vanity, blinds, curtains, kitchen chairs...*

***

Gabriel was in his office working on his laptop when Luke arrived in the open doorway. "Who the fuck do you think you are?" Gabriel ignored him. Luke walked up to his desk. "I said, who the fuck do you think you are?"

Gabriel sighed and answered without looking up, "I warned you about keeping shit out of the club, Luke. That includes setting people on fire."

"What's wrong? Bring back bad memories?" Luke sneered.

Gabriel's eyes narrowed. "No."

Luke leaned in threateningly. "You don't tell my men what to do. *Ever!* I call the shots in this club. Not you."

"The only business you're capable of calling the shots for is selling drugs to school children."

"Don't push it."

"I'm trying to keep the place looking legit. You may not realize it, but you actually need that."

"I don't need that and I don't need you!" Luke screamed as he grabbed the laptop and threw it across the room. "Cross me once more and you're gonna wish you'd never made it outta that warehouse alive. I don't give a shit what the will says."

Sam arrived at the door. "Everything okay?"

Luke turned and stormed out of the room.

"Why do you keep poking the bear, Gabriel?" Sam asked.

"I dunno. Can't help it."

Sam shook his head and left.

He's right, Gabriel thought. *Why do I keep poking the bear? Especially now. I have more to think of than just myself. That was stupid.*

He picked up his laptop. Good thing he had automatic backup because he was going to have to replace it.

***

Saint Patrick's was one of those old gothic-style churches with opulent interior that was as awe-inspiring as its tall spires and pointed arches.

Father Michael, a newly ordained priest in his twenties, stood leading the choir in practice. He wore the traditional black cassock, as did all the clergy at Saint Patrick's. When not on church property, they could be found wearing simple black suits and white clerical collars. Father Michael actually preferred the cassock; he felt it represented humility plus, as a bonus, the fabric was comfortable and cool in the long, hot summer months.

As a solo piece approached, he motioned to Tessa. She held tightly to the delicate gold cross hanging on the chain around her neck and stepped forward. It was her first rehearsal as a soloist, and she really didn't want to disappoint him. The crucifix gave her the courage she needed, and she gave it her all. Once her solo ended, Tessa backed into the group as they sang the last verse of the chorus.

Father Michael was so moved that he made a mental note to add an extra prayer of thanks to his daily devotions. And, of course, to ask God to find a way for him to buy new robes to replace the frayed ones the choir had to wear. He raised his hands. "That's enough for today, ladies. See you on Wednesday."

The choir shuffled off to store their robes. He gave a thumbs up to one of the youngest members, a cheery teen with a brow and nose ring, as she passed by. "You've been practicing, Juliette. It shows." She returned a double thumbs up and skittered off.

Tessa approached him shyly and he patted her shoulder. "Nicely done, Tessa."

"I'll do better next time. I was a little nervous."

He laughed. "If that's nervous, I'm looking forward to hearing what you can do once you get comfortable. Ready to take on another?"

"Definitely."

"Well, okay then." He took a few pages off the music stand and held them out to her.

"Thank you, Father." Another solo? This day could not get any better.

Tessa grabbed the pages and raced to the storage room, a tiny space with barely enough room for the two wooden benches and robe closets. The last few choir members, eager to leave, pushed past her to hang their robes as she stuffed the music sheets into her backpack.

Carmen, a girl Tessa's age, sat on one of the benches, engrossed in her phone. Her robe lay in a pile next to her. Shoulder-length auburn curls and an olive complexion served to accentuate her striking gray eyes. She had unbuttoned her blouse to reveal a healthy amount of cleavage, and her pink, pleated skirt was rolled up to bare a large portion of her thighs.

Tessa couldn't help but scrutinize the girl as she removed her own robe to reveal a high-collared blouse tucked into a simple, knee-length plaid skirt. She felt rather plain in comparison. She turned to hang her robe in one of the closets when Carmen let out a blood-curdling scream.

Tessa jumped and yelled, "Wha…?"

A spider had crawled onto Carmen's foot. She pushed it off with her phone and jumped up on the bench, then pointed to the floor where the arachnid was making its way toward the closet. "Spa-spider! Step on it!"

Tessa laughed, bent down, and cupped it in her hands.

Carmen yelled, "Kill it!"

"It's just a harmless, little spider. It would only hurt a fly." Tessa giggled. "And we're not flies, are we?"

Carmen shuddered, got off the bench, and backed away. "Ha. Ha. Kill it."

Tessa took the spider to the open window and released it on the windowsill. It scrambled off and down the exterior wall.

Carmen rushed over and slammed the window shut. "Gives me the heebie-jeebies. I saw a video about spiders. Did you know when they have babies millions come out?" She shuddered again, closed her eyes, hugging herself protectively. After a moment she opened her eyes. "Didn't mean to freak out. Hate creepy crawlers." Carmen picked up her robe and unceremoniously threw it over a hanger in the closet. "There's a reason they're black, you know."

"Huh?" *She's funny,* thought Tessa.

"Black is not a good color! Darkness, pain, sadness. Scary."

"People can be a lot scarier than spiders."

"True. But not *all* people. Like *all* spiders."

"Right. Not all people."

Carmen held her hand out. "You're cool. I think we should be besties."

Tessa smiled and shook her hand. "Me too!"

Carmen patted the bench. "Sit beside me." Tessa sat next to her and they took a few selfies together.

"I haven't seen you at choir before. Were you on vacation?" Tessa asked.

"Just joined. I used to sing at Holy Ghost. My family's *crazy* into religion. Mama goes to mass every morning, twice on Sundays, *and* teaches Sunday school. It's ridiculous. My brother's an altar boy, and Papa's a part-time groundskeeper there."

"Wow," Tessa whispered.

"Wow's right. They're waaay old school. Papa thinks girls shouldn't be allowed to go anywhere on their own." Carmen sighed dramatically. "Basically, I'm a prisoner."

"A prisoner?"

"Yeah. It's okay, though. I got around it. I saw on a choir website that there was a spot open for a mezzo-soprano at Saint Pat's. Holy Ghost already had too many sopranos, so it was perfect timing. I literally ran here and begged Father Michael to let me join his choir. Papa said if he promised to keep an eye on me it would be okay. So, here I am. Can you believe it? It's not real freedom because my brother drives me here and picks me up after practice and mass, but it's better than nothing. At least he and his friends can't watch me like hawks all the time."

"I'm really glad you're here."

"I'm Carmen."

"Tessa."

"Tessa." Carmen picked up her phone and googled the name. She read out loud, "*The name Tessa means 'harvester' or 'reaper,' i.e., someone who gathers or collects things.* Do you collect things?"

"I don't think so. Do albums count? I have a few albums."

"Don't know. Could, I guess."

"My mom named me after a character in an old movie. *Tess of the d'Urbervilles.* She really liked the name but said it needed another syllable to make it right. So, I got Tessa."

"Hmmm. Is the movie any good?"

Tessa shrugged. "Don't know. Haven't seen it."

"You should. I'll look it up later."

"'Kay."

"So, Tessa of the uber villes. What's your story?"

"Um. Well. Uh, my dad is in the army. He's stationed overseas right now."

"What about your mom?"

"My mom died."

"Oh! That's awful." Carmen took Tessa's hand. "You must be so sad. I know my Mama gets on my nerves a lot, but I would just die if anything happened to her."

"I'm okay. I do get really sad when I think of her." Tessa couldn't believe how nosey Carmen was, but it gave her the chance to tell at least one truth. She really did miss her mom more than she could say.

"How did she die?"

"She got sick."

"So, you have to live with the relatives now."

"I don't have any. I was an only child and so were my parents."

"Grandparents?"

"They're gone too."

"Oh. You are not lucky. Maybe you should stop wearing anything black for a while."

"Why?"

"Like I said. It's an unlucky color. And it looks like you've had a lot of bad luck. You live in a shelter or a group home? That's awful!"

"No. I live with a friend of my dad's."

"Wow, a friend of his took you in. Just like that?"

"Uh huh. And he's nice. So, see? I am lucky."

"Girl, you're so unlucky you could be in an opera."

For a minute, Tessa was nervous that Carmen didn't believe her or would tell someone. But she didn't have to worry, as Carmen didn't give it a second thought.

Carmen took Tessa's hand and walked her out the side door. Carmen plopped herself down on the grass and pulled Tessa down next to her.

"I'll tell you a secret. My real name is Natalya. I hate it. Everyone in my family calls me that, so I decided I only wish to be known as

Carmen. It's from the opera *Carmen*. You know it?" Without giving Tessa a chance to answer she continued. "Carmen is this gypsy. A beautiful, exotic gypsy who dances for her lovers."

Carmen stood and twirled. "And she sings, of course, but that's only because it's an opera. She has to sing. But, her dancing, her dancing is what's important. It makes men love her."

Tessa was mesmerized. Carmen dropped down next to her. "She had two lovers, you know."

"Two?"

"Yes. One could think that it would be good to have two men in love with you at the same time." She sighed loudly. "But, alas, not for Carmen."

"Why not?" Tessa was impressed by Carmen. She seemed so worldly. And a little wild.

"One of them killed her."

"Killed her. Why?"

"Jealously, of course. The green-eyed monster."

"That's sad." This story only confirmed what her mom always said. People can be scary. Especially men.

"Uh huh. But it's still a beautiful story because she dies in the arms of someone who loves her so very much."

"I'd prefer a happy ending. Where she doesn't die." Tessa sighed. "Like in *Twilight*. Edward and Jacob are both crazy in love with Bella. And she gets to live happily ever after with her favorite."

"True. I think all operas end shitty." Carmen jumped up and twirled around again until she fell on the grass laughing.

Tessa whispered, "I want real love. The kind that lasts forever."

"Ha. Good luck finding that."

"I will. I know I will."

"Hmm."

They lay in silence for a while.

"Is that the kind of music you like? Opera?" Tessa thought it didn't seem to suit Carmen. She figured she'd prefer anything but that.

Carmen sat up. "Hate it. Ab-so-lute-ly hate opera."

"You do?"

"Of course. Unfortunately, Papa loves it. It's practically all he listens to. *Carmen* was on TV once, and he made the whole family watch it with him. When it was over, I knew I was a Carmen, not a Natalya."

"Makes sense."

"So. How do you earn your keep at this guy's house?"

"What do you mean?"

"What does he expect?"

"Expect?"

Carmen grabs her breasts playfully. "You know, expect?"

"Oh?" Tessa's face turned bright red. She's couldn't imagine how Carmen could even think that, never mind say it to her. "No, no, no. I just keep the house clean and cook the meals. I like doing that."

"Does he pay you?"

"In a way. He gives me a sort of allowance. I'm saving for college. I'm gonna study equine sciences."

"Equine?"

"Horses. I love horses."

"Hmm. Cool. But why save for college? I bet your dad will pay for your college when he comes home."

"Oh. Right. He probably will."

"I would love to go to college. Papa says I have to take my college courses online. I don't wanna do that. I wanna be independent, you know. Finally get to meet men."

"What about your brother's friends. They're men. You talk to them, right?"

"They're not really men yet. Besides, my brother, who is a real asshat, won't—"

"Asshat?"

"Look it up. Describes him perfectly."

Tessa pulled out her phone and googled it.

"Besides, he won't let his friends near me."

"How 'bout when you were in high school?"

"Nope. I was forced to go to an all-girls school." She smirked. "Not a boy in sight. The teachers were nuns. There weren't even any priests, except for their boss, who was at least a hundred."

She whispered, "So, what's your body count?"

"Body count?"

"Body count. Ya know? Sex. With guys." Carmen pulled her finger in and out of her rolled fist. "How many?"

"None." Tessa blushed again, touching her ring, but she didn't want to explain the meaning of it to Carmen. Not yet anyhow.

"Didn't you meet guys in high school?" Carmen asked, hoping Tessa would have some good stories to share.

"I was home-schooled."

"You were? How awful."

"I loved it."

"No way."

"I did."

Carmen looked at her pitifully. "Whoa." They lay back on the grass in silence for a few minutes, enjoying the soft, cool feel of it on their skin.

Tessa worried that Carmen might not want to be friends if she thought she was too innocent or nerdy, so she tried to sound worldly. "There were boys in the choir at my church. They were fun. And there were men that worked on the ranch where we lived."

"Sooo lucky. Did you have a boyfriend, at least?"

"Uh, no. But I talked to them. A lot."

"Well, I guess that's better than nothing."

Tessa wanted to steer the conversation back to Carmen, so she racked her brain for something interesting to talk about. Nothing came to her, except… "You should get a job. Then you could meet guys and even go on dates."

Carmen sat up. "Clean the wax outta your ears, girl. My papa would never let me get a job. That's exactly what he's afraid of. That I'd meet somebody who would steal me away. I tell you. I am a prisoner."

"Geez!"

A car pulled up and beeped the horn four times. Carmen yelled, "Alright! I'm coming!" Then she turned to Tessa and said, "That's Alex, my brother, asshat, and jailer. I gotta go." She turned her back to the car, pulled a dog-eared paperback out of her knapsack, and slipped it to Tessa. "Hold on to this for me." She buttoned her blouse, unrolled her skirt, then stood and ran to the car. As she opened the passenger door, she waved at Tessa. "See you Wednesday."

Tessa watched them drive away. *I can't believe I already have a best friend,* she thought. *This is better than I could have hoped.* She put the book in her backpack and twirled around, imitating Carmen.

CHAPTER FOUR

The agent sat behind an oversized oak desk with matching swivel visitor chairs. He wore his best "Hollywood" finery, and both his demeanor and the room exuded success. Posters of the latest blockbuster films lined one wall and photos of hot young celebrities, along with prestigious industry awards, covered another. Television scripts were piled on the desk, with one open in front of him.

Iesha, a pretty teen in skin-tight jeans, a plunging V-neck sweater, and black patent stilettos sat across from him. She was posed to show her physical assets to their best advantage.

Iesha was trying to make it big as an internet influencer. She had over a thousand followers and more were signing on every day. Her specialty was modeling the latest lingerie and undergarments. The skimpier the better, as it attracted male followers. She didn't have any sponsors yet but knew they'd come eventually. Until then, she simply purchased the garments and returned them after each shoot.

In high school, she'd played the lead in a student film, and everyone said she was destined to be famous. She believed them and was sure she'd eventually get noticed by an agent or casting director.

She didn't know how his assistant got her number, but when he texted her about participating in the next hot reality TV show, she wasn't surprised. She'd sent him a rather risqué video in the hopes of catching the producers' attention. They had to know she was serious and open to anything.

The agent leaned back and lit a cigar. "As I said, the director is lookin' for fresh faces. His show promises to be a step up from *The Bachelorette*. Even more dynamic than *Below Deck*. They're expectin' a much larger viewership, if you can imagine that."

This is it, Iesha thought. *My chance at the big leagues.* "And he likes me?"

"As soon as the director saw your demo, he called us to say he wanted to meet you. Honey, after this show, I reckon the opportunities are gonna be limitless. Personally, I think you could be the next Halle Berry."

Iesha batted her fake lashes. "You think, Mr. Morris?"

"I do. Now, only a few agents have been given the go-ahead to submit someone. That's why we're keepin' it under wraps."

"I understand. No one knows about this. None of my friends, my parents, no one. I promise."

"That's my girl."

"You know, Mr. Morris, I'm willing to do anything. Anything."

He gave her a fatherly grin. "I know, Iesha." He looked at his watch. "It's ten o'clock. Let's get on over to the studio." He got up. "The screen test is scheduled for eleven."

Iesha stood. She looked down at her jeans. "Do I look okay?"

"Beautiful. Don't worry, they'll have a change of clothes if Josh wants to see you in somethin' else." He opened the office door. Iesha stopped at the doorway and leaned against him. She kissed his cheek and whispered in his ear, "Thanks again."

"Just doin' what I do." He led her out of the office and they continued down the hall, then took the elevator to the basement.

His SUV was parked next to a non-descript black van. When they reached the SUV, the back doors of the van opened and two men jumped out. Before Iesha could react, one of the men covered her head with a burlap bag while the other grabbed her arms and pulled her into the van. They closed the doors and, moments later, drove off.

Charley stood by the SUV and watched the van leave before returning to the office. He grabbed a box from behind the desk and filled it with everything from the desk and walls. He then took a rag and gloves out of a drawer and wiped the desk and door handles. He took a key out of his pocket and wiped it before dropping it on the desk.

He pulled out his cell phone and dialed Luke's number. "Order's complete." He hung up, picked up the box, and left.

***

Sam was sitting in Luke's office with his feet up on the desk, engrossed in watching a game on his phone. "Whaaat?" he screamed and bolted up. "Argh. Fuck. Fuck. Fuck." He banged his phone down on the desk.

Luke entered from the bedroom barefoot and in jeans, pulling a T-shirt on over his head. "Upset much?" he chided.

Sam growled. "I'd won. It was perfect. I hit the parlay." He leaned back in the chair, closed his eyes, and muttered, "Then a fumble that was returned for the touchdown was called back because of a lousy holding call on the play."

"Ouch." Luke tried to sound concerned.

Sam looked up. "No fucking kidding."

"I keep telling ya, Sammy. Stop the complicated betting."

"For example?"

"Just bet the spread. Like I do."

"What's the fun in that?"

Luke sat at the desk and responded snidely, "Won five hundred bucks last week." He pulled out a bottle of tequila and poured them each a shot.

Sam leaned forward and grabbed the bottle. He took a long drink, put the bottle back on the table, then picked up his glass and knocked it back.

"Feel better?"

"You're a son of a bitch," Sam growled.

"I know. How much did ya lose?"

"Too much."

"Need help covering it?"

"No. Marty's cool. Besides, I'm not worried. There's a game on Thursday. Dallas–Green Bay. It's a shoo-in."

A petite blonde, one of the Vox dancers, came out of the bedroom holding her stilettos and buttoning her dress. She stopped at the suite door. "Want me to close the door?"

Sam turned and smiled at her. "Yeah, thanks, Suzanne."

She waved at Luke and left, closing the door behind her.

Luke turned to look out the window, even though the view was simply the brick wall across the alley. "Got a call from Charley. We unload the merch tomorrow."

"Great," Sam replied sarcastically.

***

Riki parked his red Porsche Boxster a block from the club. He loved his car. Bought it secondhand but treated it like it was new. He even took it for special detailing once a month. He could sit in it all day, and he'd been doing just that for the past two days as he followed Luke to find out what new racket he was into. He checked the time on his phone. Midnight. He snorted a few lines and sang the lyrics to the rap song on his phone. He got most of the words wrong but didn't care. It was about the singing not the accuracy.

Sam and Luke exited the club. Luke was talking on his phone while they waited for the valet to arrive with the silver-gray sedan. Riki sat up, excited. *Okay, motherfuckers. Let's see what you're up to. Can't keep secrets from Riki. Cuz he's smarter than you could ever know. A lot smarter. And, you should know that.*

They got into the car and Riki followed them, at a reasonable distance, onto the highway and outside the city to cottage country. He switched off his headlights when they turned down a dirt road and continued to follow them using the light from the full moon. When they reached a laneway, Riki decided not to chance them seeing his car and parked up the road. He ran up the lane under the cover of trees, knowing that if he was caught, there'd be no Gabriel to rescue him. They'd kill him.

Sam and Luke parked in front of the cottage, exited the car, and went around to the back. The door opened and Charley stepped out. Riki ducked behind a tree. Charley and Luke exchanged words Riki couldn't hear, then Charley reentered the cottage and Luke and Sam continued to a yacht moored at the dock.

Moments later the cottage door opened, and Joey came out pulling a rope with eight girls tethered to it, one after the other. Snake was behind them, holding a semi-automatic pistol.

The women's wrists were bound and they were blindfolded. The last woman tripped, dragging the others down with her. Snake kicked the woman who had fallen first. Charley stepped out, pulled Snake away, and helped the woman up. He looked at Snake and shook his head. "Easy. You've already had your fun." Snake shrugged then helped the other women up. Joey continued to lead them to the yacht, and Charley followed them.

Two men stayed on the yacht, keeping watch with automatic weapons, and two men climbed off to stand next to Luke and Sam. One of them was in his twenties and the other looked to be in his sixties. The young man had a gun and the older man carried a briefcase.

When the captives reached the yacht, the younger man removed the blindfolds as he inspected them one by one. The girls' faces were streaked with muddied tears, their eyes wide with fear. He grabbed the buttocks of the last woman, causing a muffled squeal. "This one's no good. Too fat."

Charley remarked as he neared him, "Big asses are in now! All the rage! You can blame the Kardashians."

"No big asses. Too fat," the younger man reiterated.

"You have a long trip ahead of you, Hamid. Plenty of time to work it off. Just don't mar their pretty faces," Charley joked. The other men laughed.

The older man handed the briefcase to Luke, who passed it to Sam. The three of them walked up the dock and entered the cottage while Joey and Snake loaded the women onto the boat.

Riki ran to the cottage and crouched down next to one of the windows. He peeked in to see Sam put the briefcase on the table and open it. It was full of money. Sam pulled out a wad and began to count it, but Luke put his hand on his arm to stop him as he looked menacingly at the man. "Omar knows better than to fuck with us." Sam closed the case, and Luke saluted the man. "Always a pleasure." He nodded, exited the cottage, and hurried down the dock to climb on the yacht. Charley strolled up to the cottage as Joey and Snake stayed by the dock and waved them off.

Luke stretched out on one of the couches and yawned like the Cheshire cat while Sam counted the money. "I can't believe it. It's the easiest eight hundred grand we have ever made."

Riki uttered, "That's a hundred grand apiece." He slapped his hand over his mouth, realizing he'd said it aloud. He snuck away and ran to his car, staying close to the trees. He got in, made a U-turn, and headed back to the city, laughing wildly. "Oh, I am gettin' in on this. I am gettin' in."

Meanwhile, Charley entered the cottage and sprawled out on the couch across from Luke. He removed two cigars from his pocket and offered one to Luke, who waved it away. "That went smoothly."

Luke responded lazily, "Yeah. But we won't get rich supplying these guys. We need to increase our customer base."

"I'm sure they'll take as many as we can get, Luke." He'd wondered how long it would take for Luke to fuck with the status quo.

"Might be time to up the price as well," Luke added.

"The price?" Charley lit his cigar and threw the match into the fireplace.

"Stop thinking small, Charley. We're taking a big risk here. Gotta make sure the rewards are just as big."

Charley nodded. "Right. I'll talk to them. And we'll need more people online if we want to increase our supply. I'll put out feelers. I know a few guys that might be interested."

We're sharing the costs, so let's see him earn his forty percent, Luke thought. "In the meantime, Sam and I will look for buyers," Luke added.

"Whatever you say, boss." Sam went to the pool table. He took balls out of the pockets and set them in the rack.

***

Riki couldn't sleep. He lay on his bed, staring at a crack in the ceiling made visible from the glare of the streetlights pouring through the window behind him. The only furnishings in the room were a twin bed and small lamp on the night table next to him. The rest of his tiny apartment was as sparse and frugally decorated as his bedroom. Riki put most of his earnings up his nose, so not much was left to afford anything better after he covered the monthly payments on his car.

The benzos weren't doing their job and there was a reason. *A hundred Gs apiece.* The words kept repeating in his head. He had to get in on it. But how? He'd barely escaped with his life the last time he talked to Luke. Bastards had tried to turn him into a fuckin' Roman candle. *Motherfuckers. Come on, think. Think.* He sat up and snorted two more lines off the night table. He got out of bed and knocked on his temples with his fists as he paced around the room.

Then it came to him. He stood still and laughed. *I got it! I buy the merchandise from Luke! I get some guys to help with the transport. I know where to get the dough. Might have to pay a hefty vig on the loan but totally worth it. Then I sell to someone willing to pay more than the Arabs.*

He figured it would be easy enough to find the buyer. His uncle Kenji.

Kenji was a high-ranking member of the Yamaguchi-gumi, the largest Yakuza family in Japan. He'd set up shop in the U.S. decades ago, governed several gangs in the region with a steel fist, and was feared by the other crime syndicates. Kenji was scary in every way! He wouldn't think twice before having someone killed for looking at him the wrong way and was definitely involved in worse crimes than human trafficking. Of that, Riki was certain. Regardless, Kenji's illegal activities remained under the radar of law enforcement. He was respected in the community, owned legitimate, mainstream companies, and had a few well-placed politicians in his pocket.

The Yakuza upheld the strictest honor codes of any criminal group. The Yamaguchi-gumi syndicate was opposed to any kind of drug trafficking, and family members were not exempt. The last time Riki had anything to do with his uncle, he had to cut the tip off his left pinky finger to make up for offending him. So Riki had learned how not to get caught.

This was his chance to get ahead, to stop having to sell dime bags on street corners. To actually earn his uncle's respect. He took out his phone and dialed. "It's Riki. I'd like to meet with my uncle."

***

Riki snorted a quick line to bolster his confidence and, without thinking, wiped his nose on his jacket sleeve. He had dressed for the occasion. He wore a suit and tie, though not exactly devoid of wrinkles. He checked his pockets and found the quaalude he'd brought along to even out the effects of the coke. He swallowed it dry and waited for it to kick in before he drove up to the enormous iron gate.

He was buzzed through and glimpsed guards stationed throughout the property as he proceeded up the driveway to an impressive mansion. He parked the car and was ushered into the house by two lethal-looking men. He followed them through an imposing foyer and down a long hallway to a library filled with wall-to-wall bookshelves and elegant furniture. An antique silk Persian rug covered most of the rosewood floor.

Kenji sat, smoking a cigarette, at a desk in the center of the room. He wore his thick, black hair in a sixties pompadour and looked like any other wealthy, slightly graying, sixty-year-old businessman in a Brioni suit. No one would guess the suit concealed elaborate body tattoos. Riki was right — although he did own several legit businesses, most of his profits came from procuring black-market commodities.

Haruto, Kenji's most trusted lieutenant, stood to his left. He had a sleek, muscular frame and wore his hair pulled back high in a messy ponytail. Haruto sported a shoulder holster and was dressed in his customary long-sleeved, black T-shirt over black slacks. His clothes also concealed full-body ink.

Riki was escorted to a chair in front of the desk. Kenji's men bowed and positioned themselves behind Riki, who also bowed.

"Kenji-san. *Go meiwaku o okake shite moushi.* So sorry to inconvenience you."

Kenji nodded. He was content that Riki had given him a proper greeting.

Riki looked up and Kenji motioned for him to sit. Kenji studied him before speaking. "How is your sister?"

"She's fine. Thank you for asking, Kenji-san."

"That is good. And how is *my* sister?"

"Mother is good. She wishes she could see you more often."

Kenji laughed. "Is that so?"

Riki squirmed a little. "Sure." They both knew Riki's mother hated Kenji. They hadn't spoken in decades, and the rare time his name came up, she would spit and call him the devil. She believed he had killed Riki's father for some minor Yakuza transgression.

Kenji leaned back in his chair. "Why are you here?" He eyed the white residue on Riki's sleeve.

Riki noticed and wiped at it. "It's not what you think. This is an old jacket."

Kenji sighed. He nodded to one of the men behind Riki who grabbed his shoulder. Riki spurted out, "I am here asking what I can do *for you*, Uncle. I have a proposition for you to consider."

"A proposition," Kenji scoffed.

"One hears rumors."

"Rumors?"

"The flesh trade has become very lucrative."

Kenji harrumphed and motioned for the man to let go of Riki's shoulder.

"I have partners with a stable of prime American fillies. Quality guaranteed."

"Do you think it wise to try to meddle in my affairs, Riki?" Kenji leaned toward him. "Failure to deliver brings dire consequences."

Riki swallowed hard but reminded himself that this was a once-in-a-lifetime opportunity. "Understood."

"Your price?"

"Two hundred K."

Kenji leaned back in his chair and lit another cigarette. Perhaps his nephew was finally growing up. He was certainly growing a set of balls. Might as well see what he has. "Six. I expect delivery by the end of the month, without fail." He stood. "Remember, if you don't deliver, things *will* go badly for you *and* your partners." He waved him away.

Riki stood and bowed. "Thank you, Kenji-san." The men led him off the property.

"Six would more than fill our latest requisition," Haruto said.

Kenji frowned. "It will not bring me pleasure when he fails, Haruto."

His lieutenant nodded. "*Hai.*"

That went well, Riki thought. Now all he had to do was finance the purchase from Luke.

CHAPTER FIVE

Everything Tessa had ordered for the house had been delivered. One might even call the place cozy. The windows all had new blinds and curtains. The kitchen had an oak table and chairs and a proper set of dishes and cutlery. The living room even had a coffee table with matching end tables. She tried to give the house a bit of a masculine flair to make sure Gabriel didn't feel like she'd taken over. Except for her bedroom. She decorated it exactly like her room at the ranch. She couldn't have been happier. She'd even talked Gabriel into recycling his newspapers — but only after they were a week old.

Although Gabriel complained throughout the transformation, she knew he liked it. He was back in his bed with a new Posturepedic mattress. That had done the trick. He admitted the twinges in his back were completely gone.

She had even managed to spruce up his leisure wear. She ordered new trainers and two blue tracksuits that brought out the blue in his eyes. He had to admit everything was pretty much as comfortable as his old T-shirts, sweats, and sneakers, which had somehow "gone missing" once the new duds arrived.

Now Tessa wanted him to loosen the reins a little. She had gone out of her way to cook the perfect dinner, hoping this would soften him up. She was going to ask him to bend a little more for her. She had a new friend, and she wanted to spend time with her.

Carmen had come up with a story for her parents so she could go to the local ice-cream shop after choir practice. She told them Father Michael was making changes to the choir's repertoire, so practice would most likely finish an hour later. She also said there might be other practices that would go a little later, as they knew psalms weren't made perfect in a day. Carmen had definitely covered her bases.

But Tessa hoped she wouldn't have to lie to Gabriel. She folded Gabriel's newspaper perfectly, set it next to his plate, and straightened the cutlery. She lit the candle in the center of the table and sang to herself as she stirred the mash potatoes and checked on the roast.

Gabriel pulled his car into the driveway. He entered the house and stopped in the hall for a minute to listen to Tessa. He was content, and he couldn't help but chuckle.

Tessa turned and smiled as he entered the kitchen. "Smells good," he said, removing his jacket. He placed it on the back of the chair, sat, and opened the newspaper.

"Roast chicken. Your favorite. With potatoes and gravy."

"Mmm."

She would have to approach this at the right moment. One thing at a time. "How was your day?"

"Mm-hmm."

She knew he wasn't listening. "Dad? How was your day?"

"Same as always," Gabriel grunted and turned a page of the newspaper.

"Father Michael gave me another solo. Are you gonna come next Sunday to hear it?"

He looked up at her, eyebrows raised. She knew he wouldn't come to the church. Not only did he not want to be seen, but he also wouldn't want anyone to see her with him even more. Besides, even if he *was* willing to be seen, Gabriel thought all religions were cults in one form or another. And Catholicism was apparently the worst.

"I know. Stupid question. I can sing for you anytime." Tessa sat at the table across from him. "I've made a friend."

Gabriel folded the paper and put it on the table next to him. He tried to sound nonchalant. "Really. Who?"

"Her name's Carmen. She hasn't been in the choir that long either. I finally have someone to talk to."

"Oh."

"I mean, you know, a girl my age. Her family are very protective of her and don't usually let her out of their sight. That makes her the perfect friend for me. Don't you think?"

Gabriel waited for the other shoe to drop. He knew she was leading up to something he wasn't going to like.

Tessa returned to the stove and filled their plates. "I love living here with you. We get along so well. Don't we?"

"We do."

She put Gabriel's plate in front of him and sat down. "Aren't you gonna eat?" he asked, pointing to the spot where her plate should be.

"Oh, of course." She giggled and returned to her plate on the counter. She wasn't hungry at all.

"It's just… it would be nice to have a girlfriend, too."

Gabriel didn't respond. He concentrated on eating.

"What do you think?" She turned to face him.

"Nothin' wrong with having a friend. It's lucky you can see her at church. You know you can't tell her anything about us?"

"Oh, I know." She brought her plate to the table and began happily eating. First hurdle crossed.

When they finished their plates, Tessa started their usual, light after-dinner banter. "Did you happen to meet anyone new today?"

Gabriel really enjoyed this game. It kept him on his toes.

"I did," he responded smugly. "Angelina Jolie's in town, so I spent the afternoon helping her rehearse lines for her role in her next film. It went so well that we've decided to move in together because we have so much in common. And you *did* say you would love to have siblings."

She giggled. "So *that's* why Brad called. It all makes sense now. He went on about wanting her back and to please ask you to get out of the way."

"Hmm. Well, a little competition is healthy."

"Don't worry. I set him straight about love!"

"Thank you."

Tessa made an exaggerated sigh. "Then I told him you were too good for her anyway, and I was sure it was purely physical. *And* I would let him know when you tired of her."

"Saves me having to tell him. Might have led to a punch-up of some sort, and I wouldn't want to mar that girly face of his." They laughed.

Gabriel pushed his plate forward. "What's for dessert?"

"More of your favorite. Apple pie à la mode." Tessa cut them each a slice of pie before adding a dollop of ice cream from the freezer.

They ate in silence for a few minutes. Tessa figured it was now or never. "I was thinking that after practice Carmen and I could go to—"

Gabriel dropped his fork on his plate and looked at her. *Here we go,* he thought.

She continued quickly. "Don't worry, we just want to go for a soda. The shop's right across the street from the church. I'd be back early."

Gabriel knew she'd eventually want more freedom. What young girl wouldn't? Would it be safe for her to spread her wings a little? This Carmen sounded pretty tame and perhaps as isolated as Tessa. The church was safe. No one he knew went to church. He doubted any of them would frequent a corner soda shop. Both were probably the safest places they *could* go. "Okay. But nowhere else, Tessa."

Tessa jumped up from her chair and hugged him.

"Whoa. And only if you promise to come straight home after you've had your soda."

"I will." Tessa immediately pulled out her phone and texted Carmen.

She returned to her chair, and they finished eating their pie in silence. "More?"

Gabriel nodded. "Sure."

She picked up his plate and refilled it. "You know, Mom is the one who taught me to cook. She could have been a chef at some fancy restaurant."

Gabriel dug into his pie. "Hmm."

Tessa smiled. "Dad?"

Gabriel answered, his mouth full, "Yeah?"

"Did Mom make you pie?"

"I don't remember." This was not a conversation he wanted to have with her. Ever. He had wondered how long he would be able to put it off. He knew she'd never let it go. She wanted to know about their relationship. She wanted them to have a beautiful love story. "It was a long time ago. We were young. Then she moved away." It was all he could say.

"Do you—"

"I'm tired. It's been a long day." He put his fork down, picked up the paper, and opened it wide to put some distance between them. He began to read.

Tessa would have to find a better opportunity and was sure it would come. She looked at her phone. "Oh geez. I'm late for choir. Don't touch the dishes. I'll do them when I get back." She chuckled. He never did the dishes.

***

A red sports car pulled up and parked opposite Gabriel's house. Riki got out as the front door opened and Tessa exited, shouting, "I won't be late, I promise."

Riki watched Tessa as she walked along the sidewalk humming to herself.

"Gabriel got himself a lady friend," he said aloud. *Kinda young,* he thought, then shrugged. *Still, it ain't natural to live without somethin' to de-stress you. Ain't natural. Good for him!* He took a snort of coke and wiped his nose. Took another, then crossed the street, went up to the house, and knocked on the door.

Gabriel yelled from the kitchen, "Forget your keys again?" He tsked as he went to the door and opened it.

"You say I'm absent-minded?" he jibed. "That's twice now, Tessa. You have to... Riki?" Gabriel just stared at him. *This is not good,* he thought. *Not good at all. How the hell did he find me? Did he see Tessa?*

Riki smiled. "Gabriel, you sly dawg. What a fine-lookin' piece." He pointed in the direction Tessa had taken. "Who is Tessa? Or should I ask *what* is Tessa?" He snickered.

Shit! It took a minute for Gabriel to reply as he gathered his wits about him. He decided it was best to ignore him. He was probably stoned. He always was. He'd forget seeing her by morning. "What the fuck are you doing here?"

"Business."

Gabriel looked up and down the street. "How did you know where I live?" If Riki found out where he lived, anyone could. It didn't matter before Tessa had arrived, but now... *Shit.*

"You'd be amazed at what Riki knows." Riki squeezed past him, and Gabriel shut the door.

Riki looked around and went to the kitchen. He sat in Tessa's chair, sniffed, and wiped his nose on his shirt again. "Nice place."

Gabriel followed and stood over him. "I asked you a question."

Riki picked a piece of pie off Tessa's plate. "Knew for long time. Waited 'til you left the Vox. Followed you. Never figured you for the suburbs, Gabriel."

"Why follow me home?"

"I like to know things."

Gabriel took the plate and put it in the sink. Without turning around, he asked, "What do you want?"

"Look. It coulda been a really bad scene at the club."

"If you're gonna lie down with dogs, you're gonna get up with fleas."

"Fleas. Right. Fleas." Riki chuckled.

"What were you doing at the Vox anyway?"

"Wanted in on Luke's new venture. Crazy fucker didn't even gimme a chance to talk."

"You're a cokehead. What did you expect?"

"That motherfucker was with Mika."

"She works there. Why so surprised?" Gabriel sighed and sat across from him.

Riki whined, "You know what he does to them. I don't want that for my sister." Riki's leg began to bob up and down. He leaned forward. "So, why'd you save me anyways?"

Gabriel crossed his arms. "Hate fire."

"Oh. Right. Yeah."

"Yeah. Now, what do you want?"

"I have this new deal goin'. It's legit and it's big, and I wanna give you a piece of the action."

"Is it the same deal you wanted to talk to Luke about?"

"No, no. That was purely speculative. I got a real deal in play now. You and me can be partners."

Gabriel knew there was a monkey on Riki's back that fucked with his reasoning. He and his pals might have a knack for selling drugs on the street, but Gabriel doubted he could be trusted with much else. "Partners at what?"

"You don't gotta worry 'bout *what*. Won't get your hands dirty. All ya need to know is you'll come out on top. Riki guarantees it."

A guarantee from Riki would be worthless at best. "Not interested."

"Come on. It's a sure thing. All I need to raise is a couple hundred gees. You'll be in on the bottom. Make the biggest percentage."

"Where do you think I would get that kinda money? And what are you planning to buy with it? No. Never mind. Don't tell me. I don't wanna know because I'm not interested. Maybe you can con Luke into backing your deal. Mika seems to be the flavor of the moment, after all."

Riki frowned at him. Gabriel had actually hurt his feelings.

"Luke don't shoot straight. You know that," Riki shouted.

Gabriel stood. "Like I said, I'm not interested. So, if you don't mind." Riki just looked at him. Gabriel nodded toward the hall. As Riki stood, he saw a magazine on the kitchen counter. He grabbed the pen beside it and wrote his number on the cover. "Think on it. Here's my number." He handed the magazine to Gabriel, who put it back on the counter. He nudged Riki toward the hall and through the front door.

"Let me give you some advice. Forget about this scheme, whatever it is. You'll live longer." He slammed the door.

Gabriel was pissed. Now someone knew Tessa lived with him. Luke would pay a lot of money for a surefire way to hurt him, and she was it. If Riki knew the value of this information, he'd sell Gabriel out without thinking twice. They'd have to leave, and soon.

Riki smiled as he walked to his car. He wasn't disappointed. It was only the first meeting with Gabriel. *He'll come around,* he thought. *All I need is another backer, and then he'll come around.*

***

Tessa and Carmen walked hand in hand toward the side door of the church. Carmen whined, "I don't know how she even got into the choir. She's tone deaf and keeps throwing me off."

"Carmen, she has a good voice. Father Michael thinks—"

"Father Michael is hot."

Tessa stopped and let go of her hand. "He's a priest!"

"So? Just because he can't check out my butt doesn't mean I can't check out his. And his butt is mighty fine. I wonder what he'd wear if he weren't a priest. I bet he wears purple boxers. Purple equals frustration. And I bet he's pretty frustrated because he definitely is *not* getting any."

"Carmen!" Tessa knew she should be shocked at the things Carmen said but, instead, appreciated how worldly she seemed, even though Tessa knew she really wasn't worldly at all.

Carmen grabbed her hand. "Don't tell me you never think about guys."

Tessa answered without looking at her. "Of course. There are a few boys in the choir."

Carmen stopped. She let go of Tessa's hand. "That's the problem. They're boys. I want a man. And if not Father Michael, then a strong, handsome stranger will do. A rapper or... an MMA fighter."

"MMA fighter?"

"Uh huh." Carmen attempted a karate kick and fell to the ground.

They giggled and Tessa pulled her up. "A knight on a white horse who'll fight the terrible dragon keeping me captive in the tower." Tessa sighed.

Carmen grabbed Tessa and held her at arms length, saying wistfully, "And when he kills that damn dragon, he'll take me into his huge, muscular arms. He'll look at me..." Carmen looked intensely into Tessa's eyes. "But not just *at* me; he'll look deep into my soul and kiss me passionately."

Carmen leaned Tessa back and kissed her. They fell over onto the grass.

"Yuck, you stuck your tongue in my mouth!" Tessa complained.

Carmen rose onto her elbow. "That's how real women kiss. Guys like it better when you use your tongue."

Tessa looked at Carmen and cracked a smile. "Oh." She was disappointed that she'd acted naive again.

"And they like it even better when you give them a blow job," Carmen whispered.

"A what?"

"A blow job!"

"Why would they want us to blow on them."

"No. Silly. On *it*."

"It?"

Carmen pointed to her crotch area. "You know, their thingy."

Tessa sat up and pushed her. "*Get out.* Why would I ever do that?"

"Because they like it. I heard my brother tell his friend that blow jobs are his favorite. So I googled it. And it has nothing to do with blowing. Here, I'll show you." She took her phone out and did a quick search. "Look." They watched the video.

"Yuck," Tessa muttered. "That's so cringy." Then she asked, "Would *you* do it?"

"If I felt like it."

Tessa whispered, "I don't think I will." She wasn't so naive that she didn't know about sex. She'd lived on a horse farm all her life and had seen horses breeding. But she couldn't imagine putting *it* in her mouth.

Carmen leaned over her. "You will when you're in love."

Tessa closed her eyes. "I dunno."

"I would give Father Michael a blow job," Carmen mused.

They giggled and their giggles turned into belly laughs.

Carmen looked at her phone. "We're gonna be late." They got up off the grass. Tessa wiped her dress and Carmen rolled her skirt. "Mustn't keep Father Hottie waiting." They ran into the church.

CHAPTER SIX

Luke sat in the darkness of the confessional with Father Thomas on the other side of the screen.

Father Thomas had been serving the congregation for sixty years. He'd heard just about everything there was to hear in a confessional and nothing surprised him, including the fact that almost all his confessors lied. He'd never understood this. What was the point of going to confession if you weren't going to be honest about your transgressions? There would be no forgiveness for the real doozies, and those sins were most likely the reason to get to confession in the first place. He believed every soul had an innate goodness and preferred to think every man, woman, and child that made up his flock were basically decent human beings.

He'd heard rumors about Luke. But he also knew that Luke supported his mother, brought her to mass, and donated generously to the church. Surely the good in the man outweighed any bad.

Father Thomas pushed the grille cover aside and made the sign of the cross. Luke droned on, "Forgive me, Father, for I have sinned.

It's been, you know how long, since my last confession. I've committed a few sins of which I'm truly sorry for. What's my penance this week, Father?"

The old priest sighed. "Why do you come to confession if you're not willing to confess your sins, my son?"

"Father, just give me my penance. That's really what this is all about, isn't it?"

"No, not really. Even before you come to confession, you should examine your conscience. Reflect on your life. Try to recall all the times you've sinned against God. And be truly sorry for those sins. As important as it is to be truly sorry, one must resolve to avoid committing those sins in the future."

"Riiight," Luke said. "That doesn't work for me, Father."

Father Thomas thought for a moment. Well, at least he comes to confession. That's something. "I imagine your sins are not too grievous, my son. There's goodness in your heart."

Luke smirked. "Yeah? How do you know that?"

"You come to confession."

Luke smiled. "My mother comes to church. I bring her. Might as well make good use of my time while I wait for her to finish her prayers."

The priest sighed again. This was not a battle he would win. "Say five Hail Marys."

"Thank you, Father. Same as last week and the week before. Maybe you can come up with something new next week. You know, mix it up a bit?"

Tessa's solo could be heard over the organ music outside the confessional. "I absolve you of all your..." Father Thomas's voice faded as Luke heard her voice.

He listened intently. It had to be the most beautiful voice he'd ever heard. Like an angel's. He looked around and smirked. *Like an angel? I'm definitely being affected by this box. That and all the bloody incense.* He stood, opened the door, and looked toward the choir. He spotted Tessa standing in front of the group facing Father Michael.

Luke watched her, mesmerized. *She not only sounds like an angel,* he thought to himself, *but she's also a stunner.* Wait, what was he thinking? How old could she be? Sixteen, seventeen? Still, he knew he'd never forget her face. She wasn't like any of the women he'd possessed.

Tessa stepped back into the group. Luke shook himself out of his reverie but still watched her as he walked through the row of pews to his mother, who knelt in prayer. She was still wearing head-to-toe black.

He sat on the bench next to her. "Are you ready, Mother?"

She smiled at him. "A few more prayers. For your father."

Luke shook his head and stood. Why does this woman wanna pray for a man who caused her grief and pain? He bent down, kissed the top of her head and whispered, "Add five Hail Marys for me."

Luke exited the church and continued down the steps to the silver-gray sedan parked in front. Sam stepped out of the driver's seat to join him. They walked to stand on the grass next to the side entrance of the church where they each pulled out a pack of cigarettes and lit one.

Sam took a long drag. "How much longer do we have to do this?"

"My mother sees herself as a wife mourning her devoted husband. No matter how ridiculous that is. I think she's talked herself into believing it. So it could be a while."

The church's side door opened and Father Michael stepped out. He walked over to Luke and Sam, searching his pockets. Luke took out his pack of cigarettes and offered him one.

"Thank you, Luke."

They watched as members of the choir poured out the side door. Tessa and Carmen were the last to exit. Carmen spied the three men and grabbed Tessa's hand, pulling her toward them.

"Father Michael. That was a *lit* rehearsal. And the new robes are so beautiful." Carmen batted her eyelashes.

Father Michael pointed to Luke. "Well, we have Mr. Verde and his mother to thank for that."

Luke smiled at Tessa. She lowered her eyes, but Carmen said confidently, "Thank you, Mr. Verde. I'm Carmen and this is my friend, Tessa."

Father Michael realized he should introduce them. "Forgive my manners. Luca Verde. This is Natalya Semenov." Carmen touched his arm, and he smiled at her. "Who prefers to be called Carmen. And this young lady is Tessa Begley."

"Pleased to meet you, Mr. Verde." Carmen reached out and Luke took her hand.

"Please. My father was Mr. Verde. Call me Luke." Carmen held tight. Luke gently pulled his hand away and gestured toward Sam. "This is my friend, Sam Hayes."

Sam took Carmen's hand in both of his. "Nice to meet you, Carmen."

"I wasn't paying attention when the other members of your choir came out. Are they all as attractive as these two?" Luke asked Father Michael.

Father Michael smiled. "Of course."

"I think I might start coming to church," Sam quipped.

Father Michael laughed. "Always looking to recruit more souls, Sam. You'd be welcome."

"Are you gonna go to the church auction next week?" Carmen asked Luke.

"Of course," Luke replied, unable to take his eyes off Tessa. "Will you be there?" he asked Tessa, who didn't respond.

Father Michael touched her arm. "Tessa?" She looked at Father Michael, who pointed to Luke, then she blushed and replied, speaking softly, "We're volunteering at the refreshment table."

"I'm sure we can count on Luke to be equally generous in his donations to our little auction," Father Michael said, certain that if Luke wasn't, his mother would be.

"We'd really appreciate it," Tessa added.

Luke laughed. "Not sure I have much of a choice. I seem to remember something about a guarantee of points in heaven."

Father Michael shrugged innocently.

Luke held out his hand and Tessa shook it. It felt like a bolt of lightning climbed up her arm and into her core. Shocked, she pulled out of his grasp.

Luke couldn't stop looking at her.

Father Michael gestured for the girls to leave. "Run along, you two. I'll see you at the auction. Don't be late. There's a lot to be done."

Carmen walked backwards as they left. "Oh. My. God. Now those were men. Aren't they the most gorgeous?" She stopped. "You gotta admit, they've got serious *rizz*."

Tessa grabbed her arm and turned her around as they continued down the sidewalk.

"That Luke. Wow. Did you see how he was checking you out? He was so undressing you with his eyes."

"He was not." Tessa snuck a look back.

"He so was! I can't believe they'll be at the auction."

Tessa had to admit she did want to see him again.

Luke watched them walk away. He knew immediately that he wanted her. It was obvious she was innocent, and girls that age always hung out in packs. He'd have to come up with a strategy that included Sam keeping the friend occupied. Luke's quick wit and ability to ooze charm in contrast to Sam's quiet, introspective demeanor made them a deadly mix when it came to attracting women, of any age, so it should prove to be an easy hunt.

Meredith exited the church. When Luke saw her, he dropped his cigarette and stubbed it out with his shoe. "Mother's ready to go, Father. We'll see you at the auction." Father Michael nodded and gave him two thumbs up.

Tessa stole another look back.

"Sammy, I want that," Luke muttered under his breath.

"Who wouldn't," quipped Sam.

Sam got in the sedan as Luke helped his mother down the steps and into the car.

***

Gabriel was sprawled on the couch in the living room, a cold beer resting between his thighs and a bowl of chips next to him. He was waiting for the game to start when Tessa entered. She picked up the remote and turned off the volume, then sat next to the bowl, leaned back, grabbed a chip, and began nibbling it. "Dad, I need a new dress. And there's a big sale at Moda Bella."

"Order whatever you need." Without looking at her, Gabriel reached for the remote and turned the volume back up.

Tessa took the remote from his hands and turned it down again. "Can't order it. There won't be enough time to return it if it doesn't fit. And I want to try a few on. Besides, this sale is in-store only. Carmen's going this afternoon and she said I could come with."

"You have lots of dresses."

"I do. But I want something special for the church auction."

"Why? What's so special about a church auction?"

"I dunno. It just is."

"You can't go downtown." He was sure this was exaggerated paranoia on his part, and he blamed that on Luke. Still, he had to be vigilant.

"Tell her you can't go."

"Why not?"

"We've been through this; I asked you not to go anywhere but church. Then you wanted to go to the soda shop. Now it's downtown. What's next?"

"Nothing. Just this. We'll only go to one store. And we'll be with Carmen's mom. Carmen says she's like a prison warden. You'd love her. She won't let us out of her sight. Pleeeease." She gave him her best puppy-dog eyes.

"No. Sorry. But no."

"I can't even go shopping? Shopping?"

He thought she was being a little overdramatic now. "You shop whenever you want. You buy whatever you want. Online!"

Tessa was getting teary. If Luke was going to be at the auction, she wanted to wear something that would make her look older. More sophisticated. "I know my clothes are nice, but I want something different. Something from Moda Bella. Every girl needs a dress for real special occasions. I want a new dress from there!"

"Then order a dress from them online."

"Geez! I explained that to you. What if it doesn't fit right?"

Tessa waited for a response that didn't come. She stood up and yelled, "Now I know how Carmen feels. This isn't a home, it's a prison!" She ran up to her bedroom and slammed the door.

Prison? That hurt. Gabriel picked up the remote and turned the volume up on the TV. He tried to concentrate on the pregame entertainment but couldn't. He turned the volume off and threw the remote to the other side of the couch. *Prison? She just doesn't get it.* He put his head in his hands and muttered, "Better a prison than a coffin." But he couldn't leave it like this. He put his beer and chips on the coffee table, went upstairs, and knocked on her door. He could hear Tessa's muffled crying.

"Tessa, please."

Tessa got up from the bed and stood behind the closed door. "What are you so afraid of?"

"I already explained that."

"You didn't really. Why would someone want to hurt us? Why?"

Gabriel sighed. "This is just temporary. Soon you're gonna have all the freedom you want. You'll be able to go anywhere, shop anywhere. I'm gonna buy us a ranch as soon as I have enough money. With horses. I know you'd like that. Just trust me for now."

Tessa went back to the bed and put her face in her pillow. That could take forever. She was only interested in *now.*

"Tessa?" After a moment Gabriel shook his head and went back downstairs. He stood at the bottom of the stairs for a moment. What was the store? Moda Bella? He sighed. "So, the monster has to venture out of his cave," he said out loud. He took out his phone, found the store address, grabbed a baseball cap and jacket, and drove to the store.

***

Gabriel stood outside Moda Bella, trying to find the courage to enter the store. He felt like the hunchback of Notre Dame. People would turn away and mothers would shield their children as he passed. He knew it wasn't as bad as that, but that's how he felt. That was his perception of reality. And for good reason. There had been times he'd been proven right.

Two girls in their late teens stood behind the service desk, fixated on their phones. A woman in her early forties was busy returning tried-on clothing to the rows of dress racks.

Gabriel entered and was immediately lost in the maze of dresses. He took one off a rack, held it up, and turned to the service desk. One of the girls looked up and stepped back. She nudged the other one, who looked at her, then at him. They just stared.

Gabriel, embarrassed, turned so they couldn't see the scarred side of his face and returned the dress to the rack. He looked around at a loss for what to do. Buying a dress would be even more of a challenge than he thought.

The older salesclerk approached him. "Buying a gift for someone?"

Relieved, Gabriel nodded.

"Know what size she is?"

Gabriel pointed to the young salesclerks.

"Okay. They're both a size two. What color do you think she'd like?"

"I don't know."

"What color is her hair?"

"She's blonde," he said, then added, "with beautiful, big brown eyes."

"What's the occasion?"

"Special. So not too plain." He quickly added, "Not attention-getting either."

She picked a short, red dress. "This one just came in. It's the latest in ready-to-wear couture." Gabriel shook his head. She took a low-cut, blue dress from the rack. "What about this? All the girls want this one. It's flying off the rack." Gabriel shook his head. He'd seen hookers with more clothes on.

She put both dresses back and laughed. "Let me guess. This is for your daughter."

Surprised, Gabriel asked, "How did you know?"

"Just a hunch. Been at this job a long time." She looked around and led him to another rack.

He pointed to an aquamarine shirtdress with lace on the bodice. "What about this one?"

She checked the sizes on several, removed one from the rack, and held it up. "I'm sure she'll like it."

"It's not too plain?" He was having second thoughts.

"No. It's perfect. Very on trend. We've sold a lot of them. And this color should suit her perfectly." She handed him the dress.

"Thank you."

"You come back anytime." She smiled. "We have a sale every few months."

As Gabriel approached the service desk, the two young clerks quickly left and, keeping their heads down, began tidying the dress racks. He put the dress and a credit card on the counter and watched them.

The older clerk noticed and shook her head as she made her way to the register. She rang the sale through and packaged the dress. "Lucky daughter."

Gabriel gave her his best lopsided smile. "Thanks again."

"Anytime."

Gabriel arrived home and was so excited, he rushed up to Tessa's room without taking his cap or jacket off. He banged on the door. "Tessa, open up."

Tessa sat at her bedroom vanity, brushing her hair. She took her time getting up to answer the door. Gabriel stood, beaming, with the shopping bag extended.

"What's this?" Tessa took the bag.

"I hope you like it." She had to. He had ventured out and into a store. Something he wouldn't have done for anyone else. "It's from that store."

"Moda Bella?" Tessa took the bag to her bed and opened it. She pulled out the dress. "Oh, it's… it's beautiful. I can't believe this." Tessa held the dress up in front of her and looked at her reflection in the full-length mirror. "You actually went into a store and picked out a dress for me? All on your own?"

"In this prison, the warden lets the prisoners wear fancy dresses. I hope it fits."

"I'm sure it will." She placed the dress on the bed. "I'm sorry."

"Me too." *Problem solved*, he thought and returned to the living room to find he'd missed most of the game. *Worth it.* He grabbed the chip bowl and now-warm beer and flicked through the stations until he found an old western. *I'll have to learn to ride a horse*, he thought.

***

The doorbell rang a few hours later. Tessa rushed down the stairs and opened the front door. Carmen entered carrying a Moda Bella bag, gushing, "Wait 'til you see what I got. I begged my brother to let me visit for an hour so I could show you."

"Your brother?" Tessa asked, then whispered, "The asshat?"

"Uh huh. Mama wasn't feeling well, and she felt bad because she'd promised to take me, so she told him he had to and to be nice. And, believe it or not, he is actually being nice. So I might not call him asshat anymore. He's still totally uncool, though."

They giggled.

"I'm really sorry you couldn't come with us. The dresses were so lit. It was like being in a candy store. I had so much trouble picking one. Look." She pulled out her phone to show Tessa selfies of all the dresses she'd tried on.

"That's okay. Because I have a new dress, too, and it's perfect." Tessa took Carmen's hand and led her to the living room, where Gabriel was watching the news. "This is my friend Carmen."

He looked over at Carmen and grunted.

It only took a moment for Carmen to recover from seeing his face for the first time. "Hi, sir. It's nice to finally meet you. Tessa talks about you all the time." Gabriel looked at Tessa, who furtively shook her head. He turned back to the news.

Unable to stop herself, Carmen rambled on, "Will you be at the auction, sir? You know there are supposed to be a lot of beautiful things. I've never seen you at church. Do you go to a different one than us? Do you—"

Tessa grabbed her arm mid-sentence. "We'll be upstairs." Tessa pulled Carmen toward the stairs. "Let's go to my room."

Carmen followed, still babbling nonstop. "What happened to his face? I saw a woman burned like that when I went to visit my uncle at the hospital. Does it still hurt, do you think?"

"I don't think so." Tessa walked over to the bed and picked up her new dress.

"How did it happen?" Carmen asked matter-of-factly.

"I don't know. He won't talk about it."

"Probably in the war. He's not very friendly. Is he as mean as he looks?"

Tessa held the dress up in front of her. "Actually, he's very sweet. He just doesn't talk much." She shook the dress. "Like it? He went and got it for me."

Carmen took the dress and laid it back on the bed. "It's..."

"What?"

"Hmmm... a bit conservative."

"Conservative?" Tessa was crestfallen.

Carmen realized she may have hurt Tessa's feelings. This was the dress she would wear to the auction, so she didn't want her to feel bad about it. "But, not too. Look at the pretty lace. And it's an amazing color."

"It is, isn't it?"

"Uh huh." Carmen searched aquamarine on her phone. "Aquamarine. Stands for purity and loyalty. That's you, don't you think? And that makes up for everything."

"Does it? I don't know..." Tessa was starting to doubt herself. Maybe the dress wasn't as great as she thought.

Carmen took Tessa's hand and had her sit on the bed. "I'm gonna do a color analysis on you. She knelt in front of her and studied Tessa's face intensely, then searched her phone again. "Here. Blonde hair and pale skin. Pale skin means you have cool undertones. Which

means your season is winter. So, blue is a *very* good color for you."
She continued searching her phone. "Oh, look, aquamarine is one of
your best blues." She showed Tessa the color chart on her screen.

"Oh good."

"Better than good." Carmen couldn't help but ask the question.
"Why does he buy your dresses? Do you have to do anything in
return?" She grinned wickedly.

"Carmen! That's disgusting! I told you. I cook; I clean. That's all.
Ugh, you have such a dirty mind."

"It's not dirty, it's creative." Carmen pulled her dress out of the
bag. It was the red one the salesclerk had shown Gabriel. Tessa
touched it. "Wow." Carmen held it in front of her and walked over to
the mirror. "*Krasnaya:* passion, pleasure, desire," she whispered.

"What?"

"Red."

"Oh."

Carmen undressed and stood in her bra and panties, looking at her
reflection in the mirror. There were crimson welts across her back.

Tessa rushed to her and gently touched the marks. "What
happened to you?"

Carmen shrugged. "Just some of Papa's discipline."

"Does it hurt a lot? It looks like it hurts a lot."

"I'm used to it."

"What did you do?"

"Doesn't matter."

Tessa stared at the welts. "Can't your mom protect you?"

"She can't even protect herself. She tells me, 'Don't worry,
Natalya, God sees everything'." Carmen exhaled. "Like he even cares."
She forced a laugh. "Enough talk." She put the red dress on and
admired herself in the mirror. "Wait until Father Michael sees me in
this." She handed Tessa her phone and posed. "Take a picture."

Tessa obliged. Carmen turned and studied herself in the mirror.
Preening and trying different hairstyles.

Tessa removed her robe and put on her new dress. She took a pair
of dark-green shoes out from under her bed and put them on.

Carmen spied her in the mirror and frowned. "You can't wear those."

"Why not?"

Carmen stood in front of her. "They're dark green. That's *plokhoy*. Bad. Really bad. Ambition, greed, jealousy."

"That's just silly."

"No, really. Take them off. Besides, they're not sexy. With that dress, you're gonna need sexy."

"What?"

"I'm joking." *This girl is really sensitive.* Carmen hugged her and went to the closet. "Let's see what else you have. Then I'll take a picture of you."

Tessa sighed and took off the shoes. This color business was a bit of a pain.

***

Father Michael and a few members of the choir placed paintings on easels and positioned past-cherished items on a large table at the front of the room. Though he and Father Thomas relied heavily on collections at mass and bingo night, the auction augmented their annual revenues nicely to help pay for unexpected repairs to the church and rectory. The parishioners not only donated items but purchased them as well. They were expected to bid high on at least one item, regardless of how small it might be. It wasn't uncommon for someone to make a donation and then win on a bid for the same item.

Carmen, wearing her new red dress, stood folding paper napkins behind one of the two tables placed together at the back of the room. The tables were covered with hors d'oeuvres, finger sandwiches, petits fours, and coffee urns. Tessa, also wearing her new dress, was on her knees neatly arranging boxes of extra supplies under the same table.

Parishioners passed through, chatting amongst themselves as they filled the rows of metal folding chairs. Everyone had dressed up for the occasion. It was a great excuse to pull out those outfits they never got to wear, and it showed. The men wore suits and ties, and the women had donned their best jewellery.

Luke entered with his mother and walked her up the aisle. Carmen saw him and nudged Tessa excitedly under the table. She said, in a loud whisper, "You'll never guess who just got here. Mister gorgeous!"

Tessa asked, "Who?"

Carmen whispered louder, "Mr. Verde. Luke." Tessa peered over the table and watched Luke as he helped his mother into her seat. He bent to kiss her cheek, then turned and saw Tessa watching him. He smiled at her and waved. Startled, she crouched down.

Father Michael positioned himself next to one of the oil paintings while Father Thomas stepped onto the platform and slowly walked to the small podium. He tapped on the microphone. "Testing one, two, three." He made a point of looking toward the ceiling as he placed his hands together as in prayer. "Can you hear me?" The parishioners laughed and he giggled.

"Thank you all for coming. I hope you've brought your check books, debit cards, credit cards, and even some cash."

A few parishioners laughed and a teenager yelled, "How else am I gonna get to heaven?"

Father Thomas looked over at the boy and quipped, "You may be right, Nicholas." Everyone found this amusing except for his parents, who sat next to him, wondering what else he'd been up to that they were not aware of.

Father Michael took a vase off the display table and held it up as Father Thomas looked down at the paper outlining the list of items. He started the bidding. "This Lalique crystal vase was donated by Miss Emma McFee." Everyone applauded. "What say we start the bidding at four hundred?"

Luke walked to the back of the room and stopped in front of the refreshment table that Tessa was still crouched under. He gave his well-practiced, *I'm a really nice guy* smile and said, "Hi Carmen. I'll have a coffee. Black."

Carmen batted her eyelashes and smiled. "Right away, Mr. Verde."

Luke raised his hands. "Luke, please."

Carmen giggled. "Right away, Luke."

"You're the young lady I met at church."

"Carmen."

"I remember. Carmen aka Natalya Semenov."

Carmen gushed, "Wow, you have a really good memory."

"I never forget a pretty face, Carmen." Luke bent over the table and looked down at Tessa. "And the one hiding under the table is your friend, Tessa."

Embarrassed, Tessa rose, straightening her dress. "Hello, Mr. Verde." She moved some cups around, trying to keep busy.

Father Michael walked over and stood next to one of the easels — a portrait of a wild stallion. Father Thomas started the bidding again. "This fine oil painting by Kim Penner was donated by Mr. Luca Verde." More applause. Luke turned and gave a slight wave to Father Thomas. "Let's start the bidding at one thousand. Do I have one thousand? One thousand, thank you, Mrs. Garcia. Do I have eleven hundred? Eleven hundred..."

Carmen handed the coffee to Luke. He took a sip as Tessa rose to her tiptoes to get a better look at the portrait. "What a beautiful painting."

"Are you into art?"

"Not really. I just love horses. And he's a beauty."

Luke was thrilled to hear the words. Common ground. That was good.

Sam entered and walked over to stand next to Luke. Luke ignored him, concentrating on his discussion with Tessa. "He's one of my most prized possessions. Name's Thunder."

"You own that horse?" It was hard for Tessa to hide her excitement.

"I do. As a matter of fact, I own a few thoroughbreds." The lie was easy.

"You do? I mean, you're so lucky." She frowned. "Why would you give away such a beautiful painting of your own horse?"

"I wouldn't." Luke laughed. The bidding for the painting was still going on and was now at two thousand. Luke raised his hand and, without taking his eyes off Tessa, yelled, "Six thousand."

Father Thomas cleared his throat and continued, "Well, well. We have six thousand from Mr. Verde. Do I hear six thousand one hundred? Six thousand one hundred, anyone? Going once. Going twice. Sold for six thousand dollars to Mr. Verde." Father Thomas was calculating how much more would be needed to fix the boiler. But then the roof also needed repair. Hoping Luke's generosity would infect the others, he continued more confidently. Father Michael removed the portrait from the stage.

Father Thomas walked over to pick up the next item on the table and returned to the podium. It was a cuckoo clock. He held it up. It was heavy and he began to perspire. "Next, we have an authentic Black Forest cuckoo clock." Father Michael returned, took it from him, and held it up. Relieved, Father Thomas continued. "Let's start the bidding at seven hundred, shall we?"

Both girls were taken aback by what Luke had done. Carmen asked, "How come you bid on your own donation?"

"Would you let it go?" Luke asked her.

The portrait had been commissioned from an award-winning equine artist, and it hung in the foyer of the main house. Luke liked it and would never have let someone else own it.

"Do you buy back *everything?*" Tessa couldn't help but be impressed. But at the same time, she wondered if he loved the painting or was just showing off.

Before Luke could respond, Sam asked, "Ready?"

Luke made a point of looking surprised. "For what? The auction isn't over yet." Sam looked confused. Luke pointed to the girls. "Sam, you remember Carmen and Tessa?"

Sam looked at them, immediately understood, and smiled. "Of course. How are you ladies doing?"

"We're very, *very* fine, thank you," Carmen quipped, casually leaning toward him.

Tessa watched her, embarrassed. She picked up a cup. "Would you like a coffee?"

Sam shrugged. "Sure."

Carmen took the cup out of Tessa's hand. "Sugar?"

Sam winked. "Lots. Got a major sweet tooth, darlin'."

Uncomfortable, Tessa began to move the plates around on the table. Luke took a pastry, stuffed it in his mouth, and mumbled, "What are you doing after?"

Tessa thought she understood him but was a little surprised. "What?"

Luke swallowed and laughed. "After the auction. What are your plans?"

Carmen jumped in. "We don't have any plans, yet." She looked at Sam and smiled.

Tessa continued to occupy herself with the plates. Luke touched her hand. There was that electricity. She pulled back, not knowing how to react. "No plans, Tessa?" he asked.

"I'm going home."

Carmen nudged her. Luke noticed and smiled. Sam looked at Luke and then pushed it. "Why don't the four of us go for a drink?"

Carmen rushed to reply, "Sure, we—"

"We don't drink," Tessa interjected.

"Then, what *do* you do?" Luke asked playfully.

"I don't go out with men I don't know." Tessa bent to get more napkins from under the table.

"But you know me. Father Michael introduced us. Remember?" When Tessa didn't respond, Luke continued. "What about ice cream? You can't say no to ice cream."

Sam muttered, "Ice cream?" He gave Luke a confused look.

Luke ignored him and pressed on. "You look like the mint-chocolate-chip type. Or maybe mocha almond fudge."

Tessa started to feel more at ease and giggled. "Strawberry. I like strawberry."

"The place across the street. Toby's. The best strawberry ice cream you've ever had."

Carmen giggled. "Did you know it won awards?"

Sam joined in. "Really? Then we absolutely have to go. We have to!"

"After the auction." Luke touched Tessa's hand again. She stepped back, rubbing her hand.

Carmen answered before Tessa could turn him down. "We have to help clean up here first. We can meet you there around five."

"Five it is." Luke nudged Sam. They walked up the aisle and sat with Luke's mother.

Carmen and Tessa continued to watch them throughout the auction. Carmen took selfies of her and Tessa. Then she took pictures of the two men, even though the backs of their heads were the only parts of them that were visible, just for the fun of it.

"Carmen, we're not going," Tessa said.

Carmen finished Sam's coffee. "Oh, yes we are."

"They're too old for us."

"No, they're not."

"They are. Luke makes me nervous."

"I don't see why. You saw what he did. He bid on lots of things, stuff I'm sure he doesn't even need. And he came with his mother, for cripes' sake."

"So."

Carmen typed "Verde" on her phone. "Verde means green. And... green stands for reliability, generosity..."

"I thought you said green was bad."

"*Dark* green. His green's okay. Matter of fact, I think he suits you."

"I just don't want—"

Carmen stopped her mid-sentence putting her hand to Tessa's mouth. She just couldn't miss out on the opportunity to go on a date. A real date. "Tessa. We have to go. I think I really like Sam. And I can't go without you. Please? Pretty please?" Carmen tugged at her arm.

"Okay. Okay. Just for a few minutes." Tessa had to admit she did want to see Luke again.

"Yippee!" Carmen hugged her and they both rushed to pack everything up.

***

Toby's was a brightly lit, modern-day ice cream parlor furnished with fifties-style laminate counters and red vinyl seating. The service counter displayed tubs filled with every flavor of ice cream imaginable next to a row of vintage soda fountains, chrome serving dishes, and old-fashioned milkshake glasses.

A group of people who had attended the auction were buying treats from the pimply-faced clerk behind the counter. Music emanated from a retro jukebox in one corner of the room.

Tessa and Carmen sat across from each other in a booth, sipping ice-cream floats. Both were nervous. Carmen played with her hair and kept looking out the window. Tessa kept straightening her dress.

"What if they don't come?" Carmen asked, not really expecting an answer. "Do you think they were just playing us?"

Tessa was wondering the same thing. "They must be at least twenty-five."

Carmen laughed. "Older than that, I think."

Now Tessa was more nervous. "Really?"

"I think I saw a gray hair on Sam's head."

"What? No! What are we doing here, Carmen? They're too old for us and too experienced. If they do show, they might expect us to... you know..."

Carmen grabbed her breasts. "So?"

"So? I'm not ready for that."

"You think Luke is handsome, don't you?"

"Uh huh."

"Don't you wanna spend time with him?"

"I dunno. Maybe, but..."

"This is what men and women do. They go on dates and then they have sex."

"Yeah, well, that's too fast for me."

Carmen shrugged. "Don't worry, we're just having ice cream today."

Tessa looked around the shop. The clerk behind the counter caught her eye and gave her his best toothy grin. She blushed. "I dunno..."

The shop bell chimed as the door opened. Sam and Luke entered as the last of the other customers left, leaving the four of them alone in the shop. Carmen waved and they sauntered over.

Luke climbed in next to Tessa, who inched away toward the wall. Sam sat next to Carmen, who didn't move, forcing him to sit close.

"Sorry we're late. We took my mother home, and the traffic was bumper to bumper."

"It's okay. We've been listening to the tunes," Carmen said.

"That looks good." Sam picked up Carmen's float and took a long sip from the straw.

Carmen laughed. "Help yourself, why don'tcha."

"Thanks, I will." Sam took another sip and Carmen giggled.

The song on the jukebox ended. There was a long silence. Sam put the float down, took Carmen's hand, and pulled her out of the booth. "Let's go pick a song; this place is too quiet." He led her across the room to the jukebox. Carmen looked back at Tessa and shrugged.

Tessa watched them for a moment, then looked at Luke self-consciously. He touched the sleeve of her dress and she pulled away gently.

He leaned into her. "You know, you really are gorgeous."

Tessa blushed and looked away. "Don't say that."

"Can't help it. You are." Luke realized he was going to have to take this a lot slower. She wasn't like the women he usually pursued, who only needed him to give them the time of day. "Sorry, I didn't mean to make you uncomfortable." He got up and slid in on the other side. "Better?"

Tessa nodded and smiled. "Better."

"I also wanted to tell you what a beautiful voice you have. Is that okay?"

"You heard me sing?"

"Of course. At mass."

"I've never seen you at mass."

"Were you looking for me?"

Tessa blushed and didn't answer.

"Well, I'm there every Sunday."

Tessa looked over at the jukebox and saw Carmen and Sam leaning against the wall, facing each other. Sam kissed Carmen's neck and Carmen giggled. Tessa turned back to Luke, who watched her, smiling.

An uncomfortable silence ensued. Tessa fidgeted with her phone.

"Take my picture." Luke posed.

Tessa looked up at him. "What?"

"Take my picture."

"Why?"

"So you'll have a visual when you think of me."

"You're kinda full of yourself."

"I guess. Take a picture?" He made funny faces. Tessa laughed but put her phone down.

He picked it up and took some comical selfies of himself.

"There. Now I'll always be where you can find me."

"Hmm." Somehow, she never knew what to say to him. "You never answered my question. At the auction. Do you buy back everything you donate?"

"Nope. But the purpose of the auction is to support the church. So, my mother and I usually bring things we know will get a good price and if not, we bid on it ourselves."

"Oh."

Another uncomfortable silence followed.

Luke broke it. "How did you learn to sing like that?"

Here was something she could talk about. "I don't know. I've just always loved to sing. It's the only time I really feel at peace. You know what I mean?"

"I think I do."

"So many thoughts running through my head all the time. But when I sing, they stop."

Luke smirked knowingly. "A kind of freedom. As if you live in a different world."

"You're the first person who ever put it like that."

"That's how I feel, but not from singing. Obviously. Couldn't hold a note if my life depended on it. But I appreciate good music. It moves me. Takes me out of my head. Believe it or not, when the choir begins to sing, it makes going to mass enjoyable."

"You wouldn't go to church otherwise?"

"I went as a child. Now I go because my mother needs an escort."

"Only for your mother. Why?"

"Things change. I grew up."

Tessa leaned forward. "You're a lot different than I thought you'd be."

"Really? What did you think I was like?

"Well…"

"Go ahead, I can take it."

"Just not like this."

"I don't seem like a guy who was an altar boy for ten years?" He didn't know why he told her that. He hadn't ever told anyone, not Sam, not anyone.

"Altar boy?"

"Yep. What? Can't you picture me as an altar boy? You know, ringing the bells?"

"No. I have to admit, I'm surprised." She wasn't sure she believed him.

Luke put his hand close to hers. "You surprise me, too."

Tessa pulled her hand back but looked at him curiously as Sam and Carmen arrived back at the table.

Tessa checked her phone. "We have to go."

Carmen pouted. "Really?"

Tessa and Luke slid out of the booth.

"I hope we'll see you again soon. I mean really soon," Carmen said, looking longingly at Sam.

Luke replied, taking Tessa's hand, "Me too." He lifted her hand to his lips and pressed a kiss on her knuckles.

Tessa felt like she might faint. That shock wave again. She quickly pulled away and stepped back. Luke chuckled.

Tessa took Carmen's hand and led her out of the shop.

Luke sat back down and Sam slid into the booth across from him. "How'd it go with your little angel?"

Luke looked toward the door thoughtfully and said, "I want you to follow them."

Sam looked at him askance. "Why?"

"I wanna know where she lives."

"Jesus, Luke."

"Just go. I'll meet you back at the club."

After Sam left, Luke sat pondering the last hour. Something about her stuck with him. She'd been on his mind since he saw her at the church. There was something he couldn't quite put his finger on. Sure, she sang like some creature not of this world, but it wasn't just that. She seemed so pure and innocent, yet at the same time he believed underneath that guileless exterior there was probably a siren burning to get out. He grabbed her glass, put the straw to his lips, and emptied it.

What am I thinking? What am I? A fucking poet now? Don't be ridiculous. She's just some fresh piece you wanna fuck. You haven't had to chase a woman before and this is a challenge. You're a sucker for a challenge. That's what this is. Leave it at that.

Tessa and Carmen walked a few blocks together, then parted ways, each continuing in the direction of their respective homes. Tessa didn't see Sam following her at a distance. Her head was full of thoughts of the man who'd touched her and seemed to understand her. She'd never met anyone so handsome. She found it hard to breathe just thinking about him. When she reached the house, she promised herself she would never think of him again. But she knew that would be impossible.

As soon as her key was in the lock, Gabriel opened the door, holding a bag of chips. "Good evening!" Tessa said cheerfully. She planted a happy kiss on Gabriel's cheek and slipped past him, rushing straight up to her bedroom. She shouted, "Don't spoil your dinner. I'm making grilled cheese."

As soon as Sam saw Gabriel, he'd bent down to hide behind a car. *What the fuck? Gabriel Douglas? That's Gabriel.* In any realm of possibilities, he would be the last person Sam would have expected to open that door. But it was definitely him. He snapped a quick picture with his phone.

Gabriel chuckled. He looked left and right before he stepped in and closed the door. He returned to the living room and continued watching the news.

An upstairs light went on, and Sam could see Tessa through the window as she closed her curtains. "No way," he whispered. He took his phone out and dialed Luke. "You are not gonna believe where she lives ... You at the club? ... I'm on my way." He hung up and started whistling to himself as he walked away.

Tessa took off her dress and changed into a comfy pair of jeans, still thinking about the most superb human being she had ever met. Mr. Luke Verde.

CHAPTER SEVEN

Luke sat at his desk handing packets of bills to Charley and Joey. Sam arrived and Luke motioned for them to leave.

Luke waited until they closed the door behind them. "Well, where does she live?"

Sam smirked. "I gotta say she's one hell of an actress."

"What are you talking about?"

"You may need to fight a duel to win the damsel."

"Stop fucking around, Sammy."

"She lives with Gabriel."

Luke gave him a fake laugh. "Fuck off!" If Sam thought he had a great sense of humor, he was wrong. And associating Tessa with Gabriel wasn't funny in the least. "I never said this before, but you are not a funny guy."

"Hey, you don't have to insult me."

"Where does she live?"

"No joke. I saw them together. Real domestic like. She kissed him and he smiled. I didn't know Gabriel could smile. It was weird."

Sam took out his phone and showed Luke the picture.

Luke frowned for a long moment. *Gabriel? Gabriel. She lives with Gabriel? How is that possible?* There could only be one explanation. "She's his cleaning lady."

Sam shrugged and lit a joint. He took a deep drag. "Cleaning ladies don't live in."

"You sure she lives there?"

"I saw her through one of the bedroom windows."

"So, she's a live-in maid. Or she rents a room from him."

"Sure." Sam took another drag and passed it to Luke, who did the same.

"Whatever she is; he's fond of her." They leaned back in their chairs passing the joint back and forth.

"Faauck!" Luke exclaimed. He told himself he should be relieved. She had made him feel vulnerable, which he equated to being weak. He didn't like it. He didn't like it at all. Now he could look at her differently. She wasn't someone he might care about. He really didn't want that, did he? No. His perception of Tessa changed in a flash. She was nothing but the means to an end. She was a weapon he would use on an enemy who didn't seem to have a weakness he could exploit. She was the chink in the ugly fucker's armor.

Luke threw the roach in the ashtray, leaned forward, and slowly smiled. Sam looked at him questioningly.

"I don't give a damn what she is. If she's living there, she means something to him."

Charley knocked on the door and opened it. "You guys comin' to the cottage?"

Sam yelled, "We're busy, Charley."

Charley shrugged and left.

Sam mused, "She doesn't look the type to fuck around. Not like that friend of hers. She was all over me." He grabbed his crotch.

Luke laughed and lit a cigarette, "That's what makes her so perfect."

"Uh huh." Sam agreed.

"Besides, she can't possibly be as innocent as she pretends to be. *No one* is that innocent."

***

Meanwhile, Mika had an hour or so before her shift, and Luke hadn't let her spend time with him in days. She decided to go to his office. The staff weren't allowed in there unless invited, but she was special, wasn't she? *I have to make sure he doesn't forget why he wanted me in the first place. He likes me because I'm strong. I'm not one of the sappy waitresses or slut dancers. I won't put up with his shit. I'll give him a quick reminder of what he's missing.*

As she passed Charley on the stairway, he stopped and grabbed her playfully. She smacked his hand. "I'm Luke's. Don't forget it."

Another fucking delusional piece of ass. Are they all really that stupid? Charley mused. "Hate to burst your bubble, sweetheart, but I fuck all Luke's women. He likes me to rate them. I just haven't got around to you yet."

"You're an asshole, Charley."

"Are you telling me you didn't know?"

She continued up the stairs. "You're full of shit. It's different with us. He would never share me."

Charley yelled back, "Good luck with that."

Mika grabbed the door handle but stopped to listen when she heard voices.

Luke leaned back in his chair, crossed his arms and turned to look out the window. "Tessa, Tessa, sweet Tessa. You're exactly what I've been looking for. My little angel."

Mika stepped back from the door. *Tessa? Who the fuck is Tessa?* She turned and ran down the stairs, vowing to find this woman and end her.

***

Riki stood in the shadows across the street from the Vox. His suit was a little rumpled but passable. He'd waited until he saw Luke leave the club then ran around the back, climbed the fire escape stairs, and jimmied the latch on the window in Luke's office. The club was loud and packed to capacity, so no one noticed him come down the stairs. That is, no one but Mika. She spotted him right away.

What is that fool up to now? If I didn't know better, I'd think he actually wanted to die. She rushed over to him, grabbed hold of his arm, and whispered in his ear, "You idiot! You have a death wish? What are you doing here?"

Riki yelled over the noise, "Gonna do a deal with Marty."

"Bullshit."

"I am. Then I'm outta here."

She looked at him for a long minute then shrugged and shook her head. "It's your funeral."

He grinned. "Wish me luck."

She watched Riki as he made his way to Marty's table, both keeping their eye out for Luke or any of his crew.

Marty Gilman was grossly overweight, with a thinning, greasy comb-over. His expensive designer suits never properly fit his frame. But Marty was also a VIP who dropped thousands in a single night without a second thought, so the dancers loved him and the waitresses fought to work his section.

He ran every betting establishment in the borough. If you were looking for venture capital for any not-so-legit business, he was also the man to go to. Unfortunately, the only time Riki would ever be able to get close to the man would be at Luke's club. Hence the need to take a chance on meeting him here.

Riki slid into the booth across from Marty, who leaned back and said, "Who the fuck are you?"

"Riki Tanaka. And I got an easy way for you to make a lotta money with no effort at all."

Marty laughed. "I already got a lotta money, Riki Tanaka."

"A lot *more* money."

"Yeah?" Marty sucked on his expensive stogie as Riki made his pitch. Every now and then Riki looked around the room to make sure none of Luke's crew were in the club, then he leaned in and continued talking.

He knew TJ was off tonight and figured the rest of them would hopefully be at the cottage.

Unfortunately for him, one of the bartenders got ill mid-shift and called TJ to replace him for the remainder of the night. TJ was happy to oblige, as he was just hanging at home and there was nothing streaming on Netflix that he'd wanted to binge.

TJ got behind the bar and immediately started taking orders and pouring drinks. In no time, he spied Riki. "I don't believe it. That guy's got some brass. I wouldn't wanna be him tonight," he mused as he dialed his cell phone. "Sam? You'll never guess who's in the club whispering in Marty Gilman's ear … Riki … Yeah, and Marty seems to be listening … I thought you might find that interesting … Sure."

***

Sam and Luke arrived at the club ten minutes later. They spotted Riki at Marty's table as they continued toward the bar. TJ poured them each a shot of tequila and yelled over the music, "Believe it?"

Sam shook his head. "He's either so stoned he doesn't know where he is or he's a masochist. Isn't he afraid we'll finish the job the guys started?"

Luke shrugged. "He's harmless."

"Yeah, but what's he doin' talkin' to Marty? And why would Marty listen?" Sam downed his shot and TJ poured him another one. "I'll go find out." He picked up the glass and walked through the crowd toward the table.

Riki spotted him. "Gotta go, Marty. I'll call ya." He slipped out of the booth and was immediately lost in the crowd.

Sam continued on to Marty's table and sat next to him. "Hey, Marty. How's it hangin'?"

"This table seems to be popular tonight." Marty took a sip of his champagne. "What's up, Sam?"

"Just wanna little information," Sam said as he motioned to a waitress to bring another bottle over.

"Oh? Of what nature?"

"Riki Tanaka. Heard he snuck in, snuck out, and had a chat with you in between."

"Surprised you're interested, Sam."

"Not really. More curious. He works for me."

"Kid's lookin' for a backer. Didn't give him much mind. Obvious he's all hat, no cattle."

"What kinda backer?" Sam was definitely interested now.

***

Meanwhile, Suzanne stopped dancing and stepped off her podium. She'd spotted Luke drinking on his own at the bar. She sauntered over and posed in front of him, then picked up his drink and took a sip before kissing the rim and handing it to him. He smirked and belted back the rest. She whispered in his ear and he laughed.

Mika watched them from across the room. She slipped through the crowd toward them, took hold of Suzanne's arm, and said, "I wanna talk to you. Follow me." She led Suzanne toward the bathroom as the dancer shrugged at Luke. "Gimme a minute?"

"Sure." Luke smiled and watched them go, then he leaned over to TJ and nodded in their direction. "Between Mika and her brother, who do you think is the most trouble?"

TJ snorted. "Hard to say."

Once they were in the bathroom, Mika grabbed hold of Suzanne's hair and bent her back over one of the sinks. She pulled a small knife out of the waist of her slacks and held it to the dancer's throat. "You may not have heard, but Luke and I are an item. I don't share. Ever. If I see you near him again, this pretty face of yours will no longer be pretty. Do you understand?"

Suzanne's eyes widened with fear. She liked to think she could hold her own, but she was also aware of Mika's reputation. She wouldn't be the first dancer Mika put out of commission. She'd heard that Mika beat a dancer senseless for fucking patrons in the men's washroom. The girl did actually deserve it, as she could have simply met up with the men somewhere outside the club. She was stupid.

"Message received. He's yours. I'll stay far away," she declared immediately. "Sorry."

Mika pushed the knife in just enough to break the skin. A drop of blood slid down the Suzanne's neck. Mika let her go, and she ran out of the bathroom holding her neck. Mika checked her makeup in the mirror and exited the bathroom, avoiding looking in the direction of the bar.

Luke watched her pick her way through the crowd. When he caught her eye, he smiled and waved. She blew him a kiss. He then grabbed one of the passing waitresses and whispered in her ear. She nodded and put her tray on the bar. Luke took her by the hand, and they walked up the stairs to his suite. Mika watched them, daggers shooting from her eyes.

Sam left Marty's table and went up to see Luke. He knocked on the door and entered without waiting for a reply. The waitress was naked on Luke's knee. Luke lifted her off.

She picked up her clothes. "Do you want me to wait in the bedroom?"

Luke replied offhandedly, "No. I'll find you later."

Sam sat in front of him and lit a cigarette. "Riki was trying to get Marty to fund the purchase of the very merchandise we've started selling."

Luke scoffed. "Who is he gonna buy from and, more importantly, who is he planning on selling to?"

"He didn't tell Marty where he was gonna get the merchandise; but it turns out he's got an in with the Japs. And they're looking to buy."

Luke raised an eyebrow. "*That's* interesting."

"A heavy. Name of Kenji. High up in the Yakuza."

"I've heard of him. One nasty motherfucker. Why would he have anything to do with a nothing punk like Riki?"

Sam muttered sarcastically, "Tight-knit family, I guess."

"Family?"

"They're related."

"Fuck off! Riki related to Kenji Ishii?"

"You know what that means. Mika is also related to Kenji Ishii."

"She just got a lot more interesting," Luke mused. He couldn't be happier.

"Gonna tell her you know?"

"Not until I need to use her. Let's keep that info to ourselves."

"Sure."

"I still don't get it. If Kenji is related to Riki, he knows he's too bloody stupid *and* fucked up to run any game."

"Riki must have been convincing. He told Marty he's repping the men holding the merchandise."

"Who the fuck is he talking about? The bikers are only interested in guns, drugs, and prostitution. The Poles are only interested in munitions, and the Puerto Ricans love their *mamacitas* too much."

"Who else, Luke? Us. Musta heard we're in the business," Sam said matter-of-factly.

"Impossible. There's no way he could know."

"What about Mika. She's been hanging around a lot. Think she heard something?"

Luke leaned forward, irritated. "And how the fuck would Mika have heard something?"

"Just asking." Sam put his hands up and smiled at Luke.

Luke leaned back and they sat quietly.

"So, Riki was planning on using the capital from Marty, or whoever, to buy from us, and then turn around and sell to Kenji. Kenji has no clue Riki doesn't have the connection."

Sam nodded. "That about covers it."

"Nor does Kenji know we'd be more than willing to deal with him directly."

"Nope."

"Looks like Riki just found us one hell of a customer, Sammy. Yakuza pockets run deep. We really should thank Riki. But first let's set up a meeting with Kenji."

Luke lit a joint and they got high in silence.

***

The silver-gray sedan pulled up in front of the church. "Come back in an hour," Luke said to Sam as he helped his mother out of the car.

Sam opened his door and got out. "Why?"

"I'm gonna sit through this one." Luke not only wanted to hear Tessa sing, but, more importantly, he also wanted her to see him at mass.

Meredith smiled to herself and took his arm. "Luca, have you had a change of heart? You know nothing would make me happier than to have you worship with me."

"Sorry, Mother. Just looking for a little peace and quiet wherever I can find it."

She squeezed his arm. "It's a beginning, Luca."

Luke laughed and cupped his hand over hers.

Sam, eyebrows raised, got in the car and drove away as Luke escorted his mother into the church.

***

An hour later, the church doors opened, and Father Thomas stepped out to acknowledge the parishioners as they filed past. Luke and his mother appeared last, and they talked with the priest as all three continued down the steps.

Tessa and Carmen, as usual, exited through the side door.

Carmen saw the sedan drive up in front of the church and ran over to it. Sam got out of the car, and she gave him a peck on the cheek.

"Hi, Sam."

"Well, hello there."

Carmen snapped a selfie of them with her phone and checked it. "We look awful good together."

Sam laughed. "Let me see." She passed the phone to him, and he deleted the photo.

"Hey! What did you do that for?"

"Do you really want your parents to find a picture on your phone of you and some strange guy?" he asked.

"You're not strange." She pouted, thought for a moment, then reluctantly agreed. "You're right. Not a good idea." She took his hand. "So, tell me what you've been up to."

Tessa smiled as she watched them, then turned away as she inserted her earbuds.

Luke saw her and left his mother to her chat with Father Thomas.

He walked up behind Tessa, pulled out one of her earbuds, and whispered in her ear, "Your friend is *very* friendly."

Tessa flinched. She turned, pulling out the other earbud. "Oh. It's you... Carmen knows what boys like."

"Boys. Not men."

Tessa was actually surprised. "Sam doesn't like Carmen being so forward?"

Luke smirked. "I'm sure he thinks it's great. But Sam and I are different."

Tessa didn't understand what he was getting at. Why was he talking about Carmen. "Maybe Carmen's just being her authentic self." She knew it was a silly thing to say as she said it.

"Authentic self?" Luke shook his head. "What the hell does that mean anyway?"

Tessa shrugged. She couldn't think of an answer. "I dunno."

They both laughed and Tessa felt more at ease.

"Listen, I remember you said you love horses."

"I do."

"Thunder is ready to breed. He's being introduced to a filly on Thursday. Would you like to come?"

"You're a breeder?"

"Among other things. It's a family business. You seem surprised."

"I'd never figure you as a horseman."

"Well, I am. Unfortunately, I don't get to ride as much as I'd like."

"Me either."

"And I'm thinking of selling. My other businesses keep me pretty busy, and the ranch needs full-time management. Now that my father has passed..."

"Oh."

"Apart from that, it's very costly to run. Upkeep of the stables, staff salaries, vet fees, medicine. The list goes on. So I'd like you to come while you can."

Tessa looked around Luke to see Carmen still flirting with Sam. She checked the time on her phone. "I have to go."

Luke saw his mother give him a little wave. "Me too. Please think about it. You'd love Thunder."

"I know I would. But I can't."

"Why not?"

"I just can't."

Luke put his hands on her shoulders. She tried not to squirm.

"Think about it. It'll be fun. You, me, and Thunder." He took her phone out of her hand and keyed his number in. "Let me know if you change your mind."

Sam got back in the car and Carmen slowly sashayed, as best she could, back to Tessa, hoping Sam was watching her.

"I won't change my mind," Tessa assured him.

Luke smiled impishly. "Thunder will be very upset," he remarked as he turned and headed back to the church steps to collect his mother.

They said their goodbyes to Father Thomas, and he walked her to the car. "Sorry to keep you waiting, Mother."

"He does tend to go on," Meredith complained. "I was given a step-by-step accounting of both the purchase and the installation of the new boiler."

"Ouch."

"I see that you and Sam are friendly with some members of the choir."

"We were introduced at the auction." Luke hoped his response seemed innocent enough.

"The young lady you were talking to is the very image of a woman I once knew."

"Yeah?"

"Sarah Begley."

Luke looked over at Tessa as he opened the car door. "Begley?"

"Yes. She worked at the ranch, and we were close. She ended up leaving quite abruptly. Your new partner was the reason."

Luke helped her into the car. "Gabriel Douglas?"

"Yes."

Smiling, Luke sat next to her and enquired casually, "How was Gabriel involved?"

***

Carmen and Tessa watched the sedan drive off. "Oh, Tessa. Sam just slays me." Carmen sighed. "What did Luke say to you?"

"He wants to take me to his ranch. To see one of his stallions. The one in the painting."

"You're gonna go."

Tessa looked at her phone. "I want to, but he scares me. I never feel like I can control what happens when he's around."

"It's great to feel out of control. Sam does that to me. It's exciting. Don't ya think? I mean, how lucky are we that we met them. At church of all places. At church! It's a sign. It was meant to be."

Tessa laughed. She may not have known Carmen long, but she wasn't surprised that she'd be able to find some evidence to validate her point of view. It wasn't a color this time, but God who put Sam in her path.

"I dunno about that."

"Did Luke tell you he owns a nightclub?"

"A nightclub?"

"Only the hottest place in town! I'm gonna get Sam to take me there. Wanna come?"

"Go out with a man, an older man, who owns a nightclub? I would get locked in my room and never let out again."

"Geez. It's not like he's your dad."

"He worries about me. I haven't lived here that long, and he wants to make sure I'm safe for his friend, my actual dad. He doesn't deserve me sneaking around behind his back."

"You're in love. He'd understand that. A girl's got a right to fall in love."

A car horn honked. "That's my brother. Text me later." Carmen quickly buttoned the top of her shirt and pulled down her skirt as she ran to the car.

Tessa walked home, thinking of Luke. She wished she was as daring as Carmen. Could she be? It would take a lot of planning. And a lot of lying. Not really something she wanted to do.

Tessa made a point of making one of Gabriel's favorite meals. They ate in silence, making the odd comment about nothing of import, simply content with each other's company.

When they finished dessert, Gabriel took a folded sheet of newspaper out of his pocket. and placed it on the table in front of her. It had a picture of a ranch house and stables with a caption reading: Acres of Prime Real Estate. "What do you think? It's a ranch in Virginia. Middleburg. Real horse country."

Tessa glowed with excitement. "Can we afford it?"

Gabriel smiled, relieved at her reaction. "Yep. You'll be able to ride to your heart's content." Tessa jumped up and hugged him. He put his arms around her tentatively, then said, "I gotta go. The game."

Tessa gave him an extra squeeze before letting go. "Yes, you go watch your game."

He picked up the ad and stuffed it back in his pocket. The sooner he could make it happen, the better. He whistled on his way to the living room.

Tessa picked their plates up off the table and started washing up. But the more she thought about it, the more she realized she wasn't as excited about the prospect of getting back to a ranch as she should be. Even though it meant going back to her beloved horses. Virginia was so far away. She'd never see Luke again.

After cleaning the kitchen, she rushed up to her room. She took out her phone and scrolled through the pictures of Luke; they made her smile Should she call him? She knew she shouldn't, but she dialed his number anyway. It rang and when he answered, she hung up. *Oh. What was I thinking,* she thought. *He knows it was me.* The phone rang. It was him. "Hello?"

"You rang?" Luke joked.

"Yes. Sorry."

"Why are you sorry?" *Definitely a reminder of how young she is,* he thought. "I'm not."

"I'd like to come to your ranch."

"Great. Nine o'clock?"

"Ten is better. After choir practice. I'll wait for you at Toby's."

"I'll be there." He hung up.

Tessa changed into her pajamas and crawled into bed with her phone, even though it was still early. She looked at his pictures again before closing her eyes. She went through everything they'd said to each other over and over in her head and when she fell asleep, she dreamed of him.

***

Tessa stood in the shadow of the ice-cream shop's entrance. She felt overwhelmed with both guilt and apprehension: guilt for telling Gabriel she was going to be at an extended choir practice, and apprehension because she didn't know what being alone with Luke would be like. "What am I doing? This is crazy," she said aloud. She turned to walk home as Luke pulled up in the sports coupe.

He put the passenger window down and called, "Hi there."

Tessa stopped and didn't move. She just shook her head. "Sorry, I made a mistake. This isn't a good idea."

Luke thought for a moment. "Okay. Let me drive you home."

"No."

"Can we talk? Just for a minute."

Tessa was afraid he might follow her home if she didn't. She looked around, making sure no one was watching, and quickly got into the car.

"I'm sorry." It was the only thing she could think of saying.

He turned off the ignition and resisted the urge to take her hand because he knew she'd pull away. "I get it. You've changed your mind. Frankly, I was surprised you called."

"Me too."

"But glad."

Tessa didn't know how to explain her change of heart. She had secrets she couldn't share, and even worse, she felt out of control when she was with him. "You must think I'm such a child, changing my mind at the last minute."

"Believe me, Tessa, I don't think you're a child. You don't know me that well, so you don't trust me yet. I get it. If it makes you feel more comfortable, we won't be alone at the ranch. Not even for a second."

Tessa couldn't help but smile.

"Change your mind. Please." The wink he gave her felt like a dare. Tessa liked the way he looked at her, and she wanted him to look at her more. She nodded. "I do wanna see Thunder."

"Great."

Luke started the car and turned on the radio. They drove out of town in silence and arrived at the ranch a half hour later.

Kevin the breeding manager, greeted them. "Luke, you're just in time." He shook Luke's hand.

Luke put his arm around Tessa's shoulder. "Kevin, this is my friend, Tessa."

"Pleased to meet ya, Tessa. Luke tells me you know horses."

"I do." Tessa blushed.

"Then I'm sure you're gonna enjoy this." Kevin led them to the stables. As they entered, two grooms were leading Thunder out of his stall.

One of the grooms slipped and almost fell, surprising the horse. Thunder neighed and reared. Tessa moved toward the stallion.

Luke shouted, "What are you doing?" He tried to grab her arm, but she slipped out of his grasp.

She approached Thunder, cooing, "It's okay, Thunder. Shh. It's okay." She grabbed the bridle and began to hum softly as she petted his shoulder. Thunder calmed and whinnied.

She pressed her cheek to his neck and ran her hand up and down his forehead. Kevin watched her admiringly and said to Luke, "She does have a way with horses."

Luke smiled proudly. Kevin took Thunder's reins and led him out of the stables to a corral where a roan-colored mare stood idly.

Luke took Tessa's hand and wove his fingers through hers in a gentle grip. She looked at him but didn't pull away. They followed the horse to the paddock.

Kevin and the grooms got up on the fence, and Tessa climbed up next to them. Luke stood beside her.

Kevin pointed to the mare. "Her name's Willow. Isn't she a beauty?"

Tessa nodded and sighed. "She sure is." She pulled out her phone and took pictures of the horses. *I can't wait to show these to Carmen,* she thought. She felt a pang knowing she'd never be able to share them with Gabriel.

The stallion approached the mare, who ran at as much of a gallop as possible within the confines of the paddock to get away from him. Thunder chased her. She stopped. He nickered and she responded. He rested his head over her neck. She neighed and trotted away, obviously wanting him to catch her. They played cat and mouse for a while and eventually Thunder mounted her.

Tessa took a quick picture. Carmen would definitely want to get the full story. She giggled to herself.

Luke put his hands around Tessa's waist. Her face flushed. She shifted her position uncomfortably and Luke pulled his hands away. She turned to look at him and he gave her a wicked smile. *He's testing me,* she thought. *Am I supposed to be shocked. Or get turned on. He forgets that I grew up on a ranch.* She returned his smile with a confidence she suddenly felt.

Thunder and Willow finished coupling. Kevin jumped in and led Thunder out of the paddock. Luke put his hands on Tessa's waist again but only to help her off the fence. She gently pulled his hands away and jumped down.

Thunder neighed as he was led into the stables. *He's obviously content with himself,* thought Tessa as she followed the stallion.

Luke caught up to her and grabbed her hand. "Whoa. My little filly. Hold on. I wanna talk to you."

"What."

"Thunder has a reputation for being difficult. He's dangerous. You took a risk in the stables that you shouldn't have."

"You're wrong. He's not dangerous at all."

"Don't be ridicu—"

"You can't take a horse at face value," she interrupted. "Or a person for that matter. It's not always about what you see. Most of the time it's what you can't see that's important."

Cocky little brat, Luke thought. *Easy to have that point of view when you haven't actually lived. I plan to hump it out of her nice and slow.* "And you gleaned this insight from your vast eighteen years of life experience?"

"You're being mean. What I meant is that I knew I could trust him. That he isn't dangerous, just misunderstood. Inside, he's gentle. He wants to be gentle. Did you see the way he was with Willow? She brought out the best in him. He wouldn't hurt her, and he wouldn't hurt me."

"What you think you see isn't always what you end up getting," Luke said a little too harshly.

"Let's take you for instance, *Mister* Verde. How do you see yourself?"

"What do you mean?"

"Are you a good man?"

"Depends what you mean by *good.*"

"You know what I mean."

"No, I don't. What I think is good may not be what you think is good. Do *you* think I'm a good man?"

"I'm not sure yet. But I'm willing to give you the benefit of the doubt." Tessa rushed ahead then turned. "Are you coming?" She swiveled and kept going.

Luke watched her. *What is it with this girl? The truth is... Is what? The truth is I want to take her in my arms and never let her go.* He growled. *Goddammit. Get a grip. She's your revenge. Don't fucking forget that.*

Thunder and Willow. Luke and Tessa. What perfect pairs. He followed her, pissed that he would even feel confused.

CHAPTER EIGHT

Carmen sat at the only computer in her home. It was on a desk in the living room where her parents could keep an eye on her and her brother when they used it. They distrusted the internet and social media in general. Both were considered the devil's toolbox. Proper young ladies, or young men, for that matter, could easily be swayed to commit any number of sins by that TikTok they'd heard about. They only allowed its use because Alex insisted they had to have a computer to complete their school assignments. Which was partially true. They didn't realize that as long as their children had cell phones, they were able to access "forbidden sites" anyway. Even Alex didn't let them know this was possible.

Carmen showed her mama where she could access a new pork stew recipe, then waited until she went to the kitchen to start dinner and googled "Club Vox." A flashy photo showed the main floor at its peak occupancy. *Wow. What a place.* She looked for the address. It was only one bus ride away. A long bus ride, but still just one bus ride. She decided at that moment that she was going to go there that night.

She waited until her parents were in bed and she could hear her papa snoring. Then she put her red dress on because Sam had complimented her on it the day of the auction. She held her high heels in one hand as she climbed out her window and ran down the street to catch the bus.

When Carmen got off the bus, she stared in awe at the Vox. There was the usual lineup down the block. It didn't deter her because she knew the most important people in the club. Excited, she snapped a selfie with the club in the background. It was a great picture. She sent it to Tessa with the caption "Livin' loud." An experience like this had to be shared with her BFF.

She crossed the street to where a doorman and bouncer stood in front of the entrance. She approached the doorman because the bouncer was too scary looking. "Hi, I'm a friend of Sam and Luke."

The doorman looked her up and down. "I doubt that, miss."

Someone exited and Carmen craned her neck to look in. She had to get past these men. She stood up straight, trying to look older than her years. "Sam is expecting me. And you'll be in a whole lotta trouble if you don't tell him I'm here. Just say it's Carmen."

The two men looked at each other. The bouncer shook his head but entered the club. After what seemed like ages, he returned with Sam.

Sam took her hand and led her away from the entrance. "What are you doing here, Carmen?"

"I wanted to surprise you."

"You did."

"Good."

Sam looked her up and down, the same way the doorman had. "Look, you're still a little girl, Carmen. This isn't a place for little girls. Go home. C'mon, I'll find you a taxi."

She stood her ground. "I'm not a little girl. Please, Sam. Don't send me away." She put her arms around his waist and held tight. "Please?"

The men at the door were watching him, and he realized she wouldn't leave voluntarily; instead of making a scene, he figured he could let her in, give her a few drinks, and take her out through the back door.

"Well, you're here. You might as well come in." He pulled her arms away, took her hand, and led her in.

Once inside, Sam asked a waitress to bring a bottle up to the VIP room. The waitress looked at Carmen for a moment and then at Sam before rushing to the bar to place his order.

Sam brought Carmen upstairs. She turned and took a quick photo from her vantage point at the top of the stairs.

Sam shook his head. *Luke owes me for this one.* He led her into the VIP room, sat, and patted the seat next to him.

Carmen was finally experiencing all the things she'd dreamed of. And she couldn't be happier. She was in a hot downtown club, in a private room, with the man of her dreams. She felt so grown-up and sophisticated. She giggled. The other day outside the church he had told her she was his girl. She was sure he was the one to free her from the strict confines of her parents' home. She pictured the two of them married and living in a condo downtown with a view of the lake. He was her knight in shining armor, and she adored him.

"So, you wanted to see the club?" Sam asked. Carmen nodded. "Get a taste of the life?" Carmen nodded again and giggled.

The waitress appeared with a bottle of champagne, two glasses, and a silver ice bucket. Carmen surreptitiously snapped another photo. The waitress popped open the cork and filled their glasses. "I'll be right back with some appetizers, Mr. Hayes." She closed the door behind her.

Sam picked up both glasses and handed one to Carmen. "Here's to a fun evening." She sipped the champagne. He figured if she drank enough, she'd probably puke, want to go home, and not show up at the club again.

"This is so good." The only other alcohol she'd ever had was the half glass of wine her papa would allow her on special occasions and the sip of wine during Communion at mass.

Sam chugged his glass and motioned for her to do the same. "Always good to start the evening with a few drinks in you." He refilled their glasses and finished his in one go. Carmen giggled and did the same.

"What do you want, Carmen?" He filled their glasses again. The more important question was how he was gonna get rid of her. He had things to do tonight, and they didn't include babysitting.

"You. I want you."

He raised an eyebrow. "Well, here I am." Carmen struggled to think of a great retort. This usually wasn't something she had difficulty with. "I wanted to see where you hung out."

"Are you old enough to even be here?"

"No." She was feeling more confident now that the liquor had started to affect her. "But you are."

Sam laughed. Carmen straightened her dress and tried to look more grown-up than she felt. All she wanted to do was please him.

The waitress arrived with caviar and all the accoutrements.

"Oh goody. Snacks. I'm hungry." Carmen's words slurred a little.

Sam poured the last of the champagne into his glass and put the empty champagne bottle upside down in the bucket.

The waitress picked up the bucket. "Another bottle, Mr. Hayes?"

"I think my guest has had enough," Sam said.

"I'd like more," Carmen chimed in.

Sam sighed, shrugged, and nodded to the waitress, who smiled and left.

Carmen was focusing on the caviar. "Wow." She pulled out her phone and took a picture. "What is it?"

Sam took the phone from her and put it in her purse. He picked up a cracker and used the small mother-of-pearl spoon to put some crème fraîche and caviar on it. He put the cracker to Carmen's mouth. "Open up." Carmen opened her mouth and he placed the whole cracker in. She made a face as she chewed. *This tastes worse than spoiled fish smells,* she thought. *But tell him it's good anyway.*

"Caviar's not really for a little girl's palate," he noted.

"I told you! I'm *not* a little girl, Sam. Please stop saying that. Besides, don't know how anyone could like this. Yuck. Tastes like something died." She couldn't help herself; the words just came out.

"Uh huh." He had to admit she was a breath of fresh air.

Moments later the waitress returned with another bottle. She opened it and poured champagne into their glasses.

Carmen picked up hers and emptied it in one go. Champagne spilled down her chin. "Oops." She wiped her chin, and Sam took the glass from her.

"Okay, you've had enough."

The waitress smiled and winked at Sam, who raised his hands and shook his head in response. *I am never gonna live this down,* he thought.

Carmen was starting to feel dizzy. *It must be because I'm finally alone with Sam,* she thought. *He makes my head spin.* Carmen slurred, "I definitely *do not* like caviar. But champagne is yum-my." She waved her hand in front of her face like a fan. "Whoosh. It's sooo hot in here."

"You're the reason it's hot in here." Sam gave her an innocent peck on her nose. "I think it's time for you to go."

"Not yet. In a minute. One more kiss first." Carmen wrapped her arms around Sam's neck and kissed him.

***

While Carmen kissed Sam in the VIP room, Luke was in his office, yelling on his phone. He was furious. "I told you the merchandise is ready for immediate delivery." He rolled his eyes. "I'm gonna say it again. That is your problem, not mine. We agreed on a price and a time and place. Do you really think you can renege on either? Pick up the merchandise on the date agreed or I will find another buyer. It's up to you … Is that a threat? It better not be … You've got two days … Yes, four, goddammit! That was the deal!"

Luke slammed his phone on the desk. He continued yelling. "You think you can fuck me over? Luca fucking Verde?" They were obviously not aware of his reputation. He'd sooner have them wiped off the face of the earth than take their bullshit. Luke picked up the phone and threw it across the room. He grabbed the ashtray and threw it too. Then he looked at his watch. "I gotta get outta here." He continued mumbling under his breath as he left the office, slamming the door behind him.

He heard giggling as he passed the VIP room and pushed the door open to find Sam with Carmen. "Well, well, if it ain't Carmen." A very drunk Carmen tried to sit up straight.

"Hi." She slumped back into the seat.

Sam sneered. "Can't hold her fucking liquor."

Carmen looked at Luke through half-closed lids. "Champagne."

"Where's your friend?" As far as Luke was concerned, where Carmen was, Tessa would not be far behind. Although he couldn't picture her here. Not here. Not her. He couldn't understand why the two were friends. Carmen was a bad influence.

Carmen struggled to keep her eyes open. "Fra… frien?"

Sam knew Luke well enough to know he was pissed. "Everything okay?"

"It seems we're stuck with the merchandise longer than expected."

"Charley said that would never happen," grumbled Sam.

"Charley's not answering his phone. He's lucky he's not here right now," Luke threatened.

Sam knew it wasn't a good idea for Luke to go to the cottage in the mood he was in. Things wouldn't go well for Charley if he was there, and they needed him. Sam checked his watch. "I gotta see Marty. Need to cover a loss. Then—"

"How much?" Luke interrupted him.

"Don't worry, I got it. Then I'll go to the cottage. Take care of things." Sam motioned to Carmen. "Wanna take her off my hands?"

Luke looked at her, shook his head, and shrugged. "Why not?"

Sam left, shutting the door behind him, and Luke sat beside Carmen. She opened her eyes and tried to focus. She put her hand on his face and slurred, "Mishter Verde? Wha dar you doon here?"

Luke smiled at her wickedly. "I'm Sam."

"You're Sam?"

"Yep."

She closed her eyes. "Kish me, Sam."

Luke kissed her and reached behind her. "Let's get you undressed."

***

Hours later, glasses and plates were scattered over the floor. Carmen was lying on her back on the low, black lacquered table. She was naked.

Her legs were spread open on either side of Luke who was on the couch facing her, asleep. His shirt was open and his slacks were undone.

Carmen opened her eyes. "Wha?" She tried to sit up and realized she was naked. Her head was pounding. She looked at Luke in horror, then reached down and felt between her legs. She was sore. She tried to cover herself with her hands and saw her dress and bra next to Luke on the couch. She scrambled off the table onto the floor, waking him. She grabbed her dress and held it in front of her.

Luke stretched and yawned. "You're awake." He zipped up his pants and began to button his shirt but stopped. "Wait. Should I…" He pointed to his pants. "Want another go?"

She yelled, "What happened? Where's Sam?"

"Hush. You don't want anyone else to know about this, do you?"

"Where… where's Sam?" she asked in a lowered voice.

"Sam left."

"How did I…" She held her dress closer, looked around, and began to cry. She tried to make sense of why she was naked and why she was with Luke.

He tossed her bra at her. "How did you get naked?"

"Huh-how?"

"You don't remember the striptease you performed for us?"

Still woozy, she shakily put on her bra and dress, trying not to show any more of herself. She found her shoes next to her purse under the table; but she couldn't find her panties.

"You wouldn't keep your hands off me. You told Sam it's always been me you wanted," Luke scoffed.

Carmen looked at him, bewildered, as tears poured down her cheeks. "I-I wouldn't—"

He cut her off again and spoke matter-of-factly. "Poor Sam. He liked you. *A lot.* But when you took your little cotton panties off and gave them to me… That's when he left. You broke his heart!"

Carmen recoiled; she put her head in her hands and sobbed. "You're… you're lying."

Luke shook his head. "I tried to resist. For Tessa's sake. But you persisted."

"I would never—"

"You would." He made a point of checking his pockets. He lifted her panties out of his shirt pocket, held them up, and waved them back and forth. "Sure you would. They were the first thing you took off." He threw them at her.

She looked at the panties, shaking her head. "Sam and I are in love. I would never do that. He would never let you..." *This isn't happening. It's a nightmare. It's not real. Wake up. Wake up.*

"And your pathetic attempts at sucking my dick were laughable. You begged me to fuck you. You weren't very good at that either." He stood and went to sit on the other side of the table. "Improved somewhat the second time, but still not great." He shrugged, picked up one of the glasses, poured champagne into it, and took a sip. "I saved Sam from that disappointment." Luke sighed. "I'm not gonna tell Tessa. It would break her heart to hear that you seduced me. She'd hate you. You're supposed to be her friend, aren't you?"

"She wouldn't believe you."

"Ah. I think she would." Luke took out his phone and showed Carmen selfies of them smiling, embracing, in various stages of undress. In one, Carmen is kneeling in front of Luke, holding his penis.

Carmen shook her head fervently. "No, no, no."

He pointed to the door. "Clean yourself up before you go downstairs. Bathroom's down the hall."

Carmen couldn't move.

Luke shouted, "Get out!"

She recoiled.

He shouted again, "Get. Out!"

She grabbed her panties, purse, and shoes and put her hand on the couch to brace herself. She got up slowly, as in a trance, and stumbled to the door. She opened it and turned to look at him.

Luke put his head back and closed his eyes. "I fucking hate everybody."

Carmen left the room and looked up and down the hall. She saw the bathroom and ran to it. Once inside, she dropped her shoes, purse, and panties on the counter and looked at herself in the mirror.

Her mascara had run down her cheeks and her lipstick was smeared. It was all too real. She sobbed, crying so hard she gagged. Kneeling in front of the toilet, she threw up until all she had left were dry heaves.

She flushed the toilet repeatedly, as if she could flush away what had happened. When she was done, she pulled herself up, went to the sink, and ran the tap. She grabbed some tissues to wipe her face, then patted down her hair and straightened her dress. She put her panties and shoes on, then opened her purse and pulled out some bills. She counted them. Enough to take a taxi home. She swayed a little, still feeling the effects of the alcohol.

She left the bathroom and walked to the stairs, looking down at the partying crowd as though nothing had happened. As though her world hadn't just come to an end. She grasped the banister tightly and slowly descended. She wound her way through the partyers and escaped into the quiet of the street.

Carmen had the taxi drop her off a few blocks from her home so she could sneak in. She removed her shoes and climbed in her bedroom window, closing it quietly behind her. She took her clothes off and hid them under her mattress, feeling that if anyone saw them, they would know her sin. Then she put her pajamas on, crawled under the sheets, and cried herself to sleep.

**

Sam, Luke, Snake, and Joey arrived at the meat-packing factory to find four guards dressed in black waiting for them at the gate.

"Check out the ninja turtles. The tall one gotta be Raphael." Joey chuckled.

Snake snorted.

"Wouldn't be funny if you met one of 'em in a dark alley," quipped Sam.

"You kidding me? I got skills, man," Joey replied, offended. "Skills you don't even know. One-on-one I could kick their asses. You're not the only tough motherfucker, Sam."

"Good to know, Joey," Luke said to placate him. Sam snickered.

The guards opened the gates, and one pointed to where Sam could park. As soon as they got out of the car, they were patted down.

They followed the guards to the side of the building where beef carcasses were being unloaded and carried into the factory by men wearing hairnets and rubber aprons and gloves. As they were about to climb the steps of the loading dock, the guards motioned for Joey and Snake to stay where they were.

Luke turned and added, "Wait here." They were his men. He was the one who would tell them what to do.

Luke and Sam were cooled by the chilled temperature as soon as they stepped inside. They could see the meat hanging in one section as they walked toward the back of the plant. Workers wearing similar gear were cutting and cleaning meat on long, stainless-steel processing tables and, further down, others were feeding the finished product into packaging machinery.

"Seems like a handy spot to make a body disappear," Luke said to Sam in a low voice. "I wonder if Kenji takes advantage of it."

"What a disgusting thought," Sam said.

One of the guards glanced at him and smiled.

They climbed the back stairs to an office with floor-to-ceiling windows overlooking the factory floor.

Once again, Haruto, wearing a black jacket over his regular attire, stood next to Kenji, who was seated behind a small metal desk. Kenji was, as usual, impeccably dressed. He certainly didn't fit the location, but this was where he conducted all his non-legitimate business.

Kenji motioned to the chair in front of him and Luke sat, leaning back comfortably. Sam hovered near him.

Kenji's men closed the door and stood with their backs to it. The clanging of the machinery below decreased to a faint buzz.

Luke looked around. "Nice place you got here."

Haruto scoffed. "I'm sorry if you consider this an inappropriate place for a meeting, Mr. Verde. However, Mister Ishii makes it a point to meet individuals in an environment reflecting their status."

"Hmm." Luke grinned. *Point made. Kenji is the alpha dog. I'll ignore the intended insult for now.*

Haruto continued, "Luke Verde. Your father is Joe Verde, owner of the Club Vox."

"Yes. Unfortunately, he just passed away. I own the club now." *He's done his homework,* Luke thought. *Big deal.* Most people who frequented the club knew who owned it, even though it was listed under a shell company. *Should I tell Kenji what I know of him? Somehow, I don't think he'd be impressed or amused.*

Luke indicated Sam with a nod of his head, "This is my associate, Sam Hayes."

"To what do I owe the honor of this visit." Kenji said. It was more of a command than a question.

"I hear you placed an order with Riki Tanaka."

Kenji leaned back in his chair. "And?"

"And he's hit a financing snag."

"I do not understand. Kindly, be more clear."

"It's simple. He wants to buy merchandise from me to sell to you, but he doesn't have the money to do it."

"I do not find you amusing, Mr. Verde." Kenji took out a cigarette. "Are you trying to back out of a deal you made with Riki?"

Haruto reached his hand into his jacket.

Whoa, thought Luke. *This guy is touchy.* He raised his hands. "Not at all. I assure you."

Haruto smiled, pulled out a lighter, and lit Kenji's cigarette.

"Point is, Riki made a deal with you but not with me. Riki is a wannabe middleman. And obviously not a very good one."

Kenji's face reddened. "That is unfortunate for Riki."

"I agree. But let's not concern ourselves with him right now. What do you need?"

"Six, by the thirtieth. Two hundred K each."

Luke looked up at Sam, then back at Kenji. "Four. That's the best I can do on such short notice."

Kenji was unimpressed with the young upstart. He'd often come across his kind. No respect for those above him. A fiery candle that would burn out quickly. Easy to put him in his place. "Not enough. We require six. No less."

"No can do. You'll have to take your chances with Riki."

Luke rose, and he and Sam walked toward the door. Kenji simply watched him, saying nothing. He leaned back and took a deep drag off his cigarette, slowing blowing the smoke out in Luke's direction. The guards at the door didn't move.

Luke realized it would be Kenji's way or... He had to save face somehow. He made a big show of shaking his head and shrugging his shoulders. He turned to Kenji, smiled, and said, "Let's say it's possible. The risk factor will rise exponentially. I'd need another fifty grand to make it happen."

Kenji smiled and nodded.

Luke decided to push it a little. "And I assume there will be more orders in the future."

"We will see."

Luke returned to the chair.

Haruto opened a desk drawer and removed a box of blood-testing kits. He handed it to Luke.

"What's this?" Luke asked as he passed the box to Sam.

"We require a sample of their blood." Haruto smiled. "No charge for these, but you will get your own in the future."

Luke stood and held his hand out to Kenji. "We have a deal."

Kenji stood but didn't shake Luke's hand. "I expect delivery on the thirtieth. No later. No excuses. And let me be very clear, Mr. Verde, I do not like to be disappointed."

I can see that, thought Luke. "You won't be. And, as a gesture of good faith, please allow me to take care of Riki."

"That is not necessary. I will deal with Riki." Kenji bowed his head slightly. Luke bowed back.

One of the guards opened the door, and Luke and Sam were escorted through the building. The guards remained at the loading dock, watching them as they continued to the car with Snake and Joey close behind.

"I'm not sure this is a good idea. The guy scares me," Sam said low enough so only Luke could hear.

"Ain't no one scarier than us, Sammy." Luke punched Sam playfully in the arm.

When they got in the car, Joey leaned forward. "Get what ya wanted, boss?"

Luke lit a cigarette. "I'd say, all in all, this was a good day's work. Wouldn't you agree, Sam?"

Sam didn't answer. He just looked at Luke, eyebrows raised. *We'll see,* he thought.

"Saudis are gonna be pissed," Joey warned.

"Fuck the Saudis," Luke quipped. "They shoulda kept to the schedule. They know that."

"We want them as enemies?" Joey asked.

Luke turned to look at Joey. "Show me a man with no enemies and I'll show you a man who never did shit."

Joey leaned back in his seat. He never really got Luke's so-called words of wisdom, but this seemed to make sense. He had a lot of enemies himself.

Sam passed the box to Joey who opened it. "What the fuck is this?"

"Kenji wants blood tests."

"Blood tests? What the fuck for?"

"Probably checking for STDs," Sam said. "Who gives a shit why."

Joey whined, "Seems like a real waste—"

Luke interrupted him. "Just do it, Joey." This could be the beginning of a beautiful friendship with the Yakuza.

***

Tessa lay back on her bed, daydreaming about a life with Luke. She was meeting him at Toby's today. He seemed to be getting serious, and she admittedly felt a little out of her element. He was so much more experienced and that scared and unsettled her. But it also thrilled her.

She'd texted Carmen several times, but Carmen hadn't responded. *Is she ghosting me? Was it something I said? Or did?* Tessa couldn't think of what the cause of her friend's silence might be. But whatever it was, she'd happily apologize. She needed Carmen's friendship more than ever. Her friendship and her advice.

She sat up and searched for the family's landline number, thinking Carmen may just have forgotten to charge her phone, or worse, her parents had taken her phone away. At least someone would answer.

Carmen's mother picked up the phone. "*Privet?*"

"Hi, Mrs. Semenov. It's Tessa. Can I speak to Carmen please?"

Her mother yelled, "Natalya, come to the phone." Carmen didn't answer her. After a minute she said, "She's not coming."

"Is everything okay, Mrs. Semenov?"

Her mother yelled louder, "It's Tessa. Your friend." After a few moments, she simply said, "She won't come." Then she hung up.

Carmen didn't want to talk to her, and there was nothing Tessa could do about it for now. She'd have to wait to see her at choir practice.

She stood in front of the mirror and studied her reflection, taking stock of herself. Her hair was tied in a ponytail. *I look like a kid,* she thought. She pulled out the elastic and brushed her hair, framing it around her face. She unbuttoned the top button of her shirt. Posed innocently and smiled. She undid the next button, looked at her reflection again and posed like she'd seen Carmen do in front of the mirror. She shook her head. "What are you doing?" She asked herself aloud then re-buttoned the second button and left the room.

***

Meanwhile, a red-eyed Carmen lay on her bed, staring at the ceiling. She had heard the phone ring and her mother calling her, but she'd ignored both. The last person she wanted to talk to was Tessa. How could she explain what had happened at the club? It was mostly a blank. She remembered being with Sam, then Luke coming into the room, but that was all. She felt sure he had forced himself on her and lied about what had happened. She couldn't explain how he had manipulated her to get those pictures. She didn't like him more than Sam and would never do that to Tessa. Still, she couldn't tell her what happened. What if Tessa believed Luke and not her?

She turned on her side and curled into a fetal position.

***

Luke wasn't at Toby's when Tessa arrived. She sat in a booth and kept nervously looking at the door. Finally, it opened. Luke entered and sat across from her.

"Well, hello." He gave her his most winning smile.

"Hi." Tessa blushed.

"You look radiant."

"I think you're overdoing it."

"Ha. Well, maybe just a little. But you are beautiful. You know that, don't you?" Tessa didn't answer. "Don't you?" he pressed.

"Stop."

"Okay. Wanna soda, milkshake, sundae, banana split?"

Tessa giggled. "Strawberry sundae."

Luke jumped up and went to the counter. When he returned with the sundae, he placed it in front of her and watched her take a few bites without saying anything. She looked up. "Stop watching me. Aren't you hungry? I thought you loved ice cream."

"I do. I'd just rather watch *you* eat. Why don't you let me take you out tomorrow night? The city's much more fun in the dark."

"I can't."

"Why not? Did the slave driver you live with give you a curfew?"

"What do you mean?"

"The man you live with."

"Who told you I live with a man?"

"I don't know. Maybe it was Father Michael. Or Carmen may have told Sam."

"Oh. Well, he's not a slave driver; he's an accountant."

"What's his name? I might know him. Get you the night off. No one can say no to me." Luke smiled boyishly.

"I don't think he'd go for that."

"Even Cinderella found a way out 'til midnight."

"Please don't ask me."

"Alright. I'll stop now, but you'll have to say yes eventually. We can't meet at Toby's forever. Even if their ice cream is the best. So... tell me all about *you*."

"There's not much to tell. My life is pretty simple." *Apart from the secrets,* she thought.

"You're not from here, are you?"

"No. You already know that I lived on a ranch. Just me and my mom. And I loved it."

"Why did you leave?"

"She died."

"I'm sorry."

Tessa sighed. "Me too. But what can you do. She was very sick, and in the end, it was really a blessing. That's what everyone said. 'Tessa, this is really a blessing.'"

"I'm sorry."

"Hmm. I get that life is always gonna have fences that you're not ready to jump. The higher the fence, the more determined you have to be. You have to adapt. That's what I did."

"That's a very mature outlook on life."

"Mature?" She straightened. "You say that like you think I'm a kid."

"No. No. I didn't mean it to sound like that. I don't handle adversity that easily is all. It's impressive."

"I lost my mom but found my dad."

"Dad?" Luke could not believe his ears. So it was true. Gabriel had gotten her mother pregnant, and Tessa was the result.

"Uh huh." *Oh, no,* she thought. *What have I done? Dad would freak if he knew. I've broken our agreement already. But Luke is so nice. And I'm sure he doesn't know Gabriel. And, even if he did, Luke wouldn't hurt a fly.*

"You live with your father?" Luke needed to hear her say it.

"Is that weird to you?"

"No. Not at all. Wasn't he in your life before? When your mom was alive?"

"Not really." She didn't want to elaborate. She was feeling guilty now. She'd already said too much.

"So how do you spend your time? I want to know everything you do." He didn't really. He had all the information he needed.

Now we're in safe territory, she thought. "I love to cook, listen to music, and sing in the choir. You already know that."

Two young boys entered the parlor with their father. Luke and Tessa turned to look. A dragonfly flew in with them and landed on the jukebox unnoticed by anyone but Tessa. She pointed. "Look! Do you see it?"

Luke looked over, squinting. He couldn't see whatever *it* was but pretended to. "I do."

"We had lots of dragonflies at the ranch. When I was young, Mom said her dad used to tell her that they were the devil's darning needles, that they would sew together the lips of wicked children while they were sleeping." She chuckled. "Some say they can bring snakes back to life. Do you believe it?"

"Once a thing is dead, it's dead."

"No, you're wrong."

"Am I?" He wanted to hear her take on death. He was sure it would be innocent, even naive. Like his mother's.

"Don't you believe we go somewhere? Somewhere better than here? Or maybe even come back one day?"

"My father's dead, and he's gonna stay dead." He looked around. "I don't see him here. Do you?"

"Be serious."

"I am."

"Well. I believe my mom lives on. Not on this plane, but somehow, she's close."

"You sound like my mother. She still talks to my father, more than she ever had the occasion to when he was alive. She actually believes, now that he's dead, she gets priority over his other interests... I dunno."

"I think your father *is* with her. I know he is."

"What makes you so sure?"

"It's just a feeling that there's more than this. There just has to be. And when we die, things are simple. We can be who we want, do what we want. Imagine being with the people you love forever, never worrying that they'll leave you." Tessa sighed.

Luke realized that he had yet to suffer from the death of someone he felt he didn't want to live without. Certainly not his father. He had loved him in a way, but never felt it was reciprocated enough to miss him. He did remember losing a beloved pet when he was young, though Tessa might not equate losing a pet to losing a family member.

"I was given a black-and-white border collie pup named Max when I was a kid. I loved that dog. Two years later, it was hit by a car. My father offered to get me another dog, but I didn't want a replacement. I wanted Max back."

Tessa put her hand on his. "Sure, why wouldn't you?"

"Hmm." Luke looked down at her hand. She pulled it away. She hadn't even realized she'd done it. It just happened naturally.

They sat in silence. Tessa checked her phone. "I have to go." She scrambled out of the booth and Luke followed her to the door.

As she opened the door, he grabbed her arm, pulled her to him, and kissed her. Her eyes opened wide, then she relaxed and closed them. It felt like everything a first kiss should be. She tried to emulate Carmen but quickly pulled away, trying to collect herself. She looked around embarrassed. She felt naked.

He decided it was time to press her. "I want you to come riding with me. All very innocent. It'll be an opportunity for you to formally meet my mother."

"Your mother? She knows about me?" She couldn't believe he'd spoken to his mother about her. He was serious. This was serious.

"Of course, she knows about you. She takes her faith very seriously, so it's not appropriate to introduce you at church. She wouldn't approve of that. Best to meet her at the house. Then we'll take a ride, and I'll show you around the property. Have a picnic. Lots of fresh air, green grass. You needn't worry that we'd do anything your father wouldn't approve of."

"I'll try."

He tilted his head, raised an eyebrow, and smiled. "Try hard."

She checked the time on her phone. "I really have to go. Night, night," she sang as she rushed away. She wanted to spend more time with him. And she desperately wanted to be back on a saddle. But

Gabriel... She'd have to come up with a reason to leave the house. Maybe another long choir practice.

"Night." Luke watched her until she turned the corner and was out of sight. Now he had to make sure they didn't run into his mother.

***

When Tessa got home, she opened and closed the front door as quietly as she could and tiptoed toward the stairs. Gabriel called from the living room. "Hey. Where have you been?"

Tessa stopped. "I was with Carmen. At the soda shop."

"I called you. You didn't answer your cell."

"My battery died. We were listening to music, and I lost track of the time."

"I thought I made it clear—"

"I know. I'm sorry. I'll start dinner in a minute." She rushed up the stairs before he could respond.

She hated lying to her dad, but he just wouldn't understand. As a matter of fact, he'd freak and never let her out of the house again if he knew. She had felt exhilarated after spending time with Luke, but now she just felt bad, guilty for deceiving Gabriel. He'd been so good to her. But Carmen was right. She was in love.

She took a deep breath and sent Luke a text to let him know she would go.

Now she had to talk to Carmen. There was so much she wanted to tell her. To ask her. This was getting serious. She tried her on her cell again. No response.

CHAPTER NINE

Sam stood behind the bar at the cottage, pouring tequila into a shot glass. He downed it and chased it with his beer. Then he poured another. He always tried to maintain a constant buzz whenever he was there.

Snake and Joey were on the couch, each with a scantily clad woman on his lap. Joey pushed his woman off, causing her to yelp. He walked toward the pool table, grabbed a pool cue from the rack, and returned to the woman. He pulled her up and handed her the cue. "Give us a dance, Trace. Let's see how hard you can make everyone."

"Sure, Joey." She did a slow dance using the cue as a prop.

Charley and Luke were playing a game of pool. Luke aimed and put the last ball into the pocket. He picked a wad of money off the edge. Charley took the balls out of the pockets and racked them up. He groaned, "Isn't your deal with Kenji enough? You gotta take my money too?"

Joey walked over to the table. "Shit, boss. You win every fuckin' game. How do you do it?"

"He's got horseshoes up his ass. That's how," Charley griped. They placed more money on the edge of the table.

Luke chalked his cue as Charley aimed, broke, and sank a ball. But he missed his next shot.

Luke lined up his shot. "Fuck horseshoes. It's strategy. I approach the ball like I approach everything. There's always gonna be factors working against you. You just have to convince them to work for you.

"You talkin' 'bout Kenji?" Charley asked.

"He's talking about Gabriel," Sam said.

Luke checked the angles, aimed, and sank two balls.

"Why not just kill him?" Charley asked.

"Anything happens to Gabriel and I lose the club. It's in my father's will. There's a no-contest clause that's tighter than a witch's twat." He took another shot, sinking his ball and one of Charley's. He walked over to the bar and downed Sam's tequila.

"You sure she *is* his kid?" asked Charley.

"Oh, she's his kid, alright. She told me," Luke remarked smugly.

Charley took his turn, then circled the table, planning his next shot. "Sam says she's never been drilled."

Luke shot Sam a dirty look. Sam shrugged innocently. Luke hit the cue ball and stood back as another two balls rolled into the pockets.

Charley snickered. "If you need help, I'd be more than happy to mine that for ya."

They all laughed.

Luke, angered, missed a shot. "Fuck!"

Sam couldn't help scrutinizing Luke's reaction. He also took the opportunity to taunt Charley. "I don't think your drill's big enough, Charley. At least, that's what the dancers are saying."

Charley retorted, "There's nothin' wrong with the size of my prick. Ask your mama."

Luke laughed, cooler now. "Besides, she wouldn't look your way if your shaft was one big, long, cut diamond and your balls were dipped in chocolate."

Joey mused, "Balls dipped in chocolate. Not a bad idea, boss. Dip your balls and send her a dick pic. She'll come runnin'. Then she'll come."

Luke pointed his cue at him. "You're an idiot."

Joey shrugged and chuckled. He thought it was pretty funny.

Charley checked the angles and aimed. He sank the white ball. "Shit! Luke, why don't you just throw her in with the next shipment."

"How about I throw *you* in with the next shipment."

Sam looked at Luke and raised an eyebrow.

Luke rubbed the tip of his cue with the chalk. "No. I want Gabriel to have to look at his little angel everyday and know she belongs to me. That he has nothing that I don't let him have. And that, my nefarious friends, is just the beginning."

Charley snickered. "Fuckin' diabolical!" He took his turn. The balls settled, leaving Luke with the eight ball at the corner pocket, surrounded by three of Charley's balls. "Ha," Charley yelled triumphantly.

Luke looked down at the table and smiled. "Like I said. Strategy. If you don't have a straight shot, you just gotta change the axis. Knock it right, and when the ball settles, you got the felt working for you." He held his cue vertically and hit the cue ball. "Then, you just stand back." The ball spun around the three balls before hitting the eight ball into the corner pocket.

Charley frowned. "Hey. That shot's illegal."

"And?"

Charley muttered under his breath as he picked the money up off the table and handed it to Luke. Luke walked over to the bar as Charley racked up the balls. Joey took a cue stick from the rack and chalked it up.

Sam poured two shots. He downed his and said in a low voice, "I think she's got under your skin."

Luke smirked and turned to watch the guys play. "You are either the hawk or the rabbit, Sammy. I prefer to be the hawk."

Sam smirked. "I don't think you can hurt her."

"You're wrong. I will. When the time is right. I will."

Charley yelled at Joey, interrupting them. "Joey, you imbecile, you're gonna scratch the table."

Luke drank his shot, slammed the glass down on the bar, and roared, "When you own the table, you can do whatever you want!" He walked over, pulling his knife out of his pocket, and slashed the felt.

Charley and Joey just looked at him, mouths agape.

Luke walked back to the bar and poured himself another tequila. He shot it back, then leaned in close to Sam and said in a low voice, "Get the table fixed tomorrow, Sammy." Then he yelled, "Time to party!" He turned around and walked toward the bedroom, smacking the dancing woman's ass as he passed her. "C'mon."

She happily followed Luke into the room, and he closed the door behind them. She turned to him and, still holding the cue, clumsily attempted to hug him. He peeled her arms from around his neck, took the cue out of her hand, and dropped it on the floor, then he led her to one of the two unmade twin beds and gently pushed her onto it. She posed seductively.

Luke walked over to the room's lone, straight-back chair and sat. He leaned forward and put his head in his hands.

She sat up. "What would you like me to do, Luke?"

He looked up at her. "Shut up and go to sleep." He put his head back in his hands.

***

Riki got a call from Haruto early in the morning, telling him his uncle wanted him at the meat-packing factory right away. When he arrived, he was met by Kenji's guards. They escorted him to the office, and one of them pushed him roughly onto a chair. Riki looked up at him indignantly. "Hey, mind the threads. This jacket is vintage aviator, bro." The guard smiled a not-so-friendly smile. "Where's my uncle?" Riki asked.

They didn't answer. Riki stood but was pushed back down. "Okay, okay, I get it. He's running late. No problemo." He put his hands in his pockets and leaned back in the chair, doing his best to appear nonchalant. His pockets were empty except for his inhaler and a single quaalude he'd been keeping for emergencies. *I think this qualifies as an emergency,* he thought. He tried to secretly slip it into his mouth, but the man next to him grabbed it out of his hand. "Hey! What the fuck? What do you think you're doing?" The man whacked him across the head. Riki shrunk down in the chair.

Oh fuck. Something was definitely wrong. There's no way they'd dare treat him this way unless they knew Kenji wouldn't care. Oh fuck. He was doing his best not to show how anxious he was becoming but couldn't stop his leg from shaking.

What could have happened? I still have lots of time to do the deal. So that can't be it. Something's happened though, and it can't be good. What? He was having a hard time getting air into his lungs. He wheezed and said, "Asthma. Need to use my inhaler." Riki raised both his hands, then pulled out his inhaler and showed it to them before using it. Once he was breathing better, he grumbled, "Don't you clean this room? All this dust is not good for the lungs." They ignored him.

I gotta get outta here. He turned to the man holding his chair. "It looks like my uncle isn't gonna show. I mean, we all know how busy the boss is. I'll just come back." He stood. The man hit him harder this time and shoved him back onto the chair.

"Shut up. Wait."

Fuck. This is not good. Not good. Riki felt like throwing up and fought to keep it down.

***

Kenji arrived an hour later and sat at his desk. He looked at Riki without speaking and shook his head in displeasure.

Afraid to stand, Riki sat up straight and bowed. "Kenji-san. How are you?"

"Do you have something to tell me, Riki?"

"Huh?"

"I warned you not to disappointment me."

"What's wrong? What did I do? Tell me. I'll fix it." He had no idea what he could have done. Unless…

"I had a visit from a Luke Verde. I believe you know him."

Riki started to sweat. How the fuck did Luke find out about Kenji? "Uh. Uh. Yeah. He's a… he's a business associate."

"That is not how he presented himself to me."

Riki couldn't think. He should have done more coke earlier, then he'd be able to think. "Look—"

"Perhaps I should be disappointed in *myself,* nephew. I allowed my sister to marry a *gaijin.* I should not have permitted it. He was never able to control his children. No honor. No dignity. His westerner ways brought great shame to my sister. You are weak because your father was weak."

Riki nodded his head in agreement.

"Your sister should have been a man and you a woman. Mika has grown into a lion while you still shuffle about looking to find a teat to suckle. She is strong. You are weak."

"My sister is a whore who works in a nightclub." *Fuck. Why did I say that? What a stupid, stupid thing to say.* He knew that would only piss Kenji off. Besides, Riki actually loved and admired Mika. She'd gotten him out of more jams than he could count.

Kenji stood and motioned to the men. They grabbed Riki, pulled him up off the chair, and pushed him over the desk.

"Wait. No. Uncle, please."

"You're lucky I do not wish to deprive my sister of her only son," Kenji said as he left the room, closing the door behind him. One of the men pushed Riki's head down on the desk and held his right arm while the other forced his left hand onto the desk.

Riki yelled, "Uncle! Please." The man pulled out a knife and cut the three remaining fingers off, one at a time, while Riki screamed. When they pulled him upright, he fainted.

He woke up in his car, his left hand covered with a blood-drenched rag. He couldn't believe it. *I'm fucking maimed. How can I protect myself on the street with one fucking hand.* But that was the least of it. His own uncle had him mutilated. Again! Only worse this time. And he hadn't even given Riki a chance to explain.

I need a hit. I'll feel better. He stretched over to open the glove compartment but couldn't reach it. Whimpering, he exited the car and walked around to the passenger's side, bumping his injured hand as he got in. He yelped and cursed as he opened the compartment and pulled out a vial of coke. He managed to get the cover off with difficulty and emptied all the contents onto the dashboard. He got as close as he could to the powder and snorted, then licked up the residue and leaned back, wheezing. He checked his face in the rearview mirror, wiped the powder from his nose, and licked it off his fingers, then he took out his inhaler, took a deep breath, and made his way back to the driver's side.

He looked at his mangled hand and wept. After a while, he collected himself, turned on the ignition and drove to the nearest hospital. He decided he'd tell the doctor he was fixing something in the garage and the saw slipped.

***

Three hours later, Riki shielded his eyes against the afternoon sun as he exited the ER. They'd stitched him up and filled him with heavy-duty painkillers. His left arm was in a sling to protect his bandaged hand.

He was walking to his car as Snake and Joey rolled up in a brown sedan. Snake jumped out of the car before Riki could react and coldcocked him with the butt of his gun. Riki fell. Snake caught him under the arms and walked him to the sedan. He looked around to make sure no one was watching, opened the trunk, picked Riki up, and put him in.

They drove about thirty miles out of the city before turning onto a gravel road in a densely wooded area thick with live oaks and brambles. After continuing for another mile, they parked on the shoulder in the secluded place where Joey and Snake went when they needed to conduct business. They pulled Riki out of the trunk and threw him on the ground. Snake lit a joint, and they passed it back and forth as they waited for Luke.

Riki woke and looked around before focusing on Snake and Joey. "Wha-what the fuck?" He tried to crawl away. They watched him, unconcerned. He hadn't gone far before he had to stop, struggling to suck enough air into his lungs. Snake walked over and stepped on his back. Riki tried to grab his boot with his good hand, but he couldn't and got another kick to the gut.

"My turn." Joey took a deep drag off the joint and then ambled over to kick him. Snake looked at him and chuckled. Every time one of them took a drag, they took a turn kicking Riki. He passed out.

Sam drove up and parked near their car. Luke stepped out and walked over to the sedan. He slammed the trunk closed and leaned on the car. "What have you got there?"

Snake and Joey picked up Riki's limp body and dragged him over to Luke. His head was dangling, so Snake grabbed him by the hair and pulled his head up. Luke slapped his face hard and Riki's eyes opened. He shook his head, trying to clear it.

"La-Luke?" He struggled to free himself, trying to kick Snake and Joey. They both kicked him hard. Riki yelped and stopped struggling.

"Our contact at emerge was thoughtful enough to let us know you were there. Carpentry accident?" Luke leaned forward and grabbed Riki's bandaged hand.

"Ow! Stop!"

"Looks to me like someone doesn't love you anymore."

Riki knew the jig was up. *There's no way I'm getting' outta this,* he thought. *Can try. But there's no way.* "Just a little disagreement with my uncle. He'll come 'round. Always does. Loves me, ya know."

"Sure he does. Now let's talk about me. What were you thinking? Trying to eat off *my* plate."

"It's not like that. I was just—"

"You were just what? You just forgot to stay in your lane?"

Luke took out his stiletto, pretending to focus on cleaning under his fingernails, even though they were dirt-free. "You were a good soldier. Once. Too bad you couldn't cut down on the blow. Hell, you've even forgotten your place."

Riki mumbled, "I'm still a good soldier."

Luke looked up at him. "What's that? I'm a dead soldier?"

Joey and Snake laughed.

"People gonna notice if I go missin'. Gonna be lookin' for me."

"If they know you, they know what a fuckup you are. I doubt they'll look too long or too hard."

"Mika will."

"I'm sure she'll miss you least of all."

Riki started whimpering. What else could he use. "I'm too young to die."

"I can see how you might feel that way. But we all gotta die someday. You're just leaving this world sooner than you expected. Be a man. Make your family proud."

Joey sneered. "Yeah, be a man, Riki."

Snake chuckled.

"I ain't *afraid* to die." Riki tried to stand up straight.

"Really? You're that brave?" Luke asked, eyebrows raised.

"No. It's *how* I die I'm worried 'bout." He looked at Snake and Joey.

"Ah, I see. Why don't we hurry things along then."

"Wait, wait. You need me, Luke. You don't—"

Luke shoved the blade into Riki's stomach. "No. I don't." He gave it a twist, then pulled it out. Riki fell forward. Snake and Joey let him fall to the ground.

"Did you forget?" Luke continued, "I. Am. The. King!"

He took a deep breath to calm himself and bent to wipe the blade on Riki's jacket. "No one tries to fuck over the king, Riki."

Luke looked at his watch and calmly said, "Get rid of the body. And be quick. I want you both at the cottage."

He closed the stiletto, walked back to the car, and got in.

"Too bad. He *used* to be a great earner," Sam mused as he pulled a flask out of his jacket and took a swig.

"We still gotta find someone to take over his territory," Luke grumbled. "Cocksucker!"

"Kenji will be pissed," Sam added.

"At who? Little shits like Riki disappear every day." Luke lit a spliff, took a deep drag, and passed it to Sam.

Sam shrugged and took a drag as they drove off.

Luke took out his phone and dialed Tessa's number. "Miss me?"

***

Meanwhile, Joey and Snake took two shovels out of the trunk. They each grabbed an arm and dragged Riki's body a hundred yards to a clearing in the woods.

Joey dropped Riki's arm. "This is good. I'm wasted *and* wasted," he complained.

Snake snickered and dropped the other arm. They began slowly digging a makeshift grave.

After they'd dug about two feet down, Snake wiped his brow, dropped his shovel, and sat on the dirt. Not the kind of work they were used to. Neither were keen on manual labor, particularly grave digging. Kill 'em. Sure. Bury 'em? They'd rather not.

Joey stopped shoveling. Snake reached into his pocket and pulled out a small baggy full of quaaludes.

"Whaddya got there, buddy? Those ludes?" Joey sat next to him and smiled in anticipation. Snake held the baggy out to him, grinning from ear to ear. Joey took two.

"I think I got somethin' to wash these down with." Joey figured if you're gonna drop ludes, you might as well make it a party. He went back to the car, searching the trunk to find the bottle of mezcal he was keeping for a special occasion. He brought the bottle back to Snake and plopped himself down. They both took a swig. Joey looked at the body. "Ya gotta admit, Snake. He was one ballsy little fucker." Snake grunted in agreement. Joey poured some mezcal over Riki's head. "Here's to Riki. May he rot in peace." They continued passing the bottle back and forth until it was empty, then they passed out.

The sun had set by the time Snake woke hours later. He sat up, moaned, and held his head. He nudged Joey several times before Joey came to. Joey scrambled up and looked around, trying to get his bearings. "Oh shit." He checked his phone. "We gotta go." He looked at the shallow hole they'd dug. "This'll hafta do." He helped Snake to his feet. They rolled the body in, shoveled soil over it, then threw some forest debris on top.

They stumbled back to the car, threw the shovels in the trunk, and sped off, tires spraying dust and loose gravel.

***

Carmen sat on the toilet, her eyes red and swollen from crying. Every time she thought of the VIP room, she cried. She took a box of First Response pregnancy tests out of her purse and read the instructions. Her mama couldn't understand why Carmen's eyes were always red and swollen, so she took her grocery shopping to get her out of the house. Luckily, Carmen was able to grab the box and pay for them without getting caught.

She took one of the strips out of its packaging, peed on it, and waited. As the two colored bands appeared, showing a positive result, she moaned, "No. No. No." She tried another one and got the same result. Tears poured down her cheeks as she wrapped the strips in toilet paper and put them and the box back into her purse.

Her phone rang. Without thinking, Carmen answered, and before she could say "Hello," Tessa started talking.

"Finally! I've been texting and calling. Did I do something wrong? You ghosted me. Why did you ghost me? And you didn't show up for choir. Where have you been?"

Carmen wasn't ready to talk to Tessa. She had no idea what she'd say, but she couldn't just hang up on her. She could at least give her a good explanation of why she hadn't returned her texts. "Papa's making me go to Holy Ghost again cuz of the 'all-girl choir' thing. Ugh. Someone saw us at Toby's and told Alex. He snitched on me."

"That's pretty drastic. Isn't it?"

"It doesn't take much. I've been major depressed."

"I miss you."

Carmen looked at her purse. "I miss you too. We can still talk on the phone for now." She tried to sound cheerful.

"Have you heard from Sam? I bet he'll be upset he can't see you."

Carmen let out a sob.

"Are you crying? Carmen? Why are you crying? Is it about Sam? What happened at the club?"

"I don't wanna talk about it. Okay?"

"Okay." It wasn't like Carmen to keep secrets. She usually couldn't stop talking. About Sam. About anything. It was weird.

"You went to the club. You sent me that picture."

"No. I left. He wasn't there. I'm just upset about something else."

"Can I come over?"

"My parents think you're a bad influence."

"Me?"

"Because you're my friend."

"Really?"

"Uh huh." Carmen rested her cell on her legs. She grabbed a handful of toilet paper off the roll, wiped her eyes, and blew her nose. She picked up the phone and, with a shaky voice, tried to sound lighter. "Sooo. Tell me what *you* been up to." She hoped Tessa would say she hadn't been up to anything.

Tessa began to get excited and said, in a lower voice, "Oh Carmen. You were right. Luke's perfect. I was just with him. He acts like I'm his girlfriend. Can you believe it?"

Carmen stood and started to pace around the tiny room.

"He kissed me. I think he's gonna want more from me, but I'm not sure I'm ready for that. It's too soon. Isn't it?"

Carmen answered carefully, "You need to stay away from him. You don't know him."

"What? I do know him. He's amazing. And I think he loves me. He already told his mom all about me."

Carmen sat on the edge of the bathtub. She put her hand on her belly. "None of it's real. You have to listen to me. Please, don't see him again. Please."

Tessa's voice rose. "Why are you being like this? Did something bad happen with Sam? Is that why you don't want me to see Luke?"

Frustrated, Carmen repeated, "Just don't. I saw that movie your mom named you after. Did you watch it?"

"No."

"You need to. Your mom didn't tell you that it's a horrible story. Tess's life was ruined. By every man she met. Your mom cursed you with that name."

"It's just a name."

"No. Luke is just like those men."

"Don't say that, Carmen. You don't know him."

"It isn't real."

"Yes, it is. We're just like Bella and Edward. It's the forever kind of love."

Carmen's father banged on the bathroom door and yelled, "Natalya, *chto ty delayesh?* There are other people in this house!"

Carmen whispered, "You don't know what I know!" Her father continued banging. "I gotta go. Believe me, he's dangerous."

"I don't understand. What do you know? Can't we meet somehow?"

"No. Not for a bit. My papa is making my stupid brother follow me everywhere."

More loud banging. "Natalya!"

"I gotta go!" Carmen yelled to her father, "*Ya idu,* Papa!" Then to Tessa, "Listen to me. Luke is not what we thought. He's been love-bombing you from the start. He's the devil. So dark, the darkest green you could ever imagine!"

She hung up, flushed the toilet, and opened the door. "Gee Papa, can't I even pee without you checking up on me?" she complained. "Girls need their privacy, you know."

"Girls, yes. Natalya Semenov, no!" He lifted his arm menacingly and Carmen winced as she rushed past him. He barked, "Don't get smart with me."

Carmen's father had been a field worker in Belarus prior to immigrating to the States in the hopes of finding a better life. His stocky, muscular frame and dark, leathery skin made him look almost gnomish. Carmen wondered if he regretted coming here, as his job in landscaping wasn't really that different and probably didn't pay much more. Maybe that was why he was mean.

Carmen closed her bedroom door gently, hoping he wouldn't follow her to exact some degree of punishment. It didn't take much to wind him up.

Meanwhile, Tessa looked at her phone, confused. *Why would Carmen say those horrible things? Luke's the devil? Why? Is she jealous? Or has Sam told her something?*

Her cell rang and she jumped. "Hello?"

"Miss me?" Hearing his voice took her breath away.

**

Tessa was quiet on the drive to the ranch. She couldn't believe Luke was anything other than the wonderful man she saw next to her.

A ranch hand led two horses out of the stables as Luke and Tessa pulled up the driveway. Luke parked the car and, as he was about to open his door, Tessa grabbed his arm.

"Luke, can I meet your mother *before* we go riding?"

Luke looked at her blankly. "My mother?"

"I'm going to meet her today."

He turned off the motor and got out of the car, cursing under his breath. He actually chose to bring Tessa to the ranch today because he knew his mother wouldn't be there. *Why did I promise her that? It was never gonna happen.*

He opened the door for her. She got out and looked at him, waiting for an answer.

"My mother left yesterday to visit a friend in Richmond."

"Oh."

"I'm sorry. I don't know how I could have forgotten. I know you were looking forward to meeting her."

"It's just that—"

Luke cut her off. "There'll be plenty of time for you to get to know each other. You don't need to push it, Tessa."

"I'm not," Tessa said, not sure if Luke was listening to her. But how could he have forgotten? Unless he didn't want them to meet. She figured she would drop it — but just for now.

He took her hand and they walked over to the horses. They mounted and raced through the fields toward a mossy green forest. She sped ahead, but Luke caught up to her, and they slowed down as they neared the trees before continuing at a trot until they reached a clearing.

"This is it." Luke stopped and jumped down, and Tessa did the same. Luke untied a stuffed blanket hanging from his saddle. He put it on the grass and opened it to reveal a small picnic basket. Tessa helped him spread the blanket. They sat and took in their surroundings.

"Wow. I could stay here forever. It's so peaceful." Tessa took a deep breath and laid back on the blanket, enjoying the fresh smells of the forest.

Luke smiled and laid down next to her. "Listen. You can hear the wind rustle through the leaves, the branches creak, and the hum of insects."

Tessa sighed and reached for Luke's hand. "I'm so happy. Everything feels so fresh and new. No past, no future, just the now."

He turned to her, resting his head on his arm. "This is where I come to think. To get away from everyone and everything. I've never brought anyone here. You're the first."

"The first?"

"You're the first and the last. This can be *our* special place now." He wondered why he would say that. Wasn't it taking the romantic gestures a little too far? But he found himself picturing a life with her. She was beautiful and untouched. Like the forest. She fit.

"Our place," she whispered. After a while she sat up, opened the basket, and took plates and napkins out. "I can't wait to tell Carmen."

Her words pulled him out of his romantic reverie and back to reality. His little interlude with Carmen ensured there would be no possible chance of a future with Tessa. Even if he wanted… No. That was ridiculous anyway. There was no future with her. *Keep your wits about you. This is a con. That's all.* Regardless, one way or the other, he had to make sure she stayed far away from Carmen.

"Why would you tell Carmen?"

"She's my best friend."

"Best friends are for children. I thought you were a grown-up."

"I-I am. Everyone needs a friend. Sam is your friend. Isn't he?"

"Sam works for me. He's an employee. That's all. You need to stay away from her. She's not the kind of friend you need."

"Why?"

Luke didn't respond.

"Why, Luke?"

The sweet guy he was making such an effort to portray faded. He leaned in and spoke menacingly, "Just do as I say."

Tessa shrank back. "You sound just like... I'm not a child. I'll decide whether or not I want to have friends, and I'm perfectly capable of choosing them for myself, thank you."

Luke realized his mistake and softened his voice. "Of course, you are. It's just... She's not the sort I want my girl associating with." He took her hand.

She pulled it away. "Funny. She said the same thing about you. She said to stay far away from you."

Luke was silent for a moment, then he asked in a low voice. "Why would she say that?"

"She wouldn't say why."

"Think maybe she's jealous?"

"Why would she be jealous?"

"Because Sam's not interested in her."

"He's not? Why?"

"It's none of our business. It's up to you, but I think you should stay away from her."

Tessa didn't respond. She started to pack the picnic away. She thought she'd found someone who'd let her make her own decisions. He was sounding more and more like Gabriel. Sure, she loved Gabriel, but that wasn't the kind of man she wanted to spend her life with. He had too many rules.

She wanted a soulmate. An equal. They'd make decisions together. He wouldn't tell her who she could be friends with. She wondered if this was all a big mistake. He was handsome and worldly, and she wanted him to love her. But what price would she have to pay?

Luke closed the basket lid. "You *are* my girl, aren't you?" She didn't respond but stared into his mesmerizing eyes, wondering what was behind them. Was he really someone she should let herself fall in love with? Or was it already too late to even ask herself that question?

She opened the lid and continued packing things away.

He touched her face. "I'm not trying to tell you what to do. It's just that Sam told me Carmen threw herself at him. He assured her there was no future with him, but she said she didn't care. That he wasn't her first."

"That's not true. He's a liar."

"What reason would he have to lie? He said they had sex. I saw them together at the club. She was all over him. So I believe him. Did she tell you she went to the club?"

"Yes."

"Why would she go there, Tessa?"

"To see Sam. She likes him. She missed him."

"She has no morals. She's the exact opposite of you. She didn't care that Sam didn't love her. She just wanted to have sex with him." Tessa didn't respond. "That's why I think you should stay away from her."

"I need to think about it."

Luke reached out to her, and she took his hand. He pulled her to him, folding her into his arms. "What we have is real. It's real. You and me. Just the two of us. From now on." He kissed her and she wrapped her arms tightly around him. They continued to kiss passionately and lay back on the blanket. His hands moved over her body.

She stopped him. "I'm not ready." She was confused. *He thought Carmen was too easy, yet he wants me to be the same.* "I'm not Carmen."

"No, you're not." Luke let go of her and sat up. He took a bottle of wine out of the basket and uncorked it. Then he pulled two glasses out of the basket and filled them. "You're right."

She sat up. "You're not mad?"

Without looking at her, he smiled and sighed. "Of course I'm not mad. I'm human is all. You're a temptation I find very hard to resist. Like strawberry ice cream." He chuckled, trying to lighten the mood. Tessa put her head down, and Luke reached out to lift her chin. "There's no rush. I'm not going anywhere."

She twisted her ring. "Are you sure?"

"Uh huh." They both took a sip of wine.

She took her ring off and handed it to him. "It's a purity ring. You need to know I feel strongly about waiting 'til I'm married."

Luke looked at her for what seemed like an eternity. *No problem,* he thought. A challenge. He smiled and put the ring on his baby finger. "I'll keep it for now. We'll honor your promise together." He would have to remember to put it on whenever he knew he'd be seeing her.

Surprised and relieved, Tessa took a sandwich out of the basket and unwrapped it. She gave half to Luke and took a bite of the other.

"At least we can take care of one appetite," Luke joked and stuffed most of his sandwich into his mouth.

Tessa laughed.

CHAPTER TEN

Luke's office door banged opened, and TJ burst in to find Luke, Sam, Joey, and Snake scrolling on their phones.

"Luke, Charley said to let him know when any hot tourists came to the club on their own. We got two downstairs. I called him, but he's not answering."

"What's that to me, TJ?"

"He seemed pretty serious about it. So I figured you might wanna know."

"How do you know they're tourists?"

"I spoke to them on my break. They're from LA"

Sam looked doubtfully at Luke, and Luke ignored him. "And no one knows they're in Houston?"

"No one. And I quote, 'We snuck off for a quick vacay, teehee, no one knows we even left,'" he said, mimicking them.

Joey guffawed. "Way too easy for you ta sound like a girl, TJ. Comes natural-like, don't it?"

TJ gave Joey the finger and continued in his own voice, "They're bragging 'bout their OnlyFans pages. And are lookin' for some 'well-to-do gentlemen' to treat them to a good time. They're up for anything."

Luke knew they had to take advantage of this gift that had been dropped into their laps. "Okay, we'll be down in a minute."

"I got them a booth. I'll keep an eye on them for you."

"Thanks," Sam muttered, not really meaning it.

"Happy to do a solid," TJ said as he left, pleased with himself that he'd been able to help Charley and Luke out. He figured they'd remember this if he ever needed their help.

Joey quipped to Snake, "What does that idiot think we're gonna do with 'em?"

Snake closed his eyes and shook his head. Neither of them could believe anyone could be that stupid.

"I don't think he's given it much thought," Luke said as he leaned back in his chair and lit a cigarette.

Sam scowled. "That's all we need. Feds sniffing around here looking for missing tourists." Sam was against getting girls from the club and he thought Luke agreed. He was actually against the business altogether. But this was particularly foolhardy. He pictured "missing girl" photos plastered all over the TV and social media and then some patron realizing they'd last seen them at the club. "Luke, I just don't think we—"

Luke cut him off, pointing to Snake and Joey. "If Charley and these two knuckleheads did their job, we wouldn't have to do this. Let's check them out at least."

Sam muttered, "This is a *bad* idea."

Luke agreed with Sam, but they couldn't pass up this opportunity. "They're expecting delivery on the thirtieth. We're short two." He tried Charley's cell. No answer. "Where is he?"

"Ya can't call Charley when he's gettin' laid," Joey quipped. "He turns it off."

"You serious?" Sam asked incredulously.

Joey shrugged. "Old men like Charley gotta concentrate when they're fuckin'."

Sam couldn't help but laugh. "Isn't that what Viagra's for?"

Joey shrugged again, then sat up straight. "Boss, let me and Snake do it."

"You'd blow it," Sam replied impassively.

"C'mon, boss. Who can handle bitches better than me?" Joey whined.

Sam, eyebrows raised, looked at Luke and snorted. "Obviously anybody."

Luke looked at Sam while he talked to Joey. He knew exactly what would convince him to step up. Worse than the idea of anyone noticing what they were up to would be the thought of losing two easy marks sitting right below them. "Okay, Joey. It's your turn."

Sam stood, pissed. He knew Luke was playing him, and he had no choice but to comply. "Alright. I'll do it. We both know Joey will fuck it up."

Joey was insulted and jumped up. "Will not."

Sam ignored him and growled at Luke, "No woman in her right mind would go anywhere with Joey. Look at him."

"You never know." Luke snickered.

"What's wrong with how I look?" Joey pouted.

Luke butted his cigarette out. "Well, Charley's not here. So, I guess it's you and me, Sam. You two stay. If what TJ says is true, we'll take them to the VIP room. Bring the van around the back, then wait here and be ready." As Luke and Sam left the room, Snake went to the window, opened it, and climbed out.

Before Luke and Sam made it to the bottom of the stairs, Luke stopped and took Sam's arm. "Look, Sammy, I'm not happy about this either. I know it's risky."

Sam nodded. Luke often threw caution to the wind. Those were the times even he wouldn't bet on Luke. One day his luck was gonna run out; there'd be a price to pay, and Sam knew he would pay that price with Luke.

Luke continued down the stairs. "If Charley thinks he's gonna get his forty percent on these two, he's gonna be disappointed."

The club was packed to capacity. Loud music beat to the undulations of the people dancing between the tables. The bar had standing room only.

TJ squeezed past one of the bartenders to get closer to the Luke and Sam and nodded toward one of the booths. Luke looked at the tourists and smiled. Easy pickings.

He took off toward them and Sam followed.

The two girls sat close together, sipping highballs with straws. They whispered to each other as they watched the dancers gyrating on the pedestals. Their too-tight, low-cut dresses and overdone makeup screamed of desperation to find some excitement. The bouncer would have let them in ahead of the line, which would have made them feel special, looked-after, and safe.

"Welcome to my club, ladies. I'm Luke. Are you enjoying yourselves?"

They nodded their heads excitedly, each thinking how wonderful it was that they hadn't even been at the club an hour and had already attracted the owner to their table. Not only the owner, but the two hottest men they'd ever seen. Then again, of course they would attract them; they were the hottest women in the club, weren't they.

"This is my friend, Sam."

Sam gave them his most disarming smile.

The bolder of the two answered, "I'm Anya, and this is Tabitha. Your club is on fire!"

Luke leaned on the table. "Thank you. We're happy to have you among us. First time here?" Luke asked.

"First time in Houston. We heard about the club and figured we'd check out the scene." She put her hand on his.

Luke gave Sam a sideways glance and Sam asked, "Would you lovely ladies like to join us in the VIP room?"

The girls looked at each other and Anya replied, "Totes." They grabbed their purses.

"Should we bring our drinks?" Tabitha asked.

"No need. There'll be champagne." Luke bent and whispered in her ear, "Room at the top of the stairs. Sam and I have to take care of some business, but we'll be right up." This was just too easy.

The girls made their way up the stairs. Luke and Sam worked their way to the bar, and TJ poured them each a drink.

Mika spotted Luke and winded her way to him through the mass of patrons. She grabbed his arm. "Hey, sexy, I haven't seen you all week."

He turned, leaned in close, and said, "I'm working. I suggest you do the same."

"Charming." Mika snorted.

Luke laughed, grabbed her by the waist, and kissed her neck. "Later. Bring that red number." He turned her around, smacked her ass, and gently pushed her away. "Now get back to work." He knew the promise of "later," whether realized or not, would be enough to keep Mika happy.

Luke left Sam at the bar and went up to the VIP room on his own. The girls were sitting on one half of the U-shaped couch, and he sat across from them. "Sorry for making you wait, ladies."

"No worries. As long as the champagne is on its way," Anya quipped. "We're ready to party." She slid over to him and put her hand on his thigh, squeezing gently as she moved it up to his crotch.

Luke removed Anya's hand and kissed it. "Then prepare yourself for an experience you will never forget."

He rose and left the room, heading to the office where Snake and Joey were waiting. "Stay in there until the club closes. I'll unlock the door then. That way you won't be disturbed."

"Good." Joey chuckled. Snake had a roll of duct tape and two syringes. He put the duct tape in one pocket of his jacket and the needles in the other, and he and Joey followed Luke to the VIP room.

"Hello, ladies," Joey said as he and Snake entered. They slid in on either side of the couch. The girls looked at each other, uncomfortable and confused. Luke stood at the door, smiling at them reassuringly. "Have fun!"

He shut the door and locked it.

***

Riki regained consciousness. He tried to take a deep breath, but leaves covered his nose and mouth. He panicked. He could move his head, but he couldn't open his eyes, and he hurt everywhere.

What the fuck. Where am I? Am I dead? He let out a muffled scream and gagged as his mouth filled with debris.

With great effort, he freed his arms and frantically pushed the blanket of dirt, leaves, and branches off his face. He got his head clear, then coughed and spit, taking deep, wheezy breaths. He opened his eyes and tried to focus in the moonlight.

Do dead people feel pain? No. No, I gotta be alive.

He gingerly checked his pocket for his inhaler. After a few deep puffs, he pushed more of the debris off himself, trying to ignore the searing pain in his stomach. He turned onto his side, lifted himself up, and struggled out of the makeshift grave.

Ha! I can't fuckin' believe it. That cocksucker thought he could kill Riki? No fuckin' way. He coughed again and spit blood, then moaned.

"Lazy fucks didn't even bother to bury me proper-like," he mumbled, looking around in the nearly complete darkness. He'd have to wait 'til the sun came up. He lay on his back, closed his eyes, and cried.

A while later, the faint hum of a truck engine pulled him out of his stupor. He struggled to lift himself and look toward the sound. He was sure he saw headlights whip by in the distance.

Riki tried to stand but didn't have the strength, so he crawled toward what he hoped was the road. He stopped once, close to fainting, but eventually reached the shoulder of the dirt road. Taking another deep breath from his inhaler, he tried to slow his breathing in an effort to stay conscious. As the headlights drew closer, he tried to pull himself up. He waved his arms at the approaching pickup truck and lifted himself higher, howling in pain.

The pickup stopped inches from Riki as he passed out. Two men in overalls got out and knelt down next to him. One felt his pulse and nodded. "He's alive." They picked him up, placed him on the cargo bed, and raced to the nearest hospital.

***

Toby's continued to be the most convenient and safest place for Luke and Tessa to spend time together. Tessa sat at a booth while Luke ordered milkshakes from the pimply-faced clerk at the counter.

Tessa checked her phone and saw she had a text. She knew it would be from Carmen, but she didn't know what to say to her. What if Luke was right? What if Carmen really was jealous of her? She knew Carmen definitely didn't want her seeing Luke. Telling her he was the devil was mean, especially when she knew how much she liked him. She needed more time to think before she responded, so she ignored the text for now and put her phone away.

Luke arrived with the shakes, placed them on the table, and slid in next to Tessa. His patience was being sorely tested. It was time to insist their relationship move to the next level. He turned to face her.

"Tessa, I appreciate your reasons for this clandestine meeting thing. But this isn't going anywhere."

I knew this would happen, she thought. *He's already tired of me.* She couldn't stop the tears that sprang to her eyes. "I just—"

He put his finger to her lips to quiet her. "I'm not a kid."

She tried to answer, but he shushed her.

"And neither are you. We need to be able to go out to dinner. To a movie." He looked around the room. "I wanna be alone with you."

"I know. I'm sorry."

"Let me take you out for a real nice dinner. I know a place downtown. No one will see us there."

"Dinner sounds—"

"What would you like to eat? Pick anything."

"I've only had lobster once."

"Lobster it is. And for dessert?"

Tessa laughed. "Not ice cream."

Luke laughed with her. He took her hands in his. "Definitely not."

Phase one accomplished; now on to phase two of a two-phase plan. This time Luke was the one to check the time on his phone. "It's late. We'd better get you home."

***

Sam and Luke parked next to a black van outside the cottage. They were about to climb the stairs when Sam said, almost as an afterthought, "Let's go down to the dock."

They sat on the edge of the dock, lit a spliff, and looked up at the starry sky.

"You don't see this in the city, do ya," Sam sighed.

"Nope." Luke laid back with his hands behind his head. "Beautiful." He closed his eyes and took a deep breath of fresh air.

They were both still, appreciating the quiet. After a few minutes, Sam asked, "Remember when you told me you thought your father didn't have a soul?"

"Uh. Yeah." *What kind of question is that. Is Sam getting all profound on me again?*

"Well, *you do*."

"Maybe lack of soul is hereditary."

"It's not."

"You don't think so?"

"I don't."

"Then why bring up something I said years ago?"

"I wanna remind you that you're not him."

"Okayyy," Luke drawled. "I'm not Joe. Where you goin' with this?"

Sam sat up. "What do you think all of this is gonna lead to?"

"All of what?" Luke looked at him.

"This." Sam motioned toward the cottage.

Luke sat up. *Uh-oh*, he thought. *Sam's having one of his existential moments.* "Hopefully it will lead to both of us becoming very rich."

"Ever wish we would have just stuck with coke?"

"No. Do you?" *Was Sam worried about Kenji or, worse, was he growing a conscience?*

Sam didn't respond.

"Because we are gonna make a shitload of money, Sammy. More than we could ever make dealing. We can't expand without attracting the attention of the Gulf cartel. You know that."

Sam closed his eyes and inhaled deeply. "Yeah. I'm just not sure this is the business we should be in. It's so fucking… There's gotta be a better way to make a lot of money."

"Yeah, how?" Luke whispered. "Got any ideas?" He knew he didn't.

"It's just... Grabbing these innocent—"

Luke cut him off. "They're *not* innocent. They'd sell *themselves* to Kenji if they thought it would make them celebrities."

"Does that make them so different from everyone else?"

"When it comes to women, the one thing I learned from Joe is that they come in two categories. Period. Madonna or whore. They're never both! And these women definitely fall into the 'whore' category."

"What categories do men fall into?"

"Easy. Predator or prey."

"And we're the predators?"

"Absolutely."

Luke leaned back, resting on his elbows. It sounded like Sam was definitely having second thoughts. "You still with me, Sammy? Because we couldn't pull out of this deal even if we wanted to."

Sam looked at Luke and shrugged. Well, he'd at least made his feelings clear. "I'm here, aren't I?"

Luke got up. "Let's go in."

Sam rose and they walked toward the cottage in silence. He made a beeline for the bar and poured them both a stiff drink.

Charley was shooting pool on his own while singing along to a country tune emanating from the phone resting on the ledge of the table. He walked over to join them at the bar.

"Sam, pour me one."

Charley downed his drink while Sam chugged back his, then poured them both another. Charley continued singing.

"Miaow!" Joey yelled. "You sound like a sick cat, Charley!"

Charley gave him the finger and mouthed, "Fuck you." He continued to sing even louder.

Snake and Joey had placed the two tourists in straight-back chairs in front of the fireplace. Their hands and feet were secured with cable ties, and they had duct tape over their mouths, leaving only their eyes to convey their terror. Their makeup was smeared, their dresses soiled, and their perfect coifs replaced with dirty, stringy tresses. The women struggled to free themselves.

Snake snickered as he took a red-hot branding iron out of the fire and turned to Anya. She squirmed, struggling harder to free herself and causing deep welts on her wrists. Snake slowly aimed the branding iron at her right upper arm.

Luke saw what he was about to do and shouted, "Snake!"

Snake stopped and looked at Luke curiously.

"What is wrong with you? Your mommy beat you too much when you were a baby?"

Snake shrugged innocently. Luke took out his knife and freed her hands. "Are you okay?"

Anya rubbed her wrists and ripped the tape off her mouth. She looked up at him, gratitude in her eyes. She put her arms around his waist and sobbed, "Thank God it's you. These animals kidnapped us. Please get us out of here. I wanna go home."

Luke gently caressed her hair and looked at her lovingly. He took her right hand. "Look at Anya's beautiful skin. You should be ashamed of yourself. Marring this perfect woman." He held Anya's arm up high and turned the inside of her arm toward Snake. "Did you stop to think of how it could affect the price? How many times do I have to tell you? On the inside, dumbass!"

Snake laughed, and Anya looked at Luke in disbelief. "What?"

Snake grabbed her arm, and she screamed as she lashed out at him with her free hand. *This can't be happening,* she thought. *He can't be serious. He owns a club. He's a good guy. Why would he do this?* "No," she sobbed. "Let me go."

Joey grabbed her other arm and tied it to the chair. He pushed the tape back over her mouth.

Luke winked at Tabitha, then went over and picked a cue from the rack on the wall and chalked it.

Sam shook his head. "Shit," he muttered under his breath.

"It's just marketing, Sam," Charley remarked. "When you have primo merchandise, you want to be clear about where it came from and where you can get more."

"They're not cattle."

"Well, they kinda are. Want a game, Charley?"

"Yep." Charley went to the table and began filling the triangle.

"Please turn that shit music off," Luke grumbled.

"Sure, boss." He switched to easy listening music and did a little two-step.

Luke laughed, took the phone, found a hard rock station, and turned up the volume.

Snake put the branding iron to the inside of Anya's arm and her flesh sizzled. She fainted. When he pulled the branding iron away, the letter V was seared into her arm. The smell of burning flesh permeated the room.

Snake untied Anya and carried her to the basement while Joey untied one of Tabitha's arms as she struggled against him.

Luke took aim and made the break, sinking two balls.

***

It took a while, but Tessa finally came up with an excuse to be away for an evening that she thought Gabriel couldn't say no to. She watched him dig into his second piece of pie. He was always in a great mood when she made him his favorites.

"Dad?"

"Hmm." Gabriel looked up.

"It's Carmen's birthday tomorrow. Her mom invited me over to their house for dinner to celebrate. I'm her best friend, so I guess they want me there."

"Where does she live?"

"In Gulfton. Not far at all. Her brother will drive us there after choir practice and then drive me home after the party."

"You can go, but call me when you're ready to come home, and I'll come and pick you up."

No, that wouldn't work at all. She had to take out the big guns. She whined, "Whaaat? Dad, please! How embarrassing for me to have to say that I can come but you have to drive me home. Geez, I'm not eleven."

They sat in silence, and Gabriel studied her. *I guess she's right, she isn't eleven.* "Okay, but I want her mother's phone number. Just in case."

"You're going to check up on me? I would die."

He knew she was right. He couldn't call. After all, she was eighteen. You don't check up on your kids when they're eighteen. He'd have to trust her. She hadn't let him down yet. "No. Of course not. I'd like to have it in case of an emergency. That's all."

An emergency? Seriously? He can't think of a better reason than that? How lame, Tessa thought. *It's because he can't bear the thought of not controlling my every moment. I'll give him the number, but it won't be my fault if there's a small typo.* She should have felt guilty, but she didn't. She only felt the excitement of a proper date with the guy she was crazy about.

"Emergency. Really, Dad?"

"I'm only trying to..." Gabriel stammered, wanting to better explain his motives.

"I understand, Dad. I'll text you her number." She removed his plate and put it in the sink. "Go stretch out and read your paper. I'll bring you a fresh cup of coffee."

Later that evening, Tessa lay on her bed, thinking of Luke. Of what it would be like to go on a real date with him. She knew she was totally and forever in love. Did he feel the same? She jumped up and grabbed her backpack, reaching inside for her phone to send him a quick text. She didn't want to seem too eager, but...

Her hand found the book Carmen had asked her to keep for her. She'd forgotten all about it. She pulled it out of her bag and studied the cover. *Rebecca's Captive Heart.* It had a picture of a ruggedly handsome pirate, shirt off, holding a pretty woman wearing an old-fashioned petticoat who seemed to be trying to escape his embrace. Hmm. She snuggled under her covers and started to read.

Halfway through the book, she fell asleep. She dreamed she was the woman and the man was Luke. She didn't escape his embrace, because she didn't want to. She woke feeling warm and sensuous, moving her body in a slow, catlike stretch. *Well,* she thought. *As long as we only do it in my dreams.*

She tucked the book under her pillow, anxious to get back to it later.

***

Riki opened his eyes, squinting at the overhead fluorescent lights. He looked at the moss green walls and whispered, "Is this hell?" He moved and felt the pull of his stitches. "Ow. What the—"

He realized he was in bed. With an effort, he pushed the sheet aside, drew the hospital gown up as much as he could, and touched the thick bandage that covered the wound on his stomach.

He started to sit up and yelped in pain as the nurse entered the room carrying a new IV bag. "You're awake," he said.

"Where am I? Where are my clothes?" Riki rasped. The nurse put down the IV bag and poured him a glass of water from a container on the night table. He inserted a straw and helped Riki take a few sips. "You're at Saint Jude's Hospice. This is the closest facility to where you were picked up."

"Picked up?"

"By some Good Samaritans. They found you on the side of the road. You were quite a mess." The nurse checked his bandage, then pulled down his gown and covered him with the sheet.

"Oh. Yeah. Right." It all flooded back to him.

"Let me get the doctor," the nurse said. He left and returned a few minutes later with a doctor in tow.

"I'm Dr. Anderson," she said as she checked his chart. "How are you feeling?"

"Good, doc."

She listened to Riki's heart with her stethoscope. "Do you know where you are?"

Riki looked from the nurse to the doctor. "Uh, hospital?" *Do these guys think I'm an idiot?*

"You're one lucky son of a gun. There was no critical damage to any major organs." She took a small flashlight out of her pocket and checked Riki's pupil reaction.

"Can you tell me your name? You didn't have a wallet on you when you were brought in."

"Of course, I can." *They do. They think I'm an idiot.*

"And it is…?"

Need a name. Need a name. What's a good name? "Kendrick. Kendrick Lamar." No way was he gonna tell them who he was. It's a proven fact that everyone knows someone who knows someone who knows someone. Case in point, the degrees of that Bacon guy. So someone could know someone who knew someone who knew Luke. Luke, the fucking murdering shit.

Doctor Anderson smiled. "Kendrick Lamar? As in the rapper, Kendrick Lamar?"

"Yep."

"Well. Kendrick. We have to call the police when someone is brought in with a knife wound."

"You called the cops?"

"It's protocol. We have to. They've asked us to let them know as soon as you wake up."

"Absolutely no need for the cops," Riki insisted. "Cooking accident. Gotta watch those Ginsu knifes. Awful sharp."

The nurse snickered and helped him take another sip of water.

The doctor sighed. "I see. And I presume that's how you lost those fingers. Careless with the Ginsu knives?"

"Uh huh."

"And the lacerations and contusions?"

"Uh huh." Riki tried to push himself up. The nurse raised the top of the bed with the remote and fluffed his pillow.

"You can explain it all to the police when they get here." She squeezed his hand in sympathy. "We've stitched you up and cleaned your wounds. You'll be ready to go home in a few days." She turned to leave and, after a few steps, turned back. "Oh, and we found a high level of narcotics in your blood. You might want to stay clean while you heal. Stick to the prescriptions we give you. Especially if you're planning on cooking anytime soon."

"Will do. Good advice, doc."

"Is there anyone you'd like us to contact?" the nurse asked.

"My phone?"

The nurse opened the drawer in the stand. "It's here." He handed it to him. "It's password protected, so we couldn't access your contacts."

"Thanks." Riki unlocked it.

"I'll leave you to it. Try to get some rest." The doctor left.

Riki dialed Mika. "Mika. Ya gotta help me. I'm at the…" Riki blanked.

The nurse chimed in as he replaced the IV bag. "Saint Jude's Hospice in Rutherford."

"I'll explain everything when you get here." He dropped the phone. The nurse put it away and left. Riki fell asleep.

***

Mika parked in front of the building, went in, and stopped at the reception desk. The woman behind the desk sensed that she was probably there to see their newest patient. She pointed down the hall. "Room two-twelve."

Mika entered Riki's room and stood next to his bed. "What the fuck have you done now?"

Riki opened his eyes. "Mika." He tried to sit up but had difficulty.

"You look like someone took a shredder to your head." She looked at his bandaged hand and whispered, "Kenji?"

Riki shrugged.

"Kenji took your fingers? What was the offence this time?" She asked, louder, not really expecting him to respond.

He tried to sit up again, grabbed his stomach, and swore. She pulled down the sheet, pulled up his gown, and saw the surgical dressings. "What's this? Did he have one of his thugs do this too? What happened?"

"Calm down, Sis."

"You calm down."

"The fingers, Kenji. The belly, Luke."

"Luke? What did you do?"

"You know our uncle. He overreacts."

She sighed. "And Luke? Did he overreact too?"

"Just a deal gone wrong."

"A deal? You were supposed to stay far away from him."

"Yeah, yeah. Well, now he thinks I'm dead."

"Dead."

"Killed me his self."

"Christ, Riki. If Luke thinks you're dead, you need to stay dead."

"I know, I know. Wanna get me outta here?"

"Yeah. I'll take you to my place."

"Thanks, Mika."

Mika went to the lobby, grabbed a wheelchair, and brought it to the room. It took a concerted, slow effort to get Riki into his clothes and into the chair, but then she quickly wheeled him out of the room, down the hall, and past the reception desk.

The receptionist yelled after them, "Hey, where are you going? I don't think—"

Mika turned back to her. "Don't worry. We'll be right back." She wheeled Riki to her car and helped him in.

"Careful," he whined.

Mika strapped him into the passenger seat, then slammed his door and got in the driver's side. She reached behind her seat, pulled a floppy sun hat out of her bag, and put it on Riki's head.

"What are you doin'?" Riki pushed it off.

Mika smacked him.

"Yowch!" Riki screamed.

She pulled the hat down hard. "What if someone sees you?"

"I don't need it. I told you, they think I'm dead. They fucking buried me."

"Buried you?" *Never mind,* she thought. She figured he'd give her all the gory details later. "Keep it on or I'll kill you myself. And I'll make sure you stay buried."

Mika turned on the ignition.

Riki put his hand inside his jacket and took a small baggie of coke out of a hidden inside pocket. He snorted a line off the back of his bandaged hand.

"What the fuck, Riki. That's the last thing you need. We both have to be thinking clearly right now."

"This helps me think clearly. Alright?"

"You're an idiot. Where'd you get it anyway?"

"Riki has his ways. Stop raggin' on me, Mika."

"Look, I've got some money saved. About fifteen grand. You can have it. You can stay at my place until you're healed, but then you gotta get outta town."

"Thanks, but it ain't enough. I gotta figure out a way to get more. Besides, I ain't leaving without you."

"I'm not going anywhere. You, on the other hand, *have* to!"

"Maybe Uncle Kenji will help us."

"You're such a dumb shit sometimes. He's obviously pissed at you. He took your fingers, for Christ's sake."

Riki raised his bandaged hand and whined, "Three."

"So, it may not be the best time to ask him for money. Right?"

"Hmm. Maybe not."

Mika drove out of the hospice parking lot and headed for the highway.

***

It had taken Tessa all afternoon to choose an outfit for their dinner. She wanted to look sophisticated, so she ended up opting for a soft-pink, silk wrap blouse that complimented her figure and a pleated navy skirt with matching navy pumps. She kept her hair loose and dabbed on some tinted pink lip balm.

She wondered what Carmen would have said about the colors she chose. She found it hard not to call her, even though she still had mixed feelings about their last conversation and Luke's poor opinion of her. She decided, regardless of what Luke said, she would call her after their date. She could prove that Luke was a good guy, and Carmen would see that she was wrong about him. Maybe Luke would eventually see that he was wrong about Carmen too. Tessa knew Carmen could be a little too forward, but she wasn't what the boys back home would call a floozy. Tessa was sure of that.

She had to keep herself from running to Toby's, even though it would have been difficult with the heels anyway.

When she arrived, Luke was in his car waiting for her. He jumped out and walked over to her. "Hello, gorgeous," he whispered in her ear. After giving her an innocent peck on the cheek, he opened the passenger door for her.

He chuckled to himself. She was obviously trying to look older, and it worked, except she couldn't change her face, which screamed "I'm still just a teenager."

They drove downtown and came to a stop in front of the Club Quarters Hotel. Tessa gazed up at the ritzy facade. "This is a hotel."

"It is. I've planned a dinner where we won't be seen or disturbed. That *is* what you wanted, isn't it? To make sure we're not seen together."

A valet rushed over to open Tessa's door. Luke got out and tossed the valet his keys. Tessa stayed in the car, her seat belt still on. The valet got in the driver's side and tweaked the position of the seat and mirrors.

Luke reached for her hand. "Gonna stay in the car?"

"I dunno."

He tried not to appear impatient, even though she was acting like a child. He would probably be embarrassed if he actually cared what anyone thought. "Do you plan on spending the evening with..." He bent and looked at the valet. "What's your name?"

The valet replied, eyebrows raised, "Ian."

Luke continued, "Plan on spending the evening in the parking garage with Ian?"

"No," she whispered, shaking her head. Now she just felt silly. *Grow up,* she thought. She undid her seat belt.

Luke took her hand and helped her out of the car. "Don't worry. I will be on my best behavior. As always."

He tried to lead her to the hotel entrance, but she hesitated and whispered, "I just don't..."

The valet turned on the ignition and sped off. "Uh-oh. There goes your ride," Luke teased, then he smiled, took hold of her hands, and chided her. "This isn't a brothel. The Club Quarters Hotel is a very classy, upstanding establishment. They don't allow mischief of any kind here. So innocent young ladies have nothing to worry about."

"That's not what I—"

"You think I'm gonna take advantage of you?"

"No. I don't."

"Gimme a hug. That'll do me for the evening," Luke joked. He pulled her to him, chuckling.

She looked at the doorman, who was deliberately ignoring them, and relaxed into Luke's embrace.

***

Riki and Mika were stopped at a red light when Riki spotted Tessa and Luke in front of the hotel. He put his nose to the glass. "Holy fuck? That's Gabriel's woman. What's Luke doin' with her?"

Mika strained to look past Riki. "Luke? Where?"

Riki pointed to them.

Mika stretched to catch sight of Luke holding Tessa's hand and whispering in her ear. It seemed so intimate.

"Who is she?" Mika asked in a whisper.

"Florisa, Carisa. Somethin' like that."

"Tessa?"

"Yeah. That's it. Tessa. I think. It's her, man. Whatever her name is. I saw her leave his house." Riki leaned back on the seat with a wide grin. "He'll be so pissed!"

Mika couldn't take her eyes off them. She remembered hearing Luke say her name in his office. He'd called her his "angel." So this was Tessa. "She's a kid," Mika said as she watched them enter the hotel hand in hand.

"Looks old enough to me," Riki said matter-of-factly.

Mika shot daggers at him. He didn't notice.

The cars behind Mika's began beeping their horns. She put her foot on the gas and sped off. Her blood was boiling. *He took her to a hotel so I wouldn't catch him,* she thought. She honestly believed Luke would care if she saw him with someone who didn't work at the club. She was sure he only fucked the waitresses to piss her off. He liked her pissed off. It excited him. So why had he brought this woman-child here?

"What is she to Gabriel?"

"Don't know. Don't care." Riki shrugged, then he added, "But this could be powerful intel."

"You think this is about him?"

"She sure ain't Luke's type, is she? Not sleazy enough."

"What do you mean by that?" Mika glared at him.

"Nuthin'." He remembered Mika had a thing for Luke.

"Why would he bring her to a hotel?" Mika thought out loud.

"How am I s'posed to know that?" Riki whined.

"Why didn't he take her to the cottage?"

Surprised, he looked at his sister. "You know 'bout the cottage?"

"Yeah. That's where they bring their skanks. Party central."

"Oh. Yeah." He was happy to know that Mika was in the dark about the true purpose of the cottage.

"Again, why a hotel?"

"I dunno. I said already. Maybe she's not skanky," Riki said and snickered.

Mika whacked his arm. She couldn't get the picture of them out of her mind. They were fully dressed, on a public sidewalk, yet they were in a world of their own. It was *too* intimate.

"Ow! Hey. Stop hittin' me. Did you forget? I got injuries."

Mika punched the steering wheel and swore under her breath. There had to be payback. Payback for her brother and payback for this betrayal.

"Ya know, Kenji may be pissed at you, but I don't think he'd be pleased to find out you were dead."

Riki nodded. "Yeah. I'm still family. Right?"

"Right. So... why don't we tell him you're dead?" She looked at him and smiled wickedly.

"Huh?"

"You want revenge, don't you?"

"Course."

When Mika stopped at the next red light, she took out her phone and dialed. "Haruto. It's Mika ... I want my uncle to know that Riki is dead ... He was murdered, and I think it was Luke Verde." She hung up.

"But I'm not dead."

"We'll tell him the truth later."

Riki pulled out his phone. "My turn."

"Whaddya mean, you turn?"

"Gonna call Gabriel. This could be worth a couple Gs."

"Why?"

"Cuz he was real cagey when I asked him who she was."

Mika was never one to miss an opportunity. If this Tessa was important to Gabriel, it would be worth more than a few Gs. Especially since Luke was involved.

She grabbed his phone.

"Hey!"

"Wait 'til we get to my place. If she means as much to him as you think she does, we can probably get a lot more."

CHAPTER ELEVEN

Carmen was asleep when her father burst through her bedroom door, red-faced, holding the used pregnancy test.

"What is this?" he roared.

She jumped up and looked for her purse. It was on the desk across from her bed, wide open. Someone must have gone through it when she took her shower last night. Who was it? Her brother or her mama? Either would rat on her. Her brother, because he would take pleasure in seeing her punished. Her mama, because she would have been beaten for not knowing her daughter was pregnant once her belly started to swell.

He threw the test at her. "I asked a question."

"Nothing, Papa," she whined. She wasn't prepared for this and couldn't think of an excuse on the fly. Or who it could have possibly belonged to. Besides, he hadn't let her out of the house, on her own, for a while now, so that wouldn't work.

"Is it true?" He wasn't really giving her the benefit of the doubt.

Carmen nodded. The truth would come out as soon as she started showing anyway. And it would be worse then.

He rushed at her and slapped her hard across the face. She fell back from the force of it. He pulled off his belt. Carmen tried to protect herself as he beat her. When he finished, he sat next to her on the bed and, head down, said in a calm voice, "You will live with your *baba*. You go tomorrow."

"No. Papa, please." This was worse than any whipping. She'd rather be beaten every day than end up in some backward town in Belarus. She would shrivel up and die there. Her brother had told her that her grandparents lived in the dark ages. They didn't have internet, a television, or even an indoor toilet.

"Don't argue. It is settled. Your mother will bring the suitcase. Pack."

"Papa, Baba doesn't speak English."

"You will practice your Russian." He rose from the bed and walked to the door.

Carmen stood. "Papa, please."

He turned to look at her. "You are my greatest regret, Natalya." He shut the door behind him.

Carmen burst into tears and fell onto her bed. She cried so hard she started to hiccup. She sat up, trying to calm down. Once in control of herself, she became resolute. "I'm not going," she whispered.

Her mother had waited until she heard Carmen no longer crying and knocked gently on the door before opening it. She placed the suitcase on the floor next to the bed.

"Mama, please talk to him for me?" Carmen begged. "Don't let him send me away." She knew it was futile. Her mother would never go against her husband's decisions. Still, she had to try.

Her mother sat next to her and took her hand. "I can do nothing, Natalya. You have made your bed, *kotenok*, now you must lie down." She got up, put the suitcase on the bed, and opened it. "Pack."

"I'll die," Carmen wailed. "I'll die, Mama."

Her mother tsked and patted her shoulder. Without another word, she left, closing the door quietly behind her.

Carmen slammed the suitcase shut and threw it at the wall. She regretted it instantly, thinking her father would return and hit her again. She held her breath and waited. Thankfully, no one came.

She had no choice; she had to run away. She would rather sleep on the street or in an alley if she had to.

She looked in the mirror and took a selfie of her flushed face and swollen tear-filled eyes.

Picking up her phone, she texted Tessa, who didn't respond. Carmen didn't think she could just show up on her doorstep, so she decided to sneak into Saint Patrick's and hide in the choir room as long as she could — or until she heard from Tessa.

She couldn't take the suitcase, so she stuffed her knapsack with her favorite clothes and a few cherished trinkets. Then she searched for a pair of sunglasses to hide her black eye and deflect from the darkening bruise on her cheek.

As soon as the house was quiet, Carmen snuck down the stairs. She took a small paring knife out of a kitchen drawer, stashed it in her coat pocket, and stuffed as many protein bars and bottles of water as she could fit into her knapsack.

**

Luke took Tessa's hand and led her through the hotel lobby. She was mesmerized by the glittering chandeliers and gold-leafed decor. She'd never seen such opulence and looked around in awe.

The doors opened as they reached the elevators. A few hotel patrons exited, but Tessa didn't move. She leaned toward Luke and whispered, "Doesn't this elevator go to the rooms?"

"And to our dinner." Luke reached for her hand. "Come on," he urged.

His voice had the desired effect. Tessa took a deep breath and stepped into the elevator. When the doors reopened, she followed him down the hall to one of the rooms.

"This isn't a restaurant."

He put the key card in the door and opened it. "It isn't. But dinner *is* being served here."

A bay window and sofa were the backdrop to a dining table covered in white linens with silver cutlery, sparkling champagne glasses, and china for two. A champagne bottle sat cooling in a silver stand next to the table. Visible in an adjacent room was a queen-sized bed covered in a quilted satin duvet, an overstuffed chair of the same material, and a door leading to the bathroom.

Luke removed his coat and threw it on the sofa. He walked to the window and looked down at the city below, then turned to find Tessa still standing in the doorway.

She eyed the bedroom from where she stood. She wasn't sure if she was still having second thoughts about agreeing to dinner in a hotel or if seeing the bedroom had actually paralyzed her.

He laughed, strode over to her, and led her into the room, closing the door behind her. She looked around nervously. Everything was so nice, so sophisticated. Why did it feel seedy?

Luke uncorked the champagne and filled the glasses as Tessa walked to the window and looked out. He followed and handed her a glass.

"Are you gonna try and get me drunk?"

"No. I don't want you drunk."

That relieved her somewhat, but it didn't make her less anxious. She turned back to the window. "Nice view. Everyone looks so small. Like ants going about their day, not people." She turned to him. "Did you know that there are more chickens than people in the world?"

"No, I didn't."

"And I bet you didn't know that mayflies only live for twenty-four hours."

"I did not know that either. Yet so interesting." He chuckled.

"Uh huh."

Luke kissed her neck. She held her breath and didn't respond. Once again, she felt as though her feet were nailed to the floor.

There was a knock on the door. "Room service." Tessa, thankful for the interruption, relaxed and took a big gulp of the champagne. She felt hot.

Luke cursed under his breath as he opened the door. The waiter pushed a dish-laden cart into the room. He placed two covered plates on the table and indicated the dessert plates and coffee pot on the cart. Luke signed the bill, tipped the waiter, and closed the door behind him.

He walked back toward Tessa. "Where were we?"

She slipped past by him and sat at the table. He sighed, turned, and joined her.

Tessa whispered, "I'm nervous."

"Not like your friend at all, are you?"

"What?"

"Nothing. I just can't believe…" He thought better of bringing up Carmen again. It wouldn't get him anywhere. "I'm nervous too, you know."

"You are? You don't seem nervous."

"Well, I am. You can be very intimidating."

Tessa laughed. "You're making fun of me."

He snickered. "Yeah. I am. Let's eat." He uncovered their plates.

"What is this?"

"Soufflé."

"I've never had a soufflé before. I thought they were just for dessert."

"Some are. Not these. They're full of lobster. I believe your favorite?"

Tessa took a bite and smiled. "Wow."

"Exotic meal for an exotic woman."

"I'm hardly exotic."

"You are to me. Let's dig in."

They enjoyed an easy silence as they finished their meal. Tessa was still too nervous to eat much, but she made an attempt to at least make her plate look worked over.

Luke, on the other hand, was ravenous and finished both their desserts.

***

Mika's condo was sparingly, but expensively, decorated with a modern feng shui vibe. The living room and kitchen were separated by a black Carrara marble counter and four black-and-white Missoni stools. An enormous flat screen TV hung on the wall across from a matching Missoni sofa and marble coffee table. A five-foot Japanese maple had been strategically placed in front of south-facing terrace doors.

Mika went to the kitchen, grabbed two espresso pods, and made them each a cup while Riki shuffled over to the sofa. He used his inhaler, leaned back, and closed his eyes.

"You're absolutely positive that this is *the* Tessa?" Mika asked. "I mean look at Gabriel. Look at her. Doesn't seem likely. Not only that. She's what, sixteen?"

"It's her, I tell ya." Mika was really getting on his nerves about this. "It's. Her!"

"Okay, it's her."

"Yeah!" Riki slammed his injured hand down on the sofa then screamed from the pain. "Yowch!" His eyes watered. "Look what you made me do."

"Idiot," Mika said under her breath and shook her head in disbelief. She went to the bathroom and removed a bottle of Percocet from her medicine cabinet. She returned and handed two to Riki, who swallowed them without water, almost choking.

She filled a glass from the tap and handed it to him. He gulped it down.

"So, knowing his archrival has this Tessa in his clutches would be worth a hell of a lot more than a few grand," Mika happily pointed out as she went back to the kitchen.

"How much do ya think?"

"I say we ask for fifty." Mika returned with the coffees and sat next to him.

"Fifty thou? Are you nuts?" Riki snorted, looking at her in disbelief. *No chick is worth that much,* he thought. *Not even Mika.* Then he felt bad for thinking it.

"You'll need at least that much to disappear," Mika added.

"No way he'll—"

She cut him off. "Give him a very, very detailed description of what you saw."

"I saw them at the hotel."

"No. You saw them *kissing* in front of the hotel. And they were really into it."

"Oh, I get it."

"Pop used to say that the icing is what makes the cake worth buying, remember?" *Makes sense in this situation,* she thought. Her father had been a con man, if not a very good one. It was what had gotten him killed. He'd tried to pull a con on Kenji.

"Yeah, and he was pretty smart, wasn't he." Riki had looked up to his father and was still on the fence as to why he had disappeared. He didn't want to believe Kenji had anything to do with it, even though his mother insisted that's what happened.

"He *was* smart. Now make the call." Mika returned to the kitchen and refilled her cup. When Riki didn't move, she yelled, "Do it!"

"Okay, okay." Riki took out his phone and dialed the Vox.

Gabriel was locking his office door when the phone rang. Irritated, he unlocked it, went back to his desk, and picked up the receiver.

"Club Vox."

"Hey, Gabriel. It's Riki."

"What do you want?"

"Fifty grand."

"I told you I wasn't interested."

"This is different."

"Why would I give you fifty grand for *any* reason?"

"Cuz I know where your girlfriend is."

"I don't have a girlfriend." Gabriel hung up the phone.

"He hung up on me," Riki whined.

"Call again." Mika was confident Gabriel would bite.

Riki dialed again, and Gabriel picked up. "What?"

"Then who's the chick I saw at your house?"

"Whaddya mean at my house?"

"I saw her. Remember? When I was there."

"And?" It had crossed his mind that, sooner or later, Riki might try to use it against him.

"Just wonderin' what she's doin' with Luke?"

"Luke?" *This better be a scam,* he thought.

"Yeah. I saw them."

Mika slapped her hand on the counter and motioned for him to continue.

"He was all over her and she was likin' it, man. I figure you'd wanna know."

"Luke could have been with anyone. What makes you think it was her?"

"I just got one of those memories for faces. Big brown eyes, great skin, long, blonde hair, and a great a—"

"Where?"

"Is it worth fifty grand to ya to know?"

"If it's true. But if it's not…"

"It's true. Gimme your word you won't screw me."

"You have my word. Where do you *think* you saw them?"

"In front of the Club Quarters Hotel on Fannin."

"Riki, if this is a scam, you won't live to regret it."

"It's not."

Gabriel hung up.

Riki looked at his cell and muttered, "Why does everyone wanna kill me?"

"'Cause you're just too lovable not to wanna kill," Mika joked.

"He's gonna pay it." Riki shook his head in disbelief. It was too easy.

"Of course he is." Mika wasn't positive he'd go for it, but she knew people, and Gabriel wasn't that hard to read.

She was exhausted. She'd had a late night at the club and spending time with Riki always drained her.

"I'm tired. I'm going to bed. Wake me when he calls back." She took a pillow and sheets from the closet and made up the sofa for him. "Don't burn the place down."

"I don't smoke."

"I know."

∗∗∗

Gabriel dialed Tessa's number. The phone rang and clicked. "Tessa, I—" He was interrupted by the recording. "Hi, it's Tessa, I can't talk now..." Gabriel slammed down the receiver. He went to the bar, opened the cash register, and took a small revolver out of the back of the cash drawer. Just in case. He put it in his pocket and hurried out of the club.

He drove home like a madman and hurried into the house, shouting Tessa's name. He ran up the stairs to her room. "Tessa?" It was empty. He pulled out his cell phone and dialed her number again. The ringing echoed through her room. He glanced around and found her phone near the charger on her bureau. She must have left for Carmen's to celebrate her birthday with her family. He picked up her phone and looked through it. He saw Carmen's home number and dialed.

Carmen's mother answered the phone, "*Privet?*"

Throwing caution to the wind, Gabriel said, "This is Tessa's father. Can I speak to her?"

"*Chto?*"

"Tessa. She's there for the party. The birthday." He couldn't keep the desperation out of his voice.

"No party. No birthday."

"Well, can I speak to—"

She hung up and the line went silent.

Gabriel was about to call her again but thought maybe they'd gone to that soda shop they liked so much, or maybe choir practice had gone longer than usual. He put the phone in his pocket, rushed out of the house, and drove to the church. He parked and ran in. It was dark and empty. He ran across the street to Toby's. A young boy stood at the counter next to his mother; his hands reaching out as he watched the clerk fill a cone with big scoops of chocolate ice cream. No Tessa or Carmen. He let out an anguished scream. The mother and boy stared at him, mouths open. Gabriel didn't care.

He ran back to his car and sped toward Fannin Street. This couldn't be happening. How did Luke even know she existed? Or who she was? Then it dawned on him. Of course. Riki. How else could he have recognized her at the hotel. He'd seen Tessa the night he came to the house. Did he get money from Luke for that information? *If he's responsible for this, I'll kill him.*

He took Tessa's phone out of his pocket to call Carmen's home again, but the battery was dead. He cursed and tossed the phone down on the passenger seat. If she was with Luke, how could he have possibly convinced her to go to a hotel with him. Tessa wasn't stupid or gullible.

He arrived at the hotel, parked across the street, and rushed in to the reception desk. There was no one registered under the name of Luke Verde. He described the both of them and showed the picture of Tessa he had on his phone. No one recognized them. He checked the hotel restaurant, hoping they were only there for a meal. But he didn't find them. All he could do was wait for them to come down from whatever room they'd gone to.

He sat in the lobby, watching the elevators. After an hour, one of the reception staff asked if they could help him, and he realized he couldn't wait there. He left and crossed the street to his car, where he could watch the hotel entrance.

He had to prove to himself that it wasn't true. It couldn't be. Tessa would never do this. Not the Tessa he knew. The darkness and night chill surrounded Gabriel as he watched patrons enter and exit the hotel.

***

Luke reached for Tessa's hand and began to lead her toward the bedroom. She pulled away, went to the window, and looked out. She didn't even want to acknowledge that there was a bed in the next room, and the window seemed to present a safe space.

Luke came up behind her and turned her to face him. "The feelings I have for you are real. Even a little overwhelming."

"Overwhelming?"

Luke kissed her nose. "Yes, overwhelming."

Tessa whispered, "I know what you expect. It's too fast."

"It's not." He took her hand and tried once again to lead her to the bedroom. She pulled back and turned to look out the window again. He took a deep breath and stood behind her.

"You're not a child anymore. You're a grown woman. A beautiful, intelligent woman. And there's nothing wrong with us wanting to be closer."

Tessa didn't respond. He turned her to face him and slipped his hand around the back of her neck, weaving his fingers through her hair and holding her gently. He kissed her, reaching under her blouse and under her bra. She placed her hands over his. "Don't."

"Remember what you said that day at the stables when Thunder took that mare? You said you knew you could trust him. I thought that meant you could trust me. And you can. Just let go."

Tessa sighed. He took his hands away and she closed her eyes. "I just…"

Luke looked at the cross hanging from her neck. He touched it and, after studying it for a moment, said, "God brought us together."

She looked at him. "You don't believe God brought us together."

"Think it's a coincidence that we met at Saint Pat's?"

"That's what Carmen said. It wasn't a coincidence that we met you and Sam at the church."

Luke smiled to himself. *Thanks, Carmen.* He continued, not wanting to give her time to think. "I wanna give myself to you. Totally. Don't you want me?"

Tessa grabbed his hand and pointed to her ring. "I thought you understood."

"I do."

Tessa needed to be sure he was sincere. "If you do, then you know God would want us to be married first."

"And God would know we will be." *It's close to the truth,* thought Luke. *If I was gonna marry anyone, she has all the qualities I want.* "We'll go together to see Father Thomas in the morning."

Tessa looked at him for a moment, digesting what he'd just said. "Tomorrow morning?"

"Tomorrow morning."

"Can he marry us right away?"

Luke laughed. "Once we get the license, it'll only be a couple of days before we can. And if Father Thomas can't do it for us, we'll have a civil ceremony at the courthouse. So by the end of next week, you'll be Mrs. Tessa Verde. That soon enough for you?"

Tessa threw her arms around him and hugged him tight. "Yes." She pulled away, took his hand, and touched her ring. "It belongs to you now. I belong to you now."

Luke took her hand and led her to the bedroom. She resisted and freed her hand from his. "We only have to wait a few days."

"Really? That's exactly what a child would say. I don't think you're ready for a real relationship, a real marriage." His voice had a chill to it. "This was a mistake. Come on. I'll take you home." He turned, walked to the door, and turned the handle.

His words sounded so final. She couldn't chance losing him. She couldn't bear that. "No. No. You... you're right. I'm so silly." She rushed to him and wrapped her arms around his chest. "Don't be angry." She reached up and kissed him long and hard, awkwardly pushing his mouth open with her tongue.

It was a little amateurish but still exciting. *This virgin thing is becoming a little too real,* Luke thought. *No. Stop thinking. Just enjoy this.* He led her into the bedroom. She followed as if in a trance, only seeing him, only wanting him.

Luke pulled her to him and kissed her deeply. She relaxed in his arms and returned the kiss passionately. The kiss deepened into a slow exploration, one that was restrained yet hinted at a far deeper desire — only a touch away from exploding. It left her breathless and giddy and had her wanting him with a fierceness she didn't understand.

He untied her blouse, removed her bra, and bent to kiss her breast. She breathed heavily and, hands trembling, began to unbutton his shirt. They continued to undress each other and slowly made their way to the bed. Tessa sighed and whispered, "I love you."

Luke made love to her slowly and gently. A first for him.

As they climaxed, he looked into her eyes and, without thinking, whispered, "I love you." He planted soft kisses all over her face, then rolled onto his back.

Tessa stretched and snuggled up to him. *This is real. I can't believe I could be this lucky. He's perfect. I could stay here forever.* She placed her head on Luke's chest and closed her eyes as she caressed his face with her hand.

Luke kissed the top of her head. The steady rhythm of her breathing revealed she'd fallen asleep, and she shifted to a fetal position inches away.

He looked up at the ceiling, deep in thought. *What the fuck am I doing? Did I actually just tell her I loved her? Buddy, you better get your fucking head straight. You do not love her. You want Gabriel to suffer. You want him hurt to the core, and the weapon is here next to you. Think, dammit. He'll never get over this. That's what you want. You don't give a shit about this little goody two-shoes.*

He looked over at Tessa. Maybe he'd even take her to the cottage. Wouldn't be hard to get her there. Just another outing to the country. *She means nothing to you.* He closed his eyes and pulled her closer to him. She roused, looked at him, and smiled sweetly. He made love to her again.

I think you're fucked, Verde, really fucked, he thought and fell into a deep, satisfied slumber.

***

The morning sun poured through the window and revealed a sleeping Tessa alone on the bed.

Luke came out of the bathroom wearing only his pants, socks, and shoes. He picked his sweater up off the floor and put it on. His phone rang and he instantly grabbed it out of his pocket, answering in a low voice. "Yeah ... Of course, I have the merchandise ... Sunday, one o'clock ... We'll be there." He hung up and put it back in his pocket.

He moved to the bed and sat beside Tessa, noticing a small red stain next to her. He touched it and smiled. *My virgin is a virgin no more.* He pulled out his stiletto, shifted next to her, and looked at her for a long moment. Slowly, he pulled the sheet down from her body, stopping below her stomach. She stirred but didn't wake. He traced a V with his knife but didn't break the skin, then he put the knife in his pocket and bent to kiss the same spot. He stood and walked to the door, grabbed the handle, turned to look at her again, and returned to the bed. He pushed a lock of hair from her face, kissed her forehead, and left, closing the door quietly.

Gabriel took a last drag off a cigarette and dropped it to land among the butts scattered at his feet. He shivered from the early morning chill and pulled his jacket tightly around him, his eyes still fixed on the hotel entrance.

The hotel doors opened, and Luke exited alone. He lit a cigarette and continued down the sidewalk.

Gabriel rushed across the street and followed him until he was out of sight of the hotel doorman. He clumsily pulled the gun out of his pocket.

Luke's phone rang and he answered just as Gabriel came up behind him, screaming, "Where is she?" Luke turned around and Gabriel whacked the phone out of his hand with the gun.

Although Luke was surprised to see him, he realized this was actually a gift. The prey had come to the predator.

Gabriel's hand shook as he pointed the gun at him. "You sick, sick bastard."

Luke looked down at the gun and, after a moment, said quietly, "Is this about your little girl, Gabriel, and what I did to her?"

Gabriel screamed, "AAAGH!" He pulled the trigger repeatedly, but the gun didn't fire.

Luke threw his cigarette at Gabriel and grabbed the gun out of his hand. Speaking to him as though he were a child, he said, "You're not very bright, are you? You forgot to take the safety off. The safety needs to be off for it to work." Luke put the gun in his pocket. "Lemme tell you, she was damned frisky for a first timer."

Gabriel lunged at him. Luke easily pushed him to the ground, then looked around before putting his foot on Gabriel's throat. Gabriel gagged, grabbed Luke's shoe, and pushed it off his neck. He tried to rise but Luke kicked him in the balls. Gabriel curled up in pain.

"And, after some coaxing, not much mind you, she gave me one hell of a blow job." Luke walked a few feet away, stopped, and turned around to retrieve his phone. "She's in room 1223, if you'd like to go get your little girl. Oh, what am I saying? She's a woman now."

Luke put his phone in his pocket and continued down the sidewalk. *That takes care of that.* He knew Gabriel would pack up and leave town as soon as humanly possible to get her away from him. He'd won. Just had to hit him where it hurt the most. He should feel great. Victorious. Why didn't he? She meant nothing to him. Nothing. Why didn't he feel great? Maybe that wasn't exactly true.

Gabriel lay there a moment. He rose slowly, straightened his jacket, wiped off his pants, and walked back to the hotel.

***

Gabriel got in the elevator. He didn't know what he would say when he saw her. He didn't want to think of any innocent girl having spent a night with that sick misogynist. But it was Tessa, his innocent girl. His daughter. He thought maybe it would be better to leave. Not tell her he knew. Let her keep her dignity. Yes, that would be better. But… No, he had to be there for her. Luke had left her and wouldn't be back for her. He couldn't leave her alone in that room waiting for someone who'd never return.

Tessa woke. She stretched and sat up. "Luke?" She looked around the room, wrapped the sheet around her, and got up to check the bathroom. "Luke?" She went back to the bed and sat, staring out the window. Where was he? Maybe he went to see Father Thomas about their engagement. Or there was a business emergency that he had to rush to. *Why didn't he take me with him. He must have left a note.*

She searched both rooms. Maybe it was lost in the sheets. She pulled the covers off the bed. Nothing, except for a small red stain. She touched it and smiled, happy to find a reminder of last night. She'd heard a hymen could be broken from a lot of riding. *Not true, I guess.* "Luke will be back soon and we can laugh about it," she said as she looked for her phone. She'd call and leave him a message. Then she realized, in the excitement and anticipation of a proper date with Luke, she'd forgotten it at home.

Gabriel strode down the hallway to room 1223. He put his hands through his hair, straightened his clothes, and knocked on the door, afraid of what he would find.

As soon as she heard the knock, Tessa jumped off the bed, ran to the door, and flung it open. He must have forgotten his key. Silly man.

"I knew you wouldn't leave m—" She stopped mid-sentence, not believing Gabriel was standing in front of her. They looked at each other, each unable to speak.

Tessa backed up, blushing, and pulled the sheet tighter around her. "What… what are you doing here?"

Gabriel entered the room and closed the door behind him.

Tessa backed up, cringing. She only had the sheet covering her and felt more naked than she ever had in her life. "What are you doing here? You followed me? Us?"

Gabriel felt her embarrassment. His embarrassment. He looked away. "Tessa, I—"

"How could you?" Shocked and mortified, her voice rose. She flew to the bedroom and gathered her clothes from the floor.

"I didn't follow—"

She interrupted him, angry now, yelling, "I'm not a little kid whose daddy has to follow her everywhere she goes." She hurried into the bathroom and slammed the door.

Gabriel sat at the table and leaned back, exhausted. He asked, knowing she couldn't hear him, "Why would you come here? With him? Why would you—" He stopped himself.

He leaned forward and put his head in his hands. He needed to figure out what to do. He knew Luke had done this to hurt him. Was he planning something even more diabolical? What could be more fucked up than this? To seduce his little girl? No, there could be more. Much more. Luke didn't like to lose, and he considered Gabriel having anything to do with his business a loss. This was a definite win for him. Now he could push the knife in deeper, as quickly or slowly as he liked. Whatever he was planning, Gabriel had to get Tessa away. Now. Somewhere that bastard could never find her. First, he had to know the extent of the damage Luke had already done.

Minutes later, the bathroom door opened, and Tessa emerged fully dressed. She felt calm. It was time for Gabriel to see that she was no longer a child. That she no longer needed to be protected. He would have to deal with her on her terms. Grown-up terms. She walked back to the table and sat across from him. She wanted to face him, look into his eyes, but found herself looking down at her hands as she picked at her cuticles. "How did you know I was here?"

"Someone saw the two of you in front of the hotel and called me."

"Why would they call you? No one knows who I am or what I am to you. Not even Luke."

"It doesn't matter who called me. Or why. The point is, Luke found out who you are and what you mean to me." His voice rose, "Of all the men you could have chosen to…"

He took a minute to calm down, then continued, speaking softly now. "How did you meet him?" He needed to know if it was Riki.

"At church. Father Michael introduced us. Luke brings his mother to mass every Sunday."

So that's how he found her. At the church. Gabriel would never forgive himself for not going with her, at least once. He could have stopped this before it started.

Gabriel looked at the unmade bed. "Did he hurt you?"

Startled, Tessa looked up at him. "What?"

"Did he cut you?"

"Cut me?"

"Yes, Tessa. That's what he does. He cuts women."

"He does not. That's a lie."

Gabriel thought hard about how he could get her to believe him. To believe what Luke would do to her. To understand the danger she was in.

"He loves me."

"He doesn't love you. Luca Verde doesn't love anyone."

"He does. And I love him."

"Love him? You couldn't love him. He's a psychopath."

"He is not. He's kind and gentle. He's a good man."

Gabriel snorted. "He's the furthest thing from a good man."

"You don't even know him." She was sure Gabriel was lying to her. Lying to keep her with him.

"He's the man I've been trying to protect you from."

"Luke?"

"Luke!"

"Why?"

"This tryst. This was meant to get at me. I'm sorry it's gone this far. You can't see him again."

"You're just jealous. You don't want him to take me away from you. You say he wants to hurt me. To hurt you. Well, I have a surprise for you. We're getting married! We're seeing Father Thomas today to book the church." Although she said it with confidence, she didn't understand why Luke had left without even leaving a note.

"Did he tell you that before or after you slept with him?"

Tessa didn't answer.

"He lied to get you into bed."

"That's not true."

Gabriel looked around the room dramatically. "Then where is he? Why are you alone?"

"He's coming back."

"This is all a game to him." He motioned around the suite.

"No!" Tessa broke down and cried. She hid her head in her hands. Gabriel went to her and put his arm around her, but she pulled away.

"He said he loves me," she murmured, feeling less sure.

"Believe me, Tessa, you are not his type. He likes his women rough and damaged. Easier to handle and easier to throw away when he's used them up."

"That's not true. And if it was true before, it isn't now."

Gabriel sighed. He had to take a different approach. At this point, he wasn't sure if she could handle more. But she had to know the real Luke. Not the innocent romantic he'd obviously portrayed himself to be.

"I need you to understand what he is."

"More lies?"

"Do you really think I'd lie to you? Haven't I always been honest? Maybe I haven't told you everything, but I've never lied to you."

Tessa searched Gabriel's eyes. "Okay. Tell me."

He would have to tell her everything he knew about Luke. She probably wouldn't believe him, but he couldn't take the chance that she'd find out the hard way.

"This guy likes to carve his initial into the flesh of the women he sleeps with, or 'fucks' is how he'd put it. He laughingly refers to it as his calling card."

Tessa jumped up. "See? You don't know what you're talking about. That's a horrible, nasty thing to say. He didn't do that to me, and we just slept together."

Gabriel pulled her gently back onto the chair. "He hasn't yet. But he will. It's his thing."

"I don't believe you."

"Did he tell you that he, and his gang of thugs, peddle coke to school kids. Did he tell you that?"

"He wouldn't do that. He loves kids."

"Jesus, Tessa. He would. Masked by those boyish good looks are half the traits of a sociopath and all the traits of a psychopath."

"You're wrong, wrong, wrong. I told you; he takes his mother to church every Sunday."

"Luke's father left the bulk of his estate to his mother. Her family also runs a very lucrative horse ranch. She plans to donate everything to her charities when she dies, and he intends to make sure she doesn't do that. So, of course, he takes her wherever she wants to go."

"See? You're wrong again. Luke is the one who owns the ranch. He took me there. He said he might be selling it because it was so expensive to run."

"He doesn't own it. It's common knowledge."

"Why would his dad not leave him anything?"

"He did. He left him half ownership of a nightclub. The other half he left to me, Tessa, because he knew Luke couldn't be trusted. If anything happens to either of us, the full ownership of the club will transfer to a church. Your church, as a matter of fact. Saint Patrick's. Luke thinks I talked his father into that, and he hates me for it. Obviously, he can't get rid of me, but now he's found my Achilles' heel. You. And he's gonna use you against me. He's already done damage."

"I don't believe you."

"How do you think I knew what room you were in. I saw him leaving the hotel and he laughingly told me where I could find you."

"LIAR!" Tessa shouted and stood. How could he… Her mind was reeling. She'd been betrayed. By Luke? By Gabriel? She had to get away. She had to try to make sense of this. She wished she could talk to her mom. She would know what to do. She ran out of the suite and down the hall to the elevator and pushed the button repeatedly.

Gabriel followed her. He yelled, "Tessa, where are you going?"

The elevator doors opened, she stepped in, and held her finger on the lobby button, desperately wanting to escape before he reached her.

As the doors closed, Gabriel shouted, "He's a cold-blooded, manipulative killer."

Gabriel was left standing alone in the hall. He banged on the elevator button. He had to get through to her. He was sure she was on her way home. He could get there before her, and she'd have to stay and listen to him.

***

Luke went back to the club. He stopped at the bar and grabbed a bottle of scotch, then continued up the stairs to his office.

Sam was passed out in one of the chairs with his feet resting on the desk. Luke pushed his feet off, and Sam woke abruptly. "What the fa—" He shook his head trying to clear it. "Luke. What are you doin' here?"

"What are *you* doing here, Sammy?"

"Can't go home. Had a lot of money riding on yesterday's game. Another fuckin' *bad beat*. Can't cover it yet. Gotta lie low for a while."

"I thought you and Marty had some kind of arrangement when you needed to cover a loss."

"We do. This wasn't with Marty."

"Well, you came to the right place. How much do you need?"

"Too much." He sat up straight. "I could use a drink."

Luke laughed. "We could both use a drink." Luke took out two glasses and filled them.

Sam looked at his watch. "I assume, from the time, that last night went well."

"Better than expected even."

"When you gonna tell Gabriel?"

"He knows."

"He knows? How? Did ya call him and say, 'Hey, Gabe, I just fucked your kid.'"

"Something like that."

"How'd he react?"

"He wasn't too happy."

Sam laughed and tapped his glass against Luke's. They downed the scotch.

"But you don't seem too happy, either."

"It doesn't feel like I won." Luke refilled their glasses.

Sam noticed the ring on Luke's finger. "What's that?"

Luke looked down at it. "It *was* a reminder."

"Of what?"

"To keep my resolve," Luke replied dryly.

"I fear the lion has fallen for the lamb."

"Don't be ridiculous. I haven't *fallen* for anyone." Luke knew it wasn't true, and he needed to admit it. Out loud. "I can't explain why, but it seems I care about her."

"I know."

"You know," Luke repeated sarcastically.

"Yep."

"How?"

Sam shrugged. "It was bound to happen with someone. Why not her?"

"That's not helpful."

"What can I say. Love hurts."

"When did you become a fucking poet?"

Sam finished his drink. He rubbed his hands together. "Gotta go." He knew Luke was better off alone.

"Sammy, take what you need from the safe."

"You sure?"

"I'm sure."

"Thanks. You know I'll pay you back."

"You always do."

Sam saluted, got up, and left.

"What the fuck am I doin'?" Luke mumbled aloud.

He emptied his glass, pulled out his phone, and dialed Tessa. She didn't answer. He leaned back and closed his eyes. After a few minutes, he dialed her number again. No answer. What did he expect. He'd sent Gabriel to her room. Still, he had to see her.

He jumped out of his chair, rushed down the stairs, and found Sam coming out of Gabriel's office.

"Gimme the keys to the sedan."

"I can drive you."

"No, it's okay."

Sam gave him the keys. "It's parked out back."

Luke knew, instinctively, where he would find her. It wouldn't be at home.

***

Luke had no idea what Gabriel would have said to Tessa, but he was ready to deal with the fallout. He screeched to a stop in front of the church and saw Tessa climbing the steps. He jumped out of his car and followed her in. She was sitting in one of the pews. He slid into the pew behind her, leaned forward, and whispered, "Hi Tessa."

She couldn't help it. She felt weak just having him near her. Without turning around, she replied under her breath, "I woke up alone." She didn't know if she could face him.

"I had to take care of some business. Couldn't be helped. When you didn't answer my texts, I figured you'd show up here eventually."

Maybe he did come on his own to make the arrangements, she thought. She slowly turned to look at him. "What did he say?"

"Who?"

"Father Thomas." She saw the confused look on his face.

"Father Thomas? About what?" *Why the hell would I talk to a priest. What's she on about?*

"Why are you here?"

"I told you. I figured you might come here. I—"

"What did Father Thomas say about our wedding?"

Oh shit, thought Luke. *Forgot about that. She's just pissed about the wedding. Easy lie.* "Haven't found him yet."

"I don't believe you."

Luke put his hand on her shoulder. "It's true."

Tessa pulled away. "I'm not sure anything you say is true."

He didn't respond. Best not to overdo it.

"You know, I spoke to my dad."

Here we go. "And what did Gabriel have to say?" Luke couldn't keep the acrimony out of his voice.

A chill ran down Tessa's spine. She'd never told him her father's name was Gabriel. "He told me you're not a good person." She started to cry, then got up and ran down the aisle and out of the church.

Luke shouted after her, "Wait." He followed her outside and caught up to her on the steps, grabbing her arm and turning her around to face him.

Tessa, frightened, screamed, "Don't hurt me!"

Surprised, Luke let her go. "What? I would never hurt you."

"I know what you do to women." She continued down the sidewalk, yelling back, "I didn't believe him. But it's true. Everything he said is true."

Luke followed her. "Just listen to me."

She turned, wiping her eyes with her hands.

"What did he say I do... to women?" *Here we go,* he thought.

"I should have listened to Carmen."

"Carmen?"

"She told me you and Sam were bad men. Did Sam hurt *her?*"

"No. I told you Carmen is pissed because Sam said he sees other women. She's jealous, that's all. You know what people are like. Misery loves company."

Tessa shook her head. "I can't believe I let myself… I gave myself to you but… but you're evil."

He couldn't help but laugh. "Evil? I'm evil. And what? Your father's a saint?"

"Compared to you, he is. He told me you're a criminal. Of the worst kind."

"Oh? Was he specific?"

She put her hands on her hips. "You and Sam sell drugs. To kids."

"We don't sell drugs to kids, Tessa. We sell to the people who come to the club. Every club owner has a side racket like that. Besides, did Gabriel tell you he was my partner?"

She didn't answer him.

"He does the books. And launders the drug money through the club. You could say I do the dirty work, and he rakes in a sweet percentage. Isn't that just as bad?" He looked at her quizzically. "Did he forget to tell you that? Yes? No? He's no different from me."

"My dad doesn't abuse women." Tessa walked away.

He shouted after her. "No?"

"No!"

"What about your beloved mom?"

Tessa stopped, turned around, and looked at him. "My mom? What about my mom?"

"You don't know? Daddy never told you the story?"

"What are you talking about?"

"Let's just say what Gabriel and your mom shared wasn't exactly consensual."

"What?" This was all too much. She wanted to cover her ears. She wanted to run. But Luke continued and she felt glued to the sidewalk.

"Your mother left town because of Gabriel. She was an innocent girl, just like you, when he raped her."

Tessa yelled, "Shut up. That's not true. You're a liar! You don't know what you're talking about. You're just trying to turn me against him."

"Your mother's name was Sarah. She had hair exactly like yours. I saw a picture of her." He touched Tessa's hair.

She pushed his hand away. She was sure he was lying. "No! They were in love. He would never…"

"I'll admit I was surprised myself. But my mother, who has no reason to lie, is the one who told me. If you need more proof, I'll—" He stopped mid-sentence as Tessa turned and ran back to the church. He ran after her.

Father Thomas was walking down the main aisle as the door opened and Tessa rushed in with Luke behind her.

Luke reached Tessa, grabbed her arm, and turned her to him. "He raped her. But I didn't rape you, did I?"

Tessa pulled her arm away and stepped back. "You need to leave."

"I can't."

"Go away. Please?" she pleaded.

Father Thomas walked up to stand between them, facing Luke.

"Good morning, son." Luke didn't acknowledge him. "Tessa. Are you alright, child?"

Tessa shook her head but didn't speak. Father Thomas put his hand on Luke's shoulder. Luke stiffened. "Perhaps you should leave."

"Perhaps you should," Luke snapped, not taking his eyes off Tessa. "We need to talk. I meant every word I said last night."

Tessa shook her head.

"I'll be at the Vox. Come tonight. Please." Luke waited for a response, but when none came, he turned and left. He wouldn't get much accomplished with Father Thomas there anyway.

The priest watched him leave as Tessa slid into one of the pews. She knelt and put her head in her hands. Father Thomas approached her. "Do you want to talk?"

Tessa nodded and moved further down the pew. He sat next to her.

"What do you do when you love someone, then find out they aren't who you thought they were?" Tessa asked without looking at him.

"Hmm." Father Thomas thought for a minute before responding. "We never really know anyone. Most of the time we see what we want to see or what they choose to let us see. We humans have many faces and rarely show all of them."

"But… What if you find out they've done things? Bad things. Horrible things. But you love them. What does that say about you if you can love someone who is evil?"

Father Thomas put his hand on her shoulder. "Never regret the affection you feel, my child. Keep in mind, it isn't your place to judge anyone. We must leave that to God." He sighed. "We must trust that there is goodness in everyone. And I can tell you, without any hesitation, that God expects us to forgive even the most unrepentant sinner."

Tessa looked at him and whispered, "We were going to get married. We were going to come and see you today, to plan the date." She wept.

He gently squeezed her shoulder in sympathy. "Let's pray together. Perhaps it will help clarify things for you." He lowered himself onto the kneeler, bowed his head, and folded his hands in prayer.

Tessa did the same and they prayed in silence.

***

Luke arrived back at the club, went to his desk, sat, and poured another full glass of scotch. He chugged it back, took out his phone, and dialed Tessa's number. No answer. He texted her, "I meant what I said about us having a future."

He couldn't understand why he had to fix this. Why he had to see her happy. Had to have her love him.

He started drinking straight from the bottle. He called her number again.

***

Tessa took her time walking home from the church, her head down, looking at the cracks in the sidewalk.

Praying with Father Thomas hadn't helped. But his advice had struck her. Did she need to forgive both Luke and Gabriel? She didn't know if she could do that.

What once had been a glorious world full of promise was now foreboding and sinister.

CHAPTER TWELVE

Gabriel arrived home and looked around the main floor, calling Tessa's name. He rushed up the stairs and into her bedroom. He'd beaten her home. He saw the magazine with Riki's phone number on Tessa's bed. Mika had confided in him long ago that she and Riki were closely related to a Houston crime family. So if anyone could get him a name, it would be Riki. He reached into his pocket for his cell phone and realized he had Tessa's. He put her phone on the bureau.

He picked up the magazine and went to his room. He ripped the cover off and tossed the magazine on the floor, then pulled out his phone and dialed Riki's number.

Riki was sprawled out on Mika's sofa, watching one of the *Housewives of...* reality shows on the TV when his phone rang. Mika was taking a shower.

As soon as Riki picked up, Gabriel asked, "You still need money for your investment?"

"Gabriel? Did you find her?" He hoped Gabriel was calling to arrange payment.

"Still looking for backers?"

"Nah. I been cut outta the deal. Luke's gonna sell the girls directly to my contact. 'Sides, I gotta lie low for a while. Real low."

"That's what you wanted money for? Sex trafficking?" Gabriel was stunned.

"Well, yeah." Riki answered, not really getting why Garbriel was acting all surprised and innocent. He was Luke's partner. Didn't he know what went on right under his nose?

Gabriel knew Riki wasn't very bright. But sex trafficking? Was he that much of an idiot? And was Luke that much of a lowlife? Never mind. It didn't matter. He needed Luke dead. That was more important than ever now.

"When can I pick up the money you owe me?"

"I wanna give you more, Riki."

"More? Why?"

"I want you to do something for me. An introduction."

"What kinda introduction?"

Mika entered the living room and Riki put the phone on speaker. She pushed him over and sat next to him.

"I wanna hit put out on someone."

"A hit. On who?"

"I need someone reliable. A pro. Not some jacked up loser. There'd be a nice bonus in it for you."

"Who you want snuffed, Gabriel?" After their last phone call, Riki figured he knew, but wanted to hear him say it.

"Do you know someone who can get it done or not?"

"Sure. But still gotta know who."

"Luke Verde."

"No big surprise."

"It has to be done tonight, Riki."

"Tonight. That fast? I dunno—"

Mika nodded fervently, mouthing the word "yes."

Riki smiled at her. "It won't be cheap. How much you willin' to pay?"

"Enough." Gabriel wasn't worried about using his savings. He'd go to the club and empty the safe once Luke was dead.

"How much is that?"

"Two hundred."

Riki put his hand over the phone and giggled. This was his ticket to get away. He could keep a hefty referral fee and that much money would get him and Mika a cool place anywhere in Mexico.

"Lemme call ya back."

Gabriel hung up. He laid back on his bed to wait for Riki's call.

"You're thinkin' what I'm thinkin'?" Mika asked.

"What? You know someone could get it done tonight?"

"I do."

"Who? Killin' Luke won't be easy. He's hard to get at."

"Me."

"You?"

"Why not?" Luke was gonna die one way or the other. Either by some hired killer or one of Kenji's assassins. Why get anyone else involved. "We can do it together. Keep all the money."

"You do have access to Luke like nobody else, Sis."

"I do."

"Except... You really like the guy."

"He tried to kill you."

"Yeah. Still. I'm only your brother."

"Fuck off." She smacked his arm.

"Stop hittin' me." He tried to hit her back, but she grabbed his arm, laughing.

"Call him. Tell him you contracted a guy for him. A real pro. And you'll call him when it's done."

"Why don't we tell him we're gonna do it for him?"

"Because everyone knows you're a fuckup."

"Gee, thanks," Riki whined.

They waited a few minutes before Riki dialed Gabriel, who picked up on the first ring.

"I gotta guy. Yakuza. Real bad rep."

Mika pulled her finger across her throat indicating for him to stop. He continued anyway.

"Word is he's killed at least a hundred."

"Really. A hundred?" Gabriel was starting to regret calling Riki.

Mika put her face up to Riki's and mouthed "shut up." He finally got the message.

"Well, maybe not a hundred. But definitely a real bad rep."

"Hmm." Gabriel couldn't think of anyone else to ask so figured he'd have to take his chances with his guy. He didn't have a choice.

"So, we'll call you when it's done. Bye."

Before he could hang up, Gabriel shouted, "Hold on! I want proof, Riki. I wanna see the body. That or no deal."

"Yeah. 'Course." Riki tried to sound indignant.

"I'll meet him at the port with the money. You negotiate your cut with him."

"No problemo. Don't forget my fifty grand."

"Don't worry. And Riki, you better not be shittin' me on this."

"I'm not."

"Tonight Riki. I'll wait for the call." Gabriel hung up and took a black satchel out of the bottom drawer of his bureau. He carried it to his closet, knelt, and lifted three floorboards, exposing a safe. He opened the safe, counted multiple packets of cash, and put them in the satchel. *Worth every penny,* he thought. He closed the safe and put the floorboards back.

Meanwhile, Mika looked at Riki in disbelief. "What were you thinking? Feeding him that bullshit? You coulda lost him."

"I was doin' what you said. I was givin' him the icing."

Mika sighed and shook her head. It was either smack him again or put some distance between them. She decided to go to the kitchen and make them coffee. She'd already started to plan how they'd do it.

Riki wasn't fully convinced Mika could bring herself to off Luke. "You sure you wanna do this?" He was having a little trouble believing she wanted him dead, even if he had moved on.

"He deserves to die for what he did to you," Mika said nonchalantly. *And for what he's doing to me,* she thought. She needed to ask one last time if it was the same girl. "You're positive Gabriel said her name was Tessa?"

"Yep. Positive. Tesssaah. Why? You hear the name before?"

"Yes."

"Where?"

"From Luke's lips."

"Huh?"

"Never mind."

Riki pushed himself up and slowly made his way to one of the stools. He leaned over the counter and proudly announced, "I gotta plan."

"You're not planning anything. You're in no shape to kill a man, never mind walk straight. I'm gonna take care of this."

Riki grunted, obviously in pain. She poured him a glass of water and gave him two more pills, then went to the bathroom and returned with a bottle of Propofol, which she emptied onto a cutting board. She took a hammer from one of the drawers and slammed it down repeatedly.

Riki watched her, smirking. "Fuck. Aggressive much?"

She looked at the hammer. "Yes." She continued hammering until the pills were pulverized, then she filled a small baggie with the powder.

"Will that knock him out?" Riki asked.

Mika smiled as she tucked the baggie into her bra. "Trust me. It could knock out an elephant."

She went to the closet and pulled out a thick comforter.

"I'll be back in an hour or two."

Riki jumped up. "You're not doin' it without me."

"Sit down. You're dead. Remember?"

"I mean it. No way you're doin' this alone."

"Fine. You can drive."

They waited for Riki's opioids to kick in, then left the apartment.

***

Since Tessa wasn't home, Gabriel figured she may have gone to the church. He'd look for her there. He was on his way downstairs when she opened the front door.

"Are you alright? Look, Tessa..." She passed him on the stairs without answering. Gabriel asked softly, "Where did you go? Were you with him?"

She continued to ignore him. "You were. Weren't you? You saw him even after I told you what a monster he is?"

She stopped and, without turning, replied in a low voice. "Monster? You say your *partner* is a monster? What does that make you, Dad? Do you feel guilty when you spend the profits from the drug money."

"I don't... I can explain."

"Can you?"

Gabriel didn't respond. Tessa continued up the stairs. "I wish I'd never come looking for you. I should have stayed in Birmingham." She slammed her bedroom door behind her.

She needed to think. They both had to let her think. She sat at her vanity and stared at her reflection. Did she deserve this? Did she deserve them?

Gabriel knocked. She sighed and called out, "Just go away. Leave me alone." She didn't want to talk to anyone.

"I can't. I need to explain." Gabriel opened the door. "Look, I admit, I'm no saint. There are things I haven't told you about myself. I admit that. But I want you to end up with someone better than me. And a hell of a lot better than Luke."

She didn't respond but watched him in the mirror.

"Say something," he begged.

"I want to know who and what my father is. I want the truth. Everything."

"Okay." Gabriel sat on the corner of her bed. *Now's the time to come clean. It's the only way I can fix this. She'll understand. I know she will.* He took a deep breath.

"When I was young, I made my living working as an accountant. I earned extra income taking the odd arson job. A skill I learned from my father. He was the best. He taught me everything there was to know about chemicals and electrical wiring. I was good — even surpassed my father. No one ever got injured. I always made sure the buildings were empty. My jobs always looked like an accident; fooled even the most seasoned fire marshals."

That may explain his scars, Tessa thought, *but nothing else.*

"The last job I took was from Luke's father. Unfortunately, one of his crew thought it'd be a good idea to hedge their bets and hire another guy to do the same job without telling Joe. Apparently, a lot of Joe's money and reputation were on the line. Turned out the other guy was an amateur and an idiot. He locked the back door of the warehouse, then broke the lock, thinking the firemen wouldn't be able to get in if they got there too soon, then threw a Molotov cocktail in the front door while I was tinkering with the wiring. No way for me to get out. I managed to escape but only by running through the flames. As you can see, my career as an arsonist came to an abrupt end. Joe Verde actually felt bad about what happened to me. It was his fault. So out of guilt, I guess, he left me controlling shares in his night club. The Vox."

She turned to look at him. "And?"

"I'm not involved in anything Luke does. I *never* have been. But you're right, I don't ask questions either."

"You make money from his criminal activity."

"No. I only deal with club business."

"You must have known what he was up to. Why didn't you just walk away?"

"It's not that easy. Look at me. You might have noticed that I'm not too good with people. But I've saved enough money now and we'll use it to start over. We can walk away together." He took the clipping for the Virginia ranch property out of his pocket and put it on the bed.

Tessa didn't respond for a moment. "Is that all you have to say? Isn't there something else?"

Gabriel was silent.

"What about my mom? I suppose you didn't rape her, either!"

Gabriel looked at her wide-eyed. "What?" It was the last thing he expected to hear her say.

Tessa stared at him. "You heard me."

"That's…" What could he say?

"Oh no! You did? You did! Oh how could you, Gabriel?" she cried.

She'd stopped calling him Dad. He'd lost her. How would he ever explain what happened in a way that she might understand. "Wait. It's not what you think."

She stood. "How could it not be what I think?" She wanted desperately to get out of the room. To get away from him.

She tried to pass by him, but he stood to block her way. "Please, Tessa, sit down. At least let me explain."

Tessa looked at him crestfallen. Too much betrayal. She felt like she was being ripped apart. Tears fell down her cheeks again. How could he ever explain what he did to her mom. He raped her. She hadn't believed Luke. She thought he just wanted her to hate her father so she'd forgive him. But it was *true!*

"Please?" It was only then that she saw his tears.

"You can try." She sat on her bed, not looking at him. Gabriel sat next to her, leaving enough space between them so she wouldn't move away.

"You might not believe this, but I was quite the looker in my day. I had my pick of any girl. But there was only one for me. And it was Sarah. And I knew she felt the same. I would have asked her to marry me. After I was burned, Sarah was the only one who tried to pretend that nothing had changed. That I was the same man I was before. But I wasn't. I was full of rage and self-loathing. She came to my apartment one night. We were on the couch watching a movie and I leaned over to kiss her. I needed her to love me, to not see the face I had now. So I held her close and just… I lost control and pushed things. She didn't fight me, but I knew she didn't want to. I knew she wanted to save herself for… The ring. She was so proud of what it meant. After, she pulled away and I realized what I'd done. The damage. That the relationship had changed. That she'd only wanted me as a friend. And I had ruined even that. She said she forgave me. She said it was okay. She was glad it was me. But I never saw her again after that night. I wrote that letter, but she never wrote back. She disappeared. And I've lived with the guilt and regret ever since."

Tessa didn't say anything. She couldn't.

He continued. "Then you showed up. I'm sorry for what I did, but I don't regret that you're the result, and I never will."

Tessa asked, almost to herself, "Why didn't she tell me?"

"In her heart, she knew I wasn't a bad man. Maybe that's why she kept my letter."

"You're an arsonist, a rapist, and who knows what else?"

"I'm not that man anymore."

"If you could change, why can't Luke?"

"Because it's not in the past for him. This is now! He's using you. Why do you refuse to believe me?"

"Everybody deserves a second chance. Even you."

He looked at her. *Should I tell her about the women? She doesn't believe how dangerous he is.* He decided she needed to know.

"I spoke to an associate of his tonight. I wasn't gonna tell you, but I think you need to know. Luke's newest venture is kidnapping and selling women to the highest bidder."

Tessa jumped off the bed. "LIAR! How could you? You thought of the worst thing anyone could do. I can't believe you'd make up such a horrible lie."

"It's the truth."

"Get out of my room," Tessa screamed.

"Tessa."

"Please. Please. Leave." She fell onto her bed crying, almost unable to breathe.

Gabriel couldn't move.

Tessa sobbed, "Please. I need to be alone."

He watched her for a moment, then left to go to his room. If anything went wrong, they would need to be ready to leave fast. He took his passport out of a drawer, threw a few things into a suitcase, and went back to Tessa's room.

"Where's your suitcase?" he asked. She pointed to her closet without looking at him. He took the suitcase out and put it on the bed. "I have to go out for a few hours. I need you to pack your things. We'll leave in the morning." Tessa didn't answer.

"Trust me. There's no other way." He sat on the bed and gently caressed her hair.

Resigned, Tessa answered, almost in a whisper, "Okay, Dad."

"You'll pack?"

"I'll pack."

Gabriel left her. He retrieved the satchel and, before going downstairs, looked in on her again. She hadn't moved. "Tessa?"

She got up and opened the suitcase.

Satisfied, Gabriel rushed down the stairs and out of the house. He got into his car and drove off. He figured he'd wait for the call at the port to save time.

∗∗∗

Tessa picked up the advertisement for the ranch and studied the photo. It was what she'd always wanted. She went to her window, wiping her eyes as she watched Gabriel drive away. She turned and looked around the room. For some reason, it felt unfamiliar now. Cold. It reminded her of the feelings she'd had after her mom died.

She went to the bed and put the listing next to the suitcase. She took her jewelry box and placed it, along with her framed photos, in the case, then emptied the contents of her dresser and her closet into it, filling it to the brim. She removed the aquamarine dress from its hanger last, held it in front of her, and looked in the mirror. She smiled, remembering the first night at Toby's. The first time Luke had held her hand. The first time he kissed her. And the first time he said he loved her. She folded the dress into the case and closed it.

Tessa sat down, going over what Gabriel had accused Luke of. She didn't believe everything. How could she? She had to hear Luke tell her it wasn't true. She felt she would know if he was lying. She grabbed her phone. The battery was dead, so she plugged it into the charger and dialed his number.

Luke jumped up. "Tessa? Tessa, please, let me see you."

"Do you kidnap women?"

"What?" He didn't realize Gabriel knew about the cottage. Who would have told him? Why had Gabriel not said anything? Maybe he'd been waiting for an opportune time to use it against him.

"Do you? Do you sell women?" Tessa pushed for an answer.

"Where did you hear that?" *Fuck owning the club. I'm gonna kill him.*

"Is it true?"

"No." What else could he say. *Think fast.*

"Are you lying?"

"You need to trust me. This morning, while you were sleeping, I got a call from Sam telling me he found out some men in our employ were involved in a trafficking ring. He probably found out about it the same way Gabriel did. Believe me, this was the first I'd heard of it. I'm furious! I can't turn them in to the police now, as they would try to implicate me. But believe me, I will find a way."

"I don't know." Tessa was confused. Should she believe him? Surely, he'd never do such an unspeakable thing.

"That's why I left the hotel in such a hurry. And when I came back for you, you were gone."

She couldn't answer. She didn't know what to say.

"You gotta ask yourself why Gabriel knew about it and didn't do anything." He needed her to remember Gabriel's crime.

He could hear her breathing almost as though he could hear her thoughts.

"My father would never—"

"You're not that naive. I'm not an innocent, but who is? Remember what you said to me at the ranch. You said one can't take a horse at face value, or a person. It's not always about what you see. Most of the time it's what you can't see that's important. I know you believe that. I know you believe I'm a good man."

Tessa whispered, "I don't know."

"I'll do whatever you want. Be whatever you want. If you want to leave here, go away together, we will. I'll come and get you now."

"NO. Don't come here."

"Okay. Then you come to the club."

Tessa didn't reply.

"You don't have to worry about Gabriel. You don't have to choose between us. He'll come 'round once we're married. He will. Because he loves you. Tessa? Please answer me. What are you thinking?"

Tessa couldn't respond. She hung up.

"Faauck!" Luke threw his phone in the drawer and slammed it shut. He took numerous long drafts from the bottle of scotch, then leaned back and closed his eyes.

Tessa sat at her vanity and looked in the mirror. *But what does he see in me? I'm a lot younger than him. I'm not worldly or that interesting. Why does he want to marry me? He could have any woman without having to marry them. So why me? Is Gabriel right? Is he that good at making people believe what he wants them to believe? Is this all a trick? To hurt Gabriel? No. That's not possible. It can't be.*

She thought of their night together. Of how gentle he was. How he'd held her all night. That's *real* love. That has to be real love. Gabriel was lying. And if he wasn't, she still needed to see him one last time.

Tessa looked at her *Twilight* poster and felt sure that what she was about to do was the right thing. She opened the suitcase, took out the aquamarine dress, and put it on. She replaced it with the clothes she'd been wearing and shut the case. Glancing at herself in the mirror, she removed her cross and hung it on the vanity mirror, then texted Luke. "I'm coming to you."

***

Riki pulled the car into the alleyway and stopped next to the fire escape leading up to Luke's office. "Wait here," Mika said as she got out and walked to the driver's side. "I'll open the window and whistle when I need you to come up."

"I don't hurt anymore. Let me do it. I—"

Mika cut him off. "Just be ready when I give the signal."

"Maybe he's not by his self."

"Not a problem."

"What if you can't get it in his drink?"

Mika pulled up her sweater, revealing a sexy bra. "I know how to get him alone and keep his attention."

Riki took the baggie of coke out of his inside pocket. There was a little left. He opened it and Mika slapped him, spilling the coke.

Riki squealed, "What the fuck!"

"Stop shoving that shit up your nose!" She turned and walked down the alley to the street.

Riki tried to snort the powder from his jacket sleeve. He licked his finger and carefully dabbed the bit off his jacket and pants and rubbed it on his gums.

Mika entered the club and looked around. Snake and Joey were nowhere to be seen. TJ was serving a scantily clothed customer who was desperately trying to keep his attention by leaning over the bar and displaying her ample breasts. Charley sat at a booth, in verbal foreplay with two women.

She walked to the stairs, took another look to make sure neither man was aware of her, and rushed up the stairs. The door to Luke's office was slightly ajar.

A drunken Luke sat at his desk, filling his glass from the almost-empty bottle of scotch. He chugged it down and lit a cigarette.

Mika looked in and smiled. She entered, closing the door behind her. "There you are. I've been looking for you." Luke didn't acknowledge her.

She walked over to stand next to him, took the glass, poured a drink for herself, drank it, and then poured another for Luke. She took her sweater off and dropped it on the floor.

He focused on her, pushed her away, and slurred, "Not in the mood. Go play somewhere else." He swiveled his chair around and closed his eyes.

Mika took the Propofol out of her bra, dumped the powder into Luke's drink, and stirred it with her index finger. She walked around the desk, took the cigarette out of his hand, and stubbed it out in the ashtray. "Let Mika make you feel better." She straddled him and put his hands on her breasts. He pulled his hands away.

"What's the matter? Tell Mika and she'll make it better." She kissed his neck and reached for his glass. Luke grabbed her hand, smiled, then took the drink and gulped it down. Mika got off him and undid her slacks. She pointed to the scar in the shape of a V on her abdomen.

"I'm yours. Remember? You said I'd always be yours." She put her hand on his crotch and squeezed.

Luke removed her hand and slurred, "Get the fuck out."

She bent and picked up her sweater, watching him out of the corner of her eye. Luke rose, swaying. Mika put her arm around him and led him into the bedroom.

She sat the drugged Luke on the bed and removed all his clothes. She watched him as he lay naked for a long time before deciding to undress herself. She climbed on top of him, put his hands on her breasts, and gyrated slowly until he got hard. She placed him inside her and continued more heatedly. After he climaxed, she climbed off and stretched out next to him, studying his face. He began to snore, and she watched him for a few minutes before rising. She kissed him and put on her bra, panties, and slacks, ignoring the sweater on the floor. She walked to the office window, opened it, stuck her head out, and whistled.

Riki took the comforter and cord out of the trunk. He slung the comforter over his shoulder, put the cord in the waist of his pants, and climbed the stairs. Mika pulled her head in as Riki arrived and shoved the comforter through the window. He took a gun out of his jacket pocket and put it on the ledge, then reached into the other pocket and took a silencer out.

The silencer slipped from his hand, crashing on the metal steps. He stood still, dumbly looking down at it. The painkillers had definitely kicked in. Mika looked up and down the alley and whispered, "Get it, quick."

Riki tried to clear his head by shaking it. He picked up the silencer and Mika grabbed it from his hand and attached it to the gun. "Make sure he's dead," Riki said as he passed her the cord. "Go," she whispered angrily and closed the window.

Mika went back into the bedroom, shutting the door behind her. She put the gun to Luke's forehead. "How you feelin' now, baby?"

Luke stirred and mumbled, "I love you."

Mika pulled the gun away and held it behind her back. "You don't know how to love."

He replied dreamily, eyes closed. "I do. I love *you*."

Mika pointed the gun at him again. She looked at him for a moment, then placed the gun on the night table. She climbed onto the bed and lay beside him, curling up close and pulling his arm around her. She closed her eyes. "I love you too. I'll *always* love you."

***

Tessa's taxi stopped in front of the club and she stepped out. Though it was somewhat intimidating, she believed her future was on the other side of the club doors. She straightened her shoulders and walked up to the doorman. "I'm here to see Luke Verde. He's expecting me."

The doorman simply shrugged and unhooked the rope. *Luke and Sam's dating habits have sure changed,* he quipped to himself. "Go on in."

Tessa entered the loud, crowded bar. She was surrounded by attractive people who were drinking, laughing, and dancing to the DJ's compilation. She imagined it felt like being in the middle of a stampede. Chaos and beauty intertwined. She closed her eyes.

A waitress stopped next to her and shouted above the din, "Can I get ya somethin'?"

Tessa shook her head. "Is Luke Verde here?"

The waitress looked her up and down wondering where they all came from and how they found him. "Honey, if he ain't down here, he's probably in his office. I'm sure he'll be happy to see ya." She chuckled and nodded in the direction of the staircase. "Second door on the left."

Tessa looked up the stairs and back at the waitress. "Thank you."

The waitress called after her as she walked away. "You may not thank me later." But Tessa didn't hear her as she made her way through the crowd.

Her mind was racing as she climbed the stairs. *He will be happy to see me, because like he said, we're soulmates. Meant to be together. No one knows what's in someone's heart. Not Gabriel, not Carmen, not anyone. Luke isn't a bad man. I couldn't love a bad man.*

She stopped in front of Luke's office and gently knocked on the door. There was no response. She knocked again, harder, and waited a moment, then tried the handle. It turned. She pushed the door open slowly and looked in. She entered, closed the door behind her, and looked around the office, noticing the bedroom door. Taking a few steps toward it, she called out, "Luke? Luke, it's me." She knocked lightly on the door.

Mika sat up. She picked up the gun, climbed out of bed, and crept to the door. She held her breath and listened.

Tessa knocked again, harder.

Mika opened the door, surprised to find Tessa standing there. She kept the gun hidden behind her.

Tessa tried to look into the room, but Mika blocked her way.

"I'm looking for Luke. I'm… I'm a friend of his."

Mika looked her up and down. "Well, if it isn't the flavor of the week. Jesus. You're just a child."

Luke called out, "Come back to bed, baby."

Tessa suddenly realized Mika was only wearing a bra. Gabriel was right. Luke was already with another woman. How could she have been so blind? So stupid?

Luke moaned, "Tess-suh, come back."

"What? I don't understand." Tessa took a step forward.

Mika looked back at Luke. Had he thought she was Tessa when he held her? She felt a fury she'd never felt before.

Tessa was determined to get to him. To find out why he was with this woman. Why he thought it was her. Was this a game? She pushed Mika, trying to get past her into the room. But Mika stood her ground and instinctively brought both hands up to push her back.

The gun went off. The bullet made a slight *pffft* sound as it escaped the barrel. They stopped struggling, both looking down at the gun.

Tessa had felt a sudden sharp pinch in her belly. She looked down and saw a slowly expanding spot painting her dress red. In shock, she tried to pat it away and looked at Mika questioningly. *Why doesn't she want me to see Luke? Why would she want to ruin my dress?*

The pinch soon transformed to a horrible burning sensation that spread as wide as the stain. She fell to the floor. *Where's Luke? Why doesn't Luke come out?* She closed her eyes and let the dark haze take her somewhere the pain wasn't.

Mika watched her, dazed. She hadn't meant to shoot her. She really hadn't. She just wanted her to go away.

She walked back over to Luke. His eyes were closed.

"Tessa is dead," she said unemotionally. "It's your fault."

She raised her arm and pointed the gun at him, her finger on the trigger. "You love *me*. Mika." Her arm fell to her side. She pointed it at him again and wailed, "You belong to me!" But she dropped her arm again. She couldn't do it. She sat on the bed.

What am I gonna do. I have to take care of Riki. Then it came to her. A body wrapped in a comforter was as good as any other. She'd wrap up the bitch and say it was Luke. They could make the delivery, Riki could get out of town with the money, and Luke could take care of Gabriel later.

She picked her sweater up off the floor and put it on. She left the bedroom, closing the door behind her, picked up the comforter, and carried it over to Tessa. "You shouldn't have come here. This is on you," she said before she rolled Tessa's body, along with the gun, onto it. She grabbed the end of the comforter and continued to roll Tessa, wrapping her in it, then taking the cord and tying it around the ankles, neck, and torso. Mika dragged the bundle over to the window, stuck her head out, and whistled.

Riki climbed up as Mika grabbed one end and lifted it over the windowsill. "Help me." She pushed it through and climbed out. As she closed the window, she felt a few wet drops on her.

"Shit. Hurry, it's starting to rain," she said in a loud whisper as she nervously looked down both ends of the alley. "Grab an end."

Riki whined, "I only have one hand! Why don't we just drop it down? He's fucking heavy. I'm wounded, man. This'll open my stiches."

"We can't drop it. It might open and we don't have time to dick around." Mika reached for the pill bottle in her pocket and gave Riki two more pills. "Get some saliva going before you try to swallow them this time." He swallowed the pills immediately, and Mika shook her head in resigned distain.

"Now shut up and grab your end." The last thing Mika wanted was for Riki to realize she'd shot Tessa instead of the man they were being paid to kill. He'd insist on going up and finishing the job. She couldn't allow that. Tessa was out of the way. From now on she was going to make sure no one else would ever come between her and Luke.

With great difficulty, they got the shrouded body down the stairs and into the trunk, Riki whining the whole time. "See what happened? Look!" The bandage on his hand was oozing blood.

Mika was tempted to swat him. "If you don't stop whining, I'll shoot you and wrap you up with him."

The rain fell harder as they drove to the port.

Riki was thinking of the money. He'd heard there were a lot of opportunities in Vegas. *Maybe we should go there instead of Mexico. Neither one of us can speak the lingo anyway.*

Mika was thinking of the money too. How it would get Riki out of town and safe so she could concentrate on her relationship with Luke.

***

The port was dark and deserted. They'd chosen to meet at a spot hidden by a pile of large shipping containers. Rain had begun to fall in torrents.

Gabriel waited in his car, chain-smoking. He wasn't happy about adding a murder to his list of sins, but it was to save his daughter. His sweet, innocent Tessa. It was worth having to pay that much money, because once Luke was out of the way, Tessa would be safe. Free to meet someone worthy of her.

He knew he wasn't considered a threat by any of Luke's associates, so no one would suspect him. Luke had enemies. The kind of enemies that could easily make someone disappear. Besides, with no body, they couldn't prove that Luke was dead. And Gabriel was going to bury him where he'd never be found.

With Luke simply MIA, the conditions of the will would still be met. He and Tessa could stay in Houston. He would make sure every part of the business would be strictly legit. Tessa would want that. He'd find another ranch, one close by. She would like that. He would have the Vox, and Tessa would have her horses.

Mika's car drove up and parked a few feet in front of Gabriel's. Gabriel pulled the latch to open his trunk, got out, and walked to the idling car. Riki rolled the window down.

Gabriel looked in and saw Mika in the passenger's seat. That's strange. He knew she was nuts for Luke. Why would she come along?

Gabriel banged the hood and yelled above the din of the storm, "Where's your guy? And where's the body?"

Riki yelled back, "Calm yer self, Gabriel."

"You better not be fucking with me."

"No, no," Riki yelled. "Mission complete. Just wanted to make the delivery myself."

He put his hand on the door handle to get out and Mika grabbed his arm. "Make it quick. Dump the body and grab the money so we can get outta here. Fast!"

"Yeah, yeah." She always had to be in charge. Do this. Do that. Hurry. Fuck.

"Riki, I mean it. Grab the money and run."

He shook her arm off. "Oh-kay."

Gabriel opened his door and Riki got out, pulling his jacket tight around himself. He led Gabriel to the trunk and opened it. With his good hand, he grabbed onto one of the tied cords and pulled the comforter halfway out before grabbing his stomach and bending in pain from the exertion. He cursed. *Probably ripped somethin' on my insides cuz a this fucking corpse.*

With a lot of difficulty, Riki pulled the bundle out onto the pavement with a thud, loosening the cord. He slammed the trunk closed. "Fuck!" The painkillers hadn't kicked in enough yet and he needed a fix.

Gabriel pointed to his car. "The money's in my trunk. It's open."

Riki went to Gabriel's trunk and opened the satchel. He laughed and started to count the wads of money.

Gabriel looked down at the comforter. "Gotcha! You motherfucker!" He kicked it as hard as he could. He continued to kick the bundle as it rolled away from the car. "You. Went. Too. Far. I hope you rot in hell!"

Mika could see him in the mirror. She rolled down her window, stuck her head out, and yelled, "Riki. Now!"

Gabriel's last kick pulled one of the cords loose and the comforter rolled half open, revealing a bit of the aquamarine dress. "What the…" He knelt and pulled the rest of it open. Stunned, Gabriel stared at Tessa, not believing his eyes. "No. No. No. No." He lifted her limp body in his arms.

Mika crawled over to the driver's window. She saw Gabriel on his knees holding Tessa.

Gabriel moved loose strands of wet hair from Tessa's face, then looked down at her bloody torso and wailed. He saw the gun next to her, put her down gently, and picked it up. He walked toward Riki with the gun pointed at him.

Mika got out of the car yelling, "Riki!" She moved toward him. Smiling, Riki looked around the trunk lid at her.

Gabriel screamed, "You killed her!"

"What?" Riki didn't understand. "I didn't—"

"Did Luke offer you more money? Enough to kill an innocent girl?"

Gabriel didn't wait for an answer. He pulled the trigger twice, sending bullets to Riki's head and chest. Riki dropped.

Mika screamed. Gabriel walked to her car as she got in and shakingly turned on the ignition. He pointed the gun at her head. "It was you. Wasn't it?"

She put her hands up. "No. It was an accident."

He fired and Mika slumped over the steering wheel, causing the car horn to blare. Gabriel dragged Riki to the car and put him in the passenger seat. He pulled Mika back, put the car in gear, and positioned her so that her foot would lay heavily on the pedal, then he steered the car toward the end of the pier. It tipped over the edge and splashed into the water.

He tossed the gun in after it and returned to Tessa, dropping to his knees beside her body. Laying his forehead on her chest, he wailed, "I'm sorry. I'm so sorry."

A gurgling sound escaped as Tessa took a breath. Gabriel's head jerked up. "Tessa? Oh God." He quickly wrapped the comforter around her and picked her up in his arms. "Don't worry, it's Daddy." He carried her to his car and put her in the passenger seat, then ran to the other side, closing the trunk as he passed. He got in and drove off, tires screeching.

Tessa's breathing was shallow. Gabriel glanced over at her repeatedly as he sped down the city streets. He reached over and touched her shoulder.

"Daddy?" she whispered.

"Yes. It's me. It's Daddy. It's gonna be okay. Everything's gonna be okay." Then he asked, almost to himself, "What happened? How could it be you and not Luke? Where were you?"

Tessa's eyes opened, she moaned, and whispered, "Had to be sure."

"Sure? Of what?"

"Luke."

"He's a dead man. I'm gonna kill him. With my bare hands if I have to."

Tessa tried to move. "No."

Gabriel didn't respond. He wound through traffic, straining to see through the rain-soaked windshield.

"Pro-mise."

"Huh."

"Don't hurt him."

After a moment, Gabriel muttered, "Okay."

"Okay."

"You know how much I love you."

"Me too, Daddy." Tessa's eyes closed.

Gabriel could see the hospital in the distance. "We're almost there. Hold on, honey. Please, just hold on."

Tessa's eyes opened to a vision only she could see. "Mom?" She smiled.

"What?"

"Mom."

"No." Gabriel felt she was drifting away.

She closed her eyes and her body slumped down as they reached the hospital. Gabriel jumped out of the car and rushed to open Tessa's door. He gently picked her up in his arms. "You have to wake up. We're at the hospital. They'll take care of you."

Blood trickled from Tessa's mouth.

"No. Stay! Stay with me," he wailed as he carried her through the downpour to the emergency entrance.

***

The rain had stopped when Gabriel exited the hospital carrying a plastic bag with Tessa's personal effects. He'd told the police they'd been mugged. That the thieves had shot Tessa and run away. He gave them a full description of Joey and Snake.

He placed the bag in his trunk and got in the driver's seat but couldn't turn on the ignition. He looked at the comforter, reached over, and touched the small pool of wet blood, then brought his fingers to his lips. For a few moments he couldn't catch his breath, then he broke down and sobbed uncontrollably.

He banged on the steering wheel as his fury unleashed itself. "You should have never come here! I told you it was a mistake! Didn't I? You would have been better off in Alabama. You'd still be alive!" he yelled.

Tears poured down his cheeks. He whispered, "You'd be singing. Your beautiful voice... We could be living on a ranch with the horses you love so much. That would have made you happy. You had a long life ahead of you. But look where you are now."

After some time, he wiped his eyes and drove home. He climbed the stairs slowly and went to Tessa's room. Her suitcase lay on the bed. He opened it. She'd packed, so why had she left? Why hadn't she waited for him?

He picked up the listing for the ranch, folded it slowly, and put it in his pocket. *We could have left, and this would have never happened. It's my fault you met that monster! My fault.* He sat on the bed and couldn't move. A glint caught his eye, and he looked up to see her gold cross hanging on the vanity mirror. "You wanted me to believe there was a god, Tessa," he said aloud. "What kind of god would give you to me and then take you away?"

Exhaustion overwhelmed him. He laid back, closed his eyes, and slept.

CHAPTER THIRTEEN

TJ dragged himself to the club early. It was his job to take the weekly inventory — and he did, every Sunday. He hated being up before noon and, even more importantly, resented having to leave last night's hottie asleep in his bed. But the club was closed Sundays, so he would have the rest of the day to do whatever he wanted. He grabbed the clipboard from under the counter and began counting the bottles on the shelves behind the bar.

Meanwhile, Carmen was forced to sneak out of the church at dawn to avoid being found at that morning's scheduled choir practice. She had tried to sleep hidden under the choir gowns but was so scared a spider might crawl on her that she could only nod off sporadically. Even though it was exhausting, she was thankful to have been able to stay hidden for at least one night.

Tessa still hadn't returned her texts or calls. So the only thing Carmen could think to do was to go see Luke and ask him for money to leave town. Maybe Luke had been out of control, crazy drunk that night. And… he hadn't meant to do what he did. And he was so embarrassed that it made him act really mean. And maybe he regretted what he'd done to her. Maybe…

Sam had told her that he and Luke could be found at the club most of the time, as that was where Luke's office was located. She decided to walk the five miles to the club and took her time, figuring no one would be there that early in the morning. When she arrived, she removed her sunglasses and took a few deep breaths to gather courage. She grabbed the door handle and turned it, almost hoping it would be locked. It wasn't.

TJ had opened the trap door behind the bar and gone down to the storage cellar a few minutes before Carmen arrived.

She entered and looked around the main room. Empty. She passed the bar and climbed the stairs. The door to the VIP room was open. She looked in. Empty. She continued down the hall and tried the handle to the next door. Maybe this was Luke's office. It was locked. She cleared her throat, knocked, and asked in a quiet voice, "Luke? Mr. Verde? You there?" She knocked again and spoke louder. "Hello?" No response.

She moved on to the bathroom, peed, and studied her face in the mirror as she washed her hands. All the feelings from that dreadful night came flooding back. The fear. The pain. The shame. She put her hand on her belly and began to cry. What was she thinking? Was she nuts?

"What if he hurts me? Why did I think he'd help me?" she whispered to herself. No. She'd go to Tessa's house. Even if Tessa was mad at her, Carmen hoped they'd at least let her in so she could explain whatever it was Tessa thought she had done. She wiped her eyes, washed her face, straightened her hair, and put her sunglasses on. *There, that's better.*

TJ whistled to himself as he lugged two more cases of beer up the cellar steps. He dropped them down next to one of the bar fridges and began filling it with the bottles.

Carmen exited the bathroom and was about to leave when she heard the sounds from downstairs. She looked around in a panic and decided the VIP room was the best place to hide until the coast was clear. Who would go there during the day? She shut the door behind her and stood with her back to it, listening. It sounded like someone coming up the stairs. Not wanting to be discovered, Carmen scrambled under the table. She could barely keep her eyes open. She was beyond exhausted. She rested her head on her knapsack, sure the coast would clear soon. But after an hour of waiting and listening, she fell into a deep sleep.

***

Charley sat with his feet on a table near the bar, chuckling as he checked OnlyFans pages on his phone.

TJ was busy changing a beer keg when he saw Luke coming down the stairs. He looked like he'd had a rough night, so TJ grabbed a glass and made Luke's favorite hangover concoction. Luke sat at the bar and TJ placed the glass in front of him. "You look like shit, boss."

Luke snorted and took a large gulp. "If I didn't know better, I'd swear I got roofied last night."

Charley snickered. "Poor little girl."

Without turning, Luke gave him the finger, then put his head in his hands.

TJ had news that he figured Luke would enjoy hearing, and he didn't want to wait until the hangover cure kicked in. "You know my friend Lisa? Works in emerge at Saint Francis. Right?"

Luke didn't bother looking up. "I know, TJ. That's how we knew Riki was there. Wanna medal?"

"No. But I thought you'd wanna know she told me Gabriel was there last night."

"Let's hope whatever it was for is terminal."

"He wasn't there for himself. It was for his kid. Did you know Gabriel had a kid?" Luke didn't reply. TJ continued in a lowered voice. "A girl. Someone capped her ass. Do you believe it?"

Luke straightened then leaned in close to TJ. "Are you sure it was Gabriel?"

"There's no confusing his face with anyone else's."

Luke tried to sound nonchalant. "How's the girl?"

"DOA."

"What?" Luke shook his head. He couldn't believe what he was hearing. It had to be a mistake.

"Dead on arrival."

"I know what fucking DOA means," Luke sneered at him.

TJ shrugged nervously. Somehow, he'd pissed off Luke. Not the reaction he was expecting. He thought he'd be happy with the news. He knew he hated Gabriel. Everyone knew.

Luke pulled out his phone. He found Tessa's last message: *I'm coming to you.*

"So, I guess he ain't comin' to the office today, huh?" Charley quipped.

Luke stood, knocking his glass over. It hit the floor and shattered. TJ looked at the glass on the floor, then at Luke. "You okay, boss?"

Luke rushed to the door. It opened as Sam entered. Luke pushed past him, and Sam looked back, startled. "Hey, where you goin'?"

Luke turned and held out his hand. "I need your car." Sam handed him his keys and Luke rushed to Sam's coupe.

Sam yelled after him, "We deliver in three hours." He entered the club, watching Luke take off behind him.

"What's going on, Charley?"

Charley shrugged. "Beats me. TJ just told us Gabriel had a kid. And the kid's dead. Luke got rankled and took off. Did you know Gabriel had a kid?"

"Shit!" Sam said under his breath. He pulled out his phone and dialed Luke. He didn't answer.

***

Luke ran through the hospital lobby to the information desk. He kept telling himself it was a mistake. Impossible. But he had to be sure. He had to see for himself.

The staffer was on the phone. Luke asked, "Where's the morgue?"

Without looking at him, she lifted a finger, indicating for him to wait and continued on the phone. "Visiting hours are from two pm to six pm … No, that doesn't apply to family members. They can visit any time … Well, neighbors really aren't family members, are they …? No, ex-boyfriends either … Well, if you were, like, engaged, I could ask someone … I believe that your sister had the same thing. But it was because she was your sister. That's a family member. You were related to her so you could visit anytime … What …? No … No … Doesn't matter … No."

A security guard stood next to a sign a few feet away that read: We will not tolerate verbal or physical abuse towards our staff. It almost made Luke laugh because he wanted to grab the receiver out of her hand and hit her over the head with it repeatedly. Instead, he took a deep breath and a different tack.

He leaned over the counter to catch her eye, gave her his most disarming, boyish smile, and waved. He mimicked writing on something. She sat up straighter, smiled, and handed him a pen and pad. She put her hand over the mouthpiece and whispered, "Blah, blah, blah, blah." She sighed loudly and continued with the call, her eyes glued to Luke. "Nope. I don't think it would help if you brought flowers."

Luke wrote "MORGUE" in large letters.

She put her hand over the mouthpiece again. "Take the north bank of elevators down to B3 and turn left. You can't miss it. Mister…?"

"Thank you."

As he walked to the elevator, she shouted after him, "Anytime. Anytime at all."

Luke descended in the elevator and pushed through the swinging doors of the morgue. He spoke to the attendant as he walked toward him. "I wanna see Tessa Begley."

The attendant rose. "You need to make an appointment."

Fists clenched, Luke responded calmly, "No. I don't." He reached into his pocket and pulled out a money clip holding a wad of bills. He placed it on the counter and pushed it toward the attendant who, without hesitating, grabbed the bills and put them in his pocket. He held out a clipboard with a pen attached to it by a string. "You have to sign in."

"Where is she?" Luke asked as he scribbled his name.

The attendant led him through a set of metal doors. The room was all tile and stainless steel with a wall of lockers. Luke was led to one and the attendant opened it. There were several trays. The attendant checked the labels and pulled one of the trays out. He lifted the white sheet to reveal Tessa's face. Although paler, she looked as though she were asleep.

Without looking at the attendant, Luke said in a quiet voice, "Get out." The attendant looked at him for a few seconds, then left. He understood. Most relatives wanted to be alone to say goodbye to their loved ones.

Luke let out a wild, painful wail that seemed to last forever. He touched her hair and caressed her face. He kissed her lips. He lifted her up by the shoulders and held her tightly to him. "Why? Why?" He held her for a long time, not wanting to let go.

He whispered in her ear, "Who did this to you?" He finally placed her back down, straightening her hair and putting her arms by her side. He pulled the sheet down and studied her body, seeing the bullet hole in her stomach. He let out another painful scream. "This doesn't make sense. Who would kill such an innocent?"

He leaned against the lockers and slid down onto the floor. He held his head in his hands. Who could possibly want her dead? Tessa only knew a few people — that little pain-in-the-ass friend of hers and the priests. No suspects there. Unless the little whore wanted revenge. No, she wouldn't have the balls. Gabriel? No. Gabriel would have guarded her with his life. Who did that leave?

"I did this," he said. She was innocent. But he wasn't. It had to be his fault. Someone wanting to get at him. Someone who knew this would destroy him. He thought of Sam. Sam knew. But he wouldn't do this to him. They'd been friends through the good and the bad. And there'd been some pretty bad things. No, not Sam — but he might have told someone, even innocently. Charley, Snake, Joey? Did one of them want him out of the way? This latest venture was making them a lot of money and would make a lot more. And he got the lion's share of the profits. Maybe one of them wanted more. Wanted to take over the operation and this was the first deep cut? No, it was too easy for any one of them to kill him and simply take over. Then who? Carlos? No way he could know about Tessa. Besides, that would take too much effort. He'd just put a contract out on him. Kenji? Had he found out about Riki? He said he wanted to punish him himself. It must have been Kenji. *He could have had someone following me. Shit. That makes sense.*

He couldn't remember most of last night after he'd returned to the club. Someone must have roofied him to make sure he was out of the way? Who could get close enough? Mika? Riki was her brother after all. Maybe she'd helped Kenji. She wouldn't. Would she? Yes, maybe she would.

"I will kill them," he said aloud. "I will kill them all." He wiped his eyes and stood up.

He touched Tessa's abdomen. "So beautiful." He reached into his pocket and pulled out his knife. He flicked the stiletto open.

After a long moment, he removed his shirt. He carved the letter T into his abdomen. Blood dripped onto his jeans and the floor. He bent and kissed her again. He touched the blood on his stomach and pressed it to Tessa's lips, then pulled the sheet up to her neck. He couldn't cover her face. He pushed the tray into the locker and closed it. He put his shirt on. The blood seeped through, creating a T-shaped stain.

Luke left the hospital and got into Sam's coupe. He sat a while without moving, watching people rush in and out of the revolving doors. *What now?* he thought. Then, in a moment of clarity, he knew what he had to do. He had to erase the past in order to move forward.

He wiped his eyes, turned on the ignition, and drove.

***

As Luke pulled up to the cottage, he saw Snake had lined the six captives up against the cottage wall and was spraying them with the lawn hose. Burlap bags covered their heads, their wrists were tied, and they were only wearing panties. The women were shivering and attempting, unsuccessfully, to protect themselves from the cold water with their bound hands.

Joey walked over to the car. "Hey boss, here to supervise delivery?"

"This a new game?" Luke quipped.

Joey looked back at the women. "Just makin' them more presentable. They were startin' to get a little ripe."

"They look presentable enough to me, Joey."

Joey turned to Snake and yelled, "Boss says they look presentable."

Snake turned off the hose and led the women to the van. He opened the back and lifted them in one by one.

Luke got out of the car and took his jacket out of the trunk to cover the dried blood on his shirt and slacks.

Snake and Joey didn't mention the blood stains. They knew how deadly Luke could be, so they figured the person responsible would have ended up much worse.

"There's been a change of plans. Go to the club. I'll take care of things here."

"Change of plans? Delivery been pushed back?" Joey asked. "We wouldn't mind more time with these sweet things." Snake laughed and grabbed the crotch of one of the women before closing the van doors.

Luke had already decided that Kenji was not going to get his delivery and that he should put them out of their misery. Whatever Kenji had planned for them was probably a fate worse than death anyway.

He could plan Kenji's demise later.

Luke tossed his car keys at Snake. "Take the car back to the club."

They looked at him, confused. But he was the boss. And supposedly knew what was what. Joey passed him the keys to the van.

Snake got in the driver's seat and turned on the ignition. They watched Luke go into the cottage.

Curious, Joey went over to one of the windows and looked in. Luke took his jacket off and placed his phone down on the edge of the pool table. He picked up a cue, chalked it, aimed and, tapped one of the colored balls. It rolled into a pocket.

Joey got in the car and uttered nonchalantly, "Delivery must of been pushed back. He's playin' pool." They looked at each other, shrugged, and drove off.

Luke aimed for the next ball and tapped it. Once again, the ball rolled into the pocket. He took his time clearing the table. Then he poured himself a healthy glass of Macallan's single malt, racked up the balls, and played another game.

His cell rang and he ignored it.

***

When Joey and Snake arrived at the club, Charley was seated at the bar having a beer, and Sam was at a table playing Tetris on his phone. TJ was busy cleaning the beer taps.

Charley looked them up and down. "Where's the money?"

"Money?" Joey asked innocently. They sat across from Sam, who looked up at them surprised.

Charley stood. "For the delivery!"

"I dunno. Ask Luke," Joey answered, unconcerned.

"What do you mean?" Sam asked, looking at Charley.

"What I said. Ask Luke. He came to the cottage, gave us his car keys, and told us to split."

"Luke made the delivery?" Sam asked.

"Can't say. He was playing pool when we left," Joey answered as he waved at TJ. "Beer!"

"Pool?" Sam looked at his watch. "Fuck!" He called Luke, who didn't pick up. Sam stood and motioned to Charley. "We gotta get to Kenji. Let him know we do have the merchandise, but delivery will be a little late. C'mon."

Charley and Sam left the club and drove to Kenji's factory.

Charley was clearly anxious. "Do you know what the fuck is going on?"

Sam shook his head. "Not a clue." And it was true. He thought he knew Luke, yet he had no idea what he was up to. Whatever it was, it didn't bode well.

"Kenji is a dangerous motherfucker who you don't screw around with. Going to him now is not a good idea, Sam."

"Got a better idea?"

"Yeah. Deliver the fucking merchandise," Charley growled.

Sam shoved his watch in front of Charley's face. "Too late."

When they arrived at the gates, four men stepped out. Two of them walked over to the car and looked in.

"There's just the two of us," Sam said to them.

They were shown where to park, then grabbed at gunpoint and roughly taken to the office.

"Told you. We're dead," Charley muttered.

Kenji sat, arms crossed, with Haruto at his side. Charley and Sam were shoved onto the two chairs in front of the desk. One of the men went to Kenji and whispered in his ear.

"Jiro tells me you have arrived without our merchandise," Kenji said, eyebrows raised.

Sam bowed his head, trying to show respect and, hopefully, lighten the mood in the room. "That's why we've come in person. To tell you there'll be a slight delay," Sam said.

"Delay?"

"Not a delay really," Charley answered. "We just—"

"A delay is not acceptable. Where is your boss?" Kenji pulled out his phone and dialed Luke.

Luke saw who the call was coming from and answered. "Yeah?"

Kenji asked, matter-of-factly, "Where is my merchandise, Mr. Verde?"

"Good question."

"Are you trying to be funny? Have you forgotten who you're dealing with?"

"Kenji, you can take your fucking threats and—"

Kenji hung up. "Where is the rest of your crew?"

"Waiting to hear from us." Charley made an attempt at bravado.

Kenji nodded to his men, who pulled Sam and Charley out of their chairs. One held his gun on them while the other tied their hands.

Sam tried another tactic. "There'll be a hefty discount for the inconvenience. You know we have the merchandise." Haruto shook his head and Jiro hit Sam with the butt of his gun. Sam fell, dazed. The men pulled him up.

Charley tried again. "I can bring you to the women, now. Right now!"

Kenji leaned back in his chair and closed his eyes. They were liars.

"You were asked a question. Where is the rest of your crew?" Haruto demanded. One of the men put his gun to Charley's temple.

"At the club," Charley answered. "At Club Vox."

Haruto smiled. "We'll go there." He motioned to his men, who dragged Charley and Sam from the office, through the building, to a van in the parking lot.

Kenji sighed and rose. "Have Shio and Adachi meet us at this Club Vox."

"*Hai.*" Haruto took out his phone and dialed.

***

Luke put his phone in his pocket, placed the cue gently down on the table, and put his jacket on. He knew that what he was about to do now was necessary.

He left the cottage, got into the van, and opened the glove compartment. He knew Joey kept a revolver there. He checked the chamber to confirm it was fully loaded, put the revolver back, and shut the compartment. He turned the ignition on and drove for about a half hour further away from the city, eventually turning onto a rough trail that led to a wooded area and continuing for a few more miles.

His cell rang again and he ignored it. Luke stopped the van, took the revolver, and tucked it into his waistband. He stepped out, opened the back doors, and helped the women out of the van one by one, then closed the doors. Even in the heat of the day, they were shivering.

He lined them up and freed their hands with his knife.

The women were so frightened that none of them moved. Each of them knew this was a trick. A game Snake liked to play. An excuse to beat them, or worse, if they removed the bags from their heads or tried to escape. These animals were sadists, every one of them, so you'd be crazy to take a chance.

He took the revolver from his waist and cocked it.

One of the women reminded him of Tessa. She had the same hair color and a similar figure. *They could all be her,* he thought. They were all around the same age. He had believed they deserved their fate. That something like this was inevitable for them. Except that now he pictured Tessa, shackled and branded.

Luke's heart began to race. He fired a shot into the air. "Run!" he yelled. The women crouched down petrified. He fired again.

"Why aren't you running?" he shouted as he walked back to get into the van.

One of the women dared to pull up her burlap bag. She watched Luke get into the van, then pulled the tape off her mouth and shouted, "It's okay. Run!" The others did the same, and they all scattered.

Luke took out his phone and dialed Sam. It rang a few times and then went to voicemail. "Where are you, Sammy?"

CHAPTER FOURTEEN

Snake and Joey were slouched at a table near the bar. Joey had his phone to his ear. "Charley's not answerin'." He hung up. "Somethin's not right."

TJ emerged from the cellar carrying a case of beer. He put the case under the bar. "Can I get you guys anything?" Joey gave him the finger.

"Asshole," TJ muttered under his breath as he returned to the cellar.

The entrance door opened, and Charley and Sam entered. Their hands were tied behind their back, and they were pushed forward by four armed men.

Joey jumped up. "What the fuck?" One of the men shot him in the leg. He screamed and fell back. Before Snake could react, the same man aimed the gun at his head. Two other men searched them, removing Snake's knife and the pistol tucked into Joey's leg holster, then emptied their pockets and shoved them back onto their chairs.

"What's goin' on, Sam?" Joey asked, shaking from the pain in his leg.

Before Sam could answer, Kenji entered with Haruto and more men carrying weapons. Kenji looked about the room. "It looks like Mr. Verde isn't here. Well, no matter."

TJ had been carrying a case of wine up the stairs. He stopped when he heard the gunshot and backed down the stairs. He put the case down and climbed the stairs again, trying not to make a sound. He slowly pulled the trap door closed and sat on the steps, praying no one would find him. He could hear everything.

Haruto pulled out a chair and Kenji sat in it. This was not something Kenji would ordinarily participate in, but this had become personal once he was informed of his nephew's murder.

Haruto took one of the men to check the main floor. Neither noticed the outline of the closed trapdoor behind the bar. They went up the stairs. Haruto entered the suite and looked around the office and bedroom. The other man opened the door to the VIP room, gave the room a cursory glance, and closed the door, not seeing Carmen hidden under the table.

They returned to Kenji. Haruto whispered in his ear and took his usual position next to him.

Two of the men pushed Charley and Sam onto chairs.

Charley stood and was pushed back down.

Kenji's men took cable ties out of their pockets and secured all four men's hands and legs to the chairs.

Sam couldn't imagine why Kenji had brought them to the club. What was this? Were they gonna torture them, cut off fingers, then leave them bloodied for Luke to find? It would definitely prove they meant business, so Luke would stop dicking around and deliver the women. *You'd better be on your way here, Luke.* He tried to calm the situation to gain them some time.

"With respect, Mr. Kenji. As we've said, we did fulfill our part of the agreement. There's simply a slight delay in the delivery."

Charley chimed in. "Primo cooch. As soon as Luke gets here, we'll—"

The man behind Charley hit him in the head with his gun. Charley's head fell forward.

Kenji had to assume they were lying. Their boss didn't sound right. Something was up and they were covering for him. He replied, without looking at any of them, "A slight delay is unacceptable. The merchandise is needed now. I value duty and honesty above all else; it is unfortunate Mr. Verde does not. Therefore, the delivery of justice must and will prevail."

Kenji checked his watch and motioned toward the entrance. One of Kenji's men opened the door and two doctors wearing white lab coats and carrying medical bags entered. Four men followed with large coolers and aprons from the meat-processing factory. The door was locked behind them.

Snake yelled, "Fuck-king low-life mo-ther-fuc-kers gonna cut us up!" The others looked at him, surprised that he'd spoken, but even more by what he'd said, even though it was obvious. They continued to struggle desperately to free themselves.

Sam couldn't imagine how they were going to get out of this. Everything was happening so fast. He hoped TJ would stay hidden in the cellar and call the cops. This was one time he'd be glad to see them. Then he spotted TJ's cell phone on the bar. *Fuck! Goddammit, Luke, where the fuck are you?* He yelled at Kenji, "This is crazy!"

"Unfortunately, you must be quiet now." Haruto motioned to his men to gag them.

The doctors put their medical bags on a table and donned the aprons, latex gloves, and plastic face shields. One removed a box of EldonCards from his bag and took samples from each of the men. He tested their blood while the other doctor laid out the contents of his bag. He looked at Kenji and nodded. Kenji's men produced knives and cut their prisoners clothing off as they squirmed, trying to free themselves.

Kenji pointed at Snake. His men cut the cable ties holding him to his chair, lifted him up, and, coincidently, spread him across the same table the men had stretched Riki out on not that long ago. They held his arms and legs down while his wrists and ankles were secured to the legs of the table. Snake's gag loosened and he spat at one of the men, who hit him in the head with his gun. Snake passed out.

"I believe I failed to mention to Mr. Verde the contribution he would have to make should he fail to deliver," Kenji said matter-of-factly. "Fortunately, gender didn't matter in this case. Product is product."

Kenji nodded at the doctors who went to Snake. "We usually administer Propofol to our donors to sedate them before we cut. We are not monsters. But it seems Dr. Shio and Dr. Adachi have both run out."

Kenji and Haruto took surgical masks out of their pockets and put them on. Their men followed suit. Two men pulled the table with the surgical tools next to Snake and placed two coolers nearby. One of the doctors made an incision in Snake's abdomen. Snake woke and screamed. His bladder and bowels emptied, and the stench quickly enveloped the area.

Joey, Sam, and Charley tried so hard to break free that their chairs fell over. Kenji's men left them on the floor. It was actually a blessing, as they no longer had to watch the horror they'd soon have to endure.

The doctor resumed cutting, and Snake passed out again. The other doctor pulled one of Snake's kidneys out and placed it into a cooler.

Kenji smiled. "The heart and liver are the most profitable. However, any butcher worth his salt would tell you that it is important to use as much of the carcass as possible. Is that not true, Dr. Shio?"

The doctor nodded as he made the next incision.

Kenji stood and added, "Not to worry, gentlemen. Your turns will come soon enough." He and Haruto headed to the staircase. Kenji stopped and turned to Sam. "Mr. Hayes, I believe you may be an honorable man, though you've tied yourself to someone who isn't. Perhaps you were unaware of his true nature. I believe you deserve more time on this earth."

The relief on Sam's face was palpable. *I might come out of this in one piece,* he thought. Then immediately started planning what he was going to do to Luke.

When they reached the landing, Kenji looked down and added, "Dr. Shio, please operate on Mr. Hayes last. When you're about to die, every moment is precious, is it not?"

"Motherfucker!" Sam yelled through his gag.

Haruto and Kenji removed their masks and continued to Luke's office.

Meanwhile, Carmen woke from a nightmare. She'd dreamt she was covered in spiders and her father just stood watching her, smiling. She heard the voices and screams coming from downstairs and crawled to the door to put her ear to it. What was happening? She shoved her fist into her mouth, afraid she might scream too. Was she dreaming? *Wake up,* she told herself. She'd never heard sounds like that. Who was it and what would happen if they found her? Coming to the club was another dumb idea that she would suffer for.

She suddenly realized she could call the police. Duh. Of course. They'd take care of what was happening downstairs and find her. She took out her phone to dial 911. The battery was completely dead. She looked for her charger but couldn't find it. She pulled everything out of her knapsack. It wasn't there. *I packed it, didn't I? I didn't.*

"How could I be so stupid!" She slapped her hand over her mouth realizing she'd spoken aloud. She scrambled back under the table. She was trapped with no possible rescue. She began to cry, sobbing into her sleeve.

Downstairs, the doctors finished harvesting all the organs, and Kenji's men lined the corpses up in front of the bar. When they were done, they joined Kenji upstairs. Kenji used Sam's cell to call Luke, who answered right away, expecting to hear Sam's voice.

"Mr. Verde, I am at your club. Thank you for the delivery. However, we are missing two." He hung up before Luke could reply. Kenji took out a cigarette. Haruto, at his side as usual, bent and lit it for him. Kenji leaned back and took a deep drag. He was content to simply wait for Luke to show up.

TJ gradually opened the trap door and climbed out. He gagged, grabbed a bar rag to cover his nose and mouth as he peered over the bar, and looked around. There was no one on the main floor. No one alive that is. He opened the cash register, removed all the bills, and shoved them in his pockets. He grabbed his jacket and phone and left through the back door of the club without looking back.

***

Luke sped down the highway, winding his way through the city traffic. What was Kenji talking about? What delivery? Where the hell was Sam?

The tires screeched as he pulled up in front of the club. He opened the glove compartment, grabbed the gun, and tucked it into his waistband. The door was locked. He pulled his keys out, unlocked it, and went in.

The smell of feces, urine, and blood filled his nostrils, triggering a gag reflex. He grabbed a napkin from the nearest table and threw up into it. Once he gained control, he wiped his mouth and continued slowly, holding the gun in front of him, ready to shoot anything that moved. There was no one there, only carnage on the floor in front of the bar: the defiled, naked bodies of Sam, Charley, Snake, and Joey. Their abdomens were now gaping holes, their chests ripped open, and their hearts removed. Bloody fissures replaced their eyes.

Fucking Kenji! Fucking insane maniac! He did this!

He knelt next to Sam and dropped the gun. He picked Sam up and held him in his arms, whispering in his ear, "I'm sorry. I'm so sorry. I know this is all my fault." He wiped the blood from Sam's cheeks. "Bet you never expected me to be this much of a fuckup," he said, rocking Sam in his arms. "You'd be happy, though. I set them free. I went to the cottage and I let them all go."

He looked up the stairs. He knew they'd be there waiting for him. If not Kenji himself, then surely his goons. Where else would they be?

"Whaddya think I should do, Sammy? Run? Fight?" He laid Sam gently back onto the floor. "Okay, fighting it'll be." He removed his jacket and laid it over Sam's face.

Tucking the gun into his waistband, he went behind the bar. He found a bottle of scotch, filled a glass to the rim, and downed it in one go. Then he lit a cigarette and took a few deep drags. He filled the glass again, chugged it, took a few more drags off the cigarette, then butted it out on the bar. He climbed the stairs, leaving a trail of bloody footprints behind him.

Carmen slowly climbed out from under the table. Trembling in fear, she put her ear to the door and listened. It was quiet. She gently turned the handle.

Luke took out his gun and opened the door, hoping he might find TJ hiding there. He was surprised to find Carmen instead.

He whispered, "Carmen? What—"

"I-I heard them. I heard them," she whimpered. "Are they still here?"

He put his finger to his lips. "Shush. Quiet. Stay here. Don't come out until you're positive that everyone is gone." Carmen nodded. He took her hand and gave it a gentle squeeze, then closed the door quietly, took a key from his pocket, and locked her in. She climbed back under the table.

The door to Luke's suite was slightly ajar. He took his stiletto out of his pocket and pushed the door open with the gun muzzle. Kenji was sitting at his desk, Haruto standing next to him with his hand on his holstered gun. One of Kenji's men, hidden behind the open door, grabbed the gun out of Luke's hand and shoved his own gun into his ribs. Luke stuck his knife deep into the man's neck, pulled it out, and hurled it at Kenji, grazing his ear. The man behind the door dropped to the floor. Haruto fired at Luke but missed as Luke bent to pick up his gun. More of Kenji's men spilled out of the bedroom. He fired at Haruto, but the shot went wide as the gun was snatched from his hand and his arms were pulled behind his back.

"I'm told my nephew is missing, Mr. Verde. Have you seen him?" Kenji enquired sarcastically.

"You're fucking insane!" Luke shouted.

"What? Downstairs? Pshaw! It was not as much merchandise as expected. But profitable nonetheless. The arrangement was delivery of six bodies, and you may have noticed, when you arrived, that there were only four. So I'm sure you would be agreeable to helping us fill the order."

Kenji's men pushed Luke into the bedroom.

The doctors stood on either side of the bed and more of Kenji's men stood nearby. Luke didn't struggle as the men undressed him. Nor did he struggle when they held him down. What was the point. Besides, this would bring him to Tessa sooner. She believed there was a life after this. Maybe that was true.

Kenji saw the bloody T on his abdomen. "I see someone has begun our work for us. As a curtesy for your acquiescence, would you like one of my men to knock you out? These procedures are quite painful. There was much screaming from the men downstairs before they passed out. You see the doctors never remember to bring any kind of anesthetic. I'm beginning to think the doctors enjoy the sound. Tsk tsk."

Luke closed his eyes. The doctor took out a scalpel and made the first cut down Luke's chest. He was drenched in sweat but didn't move or utter a sound. The surgeon reached in and pulled the ribs apart. Luke screamed!

***

Gabriel woke with a start. He knew what he had to do next. He had to kill Luke himself, even if it meant he might die. It didn't matter that he'd promised Tessa he wouldn't. She'd have to forgive him, wherever she was, because he couldn't live knowing that Luca Verde was alive and well.

Apart from the gun in the cash register, there was another loaded gun in the safe in his office. He got into his car and sped to the club.

Inside, Carmen heard the men leave Luke's office and go downstairs. After what felt like forever, she gingerly turned the doorknob again and again, then remembered she'd heard Luke lock the door. Hopefully, someone would find her — someone safe. She got back under the table to wait.

Gabriel parked in the back of the club and entered cautiously. He stopped abruptly and covered his face with his hand as the smell struck him. "What the…?"

He rushed to his office and took the gun out of the safe. He left his office and saw the bodies lined up in front of the bar and the mess all over the tables and floor. He checked the rest of the room and looked up the stairs. The suite and VIP room doors were closed. He climbed the stairs quietly and stood outside the suite, listening to see if anyone was there. Silence.

He entered the office; it was empty. He opened the bedroom door to find Luke's naked body on the bed, his arms outstretched. His eyes had been removed and his chest and abdomen were a bloody gaping hole. Yet, he seemed to be smiling. Gabriel went to the bed and saw Tessa's ring on Luke's finger. He twisted it off and put it in his pocket.

"I hope they kept you awake during the whole ordeal, and it hurt like hell, you motherfucker!" He left the room, continuing to curse Luke out loud.

Carmen heard Gabriel and jumped up. She banged on the door.

Gabriel stopped and tried the handle. The door was locked. "Who's in there?"

"I'm locked in."

Gabriel put the gun away, pulled a set of club keys out of his pocket, and opened the door. He recognized her immediately. "Carmen? What are you doing here?"

"It's you!" She threw her arms around his waist. "You won't believe…" She started crying again and, between sobs, asked, "Is Sam okay? I think I heard his voice. Is he okay? They were yelling and then screaming. Awful, awful screaming. It was horrible. What… What happened?"

"It's over now."

"Was it Sam? Is he okay?"

"I'll take you home." He wasn't going to give Carmen the grizzly details. She didn't need to know. She'd been through enough. She didn't need the nightmares.

He bent and picked up her knapsack. "I want you to close your eyes and breathe through your mouth." Carmen knew she should do as he asked. Whatever had happened, she didn't really want to know.

Gabriel picked her up in his arms. "Keep your eyes closed."

He carried her down the stairs and out the back to his car. He opened the passenger door and Carmen got in. "I'll be back in a minute." He shut her door and reentered the club.

He went to his office, took his laptop, and removed the documents and cash from the safe. He put everything in a briefcase and left it outside the door.

Then he went to the bar, opened two bottles of vodka, and poured them over the bodies. Using the baseball bat hidden under the bar, he smashed the other liquor bottles and walked around to the front of the bar. He lit a match while it was in the pack and threw the pack on the spilled liquor. The bar went up in flames. He picked up the briefcase and left the club.

He put the briefcase in the trunk, started the car, and drove away. When they stopped at a red light, Gabriel turned to Carmen. "What were you doing at the club?"

"I ran away. I had nowhere else to go. I knew this was Mr. Verde's club. I thought maybe he would help me."

Jesus, she actually knew Luke well enough to ask him for money. Gabriel couldn't wrap his head around it. How long had it all been going on? "Why go to *him,* Carmen? Why not call Tessa? Aren't you best friends?" He realized what he'd just said. As though she were alive.

Carmen sat up straight. "We *are* best friends! I thought she would let me stay with you for a little bit. But I called and I texted her. She wouldn't answer. So I came here. But I changed my mind and was gonna go to your house anyway. And then I couldn't leave. I had to hide."

"What happened to your face?"

"My papa happened to my face."

It looked like Carmen needed to be protected, even if it was from her family.

"How come *you* came to the club? Do you know Luke?"

"I work there."

"You work there?"

"I work there." Gabriel repeated.

Carmen's head was spinning. It was like she was in an alternate reality where monsters like Freddy Krueger and Jason were real. She'd heard their victim's screams. She needed something normal. She needed her friend — needed to tell her everything. Tessa would be so shocked to hear what she'd been through.

"Where's Tessa?"

Gabriel cleared his throat, holding back his emotions. "She's gone."

"Gone where?"

Gabriel couldn't answer.

"Did her father come and get her?"

"I'm her father."

"Her father? But…" Carmen started to feel uncomfortable. "I don't understand. Did something happen to her? Where is she?" She had the foreboding sense she was about to hear something even more terrible than what she'd just been through.

Gabriel looked at Carmen. A tear fell down his cheek and she realized the impossible. Her hands covered her mouth, and she screamed through her fingers. "No, no, no, no!" She broke down. She just couldn't handle any more. It was too much.

***

Carmen couldn't stop crying. Gabriel tried to console her by patting her shoulder as he drove to his house. They went in and she followed him to the kitchen. He pulled out a chair, grabbed a few pieces of paper towel, and handed them to her.

"I'll be back in a minute. I have to do a few things."

Gabriel went to his bedroom and began packing the rest of his clothes into a second suitcase.

Carmen wiped her eyes and blew her nose, but she couldn't stop crying. She had believed Gabriel's story of them being mugged. She hadn't asked any questions. She didn't want the details. She'd had enough gore to last a whole lifetime.

She didn't know why but she needed to go up to Tessa's room. Maybe she'd be there, waiting for her. Maybe her father was wrong. She wasn't dead. She was alive.

She climbed the stairs, went into Tessa's room, and sat on the bed. Of course, she was the one who was wrong. She looked around the room. It felt weird being there surrounded by Tessa's things, but, at the same time, it was like she was there with her.

She went to the bed and touched the suitcase. "Is all your favorite stuff here?" She opened it and looked through Tessa's things, smiling and crying at the same time as she picked up clothes she'd seen her wear. She put the picture of Tessa on her horse into her knapsack.

She lifted the bed covers, got in, and curled up, thinking about when she'd met Tessa. She so wished she could go back to that day.

Carmen felt something hard under the pillow. She reached in and found the paperback she'd asked Tessa to hold for her. "Stupid fairy tales!" she cried, throwing it across the room. But then felt bad about messing up Tessa's room. She got out of the bed and put it in the small trash can under the vanity table.

That's when she noticed the cross hanging on the mirror. She picked it up and decided it was somehow important that she wear it. "Now you'll always be with me, Tess of the d'Urbervilles," she whispered. She sat at the vanity, toying with the small gold cross, tears falling down her cheeks.

Gabriel looked around his bedroom and snapped the case shut. He carried both suitcases to his car and put them in the trunk.

He returned to the house to get the satchel from the kitchen cupboard where he'd hidden it. Carmen wasn't there, but he figured he knew where she was. He took out a few wads of cash and put them on the table, then went upstairs.

Gabriel knocked on the door before opening it.

Carmen didn't know how he'd respond. If she'd overstepped. "I didn't think you'd mind if…"

"I don't mind. You'll probably be sleeping in here until you decide you can go home."

"I can't go home. Ever."

"Maybe your father has calmed down."

"My papa is a very unhappy man. He has a black soul. Not the forgiving kind."

Surely, her mother could protect her. "Carmen, your mother could call—"

"My mama goes along with anything he says, cuz he treats her the same as me. She watched him beat me for the thousandth time, then let him throw me out with the trash. Would you go back?"

"I guess not." He saw she was wearing Tessa's gold cross.

She touched it. "I didn't think you'd mind if—"

"It's okay. Makes sense." He took out his house keys and put them in her hand. "I need a fresh start. Stay as long as you want. This house isn't under my name, so no one will come looking for me. The bills are paid online, so don't worry about that. I left money on the kitchen table. It'll last you a while."

Gabriel left, closing the door behind him. Carmen stared at the keys. She knew she couldn't stay hidden for long. She knew her father was looking for her and would eventually find her. Not to take her home, but to put her on a plane. Besides, she didn't want to stay in the house alone, without Tessa or her dad there. No. She couldn't. She picked up her knapsack and Tessa's suitcase and ran down the stairs to the kitchen.

Gabriel put the satchel in the trunk, got in his car, turned on the ignition, and backed out of the driveway.

Carmen grabbed the money off the table, shoved it in her knapsack, and rushed out of the house. She ran after the car and banged on the window. It stopped. Carmen opened the passenger door and got in, managing to put both her knapsack and the suitcase on her lap.

Gabriel watched her. "What do you think you're doing?"

"I'm coming with you. I don't want to stay here alone. Tessa said you were a kind man. And it's true."

Gabriel didn't respond. He didn't relish the prospect of living alone again either. But...

Without looking at him, Carmen said in a low voice, "I went to the club to see Sam. But then Luke, he... I'm gonna have a baby."

"A baby? Luke's baby?" He almost laughed at the absurdity of it all.

"Yes. But... but mine too." Carmen began to cry again. "It's my baby too."

He didn't know how to respond. That fucker had managed to corrupt everything in his path. Again, Gabriel hoped he had died screaming!

What to do about Carmen. He blamed himself for Tessa's death. He hadn't kept her safe from Luke. She'd still be alive if he'd just taken her away. But he hadn't. He had to get his revenge. He fucked up. Maybe this was a second chance. A chance to make sure Carmen had a life *she* deserved.

He turned off the ignition, got out of the car, and walked around to her side. Carmen was sure he was going to make her get out, so she held onto the knapsack and suitcase with an iron grip. Instead, Gabriel said, "It's okay." She let go and he took the suitcase and knapsack off her lap and closed her door. He put them in the trunk and got back in the car.

"You like horses?" he asked.

"Horses?"

He took the newspaper listing out of his pocket and handed it to Carmen. She unfolded it. "What's this?"

"Our new home," Gabriel replied.

"Our new home," Carmen repeated. She smiled and put her seatbelt on. "Could you call me Natalya from now on? I don't think I want to be Carmen anymore."

"Sure."

She touched his shirt sleeve. "Bianco."

Gabriel looked at her questioningly.

"White. New beginnings."

He nodded, put the car in gear, and they drove off.

Natalya stretched and put her feet up on the dash.

"Down," Gabriel said without looking at her.

She quickly removed her feet, sat up straight, and smiled.

They drove off without another word.

GLOSSARY

It felt more authentic at times to let the characters use their native language.

Russian

baba: grandmother
chto: what
chto ty delayesh: what are you doing
kotenok: kitten
krasnaya: red
Mama / Papa: Mother / Dad
plokhoy: bad
privet: hello
ya idu: I'm coming

Machanka is a Belarusian stew

Japanese

Kenji-san: a title of respect added to a Japanese name
hai: yes
gaijin: foreigner
Go meiwaku o okake shite moushi.: We apologize for the inconvenience.

ACKNOWLEDGMENTS

Endless gratitude goes out to Catherine Frid, Pat Folliott and Dyan Aitken, whose support and brilliant feedback not only made my story stronger but also made me a better writer. I'm grateful for their meticulous and invaluable notes. I consider myself very lucky to have such brilliant friends.

To my wonderful husband, Ian, for tolerating my obsession and suffering through the chapters given to him to read, out of order, with an expectation of his opinion. And for the necessary reminders to not go too far with the darker stuff.

Thank you to my readers for letting me share this story, these people and this world with you.

Ramona Baillie is a seasoned writer and creative professional with a sharp eye for life's grittier edges. Born in Westmount and raised in Pointe-Aux-Trembles — then one of Montreal's roughest neighbourhoods — her childhood played out against a backdrop of gangs, BB guns, and street-level crime. By age nine, she was navigating dangers most adults never face, from attempted abductions to daily fights. Even the first — and only — bike she and her brother owned was stolen the day after they got it. Those early experiences gave her a crash course in resilience, street smarts, and human complexity — all of which now shape her distinctive narrative voice.

Her work is unapologetically honest, often exploring the messier, more off-center parts of life. As one colleague put it, Ramona has "a distinct affinity for the messy and off-kilter," and she's not afraid to go there. While happy endings sometimes find their way in, her writing lives firmly in the real world.

Professionally, Ramona has built an impressive thirty-year career in the staffing and HR industry, earning an Honorary Life Award from the Human Resources Professionals Association for her outstanding contributions. She has served on corporate and non-profit boards and brings a strong leadership mindset to her creative projects.

As a playwright, screenwriter, and producer, Ramona has had six of her plays performed across Canada, and her film scripts have garnered awards internationally, with productions in Canada, Europe, and the U.S. She's also spent time in the vibrant arts scene of South Beach, Florida, before settling in Toronto, where she now lives with her husband.

Ramona continues to explore the shadows of human experience through story — where the darkest green often hides the richest truths. Ramona's debut book, *The Darkest Green*, is as unfiltered and grounded as the life that shaped it.